A LIFE IN THE BALANCE

"Suppose the treatment you propose works, at least for a time? What does that prove?" Carhill asked. "What statistical significance does it have? Or suppose it ends in disaster? Now if your hospital's hem-oncology group were to propose to treat a series of such patients, I would be more than happy to consider a collaborative venture. Even though we've entered into preliminary discussions with other hospitals regarding such trials, there's no reason your fine clinical facility can't be included. Honestly now, wouldn't that be a more suitable arrangement?"

"For my fine clinical facility, it would," replied Dan Lassiter. "But I'm not representing it at the moment. I'm the advocate on one fourteen-year-old boy who's dying of leukemia and doesn't give a damn about statistical significance!"

"Now, now," soothed Carhill. "No need to get emotional. I'm not heartless, Dr. Lassiter. I'm merely a scientist trying to act responsibly. I'm afraid I'd feel the same way if the boy were my own kin."

I'm afraid you would, too, thought Dan grimly.

Also by Marshall Goldberg, MD:

THE KARAMANOV EQUATIONS
THE ANATOMY LESSON
CRITICAL LIST
SKELETONS
NERVE

With Kenneth Kay:

DISPOSABLE PEOPLE

MARSHALL GOLDBERG, M.D.

NATURAL KILLERS

LEISURE BOOKS NEW YORK CITY

For
Barbara Young
(a.k.a. my wife)
and
the ghosts
of
Sylvester Manor

A LEISURE BOOK

Published by

Dorchester Publishing Co., Inc.
6 East 39th Street
New York, NY 10016

Printed in the United States of America

NATURAL KILLERS

Author's acknowledgments:

In May of 1981, while working parttime as medical correspondent for ABC-News, I broke a story on "World News Tonight" that I thought then and know now is one of the greatest medical discoveries of the century, perhaps *the* greatest. The story concerned the laboratory creation of monoclonal antibodies and the 1984 Nobel prize in medicine was subsequently awarded to their creators, Drs. Cesar Milstein and George Kohler. The scientists I met while reporting this story led me into cancer research myself and the writing of this novel; but being new to the cancer field I needed, and got, much valuable advice from the following experts: Dr. Robert Gallo of the National Cancer Institute; Dr. George Todaro of Seattle's Oncogen Corp.; Drs. Hilary Koprowski, Zenon Steplewski, Carlo Croce and Giovanni Rovera of the Wistar Institute, Philadelphia; Dr. Ken Foon of the University of Michigan Medical School, and Dr. Harland Verrill of the Hurley Medical Center, Flint, Michigan.

I am also deeply indebted to my close friend and collaborator on other novels, Lieutenant Colonel (ret.) Kenneth Kay; my sister, the late Dr. Toby Goldberg; my superb secretary, Wilma Kingsley; and my editor, Jane Thornton.

I humbly thank them all.

Marshall Goldberg, MD

PART ONE

THE ANTIBODY

Chapter 1

FEW FOURTEEN-YEAR-OLDS THINK much about death. Billy Freiborg was an exception. For several weeks, ever since it became increasingly clear that his Mayo Clinic doctors would be unable to save him, he thought of little else.

A lanky, sandy-haired farmboy and straight A student from Bemidji, Minnesota, Billy had leukemia—no longer an automatic death sentence, he knew, but never easy to cure. None of his doctors even mentioned the world "cure." Instead, they kept talking about five-year survival rates—as if five more years would give him a fair amount of living. At nineteen, he'd barely be old enough to vote or drink in bars or get much taste of college life.

Sometimes, Billy shut his eyes and tried to imagine what it would be never to open them again. It was dark behind his lids, but not black; he could see dots and wavy lines and the faint afterglow from his bedside lamp. The other evening one of his doctors had spent a couple of minutes looking into his eyes with an instrument. What did he see that was so interesting? Clumps of leukemia cells? Billy wanted to ask if he might go blind, but he didn't, doubting that he would get a straight answer.

"Explanations around here are like ice cream cones," Chad Petersen, his former hospital roommate, had once told him. "They come plain and sugared. Stick with the plain kind."

Some older nurses looked Billy in the eye when they spoke to him, but most of the younger ones didn't. He could almost hear them telling others about the fourteen-year-old kid who seldom spoke, just stared. Just once, he wished one of them would ask the question that must be on all their minds, and he would answer, describe how dying, or at least the thinking about it, felt inside: it left a hard-to-breathe ache.

With a similar ache, Presidential Advisor Nelson Freiborg ended his conversation with his younger brother, Sven, and hung up the phone. Sven had just talked to the Mayo Clinic doctors caring for his son, Billy. Their report had been dismal, their recommendations frightening.

Moving to the window of his West Wing office, Nels gazed out at the White House lawn. Beyond the gate sprawled the world's most vibrant capital city. At times, he could scarcely believe his good fortune in being at its epicenter; at other times, he could barely wait to outscheme the schemers against the President's policies one last time and get out. Now, in place of controlled anger, his usual anodyne against frustration, he felt only numbing despair. Horrible though it was to contemplate, the death of Sven's young son—his only nephew—looked more and more imminent and there didn't seem to be a damn thing that the vaunted Mayo Clinic staff or anybody else could do about it.

Billy's white blood cell count, numbers more important than federal trade deficit figures or Dow-Jones averages to Nels now, had stubbornly refused to yield to the four and five chemotherapy drug combinations he had gotten. Having run out of remedies of proven or even marginal benefit, Billy's doctors proposed to plunge him into the dark realm of the experimental. Should he let them? Sven had asked in a choked voice. Or should he take Billy home to their small farm near Bemidji to die in peace? What would he do if Billy were his son?

Nels had not known how to answer. Had the dilemma involved a major American corporation facing insolvency or a debt-ridden country like Mexico about to default on its multi-billion dollar loans, he would have known precisely what to do. These were man-made crises that experts in the intricacies of the world's monetary system could usually solve. But what did he know of leukemia, of medical decision-making? How could anyone, however clever or determined, face down cancer?

At the soft knock on his door, Nels spun around and, louder than intended, barked, "Come in!"

Jeff Darnell, youngest and brightest of his three assistants, entered hesitantly. "Hope I'm not disturbing you . . ."

"Not you—life," said Nels. "What is it, Jeff?"

"Just wanted to remind you of the Health Care Costs Commission meeting tomorrow morning. Will you be attending?"

"When and where?"

"Nine o'clock. The HHS building."

Picking up his desk calendar, Nels stared at it while seemingly unrelated thoughts suddenly connected in a promising pattern. Dr. Daniel Lassiter, general director of Boston's Commonwealth General Hospital and a friend since their freshman year at Williams College, would be in town for that meeting. Although a bit of a maverick about medical politics, Dan was as honest and informed and dedicated a physician as he knew. It was these attributes, more than friendship, that had prompted Nels to recommend Dan's appointment to the Presidential Commission on Health Care Costs and keep him in mind for even bigger jobs. Yes, Dan Lassiter was just the man to ask about his nephew. What he knew about treating leukemia did not matter; what mattered was that no one understood the workings of the American medical system better.

Suddenly reminded of his assistant's unanswered question, Nels cleared his throat and said, "Uh, no. I won't be attending. Have to be on the Hill then. But make a luncheon reservation for two tomorrow at *Hugo's* and get Dr. Dan Lassiter on the phone for me."

During his sixty-seven-day hospital stay, Billy Freiborg had had four roommates—the latest, twelve-year-old Henry Wedemacher was another leukemia victim. Liking his privacy, Billy did not welcome the new arrival's company, especially after learning his diagnosis. Not only would they have to share the room, but Billy would have to explain the routine and other things to him, as Chad Petersen, Billy's first roommate, had done for him.

Following his bone marrow transplant, Chad had been moved to an isolation room. That was the last Billy had seen of him. He didn't even know if Chad, or any of his friends on the pediatric cancer ward, were still alive. Chad himself had convinced him it was better not to ask.

Well, thought Billy, glancing across at his new roommate, he won't be asking any questions for a while. A four-tuber was usually too sick.

It was Chad who had taught him the importance of tube-counting. The intravenous tubes were nothing, merely "standard issue." The stomach tube irritated your nose and the bladder catheter the tip of your penis, but neither meant much. Beyond those, though, the outlook got pretty grim. The long plastic tube they stuck into your wrist artery for blood pressure measurements didn't hurt but indicated you were in big trouble. Worst of all was the trach tube. Not only couldn't you talk with one of those monsters jammed down your throat but you felt as if you were choking most of the time. The most Billy had experienced so far was three tubes, but Chad, in the third year of his illness, had had them all—he was one of the few seven-tubers to ever survive. He didn't brag about it, didn't even like talking about it, but Billy, wanting to know as much as possible about what lay ahead, kept after him until he did.

Some of the nurses on the ward thought Chad was sullen and resentful; a real loner. Billy had thought that, too, until he got to know him. Chad's dad, a bemedaled Marine Corps captain, had been killed in the last year of the Vietnam War. Chad kept one of his medals in a satin-lined box by his bed and would squeeze it hard whenever he was in pain. That's when they would talk the most, and not about the things fourteen-year-olds usually discussed. Neither cared what record was "top of the charts" or how the Milwaukee Brewers were doing in the pennant race. Instead, they talked about God and cancer and death—subjects Billy had once thought himself too young to understand; but, as Chad pointed out, you understood what you had to.

Hearing Henry Wedemacher moan, Billy said, "Hey, Henry, you want a pain shot? Want me to call the nurse to give you one?" Get a pain shot, he thought. It'll keep you quiet.

"W . . . What?" gasped Henry, coming awake and struggling against his arm restraints. "Who's there?"

"It's me, Billy Freiborg. Your roommate."

"Why am I tied down?"

"So you won't rip out your IV's is why. Know where you are, Henry?"

"Billy . . . ?"

"Yeah."

"Billy . . ."

"What?"

"I . . . I . . ."

As Henry's voice trailed off, Billy propped himself up on an elbow and leaned over to check his breathing. The least leukemics could do was look out for one another. He thought back to waking in terror his first night in the hospital and crying out, "Where am I?"

"You're in a war, kid," Chad had replied coolly. Probably because of his dad, Chad liked to talk in military terms, and that's how he explained the disease. Their bodies had been invaded and almost overrun by the leukemia cell enemy. Their defensive forces, loyal white blood cells, were doing their best to halt the spread, stabilize their front lines, but needed help.

"From where?" Billy had asked.

"From The General."

"The General" was what Chad called the ward chief, Don Henley. They didn't see Dr. Henley too often—usually only on Friday afternoons when he made his weekly inspection tour—but Chad claimed to know what he was thinking through an informer on his staff, a fourth year medical student named Madeline with big blue eyes and a neat figure. When Billy first heard this, he was skeptical; but, like everything else Chad told him, it turned out to be true. Almost every night Madeline would drop by to fill them in on their latest lab tests and what was planned for them next. Billy really looked forward to her visits. He might have fallen in love with her if Chad hadn't first. Then, unaccountably, Madeline stopped coming around. And shortly after that, Chad surprised and shocked him with an even more upsetting development. The war inside him was going badly, he said, so The General was bringing up his heavy artillery.

"What do you mean?" Billy had asked.

"They're going to blast my bone marrow to bits with X-rays and replace my whole front line with fresh troops from a bone marrow transplant."

"Whose?"

"My mom's. We're a pretty close match."

"When?"

"Tomorrow. Which means we won't be seeing each other for a while. But don't feel bad. If this new strategy works on me, it will on you, too."

That had been almost a month ago; Billy had not seen nor heard from Chad since. Once, while being wheeled to the X-ray department, he had ridden down the elevator with Madeline. Though they exchanged looks, neither spoke. Was Chad dead? Billy sensed that he was, and prayed he was wrong. But never ask, Chad had warned, and he hadn't—not about him or his two other former roommates.

Maybe it would be best if he didn't make friends with this Henry Wedemacher after all, Billy thought. Just because Chad had taught him the ropes didn't mean he had to keep teaching them to others like some sort of tradition. But he just couldn't let the poor kid lie there, lonely and scared. When Henry was ready to listen, he would tell him what he could. Then, one way or another, he too would check out. He hoped it would be for home, but knew his chances were slim because he wasn't responding to treatment.

At noon, following a three-hour meeting of the National Commission on Health Care Costs where prophecy, not policy, was discussed—which regulatory agencies would be funded and which would get the axe in the wake of the latest budget cuts—Dan Lassiter left the Health and Human Services building to meet Nels Freiborg for lunch.

The restaurant Nels had chosen was locally renowned and a beehive of activity. As the maitre d' showed Dan to a table, he received the obligatory glance from diners around him to see if he was newsworthy or notable. None gave him a second look except for two stylish young matrons who found his rugged features and purposeful manner intriguing.

Soon Nels Freiborg came striding up. It had been over a year since they had last seen one another and Dan smiled warmly at his college friend. Nels was barrel-chested, balding and florid faced, a man of incisive manner and a solid reputation for getting tough jobs done. An economist by training, he possessed a rare linguistic talent: the ability to translate the lexicon of economic theory into the lingo of politicians. Following a brief stint as Assistant Secretary of Commerce in the Ford administration and a longer one as head of his own Washington-based consulting firm, Nels had recently been appointed Chief Domestic Advisor to the President.

"I'd like about three of those," Nels said as they shook hands and he eyed Dan's whiskey and water. "But I've got a cabinet meeting at two. Anyway, glad to see you, Dan, and let's hear what you and your commission's been up to."

As Dan talked, Nels tried to look attentive, but it became increasingly obvious that he was preoccupied by other matters. Finally Dan demanded, "All right, let's hear it. What's your chief complaint?"

Nels started to speak, faltered, and rubbed his brow as if in pain. "This may be taking unfair advantage, Dan—I don't know—but all of a sudden the Freiborgs of Bemidji, Minnesota, seem to be an endangered species. I'm divorced and childless, my sister Ruth is a spinster, and my brother Sven's fourteen-year-old son, Billy, has leukemia."

Dan grimaced. "What kind?"

"Initially, they didn't know. Called it stem-cell leukemia. Now, based on some new tests, they're pretty sure it's the acute lymphoblastic variety."

"Better than the other kind," Dan said. "They're getting more and more long-term remissions with it, even cures."

"That's what Sven was led to believe, too, but it doesn't look like Billy's going to be one of them. As if leukemia isn't bad enough, he has something called refractory T-cell leukemia. The specialists at Mayo's have tried all sorts of drug combinations without any response at all. Now they want to turn him over to the experimentalists—treat him with total body irradiation and a bone marrow transplant. My question to you: Is Mayo's the bést place for him or would Boston be better?"

"I'm not a hem-oncologist, Nels. It's not my field."

"No, but you're a friend. You'll level with me. They claim they're doing everything possible, but you know doctors and big, impersonal medical institutions. Sven's a farm engineer—nobody important. Billy's a helluva kid to us, but just another leukemia case to them. So I don't know, Dan. They say they're doing their best, but are they? Who's doing it—an intern, a section chief, a world authority who's off lecturing most of the time—and just how good is that? How can I—how can any lay person judge?"

Dan met Nels' anguished eyes for a moment and then dropped his gaze to the table. Although his administrative duties kept him from seeing many patients, he saw a few and when he told one that he—his hospital—was doing everything possible he meant it. There was a routine he followed: consultations with more expert colleagues, computer searches of the latest medical literature, telephone calls to researchers at the frontier. It was a tedious process that he undertook reluctantly, particularly when the case seemed hopeless, but unless he did it, he couldn't state with conviction that he had done his best. No doubt Billy's Mayo Clinic doctors were competent and caring. The nagging question was, did he, as head of a major hospital with access to certain pertinent but unpublished information, know something they didn't know?

"Well," Nels prompted, "what do you think? Am I off base asking you such a loaded question and advised by your silence to back off? Or should I badger you some more? I guess what I'm really asking, Dan, is—should I tell my brother that Billy's doomed anyway, so let them go ahead and experiment? Or that a top-notch doctor I know has something better to offer?"

"You're putting me on the spot, Nels. I know Don Henley and his hem-oncology group there and respect them. You're asking me to second-guess one of the best."

"I know, Dan. If your computer-like brain is flashing INSUFFICIENT DATA right now, I certainly understand."

Dan almost wished it were so; that he had not picked up two important bits of information recently —one, from an article he had reviewed for publication in *The New England Journal of Medicine;* the other, something his hospital's leading cancer researcher had told him at a cocktail party two nights before. His dilemma was whether to pass such speculative information on to his friend; raise Nels' hopes at the cost of shaking his confidence in his nephew's doctors. "All right," he finally said, "as information for information's sake, maybe I can offer something helpful. You know, Nels, from the howls coming from your cronies on the Hill, the war on cancer seems like a big flop so far; a billion dollar boondoggle. And the National Cancer Institute is catching hell for it. But before you come up with a cure, you've got to have a solid concept of what you're dealing with. And out of some concepts that have emerged lately we may soon be able to construct some pretty big guns. For instance, did you hear of tumor-associated antigens?"

"No," said Nels. "I'm not even sure I know what an antigen is."

"Neither do most doctors, exactly. Simply put, an antigen is anything the body perceives as foreign or different from what it's supposed to be and manufactures an antibody to destroy. It's the way our immune system, when it's working right, deals with invading microorganisms and early cancers. Follow me so far?"

"Pretty much," said Nels. "But before you go on, please tell me this: Are you saying that Billy has a chance?"

Slowly, tentatively, Dan nodded. "He just might—a chance worth taking."

Nels closed his eyes in what Dan guessed was silent prayer. It was the most emotional he had ever seen this tough-minded Swede. Touched, and more than a little troubled by the implications of what he was about to say, Dan looked away until Nels said, "All right, let's order a round of drinks and then you tell me all about these tumor-antigen things."

Chapter 2

"WOW!" EXHALED TED SWERDLOFF, chief of research at Commonwealth General, when Dan related the gist of his conversation with Nels Freiborg the day before. "I hope you realize what you're getting yourself into."

Dan stared at Swerdloff, a medium tall, thick-set man in his early fifties who divided his time between cancer research and pediatric hematology. "I hope *you* realize you're partly responsible."

"Me?" exclaimed Swerdloff. "I never claimed I could cure T-cell leukemia. Not cold sober, anyway."

"So you *do* remember!"

With his round face, aquiline nose and thin fringe of hair rimming his bald pate like a laurel wreath, Swerdloff always reminded Dan of a Roman senator, especially when he was in his cups. The more Ted imbibed, the more loquacious he became—and the more entertaining. He was as essential to the merriment of any staff party as a good bartender.

Unable to sustain his look of wide-eyed innocence, Swerdloff smiled sheepishly. "I do have a *vague* recollection of cornering you last Saturday night to propound some wild new theory."

"Wild theory!" mocked Dan. "You made it sound like the surest cure since vitamin B-12 for pernicious anemia!"

"Well, maybe I did slip off the edge of the scientific data on a few turns. But I was just back from the big *hybridoma* meeting in Los Angeles and the enthusiasm of that bunch was contagious. The monoclonal antibodies those guys were churning out seemed capable of curing everything from cancer to baldness. I'm sorry as hell if I gave you the impression . . ."

"Never mind, I'm committed to trying it. I said you were *partly* responsible, Ted. So is Gregory Carhill."

"*Sir* Gregory?" said Swerdloff, surprised and intrigued. "How does the impressario of cancer research figure in this?"

"His group at the Bethune Institute recently submitted a paper to *The New England Journal of Medicine* that I reviewed. It's Nobel Prize material—if true."

"What do you mean, 'if true'? Despite his pomposity, Carhill's a scientist's scientist. His work on tumor viruses is the Gold Standard, unoriginal as much of it is."

"Well, far as I can tell, this latest stuff is not only original but a medical milestone of sorts. Carhill claims he's found a cell-surface antigen that's absolutely specific for virus-induced mouse leukemia cells—isolated it, determined its molecular structure and modified that structure enough to make a vaccine that's almost one hundred per cent protective. Never again will lab mice have to succumb to the ravages of virus leukemia. But that's not all. In some of the most understated prose since Watson and Crick remarked on the genetic implications of DNA's double helix structure, Carhill speculated that the same methodology will shortly lead to the isolation of similar antigens for all types of human leukemia."

"Hmm," said Swerdloff, and paused to sip the coffee on the table beside him.

Impatiently Dan waited for him to continue. "Hmm, even hmmm, is a rather noncommittal comment, Ted. Under the circumstances, I need more than that."

Swerdloff shrugged. "What can I tell you? Immunologists have been racing to find the first tumor-specific antigen since Foley's time thirty years ago. Things really speeded up after Kohler and Milstein in England created the first hybridoma in 1975. Now, maybe, that race has been won—though I always figured Stefan Sigourney's team in Philadelphia, not Carhill's, would be first across the finish line."

At mention of Sigourney's name, Dan flashed back to a lank, lean, almost gaunt, researcher he had known two decades before. Early in their medical careers, the two had shared the same mentor—the late Curt Anders Gundersen, founder and fashioner of the new Commonwealth General Hospital out of the ramshackle, graft- and scandal-ridden ruins of the old one; a legendary figure in American medicine, though a tragically flawed one to those who knew his quirks.

In 1960, Dan was Gundersen's chief medical resident and Steve Sigourney his research fellow. Steve practically lived in Curt Gundersen's hematology lab in those days, trying to perfect a bio-assay for erythropoetin, the kidney hormone that stimulates the bone marrow to manufacture red blood cells. Gundersen himself suffered from a chronic, cancer-like disorder named polycythemia vera in which his blood thickened dangerously unless thinned by periodic blood-lettings. And it was Steve's misfortune to be assigned this particular research project rather than one for which Gundersen could exercise his usual cool objectivity.

Under relentless prodding and, as Dan later learned, from clinical data furnished by Gundersen that contained falsified diagnoses, Steve published a paper claiming success for his assay—a result that could never be reduplicated by others in the field or even by Steve himself. For a young researcher, it was the professional equivalent of cheating at high-stakes poker or faking a winning golf score—grounds for ostracism, if not lifelong ignominy. The debacle might well have dealt Steve's career a death blow had not Gundersen, out of his own guilt, helped him obtain a junior faculty position at New York University. From there, he moved on to the University of Pennsylvania and eventually to the directorship of his own institute. Stunned and embittered by Gundersen's duplicity, Steve did not publish another major paper for almost ten years. When he finally did, however, his findings were so integral to the fledgling field of cancer immunology that it put him in contention for the Nobel Prize.

"Steve Sigourney, huh?" mused Dan. "Haven't seen Steve for years, but I knew him when he worked here back in the early sixties. At least, I knew him well enough to consult on laboratory procedures and chat with over coffee. He was a real recluse in those days. Had a hospital pallor that made him look terminally anemic."

"Still does," said Swerdloff. "He was at the hybridoma meeting in L.A. and looked like he hadn't shaved or slept in days. I swear, Dan, if it weren't for his eyes—those feverishly bright, incredibly alert eyes—and the razor-sharp comments he makes, he'd be shunned, even ridiculed as 'The Howard Hughes of

Science.' Instead, he's deferred to. Which is understandable, I suppose, when you consider all the virology, immunology, molecular biology, and God knows what else he's mastered. Was he always so eccentric?"

"In his dress, yes. Otherwise, I don't know; I didn't see that much of him. The longest conversation we ever had was over a late night meal in the cafeteria. Know what we—or rather he—talked about? The importance of electron spin resonance to the clotting process!"

"Huh," grunted Swerdloff. "Must be a peculiarly Hungarian obsession. Albert Szent-Gyorgyi was always theorizing about that, too . . . You know about Sigourney's long-running feud with Carhill, don't you?"

"I've heard talk. How did it get started?"

"Nobody seems to know. But it's gotten steadily worse over the years. You should see those two go at each other at meetings."

Dan glanced at his watch. As usual, he was running late. "Getting back to our boozy discussion of the other night, tell me again how you hope to cure refractory leukemia—Billy Freiborg's leukemia in particular."

Swerdloff sighed. "Well, it all hinges on making a hybridoma that produces a monoclonal antibody that selectively recognizes your patient's leukemia cells, targeting only those cells for destruction."

"Ted," interrupted Dan, "since I'm the middleman here, and no immunologist, it's imperative that I follow your reasoning every step of the way. So check me out on this: a hybridoma is a hybrid cell formed in the laboratory by the fusion of a cancer cell, which is immortal in the sense that it reproduces endlessly in a nutrient broth, and a lymphocyte that contains the blueprints for making a certain antibody. Once the fusion is achieved, the hybrid keeps cloning itself and turning out tons of that particular antibody—right?"

"Right. Nothing in nature can copy so exactly. The trick, of course, is fusing the right cancer cell with the right lymphocyte to make the precise antibody you want. It's a tedious, trial-and-error process that can take months, even years."

"Which in Billy Freiborg's case we don't have."

"True. So we've got to borrow the hybridoma we want—if, in fact, one exists. If so, we're in business. In a three- or four-step process, all fraught with potential pitfalls, we can try for a cure."

"Go on," said Dan as Swerdloff sipped more coffee.

"Well, let's say Billy's leukemic cell population is around two trillion right now. Ordinarily I'd first try to knock the count down as low as possible with combination chemotherapy. But since that hasn't worked in his case, I'd go to step two. Using a blood separator, like a plasmapheresis machine, I'd remove blood from his body a pint at a time, mix it with the monoclonal antibodies to destroy his leukemic cells, and then give the purified blood back to him. If it works—admittedly a big if—that leaves us with the malignant cells in his bone marrow and infiltrating his tissues. To achieve total leukemic cell kill essential for a cure, I'd next inject the monoclonal directly into his blood stream. That, of course, is the hairy part, since there's always the danger of a fatal allergic reaction . . . Funny, how it sounded so simple and sure-fire the other night, and so iffy this morning."

"Funny to you and me, maybe, but not to a fourteen-year-old kid dying of leukemia. All right, Ted, let me ask you this: is there any treatment you know of, any you've even heard rumored, that stands a better chance of saving him?"

Swerdloff pondered. "Not from what you've told me about his case so far."

"That's Don Henley's feeling, too. He's a straight-shooter and he readily admits that his results with such leukemia patients to date have been dismal. So, skeptical as he, as any good oncologist would be at this stage, he's given us his blessings. Which brings us back to Gregory Carhill. Assuming he has the specific monoclonal antibodies we need or can make them in a hurry, think he'll hand them over?"

"To me, no. I'm one of those cut-throat cancer researchers he's always complaining about. But with your political clout, your pipeline to the federal funders, you might get lucky. Just remember what Marcel Proust once said about concupiscence: 'Any woman can be seduced if you're willing to stay up till four o'clock in the morning listening to her bitch.' "

Dan smiled. "What's that supposed to mean?"

"It means Carhill's a bit of a windbag; what my teenage daughter would call a motor-mouth. At least, that's been my experience with him at meetings. He just likes center stage too much to relinquish it with simple yes or no answers. So try to set up a pre-lunch appointment with him. Maybe hunger will hurry his decision along."

Dan rose and walked Swerdloff to the outer door of his spacious office. "Tell me, Ted," he said, "even if Carhill comes through, do you think we should still go ahead with this half-baked protocol? Or should we bow out now?"

"Go ahead," Swerdloff said without hesitation. "The odds are it won't work. But I can't help thinking of the British doctor who thought the same thing when he first treated a patient dying of pneumonia with penicillin."

A little after eleven, Dan's wife, Kristina, also an internist, came out of her study to join him in the living room as he sat watching the late evening news.

From the corner of his eye, he saw her gazing at him, not the television screen, and gave her a questioning glance.

"Coming to bed?" she asked.

He yawned and stretched. "Not just yet. Ted Swerdloff lent me some hybridoma articles I want to read."

"Hybridomas, huh? Complicated stuff. Why the sudden interest?"

"Has to do with Nels Freiborg's nephew, the one with leukemia. Ted thinks it might be possible to treat him with monoclonal antibodies."

"Oh? Has that ever been done before?"

"Not successfully. But according to Ted, that's where cancer therapy is heading."

"I didn't know Ted had the set-up for producing monoclonal antibodies."

"He doesn't—yet. He's pushing me hard to fund it, though, and if they work on Billy Freiborg, I will."

"Then where are you going to get them?"

"From Gregory Carhill, hopefully. I know, from the article of his I reviewed for *The New England Journal*, that his group at the Bethune Institute has quite an assortment of them. My job tomorrow will be to persuade him to part with the ones we need."

"What if he won't? After all, if they're the coming treatment for cancer, why let you share in the glory?"

"Then I'll have to scrounge around elsewhere. Maybe try Steve Sigourney's place."

Kris's eyebrows arched. "What makes you think Sigourney will be any more forthcoming?"

Dan shrugged. "We used to be friends."

"Friends! You haven't seen him in years. Neither have I, though I'm certainly not complaining. The last time we bumped into one another at a medical meeting, he tried to knock me down, or at least my arguments. Before the whole assembly, too, which didn't exactly endear him to me. Oh, I admire his

Einsteinian intellect. How, in fairness, could I not? But raw intellect is like raw meat—hard to swallow sometimes."

"Meaning what?"

"Meaning he's a Cossack who loves to ride roughshod over people. Always spoiling for a fight, a chance to slash away at others with his barbed comments. He's rude, arrogant and thoroughly unattractive." Kris knew she was exaggerating, but Dan's disapproving look goaded her on. "Yes, unattractive! That smirky smile. Those terrible teeth. And that rash—that ugly rash smeared like strawberry jam over his face. Why can't he see a dermatologist and get it cleared up?"

"From what I understand, it's a nasty neurodermatitis. Refractory to the usual treatment. Breaks out whenever he's under too much stress, which is most of the time."

"Then why doesn't he take tranquilizers, get laid, do whatever it takes to get rid of it? Rash or not, I simply don't understand why he has to look so scruffy all the time."

"Come on, Kris. The DNA strands and monoclonal antibodies Steve works with don't care how he looks."

"Oh, I suppose," she said, relenting. "But if it weren't for Steve's intense hatred of Carhill I doubt if he'd have any human emotions at all. Now, come to bed."

Dan stared. Kris hardly ever nagged. "Okay, but what's going on with you?"

"It's not what's going on, it's what hasn't! You've been out of town a lot lately and I'm a normal, healthy woman with normal, healthy desires. So what interests you more right now—me or hybridomas?"

Dan grinned up at his wife of almost three years. Even in baggy sweater and jeans, she was still the most exciting woman he knew; the best companion. Extending an arm, he said, "Help me up—from the couch, that is. I won't need help after that."

"You never have yet," she murmured and pulled him into her arms, hugging him tightly. Despite his moody complexity and the stern, almost cruel, set of his mouth in repose, Dan was the gentlest of lovers.

Her anticipatory pleasure as she undressed in their bedroom made Kris wonder why she had felt so antagonistic toward Steve Sigourney earlier. Years before, when he had temporarily set aside his cancer research to dabble in the field of neuropeptide control of glandular function, she had engaged him in heated debate at an Endocrine Society meeting. But Kris was reasonably certain she bore him no grudge for that; not even for his argument eventually proving to be correct. But before she could deduce her real reason for disliking the man, thoughts of the bliss she would soon share with Dan intervened. Even if Steve Sigourney did win the Nobel Prize, she mused, he would never know such sustained happiness as hers.

Chapter 3

THE BETHUNE INSTITUTE, named after the British textile magnate who had founded it in honor of his Boston-born mother, was a research center whose reputation was rapidly on the rise. For years a leader in the development of vaccines for viral and bacterial diseases, it had gradually shifted its focus to the frontier science of cancer immunology until it became pre-eminent in that field. Its director, Gregory Carhill, M.D. and Ph.D., professor of bacteriology at Harvard medical school and former chairman of the scientific advisory council of the World Health Organization, was equally renowned, not only for his prolific publications but for the large number of basic scientists from all over the world he had trained at his institution.

Despite certain British affectations of speech, his wife's ancestral estate in Surrey and their winter retreat in Bermuda, Gregory Carhill had not been born in England. Some of his detractors sneered that this was one of the two biggest disappointments of his life—the other being his failure to win the Nobel Prize, along with his mentor, John Enders, for their pioneer research on viral replication that laid the groundwork for the polio vaccine. Actually, Carhill had been born and raised less than ten miles from where his world-famous institution now stood, in a respectable but middle-class neighborhood bordering Dorchester. His mother was a high-school science teacher whose students consistently outscored those of other schools in competitive city-wide exams; his father, an engineer who, through powerful political connections, got into ship building shortly before World War II and became wealthy just in time to provide his only son a quality education. Gregory, an exceptional student, spent two years at Harvard College before being accepted for their accelerated M.D. training program. After graduating top of his class in 1945, the army sent him to Cambridge, England, to do research in bacteriological warfare.

At first, Carhill had serious misgivings about the assignment—his father was dying of bone cancer and the concept of germ warfare was repugnant to him—but it turned out to be the pivotal event of his life. In three years at Cambridge, he acquired a solid foundation in the emerging field of virology, a plain but well bred, witty, and exceedingly wealthy wife, and a taste for upper class British conveniences and customs.

From Cambridge he moved to Washington, D.C., spending two years in the virology section of the N.I.H. before accepting an assistant professorship at the Harvard medical school to work with the Enders group, contributing substantially to their methods for growing viruses in embryo cultures but not enough to be recognized for it by the Nobel Prize selection committee. Carhill was deeply wounded by the slight; for a time just being in the same room with Enders, Fred Robbins or Tom Weller sickened his stomach with jealousy. Ironically, though, the losers in the "polio prize" eventually did as well as the winners, Hilary Koprowski going on to head the Wistar Institute, Carhill the Bethune, and Jonas Salk accumulating sufficient wealth from his licensed patents to found an institute of his own.

With two fortunes to draw on—the Bethune trust and his wife's inheritance—Carhill set out to develop the finest biological research facility in the world. While concentrating on vaccines for such common infections as influenza and pneumococcal pneumonia at the start, his ultimate goal was a poly-vaccine against the family of viruses believed to cause or contribute to human leukemia. It was a formidable task, Carhill knew, but not beyond his capabilities. To achieve it he not only had to keep abreast, even a bit ahead of the rapid technological progress in the field of molecular biology, but recruit a loyal and diversely talented team of assistants. It was in the latter requirement that Carhill excelled.

A baseball player in his youth and a lifelong Red Sox fan, Carhill perceived certain parallels between the pursuit of pennants and scientific discoveries. American-trained researchers were much like free agent players. It took at least five years of intense personal supervision to train them to the point of real proficiency; then the good ones were apt to be hired away by universities offering chairmanships, or pharmaceutical companies promising that they could direct their own labs. By contrast, foreign researchers were just as well trained in the basic sciences and far more likely to remain loyal. The Chinese and Japanese, in particular, made excellent biochemists; the Swiss, immunologists. What he needed, Carhill had realized, was a farm system in the guise of a scientific exchange program. Thereafter, his countless trips abroad to lecture or to receive honorary degrees had two purposes: to enhance his international reputation and to recruit promising rookies for his team.

Unlike his arch rival, Stefan Sigourney, Carhill was neither a loner nor eccentric. Like him, however, he was a very private person. In odd, introspective moments he sometimes suspected that Sigourney understood him better than anybody else, even his own family. He was continually amazed at how similar their ways of thinking and operating seemed to be. Both were exceptional organizers and conceptualists, able to spot links between other scientific disciplines and their own and take advantage of them long before their competing colleagues. At such times Carhill not only regretted their fierce feud but remained a little vague on how it got started.

Unlike other bitter rivals—Freud and Jung, Andrew Schally and Roger Guillemin—who had worked together in harmony until their falling out, he and Sigourney had never even collaborated. All Carhill could recollect was a seemingly minor run-in at an immunology meeting ten or so years ago. After delivering a painstakingly prepared state-of-the-art lecture which introduced a new theory of antigen recognition, Sigourney had approached him to point out certain inconsistencies in his reasoning. With the thunderous applause of his colleagues still resounding in his ears, Carhill had regarded this unknown and tackily dressed upstart with barely concealed contempt and politely brushed him off.

From the speaker's platform the following morning, looking even more bleary-eyed and unkempt than the previous day, Sigourney had departed from his prepared lecture to blast Carhill's theory with a barrage of facts, mostly gleaned from the foreign literature, and propose one of his own that purportedly better fit those facts. That much was tolerable; after all, science thrived on controversy. But Sigourney didn't stop there. In closing, he looked straight at Carhill while reminding the audience that flimsy theories like flimsy toys, while cheap and easy to construct, were not made to last.

Angered by the affront, Carhill had returned to his institute determined to prove his theory right and Sigourney's wrong. But such proof was not easy to come by for either him or Sigourney. So at the next big immunology meeting they were at each other again. And the next. . . .

"Of little acorns, great oaks grow," mused Carhill as he now waited in his office for his last visitor of the morning. At times, he relished their intense rivalry; it spurred him on to greater efforts. At other times, he deplored it as energy-wasting and excessive. Worst of all, it demeaned both of them in the eyes of the phlegmatic Swedes who sat on the Nobel Prize selection committee. More than once he had been warned that they tended to shy away from, even exclude from consideration, participants in a bitter personal feud. And the Prize was the thing, Carhill told himself; the ultimate arbiter of who was the better scientist—the better man.

A little before noon, a hospital car dropped Dan Lassiter off in front of the black marble entrance to the fifteen story Bethune Institute on the Boston waterfront. Carhill's office was on a middle floor at the end of a long line of laboratories. An attractive, middle aged female secretary greeted Dan with a cheery, French-accented, "Allo" when he entered.

"You have to be Dr. Lassiter," she continued. "Dr. Carhill predicted a busy man like you would be punctual. Please go right in, Dr. Lassiter."

Though never formally introduced, Dan had heard Carhill speak at so many medical meetings that he knew the well-tailored, silver-haired man on sight. Only baggy eyes and a fleshy lower lip detracted from his otherwise aristocratic features. With a sweep of his hand, Carhill removed his rimless glasses and came around his desk to shake Dan's hand as he entered.

Dan was more accustomed to having research scientists greet him in shirt sleeves or rumpled white frocks, but Carhill's pinstriped tailoring and jade cufflinks were the essence of Bond Street elegance. Just as Curt Gundersen had used his capacious office, with its forty foot walk from door to desk, to intimidate and impress, Dan suspected Carhill dressed as he did for the same reason. Though almost shabby by comparison, Dan's favorite flannel suit was at least lint free, he thought.

"Well, Dr. Lassiter," began Carhill, moving back behind his desk, "after reading the book *Power Through Intimidation* I have to ask where you would feel most comfortable sitting. Here?" He indicated the chair by the desk. "Or across from me at the coffee table over there?"

Hoping Carhill's friendly overture might presage a successful outcome to their meeting, Dan smiled and took the chair in front of him.

Carhill nodded and sat down behind the desk. "Well, I must say I was pleasantly surprised by your phone call and delighted to arrange this little get-together. From all I hear, you're extraordinarily effective in your job, and it's high time we met. Tell me, is running a 1200 bed hospital as exhausting as running a 200 man research institute?"

"I suspect so," said Dan, shifting position to avoid a beam of sunlight in his eyes. "Your scientists aren't unionized, are they?"

"Worse—they're free thinkers!" After an exchange of smiles, Carhill leaned back, tented his hands, and asked, "Well, Dr. Lassiter, how can I help you?"

Dan felt a sudden twinge of trepidation, generated

not by Carhill's imposing presence but by the presumptiveness of his request. "No doubt you've heard of Nelson Freiborg?" he began.

"The economist? One of the President's better appointments, I'd say."

"He'd be pleased to hear it. Anyway, my long friendship with Nels Freiborg is the reason I'm here . . ."

Carhill listened impassively until Dan got to Billy Freiborg's leukemia. Then, after making sympathetic sounds, he displayed a deepening frown. "If you're asking my advice on the treatment of refractory leukemia," he said, "I'm afraid I've none to offer. I'm not a clinician. The best I could do is give you the names of the two or three chemotherapists I consider farthest along in their treatment methods—hardly enough to repay you for your kind visit."

"I'd welcome them all the same. But I'm asking for more: I'm asking for the monoclonal antibody I've reason to believe your group has against lymphoblastic leukemia of the T-cell subset."

Carhill's eyebrows lifted. "Are you! And what leads you to believe we possess such a tumor-specific antibody? That's certainly not common knowledge. Otherwise we would've been deluged by similar requests from half the leukemia specialists in the country by now."

"No great mystery," Dan replied. "As associate editor of *The New England Journal,* I read the paper on mouse leukemia your group recently submitted for publication. It caused quite a stir at our editorial meeting, I can tell you, especially the remarks you made pertaining to the prevention of human leukemia in the discussion."

"Not *my* remarks," Carhill corrected. "I was strongly opposed to any mention of its potential human application. But my younger, more impetuous co-authors insisted. Your presence here today is proof of how right I was. But now that the cat is out of the bag, so to speak, I hope you'll use all your influence to hasten publication. That report represents years of arduous effort. I would hate for a rival group to rob us of our rightful priority by the simple expedient of publishing first in *Science* or *Research Reports* or the Frenchman's favorite, *Comptes Rendus*, which rushes scientific articles into print faster than the wire services' news bulletins."

"I understand," said Dan, "and I promise I'll pass on your concern to our editor."

Carhill paused, patting his finger tips together. "Ungracious as it may sound, I'd like you to do more than that, Dr. Lassiter, especially in light of what brought you here today. Please tell your editor that if he cannot promise publication within three months to so inform me immediately."

"As you wish," said Dan reluctantly. "But in my opinion that would be pushing it."

"Perhaps. But you leave me no alternative."

"Me?" Dan protested, dismayed that their talk had gotten sidetracked and irked by Carhill's evident lack of trust in his discretion. "Look," he said forcefully, "I've discussed the gist of your paper with just one person, Ted Swerdloff, who'll be supervising Billy Freiborg's treatment, and I'm sure the other members of the journal's editorial board have been just as discreet. It's not state secrets we're talking about, Dr. Carhill, it's scientific data, and the usual reason you submit them for publication is to inform the scientific community. Otherwise, why bother?"

Carhill smiled tolerantly. "In an earlier and pleasanter era, Dr. Lassiter, you'd doubtless be right. But you know perfectly well that that era went out with ballroom dancing. But to get back to your patient. What makes you think I have the monoclonal antibody you're after?"

Dan sighed. Not only did he sense defeat, but now Carhill was acting coy. "*Do* you?"

"As a matter of fact, we do. At least, we have hybridomas that manufacture antibodies we believe are specific for T- and B-cell leukemia. Whether one of them precisely fits the antigen on the surface of your patient's leukemic cells remains to be seen. Even if it doesn't, there's an excellent chance we can make one that does in short order."

"I'm happy to hear it," said Dan. "I'd be even happier if I didn't sense a 'but' in your voice."

"You do, indeed. Even though we can probably provide you with the most essential ingredient in your dubious treatment protocol, and though it stands a slim chance of succeeding, I'd consider it the height of folly to release it to you. It would be ill advised, to say the least, and irresponsible of me to be a party to it. Need I elaborate?"

"That would be decent of you," said Dan, his voice hard-edged, " . . . if you can spare the time."

"Very well. A favor for a favor," said Carhill. "I expect your help at the *New England Journal of Medicine*, don't forget. It's true, we've cured mouse leukemia with our monoclonals, but that result doesn't translate easily into the human kind. Murine leukemia has been studied in the laboratory for years; it's clearly virus-induced. Who can say if acute human leukemia has a similar origin? Or even a single cause? The odds are it's multi-factorial—heredity, retroviruses, chemicals, all contributing to its expression. Moreover, I despise anecdotal reports. Suppose the treatment you and Swerdloff propose works, at least for a time. What does that prove? What statistical significance does it have? Or suppose it ends in disaster. After all, you'll be introducing a mouse protein into your patient's blood stream. What's to stop him from having a fatal allergic reaction? All that'd accomplish would be to worsen the 'mad scientist' reputation researchers in the field already have. Now, if your hospital's hem-oncology group were to propose to treat a *series* of such patients, one large enough to achieve statistical significance, I would be more than happy to consider a collaborative venture. Even though we've entered into preliminary discussions with other hospitals regarding such trials, there's no reason your fine clinical facility can't be included. Honestly, now, wouldn't that be a more suitable arrangement?"

"For my fine clinical facility, it would," replied Dan. "But I'm not representing it at the moment. I'm the advocate of one fourteen-year-old boy who's dying of leukemia and doesn't give a damn about statistical significance!"

"Now, now," soothed Carhill. "No need to get emotional. I'm not heartless, Dr. Lassiter. Nor am I the director of a treatment center like the Dana-Farber Institute. I'm merely a scientist trying to act responsibly. I'm afraid I'd feel the same way if the boy were my own kin."

I'm afraid you would, too, thought Dan.

"All right, Dr. Carhill, I won't belabor the issue. But neither am I quite ready to admit defeat. Since you won't supply us with the antibody we need, perhaps you can recommend another source . . ." When Carhill looked doubtful, Dan snapped, "Surely you know who your closest competitors are—the ones you're so afraid will beat you into print?"

"Of course," said Carhill stiffly. "There are several groups trying to isolate specific tumor antigens for the lymphomas and leukemias."

"And the closest?"

Carhill sighed. "Sigourney, as always. He's concentrated mainly on the antigenicity of solid tumors, but I wouldn't be at all surprised if he's studied leukemias, too." He sighed again. "Nothing that man does surprises me anymore. But frankly, Dr. Lassiter, I doubt his attitude will be any different from mine. He's not totally mad."

"No," said Dan. "He's certainly not. I haven't seen Steve in many years, but we were once friends. We both trained together at the old Commonwealth General."

"Did you? I'm relieved to hear it."

"Relieved?" Dan was puzzled. "In what sense?"

"In . . . in what I'd consider an ethical sense. It's my understanding Sigourney was asked to leave Commonwealth General after publishing a paper that contained certain, uh, faulty data. Since you were there at the time, you must have heard talk about it and . . ."

"I heard more than talk," Dan interrupted. "I heard the facts. And I strongly advise you never to make such an accusation again. Some of the data—the clinical data—were, indeed, 'cooked,' but by Curt Gundersen, not Sigourney. This, by Gundersen's own admission. He was a sick man at the time, mentally as well as physically, and he desperately wanted to be first to develop a reliable erythropoetin assay. So he changed some of the clinical diagnoses to fit Steve's assay results, hoping subsequent improvements in the method would ultimately establish its worth. Also hoping to stake out that same priority of discovery you were stressing earlier.

"Unfortunately, he never admitted this publicly, and Steve Sigourney was too much of a gentleman to place the blame where it belonged—on his once great but dishonest mentor."

"I see," said Carhill, looking abashed. "I'm grateful you told me. I wish I could be more charitable toward Sigourney but, alas, our enmity runs too deep."

Dan regarded him curiously. "Mind telling me why?"

"Mind?" Carhill cocked an eyebrow. "After that come-uppance you just gave me, I'm afraid I *do* mind. But I wish you luck with Sigourney, and especially with your patient, all the same. Good day, Dr. Lassiter."

"I'm not surprised," said Ted Swerdloff after Dan related the outcome of his meeting with Carhill. "Even though they're pretty cold-blooded, his reasons are hard to fault. Are you going to contact Sigourney?"

"I already have," Dan told him. "It wasn't easy. According to his secretary, he neither takes nor returns phone calls between eight and four. Not a bad idea when you think about it. But she called a little while ago to say Steve would be willing to meet me tomorrow evening in his lab. Want to go down to Philly with me and see his set-up? After all, you're expecting me to fund a hybridoma farm of your own."

"Believe me, Dan, it's a real growth industry."

"For the three hundred grand seed money it takes, it had better be!"

Chapter 4

"HOW DO YOU BECOME a famous scientist? You do it in three stages," Steve Sigourney once told a student reporter. "First, you work very hard in the laboratory for many years. Second, you hire others to do the lab work while you go around giving lectures. Third, you show off your own institute."

Steve was not being entirely facetious. In the absence of a monarch bestowing peerages or a State Central Committee awarding dachas, that was the American way and he had followed it—though, in his case, the second stage had been remarkably brief. In 1975, a huge cash grant by an anonymous donor paid for the conversion of an old armory on the north edge of the University of Pennsylvania campus into a research institute where Steve could pursue his innovative work in molecular biology. In a hurry to make the most of the opportunity, he left the armory's exterior intact. Under its sandstone shell, the Sigourney Institute was a makeshift affair of offices, laboratories, conference rooms and animal quarters. Someday Steve planned to remodel it, turn in into a showplace of elegant design and efficiency, but right now all available funds went for the purchase of the latest equipment and salaries for his fifty-two fulltime employees.

Returning to his office in late afternoon, Steve was surprised to see a telephone message from Dan Lassiter urgently requesting a meeting, and after a moment's deliberation, he agreed to it. He remembered Lassiter as an intense, inquisitive medical resident who spent almost as much time on the wards as Steve did in the laboratory. If he saw any medical doctor in the hospital cafeteria at two in the morning, it was likely to be Lassiter. He also recalled that, for reasons never made clear, Lassiter was death-haunted; personalizing it, openly declaring unnatural death his mortal enemy. From emergency room to intensive care unit, the hospital was a field of combat on which Lassiter fought death tenaciously. Such drive made him a Gundersen favorite and his eventual successor—though for several interim years, he had been banished to a community hospital in mid-Massachusetts, made to do penance for daring to rival the Great Man's clinical skills and popularity with the house staff.

Parallels between Lassiter's ties to Gundersen and his own raised unpleasant memories, but Steve had no time to dwell on them; he had a more pressing problem.

Nicole Brueur, Hungarian born like himself and niece of an old family friend, was a Ph.D candidate in biochemistry at the University of Pennsylvania who had spent the last six months working for him. In his weekly seminars with his quartet of graduate students, Steve had been impressed with her. She was knowledgeable, hard-working and fluent in several languages, an immense advantage in scientific literature searches. Sometimes he would even speak a few words of Hungarian to her. She was easily the brightest of the four, and to be fair, not sexist, he should not hesitate an instant to offer her the full-time staff position they all coveted. But he was running a research program, not an equal employment enterprise, he told himself, and Nicole presented a peculiar problem: she was simply too attractive. A disruptive influence. It was pitiful to see how her male co-workers' concentration lapsed and their speech faltered when she came into a room; how the crossing and uncrossing of her legs drew their eyes. It was not merely lustful young men she had this effect on; some of his senior scientists were equally susceptible.

Steve understood why. Her smile, which at first he had considered merely pleasant, even winsome, was more than that; it was dazzling. Her russet hair had a natural sheen no commercial shampoo could lend. Her lustrous eyes were distractingly changeable—innocent one moment, shrewd and knowing the next. At unguarded moments, while she was listening to a dull lecturer or doing rote tasks in the lab, Steve sometimes caught a look of sadness in them so deep as to resemble bitterness. He supposed it stemmed from her personal history.

According to her uncle, who had persuaded Steve to recommend Nicole to the admissions committee of her Ph.D program, her industrial-chemist father and politically active mother had fled Budapest for Paris after the bloody uprising of 1956. Nicole had been briefly, miserably, married to a French film-maker, then engaged to an American medical student—her reason for coming to Philadelphia. That relationship must have foundered, too, and from her long hours in the lab Steve suspected there was no new man in her life.

In an obvious effort to minimize her sexual allure, Nicole wore white frocks buttoned almost to her neck and pinned her shoulder-length hair back in an old-maidish chignon. But it did little good: beauty concealed could be even more tantalizing than beauty flaunted and Nicole's male co-workers still stared.

Steve had to admit that at times she exerted a strange effect on him, too. It was as if he had known her intimately years before—impossible, since she was thirty-one and he was forty-six. Whatever the attraction, he knew it wasn't sexual. He had not felt that emotion in years, sublimating it to his work as a monk must to his religion. Yet he could not deny it—he felt a strong current of tension, of nameless emotion, in her presence. It was distracting, perplexing. Once, while leaning over her shoulder to point out something through the lens of a binocular microscope, the fragrance of her hair had momentarily made him light-headed.

But a relationship with her—with any woman—was out of the question. How does a man introduce a woman he desires into his private world when that world consists of a special madness?

Steve knew he was not insane, not in any clinical sense. Nor did he really feel he was any kind of genius. If *genius* implied extraordinary powers of intuition and perception, he would hardly have to work so hard to progress so slowly. Besides, his uncle Anton was the purest intellect in the family. Emeritus professor of philosophy at Columbia University, theological scholar, collector and translator of rare religious tomes, Anton was even more reclusive and miserly with his time than Steve himself. In their ritualized, twice-yearly visits, his uncle both fascinated and infuriated him. Steve could tolerate Anton's mysticism, but his anti-science arguments were so abstruse as to be incomprehensible. If God had two faces, two altars, Steve and Anton stood on opposite sides of Him. . . .

But his mind was wandering again, he realized,

taking him in the opposite direction from where he needed to go.

He had procrastinated long enough; he must make a decision in Nicole's case now. In a few minutes she had an appointment with him, at which time he felt obliged to tell her whether or not she would be offered a position on his full-time staff. The prerogative was his; he had guarded it zealously. But just this once, couldn't he make an exception? Let a committee of senior scientists decide? No, he concluded reluctantly. Not only would it be setting an unwanted precedent, but they would almost certainly vote to keep her on the basis of merit alone. So why was he still agonizing over it? What possible threat did she pose?

Stefan, he said aloud. Get a grip on yourself. Where is your vaunted ruthlessness? Look her in the eye and firmly but tactfully fire her. Give yourself some peace!

Virtually on the stroke of five o'clock, Nicole entered his inner office with a steaming demitasse rattling slightly in its saucer.

"Cafe espresso from Carlo's lab,"she announced. "I thought you might like some."

"Thank you," said Steve, taking the cup from her and smiling through compressed lips, as he habitually did to hide his crooked teeth. "That's very thoughtful of you. Sit down, Nicole. Sit down. How's the work going?"

"A good afternoon. We harvested over two hundred hybridomas from the last batch."

"Excellent . . . excellent," he said and sank down in his desk chair. He must stop saying everything twice, he told himself; it was too obvious a sign of nervousness. "Well, Nicole, well . . ." he began and faltered. He felt uncomfortable addressing her by her first name. But he couldn't call her "Miss Brueur" when he was on a first-name basis with her fellow graduate students, and he couldn't call her Dr. Brueur for a few weeks yet.

"Yes, Dr. Sigourney?" She sat erect and expectant-looking, hands folded demurely in her lap.

Steve took a quick sip of the strong coffee and sighed. "You've been with us six months now and your work . . . well, aside from your work, which has been quite satisfactory, it's been a pleasure having you here." Again he smiled through tight lips.

"Thank you, Dr. Sigourney. It's been . . . it's been one of the great experiences of my life."

An exaggeration? he wondered. Perhaps not. She had been taught scientific discipline; he had made sure of that. And the excitement generated by their research was contagious. Otherwise he would not have such a long list of graduate students eagerly waiting to fill each available spot. "I'm pleased to hear it. Nonetheless . . ."

"Yes?" she asked, puzzled by his sudden grimace.

"Nonetheless, Nicole, I don't think it would be advisable for you—your career—to stay on here. I don't think this is the right place for you."

There, he thought with grim satisfaction, the hurtful words were out. He steeled himself for her response.

To his surprise, she didn't even blink. Exhaling a sigh, she said, "Regrettably, I agree with you."

"Oh?" he uttered, taken aback. "Are things not to your liking here?"

"Oh, no," she said hastily. "It's not that at all. I've never been happier anywhere in my life. Never so productive. It's just that . . ." Her voice trailed off and she slumped in her chair, hugging herself with her arms.

"Yes?" he prompted. "Go on."

"This is difficult . . . so difficult," she said softly, her gaze on the floor. When she looked up, he was startled to see moisture in her eyes. "I'm not sure I have the courage to explain."

"I insist!" he said, regretting his imperious tone but totally confused now.

"Very well," she said resolutely and drew herself erect again. "Who were *your* mentors, Dr. Sigourney? The scientists you studied under who had the greatest influence on your career?"

"Mentors?" Steve repeated. "I've had several, from Krebs and Kornfield in England to Speigelman here."

"All men?"

He shrugged. "Of course. The women's movement was not upon us yet. What is your point?"

Boldly she said, "My point is this: you have been more than just a mentor to me. You have filled my fantasies like no other man before. Naturally, you have done nothing to encourage this. It is merely something I feel, and will go on feeling. But it's an impossibly one-sided situation, of course, so I think it's best that I leave."

Steve's first reaction was utter disbelief, then anger. Surely this was some kind of a joke—a joke with a cruel, cutting edge! How dare she taunt him this tasteless way? He started to speak sharply when he saw her recoil at his facial expression and reconsidered. Logic was too integral a part of his thought processes to be ignored now. If it *was* a joke, what was its purpose? What could she possibly hope to gain by offending him?

"Nicole," he began and sighed deeply. "Naturally, I'm nonplussed. Perhaps you'd better explain."

"Explain what?" she replied defiantly. "A feeling? A fantasy? What do you want explained—its molecular structure, its physiology? I've embarrassed you, I know. I can see it. Possibly disgusted you . . ."

He shook his head.

"I never should've mentioned it," she went on.

"But I was hoping—a slim hope—that you might be interested in me, too. It was foolish, I realize now, but no caprice. You'll never know how I agonized over whether to tell you. But I assumed you'd offer me a position here and be hurt when I refused. That, of course, was my second bit of wishful thinking, since you didn't even do that. Why?" she demanded. "Why was I not offered a position?"

Steve smiled wanly. "I had a little speech prepared but it's flown completely out of my head." Good God! he thought. He couldn't possibly tell the truth now; he would have to improvise. But he had neither time nor stomach for it. How could he be so craven as to reward the courage she had shown with self-serving lies?

As if sensing his discomfort, she suddenly rose. "Do you wish me to leave?"

He gazed up almost pleadingly. "Perhaps it would be . . . No! I do *not* wish it. Sit down, Nicole. Sit down and let me repay the great compliment you've paid me with the not so complimentary truth. From the quality of your work, the evaluations of your supervisors, you deserve a full-time position here. But I was reluctant to offer it. In fact, I was determined to get rid of you." Awkwardly, he explained why.

When he finished, she barely concealed a smile. "But if I am so irresistibly attractive, such a *femme fatale*, why weren't you attracted to me, too?"

"I didn't dare let myself be. After all . . ." he spread his hands, "I'm hardly a matinee idol."

"Hardly," she agreed. "Nor particularly *au courant* about the ways of modern women. Not only are we more independent, but a little more discriminating, too. You talk about matinee idols. Well, I've dated a fair sampling, but seldom more than once. I like my brain exercised as well as my body. You, on the other hand, have enthralled me for months. Your lectures are brilliant; your staff conferences are even better. I could hardly wait for the others to finish their reports so you could comment, so I could marvel again at how clearly you think . . . I cannot help the way I look, Stefan. Oh, I suppose I could dress dowdily, make myself less appealing in other ways. And you—you could do the opposite. But I, too, put less value on form than substance. You know as well as I that there is as much romance, as much a mixture of thrill and risk, in science as any amorous adventure —and who is your equal there?" She paused for breath, waiting for him to reply. When he didn't, she said exasperatedly, "Oh, for God's sake, give me credit for some maturity, for wanting to make as exciting a life for myself as I can! And you, I presume, want the same. Research can't possibly fulfill all your needs. Don't you ever get lonely? Want somebody to reach out to at night? Is your life so different from other mere mortals?"

"You know nothing about my life!" he said defensively.

"No. I know nothing of how a television set works either, but I can judge the quality of the picture it projects. Or am I being presumptuous—not about your life but about your feelings? Perhaps I'm simply not enough of a challenge for you."

"Or perhaps too much. A worker ant can't change its nature."

"That is merely an assumption. Where is the proof?"

Steve stared at her for a long moment, his scalp tingling with strange excitement, his brain in turmoil. He really didn't know how to converse with a young woman. But she was a scientist, too, he reminded himself. He could talk to her in scientific language. "All right, all right, I admit the bare possibility of an affinity, a reaction, a positive result. But *you* plan the next step in the experiment."

She smiled triumphantly. "I will!" Reaching out

and seizing his desk calendar, she turned it toward her. "According to this, you're free the night after tomorrow. Dinner at my place? Eight o'clock?"

Slowly, reluctantly, he nodded. "It's madness," he muttered. Then, recovering his voice, he warned, "Just remember what Claude Bernard once said: A scientist does not conduct experiments to confirm his ideas, but to control them."

"And you want me to control what? My fantasies? I thought we'd already been through that. I don't deny I'm excited, Stefan. Who wouldn't be? After all, for the small bother of cooking dinner I'll get hours of uninterrupted conversation with one of the world's great minds!"

"Out!" Steve ordered with genuine impatience. "Even insouciance has its limits."

"At once, *Monsieur le professeur. Bon soir and mille merci.*"

After Nicole had left the office, exchanging cheerful "Good evenings!" with his elderly but invaluable secretary, Marta, Steve tried to compose himself, clear his mind for the hours of work ahead. He plucked the top manuscript from the stack on his desk and tried to concentrate on it, but it was no use; his brain still whirled in confusion and the typescript was a blur. Wearily he rose and went into his private bathroom to douse his face with cold water, to restore his vision, if not his critical faculties. But before he did, he could not resist staring at his reflection in the mirror. His face contained a little more color than usual—otherwise, no change. Had he expected any?

An affair—a physical relationship—with Nicole was unthinkable. He had sworn long ago never to become vulnerable to another person's whims again. Yet he had to admit she was charming. And she certainly spoke her mind. And there was a vitality about her that he couldn't help envying. Unlike the rut he was in, existing only for scientific facts, for measurable truth, for the prize offered annually by the inventor of dynamite, Nicole's life seemed vibrant with possibilities.

Returning to his desk, he again picked up the manuscript entitled *Idiotypes, Anti-idiotypes and Immunogenic Determinants*, and sighed. Technical concepts he could understand. They were logical, provable, reasonably predictable—all the things that limited experience had taught him love between a man and woman was not.

Billy Freiborg never did get a chance to talk to his new roommate. During their first night together, Henry Wedemacher began to hemorrhage from his nose and mouth and was immediately transferred to the pediatric intensive care unit. The next morning Billy saw Henry's parents, whom he had met when the boy was first brought in, at the nursing station signing papers of some kind. His mother, a nice looking woman, was in tears. His father had his arm around her shoulder and looked dazed. Nobody seemed to notice Billy as he walked past, but he heard the nurse mention the name of a funeral home.

Jeez, he thought, poor Henry had died, bled to death or something! But how could that be? They had plenty of blood in the blood bank. Both Billy's parents and his uncle Nels had donated some. How could Henry's doctors have let him just bleed to death?

Chad had told him, and Madeline had confirmed, that even with the best available treatment, only forty to fifty percent of leukemic kids made it five years. It was like a coin flip—half lived, half didn't. So, Billy told himself, it shouldn't really shock him that some went on to die right here at Mayo's. But somehow it did. He wished he hadn't found out about Henry. He sure didn't want to know about any of the others, especially Chad. Yet, loath though he was to admit it,

Henry's death raised questions that needed answering.

That evening when the shift nurse, Miss Jones, brought his supper tray, Billy asked, "Hey, Jonsey, how can I get hold of Madeline Hershey?"

"Madeline's not here any longer, Billy. She got her M.D. last week and went off to California somewhere to take a residency." The matronly nurse smiled. "As med. students go, she was a nice one, wasn't she? Pretty, too."

"Yeah—both."

"Anything I can do?"

"Naw. Not unless you know a way to get me out of here."

"Sorry, pal. That's for others with more authority than me to decide. Now," she said, picking up a knife and fork, "since I don't want you jiggling your intracath too much, let me cut up some of your meat."

"Henry Wedemacher sure didn't last long, did he?"

The nurse dropped the utensils and turned to stare. "You know about him?"

"As much as I want to."

"It doesn't usually happen that way, Billy."

"I bet. You wouldn't have many patients if it did."

"Want to talk about it—if not with me, then with Dr. Hendricks?"

Scornfully, Billy said, "That psychologist guy, or whatever he is? No, thanks. He's writing a book and I don't want to be in it."

"Anybody else then?"

"My folks—only I won't. I tried once before to talk to them about dying and you should've seen the looks on their faces! Like I told them I was gay or something."

The nurse nodded sympathetically. "If you like, I could sort of hint you wanted to talk about it when your dad comes by tonight."

Billy hesitated, then shook his head. "Naw, forget it. With all the farmers in Northern Minnesota going broke, he's got enough on his mind."

"Well, just let me know, Billy, if you ever do."

"Sure, Jonesey. Thanks."

When the nurse left, Billy picked at his food for a while and then pushed the tray aside, wishing he could push away the thoughts in his mind as easily. The image of Henry Wedemacher's parents at the nursing station still haunted him. He hated to think of his own mom and dad looking so forlorn about him someday. But it would be too late to comfort them then, and he didn't know how to prepare them now.

Only with Chad Petersen had he ever talked about death and Billy hadn't had much to say. Nobody important to him, not grandparents nor close relatives nor school chums, had ever died. He had never even attended a funeral. At least Chad had been to funerals—his dad's, his cousin Heather's, who was so great-looking she had been a fashion model in Chicago before she'd been mangled in an auto accident. Once, when Billy had asked about them, Chad had wrapped a hand towel around his neck to resemble a clerical collar and intoned, "We are gathered here today to mourn the passing of Billy Freiborg, who, in fourteen years of hard living, smoked pot only once, played touchie-feelies with his girl only once, and jerked off never! He died as he lived—never knowing what it was all about."

"Hey, cut the clowning," Billy had complained. "That's not funny."

"Okay. How's this: Here in this beautiful pine casket, a four-hundred-dollar value, specially priced all this month for two ninety-five at the Bemidji Funeral and Massage Parlor, lies Billy Freiborg. But just remember, folks, it's only his shell—the nut is gone! Better?"

"Not much."

"Or— Here lies Billy Freiborg who, in his brief time on this earth was his father's pride, his teacher's pet, and the Mayo Clinic's case 43132, deceased."

"You're sick!" Billy accused.

"So are you, kid. Why else would we be here?"

Billy smiled at the memory and turned on the TV to his favorite show, *Barney Miller*. Having seen tonight's rerun at least twice before, however, he soon dozed off.

Chapter 5

ALONE IN HIS STUDY THAT evening, his brain buzzingly fatigued from trying to digest the glut of facts just fed it, Dan Lassiter put aside the medical articles piled on his lap and came to some sweeping conclusions.

Life, he decided, was a movie, and man a comically arrogant movie-goer who had arrived in the middle and watched for all of five seconds before bitterly complaining that he didn't understand the plot.

Moreover, in a world of grown children disenchanted by happily-every-after, science was the ultimate bedtime story, an endless source of fascination and wonderment. The universe was expanding at an incredible rate. Expanding into what? Positively charged sub-atomic particles must be balanced with negatively charged ones, the Yin with the Yang. Why? How does the body process the billions of viruses, bacteria and chemicals that invade its blood stream each day and decide which is "self" or "non-self," friend or foe?

And cancer—innumerable questions there. Is cancer a natural force like fire, wildly destructive when unchecked, indispensable when controlled? Unlike normal human cells, which can only divide forty to sixty times in tissue culture, cancer cells reproduce endlessly. Such behavior, under artificial conditions, was considered an anomaly. But as scientists have long appreciated, anomalies are often the first clue to some deeper discovery. Could cancer possibly by trying to teach us the secrets of immortality?

Dan had been plunged into this contemplative mood by reading the collection of hybridoma articles Ted Swerdloff had lent him earlier. Ted's claim that the creation of the hybridoma was the equal of recombinant DNA as a technological triumph and the equal of penicillin as a therapeutic tool—in short, the medical break-through of the decade, possibly the rest of the century—Dan had first dismissed as hyperbolic. But now, after pondering the implications of the reports he had just read, he thought Ted might be right.

For years, immunologists had been stymied by their inability to make pure antibodies, as essential to their work as sharp scalpels to surgeons. These tiny bits of protein were manufactured in that sub-group of white blood cells called lymphocytes, the supply factories for the body's immune, or policing, system. Although people took the workings of their lymphocytes as much for granted as the oxygen content of the air they breathed, they were truly one of Nature's wonders, each of its protein policemen having "eyes" so keen they could recognize one biologically active molecule out of the millions on a cell's surface, and "claws" to seize it. For reasons unknown, however, lymphocytes did not survive long enough in culture dishes for their specific antibodies to be harvested.

The immunologist's only alternative was to use laboratory animals to generate crude mixtures of antibodies containing the one they sought. But because of the immune system's ultrasensitivity to even the most minute amount of foreign protein, this method was highly fallible. When a foreign substance like hepatitis virus was injected into an animal, its immune system responded not only to the virus itself but to whatever other protein molecules were stuck to its surface, producing a hodgepodge of antibodies of only limited use. For the immunologist, this meant a task as tedious as trying to fish out a rainbow trout in a pond full of speckled ones. What was needed was a way for him to breed his own rainbow trout—a procedure heretofore impossible because lymphocytes refused to replicate under laboratory conditions. The creation of the first hybridoma in 1975 provided a possible solution. When a cancer cell fused with a lymphocyte, it endowed this "marriage of necessity" with its unique immortality, it's ability to clone itself exactly and endlessly. And a single lymphocyte produced a single "monoclonal" antibody that could be isolated, preserved, and stored in limitless quantities.

This much Dan could deduce from the highly technical terminology of the articles. What was left for him to do was to persuade Steve Sigourney, the premier explorer into this microcosmic world, to focus his genius on the plight of one fourteen-year-old boy.

A little before ten, Kris finally came home from the hospital. Joining her in the kitchen as she fixed herself a sandwich, Dan said sympathetically, "Rough day?"

"Rough day *and* night. We had three empty bed on the ICU this morning, but by evening it was standing room only. The last admission was the worst. A sixty-year-old Englishman, disappointed in love, who tried to kill himself. Watch out for suicidal Englishmen," she said between bites into a tuna salad sandwich.

"Why?"

"Because they know something most Americans don't: that a bottle of *Tylenol* is a lot deadlier than a bottle of aspirin."

"Did you give him the methyl cystine antidote in time?"

"Can't be sure. We'll know by morning. If not, we'll put him on charcoal dialysis . . . How'd you make out with Carhill?"

Dan made a thumbs down sign. "Worse yet, he lectured me."

"On what?"

"On the sanctity of the scientific method and its deplorable corruption by well-intentioned dunces like me. One thing came through loud and clear, though. He hates Steve Sigourney with a passion."

"Steve? Did he say why?"

"Not after I defended Steve over the bum rap Gundersen laid on him. You know, the erythropoetin assay."

"I thought that was ancient history."

"Not to Carhill."

"Well, what now?"

"I go hat in hand to Steve. Ted and I are meeting with him in Philly tomorrow."

A violent electrical storm over New Jersey made Dan's flight to Philadelphia bumpy and more than a little frightening. With relief, he felt the wheels of the DC-9 grip the runway only ten minutes behind schedule. "If God had meant for man to fly—" he muttered to Ted Swerdloff as he unbuckled his seat belt.

"He would've made him jet-propelled from mouth to arsehole."

"That's original," said Dan dryly. "Just save some of your celebrated wit for Steve Sigourney. Or has he lost his sense of humor?"

"Humor? I've never even seen him smile. Almost —but not quite. Want to hear about it?"

"Go ahead. I'm through praying."

"Well, it happened at an international workshop on major histocompatibility antigens in Mexico City a few years back. A lot of big guns were there trying to shoot each other's pet theories down and the flak rose hot and heavy. Anyway, during one panel discussion moderated by Baruj Benacerraf and including Carhill but not Sigourney, someone from the audience asked a question that stumped the four panelists. So Benacerraf said, 'I see Dr. Sigourney in the room. Perhaps he knows the answer.' Steve ambles up to the aisle mike and says, 'Of course I know the answer. But since you didn't invite me to be a member of your panel, I'm not going to tell you!' and sits down. That's the closest I ever came to seeing him smile."

Dan laughed. "That's outrageous, but funny. I just hope our old friendship counts enough to make him a little more tolerant of us."

Forty minutes later, Dan and Ted arrived at the Sigourney Institute and were escorted to Steve's ground floor office by a security guard. A white-haired secretary told them Dr. Sigourney would return shortly and ushered them into his inner office. Dan spent a few minutes inspecting the awards and mementos hung on the walls and then, realizing he was pacing, stood by the window, wondering again why he had ever involved himself in such a heroic undertaking.

Moments later, Steve entered the office, put the stack of books he was carrying on the desk and offered his hand.

Dan was pleased by the warmth of his greeting but shocked by his appearance. Steve was even gaunter than he remembered. His hair was completely gray, thinning on top, and flecked with flakes from a rash on his forehead. Another rash, reddish and pustular, spread out from the sides of his nose in a butterfly-like pattern, making Dan wonder if he had lupus erythematosis. From bloodshot eyes to twitching eyelids, Steve not only looked exhausted but as if he were running on nervous energy alone.

Dan was not surprised that Steve's greeting of Ted Swerdloff was more restrained, almost perfunctory. To his "us or them" mentality, Ted represented competition.

Waving them to the couch, Steve sat opposite and said, "Well, tell me about your urgent problem."

After reporting the bare clinical details of Billy Freiborg's case, Dan asked Swerdloff to describe his proposed treatment.

Steve sat rubbing his eyes and scratching his cheek restlessly but heard them out without interruption. "Okay," he finally said. "So you want to try monoclonal antibodies to cure a case of leukemia. That might be jumping the gun a bit, considering the current state of the art, but that's not my concern. My question to you, Dan, is why?"

"What do you mean?"

Steve gestured impatiently. "I mean, the boy is no kin to either of you. You haven't even met him. Why get so involved?"

"I've asked myself the same question countless times," Dan admitted. "I could say I'm doing a favor for an old friend who's also a Presidential advisor and could return the favor in any number of ways. But I'm just not that political an animal, Steve. I get enough grief from the medical politicians in my own back yard not to want to enlarge that constituency. I suppose I got involved to meet a need. Now that the field of immunology is finally coming into its own, I need some stimulus to keep up with it—to make me feel I'm still a front-line physician. After all, applying new facts to the care of patients is the main way doctors like me learn."

"You want a . . . therapeutic adventure?" asked Steve dubiously.

"Something like that."

"Interesting," Steve mused. "I'm not overly fond of dilettantes, even though I was one myself for a time, and I'd certainly feel more at ease if you'd skipped the self-help part and simply stated you wanted to be the first to come up with a new treatment for leukemia. But . . ." he shrugged, "I accept your explanation. What do you want from me?"

"The monoclonal antibody to destroy malignant T-cells. As much of it as you can possibly spare."

"To treat *one* patient?"

Dan braced himself for a repeat of the same arguments against such a risky and unscientific course that Carhill had used. "Just one—at least to start. Can you help us out?"

Steve hesitated. Then, to Dan's relief, he nodded. "There's a good possibility that I can. One of my project directors, John Wendall, has been accumulating a library of monoclonals against various types of leukemia. Naturally he'd have to have a sample of your patient's blood to check, but I'd be rather surprised if he didn't have an antibody to match it."

"And you'd be willing to collaborate with us on the treatment?" asked Swerdloff.

"Collaborate—no! Officially, I want nothing whatever to do with it. But cooperate—yes. After all, I have what you need. It's for a worthy cause. Why shouldn't I be generous?"

Dan exchanged glances with Swerdloff and said, "I'm deeply grateful, Steve."

"I'm sure . . . Why do you look so surprised?"

"I hoped, but hadn't really expected you to agree so readily. Before imposing on you, I tried to get the monoclonal we need locally. Carhill turned me down flat and predicted you'd so the same."

"Carhill makes a lot of uncharitable predictions about me. But two things I won't discuss in this office, lest I get carried away. One is nuclear proliferation, and the other is Gregory Carhill." Steve glanced at his watch. "Now, is there anything further I can do for you two?"

Swerdloff said, "I'd like a quick tour of your hybridoma labs, if it wouldn't be too much trouble."

"Of course." Steve buzzed his secretary on the intercom. "Marta, tell Wendall I have visitors who would like to tour the third floor labs. They'll be up shortly."

Steve rose and escorted them to the door. He shook Swerdloff's hand and then turned to Dan.

"Steve, I don't know how to thank you . . ."

"It's nothing. Carhill and I are just heartless in different ways. Besides, it's a real pleasure to see you again."

"For me, too," said Dan. "After all, we were both Gundersen proteges in the good old days."

"The *not*-so-good old days," amended Steve with an accusatory glint in his eyes. Taking Dan by the arm, he said, "Could I have a word with you in private? My secretary will help you catch up with Swerdloff later."

"Of course," Dan agreed and followed him back inside the office.

Once reseated, Steve said, "I may be mistaken, but it's my understanding you were the first to find Curt Gundersen's body after he committed suicide."

"Actually a cleaning lady did. She called me."

"Did he leave a note?"

Grimly, Dan nodded. "It was terse, melodramatic and haunting: 'No wife, no kin, no hope.' "

"Anything else in the way of personal papers? A diary perhaps?"

"None I know of."

"I see," said Steve, frowning. "I was hoping . . ."

"I think I know what you were hoping for," Dan ventured. "A confession of sorts—something—to absolve you of blame in the erythropoetin assay debacle. But he didn't leave one."

"You *knew* about that? You knew he furnished me with faked data? How?"

"From my wife. You may remember her: Kristina Torvald."

"The endocrinologist! From—from St. Louis. I remember her well. We crossed swords once at an Endocrine Society meeting and she more than held her own. You married her?"

Dan grinned. "I had to. I was determined to get her to join our staff and she spurned every offer I made except one. Fact is, we first met at Gundersen's funeral . . . This is confidential, Steve, but Gundersen was one of her med. school professors. And, for a brief time, her lover. It was around the beginning of his mental breakdown and he desperately needed a confidante. Among other things he confided to Kris was how he made you the fall guy for the failure of the assay. After they broke up, he tried to victimize her, too—nearly forced her to drop out of medical school. But she's tough. She not only survived but vowed to get back at him in the only way that counted: by outshining him as an internist and researcher. Even before we met, she resented me for being named Gundersen's successor, the job she wanted above all else." Dan smiled wryly. "Funny, how Curt roused such fierce, vengeful ambitions in the few people he let get close to him . . . But back to the erythropoetin assay. If it causes you further difficulty, I'm sure Kris would be a willing witness on your behalf."

"It's caused difficulty enough," said Steve ruefully. "But thanks for sharing that information with me. In return, I must be equally candid with you. I seriously doubt that Swerdloff's treatment will work. I give it one chance in a hundred, at best."

"Why?" said Dan, dismayed.

"The animal experiments aren't very encouraging. Oh, the monoclonal certainly lowers their leukemic cell population, even as much as a thousandfold, but it never achieves total kill. Something happens, the count stabilizes, and once the monoclonal infusions are stopped, it rebounds higher than before."

"Any explanation?"

Steve shook his head. "Theoretical possibilities galore, but no solid proof for any of them. To make matters worse, we have observed the complex phenomenon of 'antigenic modulation.' "

Steve explained as best he could. When he finished, Dan sighed and said, "That's really discouraging. What do you suggest we do?"

Steve deliberated. "I suggest you try it. Go the limit. Maybe Swerdloff's idea of mixing the monoclonal with the leukemic cells outside the body will obviate some of the problems we've encountered in our animals. If not . . ." he smiled faintly, "come see me again. Who knows? I might have a few more tricks up my sleeve by then."

"That's a little vague, Steve."

"Intentionally so. Unfortunately, biomedical research institutes like mine aren't what they used to be. They've become mini-Pentagons with vaults full of military secrets. Some even employ spies. Paranoid as it sounds, I'm convinced Carhill has one in my lab . . . I won't comment on whether I have one in his."

"You can't be serious!"

Steve laughed mirthlessly. "There's an old

European saying: 'When you run with the wolves, you howl with the wolves.' You've doubtless heard of industrial espionage. The Russians are particularly adept at it. Well, we researchers represent an industry, too—an increasingly profitable one. Our corporations are big sellers on the stock market."

"Steve," Dan interrupted, "before you go on, there's something I *must* know, and I beg you in strictest confidence to tell me. Although Ted will be directing Billy Freiborg's treatment, I feel personally responsible. If you're right, if it fails, I've got to know for sure there's something more we can do that stands a reasonable chance of succeeding. Otherwise I'm ready to back off now and leave him in the hands of Don Henley at the Mayo Clinic."

Steve paced about his office a few moments, then turned back to Dan. "For the past two years we've published few papers here—not because we've run out of reportable results but because we're overflowing with them: a surplus we're not quite ready to share with our competitors. We've made such incredible progress in the cancer field, Dan, it would take a full day to describe it all. And next month we start publishing; a major paper a month for the next twelve to fourteen months. A veritable barrage! It will stun the scientific world, smash the logjam in the cancer field, maybe even win me the Nobel Prize. So you must try to understand my secretive mentality."

At Dan's uncertain frown, Steve smiled sardonically and snapped, "But you—I can see *your* mentality hasn't changed a bit. What do you care for science prizes or even young leukemia victims? You just want to win one more against your archenemy, death . . . Oh, I haven't forgotten the late night conversations we used to have."

"Evidently not," said Dan, impressed by both his memory and his insight. "And you might well be right. But . . ."

The intercom buzzed. Scowling, Steve seized the phone and barked, "Yes . . . Oh, yes, Marta. I completely forgot. Please tell Andre I can't meet with him until six o'clock. That I'm entertaining an old friend . . . No, six will be fine. Thank you."

"Steve, I really appreciate this," said Dan when he hung up.

"Appreciate what? A rare chance for friendly, honest talk? What do the psychiatrists say—that for most of us sanity is simply *controlled* obsession . . . Well, here we are, two doctors with uncontrolled obsessions—you by death, me by cancer. All right, you insist on knowing what my fall-back strategy will be if the treatment you intend for your patient fails, and I'll tell you. But not a word of this to Swerdloff, understood?"

At Dan's nod, Steve took out a ring of keys from his lab coat pocket and unlocked a filing cabinet. "Come over here," he said, "and I'll show you some data that will absolutely astound you . . ."

"You're strangely silent," remarked Ted Swerdloff toward the end of their flight home.

"Just strange," replied Dan. "Hospital director's disease." He wished he could tell Ted about their reserve weapon, or the other mind-boggling discoveries by Steve's team mentioned merely in passing, but he was sworn to secrecy. In his mind, Dan pictured a marathon among cancer researchers run at a snail's pace for the last fifty years. Suddenly two new technologies, recombinant DNA and monoclonal antibodies, had given the runners their second wind and a dozen or so were sprinting hard for the finish line; the ultimate winner, of course being mankind.

Much as he admired Sigourney's accomplishments, the man himself interested Dan more. Why, he wondered, had Steve been so candid and cooperative? Did the shared ghost of Gundersen bind them together? Or was Steve merely hungry for a confidant whose own quirks made him trustworthy?

"Think we're ready to have Billy Freiborg transferred to us?" he asked Ted a moment later.

"Ready as we'll ever be."

"Good. I'll call the Freiborgs and Don Henley when I get home."

The hesitant note in his voice prompted Ted to ask, "Having second thoughts?"

"More like ninth or tenth, especially after Steve pinned down my motive."

"There's nothing wrong with therapeutic adventures," said Ted, mistaking Dan's meaning. "Not so long as you're clear of head, pure of heart, and well versed in *Murphy's Law.*"

Chapter 6

FIRST NICOLE, NOW DAN LASSITER—he was in danger of losing his misanthropic reputation, thought Steve as he trudged home that night. If the trend continued, he might even join a country club and start sending out Christmas cards!

At least he didn't have to worry about money. While other researchers scrounged for federal grants and private donations, Steve had no such concerns. Thanks to his friend Georgi Kosterlitz, his institute was literally living off the fat of the land. As long as there were rich, vain, gluttonous people in the world begging for admission to the Kosterlitz Clinic, he and Georgi would prosper.

What the two of them had launched years before was one of the strangest medical experiments ever, and one of the most profitable; a clinical trial of unprecedented scope and span. The study was as comprehensive as any devised by a pharmaceutical company and its twenty-five year duration more than ample to detect any delayed side effects from the appetite-killing hormone they were testing. Nonetheless, Steve had persistent misgivings about his silent partnership in the clinic. How would it look to the Nobel Prize selection committee if they ever learned that he had made a major discovery fourteen years before and kept it secret for monetary gain?

If he'd had any inkling back then of the heights his scientific career would reach, he would never have become involved in Georgi's audacious scheme. But what was done could not be undone, thought Steve, reflecting on the compelling circumstances. . . .

In 1965, toward the end of his second year at the University of Pennsylvania, Steve had received a letter from Kosterlitz inviting him to London, England, to discuss a scientific collaboration with his privately owned pharmaceutical company. The engraved letterhead on the stationery and the titles under Kosterlitz's signature were impressive, as was the thousand dollar cashier's check enclosed to pay Steve's travel expenses. Apart from surprise at hearing from Kosterlitz, a medical school classmate at Cambridge whom he had known only slightly and liked even less, Steve's first reaction was to return the check immediately and dismiss the matter from his mind. But a follow-up phone call from Kosterlitz urging Steve to hear him out and a desire to see his ailing father, Maurice, after a four year absence, finally persuaded him to make the trip.

A week later, he and Kosterlitz lunched at Claridge's. Georgi, tall, trim and even more handsome in his early thirties than in his student days, certainly looked as prosperous as he claimed to be. But in spite of the costly comforts he had arranged for Steve, booking an entire hotel suite for him, some barely hidden urgency in his tone and manner suggested an underlying desperation that made Steve wary.

"Well, let's get down to business, shall we?" Kosterlitz said over coffee and brandy.

"Let's, indeed," replied Steve, weary of pointless reminiscences.

"Firstly," began Kosterlitz with disarming candor, "I'm afraid your impression of me—based, in part, on my mediocre performance at Cambridge and my pretentious living style—is only too correct. I'm not a scientist and not much of a physician either. Oh, I have a thriving Harley Street consulting practice and my own company to manufacture harmless, high-potency vitamins, but . . ."

"Georgi," Steve interrupted. "Spare me the apologia and please get to the point."

"At once," Kosterlitz said with a good-natured grin. "What do you know of the anorexigenic factor Lars Nyquist in Oslo isolated from the urine of women with anorexia nervosa?"

"Not much," admitted Steve. "I vaguely remember reading his report in *Nature* and thinking he might be onto something. That's about it."

"He *was* onto something," Kosterlitz stated. "But from our last conversation, he seems to have lost his way."

"Meaning what?"

"His initial extracts were remarkably potent, inducing food refusal in laboratory mice and reducing their body weight by forty percent in a few months. Nyquist even thought he had identified the active ingredient, an amazingly simple polypeptide comprising only three amino acids. But then things went awry. Subsequent extracts proved inert, and all attempts to synthesize the polypeptide have failed. Could *you* do it?"

"Possibly," Steve mused. "I might just know a few

things about the stereochemistry of glutamic acid that Nyquist doesn't. But why would I want to?"

"Two reasons. For the scientific challenge, and for a great deal of money."

"Go on," said Steve, only mildly interested.

"I have a dream—a rather splendorous one. Instead of injecting rich patients with minced monkey glands or *Gerovital*, a worthless procaine solution, I want to inject them with something that really works."

"The anorexigenic peptide?"

"Exactly. But only while they are residents at my own clinic, so I can keep a careful eye out for side effects. What I envision, Steve, is a large group of fat (or at least unfashionably plump) filthy rich patients who would spend one or two months a year with me losing the weight that they'll inevitably regain on the outside, and paying exorbitantly for the privilege. What do you think?"

"Forgive me," said Steve with a look of disdain, "but it sounds quite frivolous."

"Oh, quite! But where's the harm if the peptide you're able to synthesize proves as safe to humans as to Nyquist's mice?"

"A *big* if," Steve reminded him.

"Agreed. But we would take the most meticulous precautions. Keep detailed records. Make it a drug trial with unparalleled safeguards."

"There are laws regulating new drug testing . . ."

"Not where I would build my clinic: Minorca, in the Balearic Islands. I've already picked the site. A garden spot. And I've held preliminary discussions with the Governor General. It'll be an enormous health complex, Steve! In addition to a small hospital with operating room suites, there'll be dieticians, dentists, cosmetic surgeons—the works! All it needs is the gimmick, the drawing card, that I'm hoping you can provide."

"It's an interesting concept," Steve conceded. "Unfortunately, it doesn't interest me."

"I'm not surprised," replied Kosterlitz with equanimity, "since it's my dream, not yours. What might yours be?"

Steve shrugged. "The dream of all scientists—to learn what was never known before."

"Sounds modest enough. But remembering you from student days, I doubt if what *you* have in mind really is. Regardless, wouldn't you like a free hand to pursue it, almost limitless funds?"

At Steve's perfunctory nod, Kosterlitz leaned closer and said, "Then let me tell you what I'm prepared to give you in the way of percentage of gross profits, if you succeed . . ."

Kosterlitz's offer, though a paper one, was impressive, even staggering. But despite this potential windfall, Steve's instincts warned against involving himself in such an unorthodox undertaking. Two considerations finally persuaded him otherwise. First, after reading Nyquist's publications, he strongly suspected he knew how to avoid the pitfall that had stymied all attempts to synthesize the appetite-suppressing tripeptide. Secondly, his father, once a highly successful music hall impressario, was now too crippled by lung disease to work and was deeply in debt. Steve had been appalled by his frail appearance, his seedy residence hotel, the woefully inadequate medical treatment he was getting from a bumbling British health service physician. When all arguments failed to persuade him to seek expert medical care in the United States, Steve resolved to provide his father with the specialists and local hospital facilities to make his remaining days as comfortable as possible. But that cost more money than Steve could afford. Thus began his collaboration with Georgi Kosterlitz.

* * *

Now, mused Steve as he entered his apartment house, the Kosterlitz Clinic was not only world famous but as much in demand among the affluent as the plushest resort. Though it had taken a year to pin down, Steve's initial hunch had proved correct. The tripeptide was inert until an amino group was added to the glutamine end, causing it to bend around itself to form an internal ring known as pyro-glutamic acid. The glycine end required a structural manipulation, too. But Steve finally succeeded in synthesizing the active compound and establishing by various analytical techniques that it was identical to the naturally occuring one. Clinical trials, first on animals, then humans, proved it to be both safe and effective. Not only did it suppress appetite, it suffused the recipient with energy—an extra benefit consistent with the fact that anorexia nervosa patients, even when emaciated to skin and bones, usually deny either hunger or fatigue.

In contrast to the medical profession's predictable denigration of the clinic—its nutrition experts insisting it was the low-calorie diet, not the bogus hormone shots that produced the weight loss—the pharmaceutical houses remained alert to the possibility that Kosterlitz had hit on a bona fide treatment for obesity. At least two had sent company spies to the clinic as patients to collect post-treatment samples of their own blood and urine in the hope of determining the chemical composition of the appetite-killing injection. But the tripeptide was too similar to other metabolic products in the blood to detect. And though Steve's brillliant biosynthetic feat was doubtless the key factor, Georgi also contributed substantially to the clinic's success. He was not only a superb administrator but a conscientious data collector, keeping detailed records on each of his patients as promised. By 1974, ten million or more dollars per year flowed from the clinic into Steve's research program via a Madrid bank whose clients enjoyed absolute anonymity, and Steve made periodic trips to Minorca to review the scientific aspects of the operation.

Yet despite the mutually rewarding arrangement and the precious time it saved him by not having to fill out grant requests, Steve had recurring nightmares about it. Over and over he dreamed of finding himself in a front-row seat at the Stockholm Concert Hall. Before him the stage was bedecked with flowers and dominated by the bust of Alfred Nobel in its center. The black-tie audience was hushed and expectant. Suddenly the orchestra struck up a solemn march, and a master of ceremonies appeared to summon Steve onstage. Waiting for him there, gold medal in hand, was King Carl Gustaf of Sweden with Queen Sylvia by his side. But the medal was never passed. Each time Steve reached for it, the King teasingly withdrew it and the spectators guffawed. Finally they rose as one and shouted, "Fake! Deceiver! Profiteer!" until Steve, eyes stinging from tears of humiliation, bolted from the stage into the wings.

Steve's two-bedroom apartment was sparsely furnished and overflowing with books. One bedroom had, in fact, been converted into a shelf-lined library and the other into an office-den. The living room contained a seldom used fireplace, a leather sofa that opened into a bed, a few easy chairs and end tables, and an elaborate stereo system with four stand-up speakers. Above the mantel hung a life-sized portrait of his mother Elena, painted by Budapest's leading portraitist when she was thirty and at the peak of her career as a concert pianist of national, if not quite international repute. The painting had been his father's most prized possession and had been willed to Steve along with trunks full of worthless memorabilia. A pair of spotlights, strategically placed, highlighted the flesh tones of the portrait, but Steve rarely turned them on. Elena, an *artiste* first and mother second, had kept young Steve in the shadow of her career so long that he preferred to keep her likeness in shadows now.

A few other paintings, including an original Miró Georgi had given him on the tenth anniversary of their clinic, adorned the walls; otherwise, the furnishings were strictly functional. Depending on his activity, whether reading or listening to music when drowsiness overtook him, Steve either slept on the couch in the den or the convertible sofa in the living room.

Pocketing his door key and hanging his raincoat in the hall closet, Steve went directly to the kitchen where he supped on a can of chunky vegetable soup and a container of yogurt. The soup left him thirsty and he was debating whether to brew tea or open a bottle of wine when he heard a knock on the front door.

From the boldness of the knock and its timing, Steve was sufficiently certain of his visitor's identity that he didn't bother to peer through the peephole. "Come in, Yuri," he said and stepped aside for his young friend to enter.

Yuri Donner was the son of an Israeli couple across the hall and the only neighbor who made a habit of dropping in. They had been friends ever since Steve had found an expensive ebony rook on the carpet outside his door and made the rounds of the tenants on his floor until he found its owner. That had led to a discussion of chess strategy and a series of matches.

"Hi, Steve," said Yuri, extending his hand. "How's your research stuff going?"

"It goes," replied Steve, marvelling as always at this pudgy-faced, bespectacled thirteen-year-old's ease of manner.

"Feel up to a match?"

"I could be persuaded. Just tell me who I'm playing tonight. Capablanca? Ruy Lopez? Paul Murphy? Whose book have you been reading lately?"

"Bobby Fischer's. His slashing style is a lot like mine."

"You ought to tell him. It might encourage him to make a comeback."

Yuri ignored the gibe. Arms akimbo, he demanded, "You want to play or you want to talk?"

Steve sighed and led him to the kitchen where they set up the board. He knew he was too exhausted to muster the concentration it took to beat this chess prodigy, but he proceeded to try. Without this distraction he would probably spend the rest of the evening booding over memories of Gundersen revived by Lassiter's visit or the disaster that he feared tomorrow night's dinner with Nicole would turn out to be.

Often, as now, Billy Freiborg's most vivid dreams came not during the night but when he was dozing in the daytime. In this latest one, he and Chad Petersen, sweating profusely in combat dress, brushing away swarms of mosquitos from their faces, were tracking a bunch of Viet Cong through the bush. Sometimes they followed a trail and sometimes they hacked out one. Lugging backpacks and submachine guns, wary of ambushes and booby traps, it was slow, tough going. Except for branches cracking underfoot and shrill jungle noises, they trudged in silence until, coming upon a clearing, Billy groaned, "I know they're out there somewhere, but where?"

"Shh," whispered Chad. Then, tensing and swinging up his gun barrel, he cried, "Look! They're all around us!" Like jack-in-the-boxes, black-clad Cong sprung up around the perimeter of the clearing. Instead of the platoon-sized raiding party they had expected, there were scores of them; at least a hundred.

Back to back, submachine guns jerking and spitting bullets and heating up in their hands, Billy and Chad emptied their magazines at the Cong. Those in the front row, and some behind them, wobbled and fell like duck pins in a bowling alley. Flinging their spent machine guns aside, Billy and Chad drew pistols and kept on firing. Neither the enemy bullets whistling past or kicking up dirt around them nor the sudden squawking of their walkie-talkie disrupted their cool concentration, their deadly accuracy: one bullet, one dead Cong. Never before had Billy felt so imperiled nor so exhilarated.

Suddenly, silently, Chad clutched his chest and fell forward. *Oh, no!* thought Billy, crouching beside him and turning him over. He recoiled in horror. Blood gushed from a hole the size of a fist in Chad's chest. Fearfully, Billy gazed at his face. Lifeless eyes stared back at him. He couldn't believe it: his best buddy was dead! And at any moment he would be, too, Billy realized, as he looked around and saw the ring of Cong, their bayonet blades gleaming in the sun, closing on him.

Involuntarily he cried, "Chad! Chad! Tell me what to do?"

And Chad, who was supposed to be dead, his heart blown away, shrugged and said, "Up to you, kid."

Okay, thought Billy with fierce resolve, if I'm going to die I'm taking some more of these gooks with me! Yanking the pins from two grenades with his teeth, he clutched one in each fist and began spinning around. Surprised by such courage, the Cong gaped. Then, snorting and shouting Oriental gibberish, they began to back away.

"Four . . . three . . . two . . . one!" Billy counted, waiting for the fuse mechanism to run down. Squeezing his eyes shut, he prepared to die. But all that happened was, he got so dizzy from whirling he sank to the ground.

Disgustedly, he asked the dead but somehow still talkative Chad, "Why didn't these damned grenades explode? Why didn't I die?"

This time, though, he got no reply. When his head stopped spinning and his vision cleared, there was no Chad and no Cong either . . .

He was seated at his homeroom desk in Truman Junior High School listening to "Shorty" Jamieson, his history teacher, drone on about the English kings. Across the aisle, catching his eye, Mary Beth Cartmill, the best-built girl in the eighth grade, leaned back nonchalantly and stretched, showing the twin bulges under her sweater.

From behind her, priggish Carolyn Brecht hissed, "Mary Beth, you *stop* that!"

Ignoring her, Mary Beth cooed, "Bill . . . ly," and dreamily cupped her breasts.

Wondering if Mr. Jamieson could see them, Billy turned round; the teacher was staring straight at him. Flinging his chalk down, he snarled, "That'll be enough of that!" and, striding up to Billy, slapped him across the face.

Astonished and enraged—no teacher before had even rapped his knuckles—Billy leaped up and cocked his fist. But before he could clobber the stumpy teacher, Jamieson's hand whipped back and forth across his face—surprisingly soft blows, more like pats on the cheek.

"Billy?" shouted a familiar deep voice, clearly not Jamieson's. "Come on, son, wake up! It's me—Dad."

"Dad?" Opening his eyes, Billy blinked him into focus. "And . . . mom! W . . . what's going on?"

"Got exciting news," said Sven Freiborg. "We're taking you to Boston!"

Chapter 7

BILLY FREIBORG WAS ADMITTED TO Commonwealth General Hospital the next afternoon. His early arrival caught Dan Lassiter by surprise. Until now, he had thought of the boy mainly in the abstract, as a tactical and logistical challenge: how to mobilize and launch monoclonal antibodies, the guided missiles of leukemia therapy, into his blood stream to kill malignant T-cells? It was not until meeting him in person that Dan realized the fallacy of such thinking. Billy Freiborg was no abstraction. He was a lanky, tousle-haired farm kid with a cynical streak and nobody was going to order him around.

Dan's first hint of this came when Ted Swerdloff phoned him at his office around four p.m. to say that Billy was demanding to talk to him.

"Can't it wait?" Dan asked. "I'm in the middle of dictating a grant request."

"I suppose," said Ted reluctantly. "But I've got

rounds in a half hour and we've got a big selling job on our hands."

Dan sighed. "I'll be right down."

Joining Swerdloff at the nursing station of the adolescent unit a few minutes later, Dan said, "All right. What's his problem?"

"It's *our* problem, I'm afraid. He doesn't know why he's here, doesn't want to stay, and doesn't want to talk to anybody but the head man about it."

Dan sank down into the nearest chair, "What does he want?"

"To negotiate terms, I'd imagine."

"*What* terms? It's not a bargaining situation. Doesn't he know how ill he is?"

"Oh, he knows, all right. He may be only fourteen, Dan, but he's been through the medical mill. He's case-hardened. You haven't treated many young cancer victims, have you?"

"Hardly any. Why? Are they that different from adults?"

"As night from day. For one thing, they haven't smoked, drunk or screwed around, so they don't feel the cancer's their fault. They don't even know what the catch-phrase 'taking responsibility for your own life' means. They only know that something has made them different from other kids."

"Okay," said Dan. "How do you suggest I handle him?"

Swerdloff shook his head. "He's a tough one. My brand of humor didn't work at all. The only smile I drew was when I accidentally dropped my reflex hammer and he called me a klutz. He knows his uncle is important, and you're important, and for a while at least he's important to both of you. Just *how* important, he's determined to find out. So steel yourself for a power struggle."

"Where are his parents?"

"Checking into a nearby motel. They should be

back shortly. Shall I send them to your office?"

"Sure," said Dan absently and paused. "Why do I suddenly feel shaky?"

Swerdloff smiled. "Because you're human, Dan, and just as confused about it as that adolescent in there."

Billy Freiborg, wearing an Indian print flannel bathrobe over his pajamas, was sitting in the chair by his bed when they entered the room. From the doorway, Dan thought he looked like any skinny, long-necked Minnesota farm boy with a prominent Adam's apple. But up close his skin was almost alabaster pale with crops of pinpoint hemorrhages reddening his neckline. "Hi! I'm Lassiter," he said. "Dr. Swerdloff tells me you want to pow-wow."

"Pow-wow?" repeated Billy with disdain. "That's pretty corny, don't you think? Can't we just talk?"

Dan shrugged and pulled up a chair. "You talk, I'll listen."

Billy scrutinized him. "You don't exactly look like a doctor."

"Oh? What do I look like?"

"A jock."

Dan grinned. "I was a boxer once. But a few broken noses convinced me to become a doctor."

"A hot-shot doctor. Not many ex-jocks get to run hospitals."

"That's right," said Dan, meeting his stare without blinking. The rash on Billy's neck worried him. The same low platelet count that produced the tiny skin hemorrhages could cause a fatal brain bleed at any moment.

"Got X-ray eyes?" Billy taunted.

"Wish I did. Would save Blue Cross a lot of money."

"Why'd you bring me here—to impress my uncle?"

"Not especially. But I hope it works out that way. He's bound to be impressed if the new medicine we plan to give you works."

Billy scowled. "The odds are against it."

"How do you know?"

"I know my disease. The five-year survival rate is practically zilch."

"That was the old ball game. Nobody's figured the odds with monoclonal antibodies."

"Oh, yeah," groaned Billy. "Monoclonal antibodies. Swerdloff tried to explain them to me. But all I got out of it was that guided missiles kill cancer."

"That's a start," said Dan. "What more do you want to know?"

"How soon I can get back to Mayo's?"

"That's the *old* ball park. What's your hurry?"

"I got friends there. *Real* friends. They level with me."

"What's to stop you from making real friends here?"

"I know the routine," Billy said sullenly. "Once my white blood cell count drops, you'll stick me in reverse isolation, right?"

"Right. But not forever. Nothing's forever, except maybe death."

"Wow!" exclaimed Billy in mock amazement. "You actually said it. My parents never mention death anymore. They think about it, though. Every time they see me—how crummy I look—they think about it."

Dan glanced up at Swerdloff as if seeking guidance. When Ted said nothing, he turned back to Billy. "Look, friend, let's get one thing straight. I didn't give you your disease. It's not my fault. I'm just trying to help you survive it. So if you're ready to talk about that, let's get to it." Dan's blunt words were not meant to scold but merely to redirect Billy's anger from his doctors to his disease.

"Okay," said Billy, unruffled. "I'm sort of running

on empty right now—meaning, out of gas—so I'm ready."

"Good. Ted tells me you want to negotiate. Let's hear your terms."

Billy paused to sip ginger ale through a straw and then eyed Dan resolutely. "I'll do what you want as long as I get straight talk and hard facts and no bull-shit. No Gray Ladies bugging me, no puppet shows, no O.T., and no medical gobbledegook. I wants kids my own age to talk to, whether they've got leukemia or not. I want science books to read and I want the new treatment I'm supposed to get explained to me, step by step."

"Sounds fair," said Dan. "Anything else?"

Billy hesitated. "One more thing. If that antibody stuff doesn't work, or if it looks like it's going to kill me before it cures me, no early Christmas, huh?"

Dan smiled. "That would scare hell out of me, too. Okay, Billy, we accept your terms. Now why don't you catch a quick nap before supper and we'll see you later."

"Oh, sure," said Billy skeptically. "I bet I'll see you two as often as I saw Don Henley—every few weeks or so."

"Wrong!" replied Dan. "You'll see a lot of us once the magic show starts. Ted and I are the chief magicians."

Chapter 8

AT 8:20 P.M., NICOLE SWITCHED from worrying about how she looked to whether Steve Sigourney would show up for dinner at all. The weather had turned wet again; sheets of rain were lashing the bay windows of her fifteenth-floor apartment, and with each passing minute the goulash in the stove was congealing further. If Stefan did not arrive soon, her main course—the evening itself—would be ruined. Was the intimate little dinner she'd planned not only ill-advised but ill-fated as well? She refused to believe it. The more logical assumption was that he had merely been held up in traffic snarls brought on by the downpour.

At last the buzzer from the downstairs lobby sounded, sweeter than any music.

She answered it and then rushed to her full-length bedroom mirror for a final inspection. What she saw reflected there was more flattering than reassuring. She never should have worn the silk, Parisian-cut blouse that clung so tightly that it quivered with each breath, nor the stylish new high-heeled shoes that might make her taller than Stefen. She doubted if he would dress to impress her—though it would certainly be encouraging if he did.

At the softer buzz of her front door, Nicole tore herself away from the mirror and went to unlock it. "Welcome!" she managed to say before her eyes widened and her hand flew to her mouth to suppress laughter.

From sodden felt hat to dripping pants cuffs, Steve was thoroughly drenched. "My God, Stefan!" she exclaimed. "Don't tell me you walked? Why didn't you take a cab?"

Through clenched teeth, Steve said, "I would have gladly taken a cab, a bus, a *gondola,* if only I could've found one?"

"Well, come in and dry off. Do you want a towel?"

Steve shook his head, splattering water on the hall rug. Handing her his hat and coat, he blotted his face with a handkerchief. "You're lucky I'm in a good mood," he said, stepping down into her sunken living room. "Andre Evashevsky finally created an antibody to the ATPase enzyme we've been studying. Our work should move much faster now."

"That's wonderful!" she said. Except for Steve, Evashevsky, a bearded bear of a man in his late thirties, was the most talented researcher at the Institute and its deputy director. A native Philadelphian despite his foreign-sounding name, he was so emotionally volatile as to make Steve appear phlegmatic in comparison. He never talked, he growled—his standard rebuff to anybody, even a complete stranger, who dared to interrupt his concentration being, "Now what?" But when his research was going well, he had a twinkle in his eyes and a roll to his ambling gait that made Nicole smile whenever she passed him in the third-floor corridor. "Andre must be very pleased with himself."

"Pleased? He's ecstatic! I practically had to restrain him bodily from rushing out in the rain to tell God the good news. Anyway," he said, turning away from perusing the contents of her bookcase to face her, "you look, uh, different."

Smilng uncertainly, she said, "An improvement, I hope?"

"Of course," said Steve, though he wasn't sure that was what he meant. Nicole looked as if she had just walked off a movie set. Her auburn hair, released from its customary chignon, hung to her shoulders. Mascara and eyeshadow gave an exotic slant to her eyes. Her tight-fitting black skirt revealed the shapeliness of hips and legs usually hidden by her lab coat. Most seductive of all were her breasts. Steve had never thought of her as large-breasted, but the clinging contours of her blouse left no doubt.

"May I offer you a drink?" Nicole asked. "A little sherry, perhaps?"

"No, thanks," he said curtly. "I like a little table wine with my dinner, but never sherry. Sipping sherry was *de rigeur* at Cambridge faculty-student parties and I grew to detest everything about it: the sticky taste, the formality, the inane prattle."

"Well, in that case, would you like a tour?"

He raised an eyebrow. "Of a one-bedroom apartment?"

"You might be surprised by all the *objects d'art* I've collected. Come," she said, taking his hand. "I'll show you."

Her touch was electric, unnerving. Almost with relief, Steve released her hand to let her precede him up two steps to the small dining area.

She stopped before a gaudily painted street scene. "The *rue* where I lived in Paris. Not great art, but for me rich with nostalgia. I commissioned an artist friend to paint it for a keepsake when I came over to the States."

"Then you were happy in Paris?"

"For a long time. As a child I couldn't wait to grow up, to wear high heels and makeup and to stroll the boulevards arm-in-arm with a boy; to kiss openly in the *Metro.*"

"And finally you did."

"Yes," she said, a hint of sadness in her voice. "A mixed blessing."

Taking his hand again, she drew him over to the life-sized bust of a man on a wooden stand. "Recognize him?" she asked.

"Sir Isaac?" He looked at her askance. "Why put him on a pedestal? Newton was a mathematician and physicist, not a biochemist."

"He was a scientist *par excellence*—probably the greatest scientific mind of his millenium. Without him, we could never have sent men rocketing to the moon."

"Another mixed blessing," muttered Steve and leaned forward to examine the bust more closely. With his thick, wavy hair, aquiline nose and well-shaped mouth, Newton had either been extremely handsome or greatly favored by whomever had sculpted him. "This is certainly art, not nostalgia," he remarked. "Who did it?"

She hesitated. "I did."

"You!" he exclaimed. "Explain."

"My closest friend in Paris was a sculptor. She taught me how."

"But why Isaac Newton?"

"I was taking a philosophy of science course at the Sorbonne at the time and his life fascinated me. For a whole winter, we were quite intimate . . . Yes, intimate. In the months it took to sculpt him, I read everything I could find by or about him, even had imaginary conversations with him. It sounds bizarre, I know, but recreating the face of a dead genius is a remarkable experience. *Very* intense. I felt as if I were communicating with him and he with me."

"Really?" Steve looked bemused. "Tell me about this mystical communication. What did you learn from it?"

"That he was a fatherless farm boy and possibly because of this never felt completely at ease in his masculinity."

"*He* told you this?"

"No, my analyst did. He threw it in free of charge."

Steve resisted the impulse to ask why she had needed analysis. "Go on," he said imperiously, as if ordering her to defend a thesis.

"In his later years, he became a complete recluse. He never married. They say he never really loved anybody."

"*They?*" he repeated contemptuously. "The anonymous, omniscient *they?* Were *they* privy to his private thoughts, his yearnings? If not, how could *they* reach such a sweeping conclusion? God knows what *they'll* say about me someday!" Moving on to a collection of Dresden china in an adjacent cabinet, he added, "It was probably just as well. If Newton was a better scientist than a social being, he was right to concentrate on his work and avoid emotional turmoil."

"Is that your philosophy as well?"

Steve stiffened slightly. It was a provocative question; if not answered circumspectly, it could lead to more of the same. Flippantly, he said, "My philosophy? Like the Shintoists in Japan, I have neither philosophy nor theology. I just *dance.* In science, fortunately, I can now dance to my own tune . . . But back to your sculpture. It's really quite good. Have you any more to show me?"

"Not here. But I'm tempted to start up again. Would you pose for me?"

He grimaced. "I've posed enough already. My behavior toward you the other day in my office was really inept. And I don't seem to be doing much better now, even though my main reason for coming was to correct any false impressions I may have given you."

"An admirable, if too modest, intention. Are you *sure* that's all you want?"

"It's not so much a question of wants as of realities. You continually amaze me, Nicóle. Forgive me if I offend you, but you're certainly more Hungarian than French in your impracticality."

A soft pinging from the kitchen spared him her retort. "The oven-timer!" she exclaimed. "Come, Stefan, and I'll prove that I'm not as impractical as you think. I can cook!"

She opened the oven door and the savory aroma of spiced beef was wafted to his nostrils. "Goulash!" he cried, delighted. "I practically grew up on goulash."

"Not like this," she said confidently. "Wait till you taste it: sauce blended to perfection, dumplings fluffier than any *quenelle*. The recipe is a family secret—one of the few useful pieces of information my mother passed on to me."

"Your mother?" said Steve, remembering something he had heard. "She was a political organizer, wasn't she?"

"That's a tactful way of putting it," said Nicole, sliding her hands into padded pot-holders. "She was a Communist. Philosophically, she may still be—I don't know."

"Tell me about your family," asked Steve, standing well out of her way as she swung the steaming pot from the oven to the top of the stove.

"I will . . . over dinner. Right now," she said, taking a bottle of red wine from a cabinet, "use those nimble fingers you splice genes with to open this *Beaujolais*."

During dinner, Nicole described her trip to Budapest as the sole family representative at her paternal grandmother's funeral the year before, her first return to her birthplace since fleeing it in 1956.

"How old were you then?" he asked.

"Only seven, but I remember it well, especially the wild train ride before the Russian tanks rolled in. Naturally the entire train was packed with people frantic to get out. Even so, there were strange goings-on in a compartment a few doors down from mine. By some tacit arrangement, it was reserved for couples, married or otherwise, to make love in. They were each allotted a half hour. I know, since a steady procession of them lined up outside my door day and night. There was so much laughing and giggling when a couple came out, and such loud arguments when any of them overstayed the time limit, that I couldn't sleep. Even more frustrating, my parents wouldn't tell me what was going on. By the time the train reached Paris, that compartment must've been swimming with sperm."

"Curious," said Steve.

"What—sex after survival? I don't know. I imagine for some it was a celebration of life; for others, a release from terror. How old were you when you left Budapest?"

"Fifteen," said Steve. Her sexual references made him uncomfortable and he was relieved to change the subject. "Those years, unhappy as many of them were, influenced me greatly. I'll never go back as long as the Communists rule, but I'll always think of it as home."

"Why, unhappy?"

Steve laughed mirthlessly. "Music may well be the food of love, but it gave me a bellyache. My mother was a concert pianist, my father a minor composer and music hall impressario, and I—well, let's say I lacked the necessary gene allignments. My parents expected their only child to be a musical prodigy, another Mozart. They never quite got over their disappointment. Professional musicians are not particularly tolerant of the untalented or the unappreciative; to win their approval, you either have to play or praise, and being an obstinate child, I did neither. Fortunately, my father had two remarkable brothers. One of them, Anton Sigourney, is a well-known philosopher; the other, Ilya, dead now, was a mathematics professor and my champion. I'll be eternally grateful to him for discovering I had an aptitude for math, if not music—similar as the two are . . ."

As Steve paused to refill their wine glasses, Nicole said, "Tell me more about your mother."

"Ah, my mother," he sighed. "I tried hard to please her and she tried to care about me. Neither of us succeeded very well. Inadvertently, she did me one favor, though—and I don't mean this to be cruel. She died of cancer, an insidious ovarian neoplasm. She was fifty and I was at King's Hospital Medical School. Somehow—I'm sure it has neurotic origins—that got me interested in cancer research."

"You have no pleasant memories of her at all?"

"Hardly any. Not of her nor any woman."

"Whose fault is that?"

"Why assign fault? Some men are just unlucky that way."

"Was it always so? I'm not asking merely out of curiosity; there are things I want to tell you and I prefer shared confidences to confessions."

Staring at her above the rim of his wine glass, Steve tried to see past her glamorous exterior to the person beneath. He wished she had dressed less provocatively; it would have made it easier for him to believe that she really didn't care about outward appearances. A trivial hypocrisy, to be sure, but it put him on guard against others. "I almost married once. A mortician's daughter," he said, smiling through tight lips. "That's a horrid description, I know, but it's how I remember her. Actually, she was a girl named Gwen I met in medical school. Her last name was Simpson and the class's alphabetical arrangement threw us together a lot. We used to spend many afternoons and some evenings working side by side in the physiology lab. She wasn't particularly pretty, but she was vivacious and witty. 'A good sort,' as the English say. One thing led to another and we became lovers. But it was an experiment with too many uncontrolled variables. It simply didn't work out. There were few women in the class and she was very much in demand. I guess it went to her head. She . . . she betrayed me. Several times." Bitterness distorted his face. "She worked her way up from an Egyptian lab instructor with soulful eyes to the assistant chairman of the physiology department. When I found out, I ended our engagement and—like Newton, I suppose—made myself face up to the fact that I lacked the emotional reserve, the resilience, to absorb such heartache. I decided it was better to gratify my ego through science than through the pleasures of the flesh." Gulping his wine, he added, "Don't you agree?"

She met his accusing look coolly. "The pleasures of the flesh, as you quaintly put it, are really perceptions of the mind—the same critical mind that perceives scientific truth. Oh, don't look so doubting. I don't pretend to know what love is, either. But I *do* know it can't be defined by science. Even with serum endorphin levels, it's not measurable. Neither is the beauty of a summer day, a rustic lake, a symphony. Yet it's still rewarding, enriching." She smiled wanly. "Or so I keep telling myself. Like yours, my experiments—unfortunately multiple—have all been dismal failures. But I'm not ready to give up. After all, one bad result, or even a string of them, proves nothing if the ingredients are wrong . . . I suppose you know that I came to Philadelphia because I was engaged to a U. Penn. medical student."

He nodded. "Your Uncle David mentioned it."

"Well, that's ended now. *Fini.* It's been over for months. Like your former fiancee, Andrew was *very* popular, too. Other problems existed that he thought we could work out once I moved here, but we couldn't." She shrugged. "If you don't mind, I'll skip the details for now. I have something tastier to offer you."

Dessert was a crisp-shelled torte topped with fresh raspberries and whipped cream, that tasted as delicious as it looked. Sighing contentedly after his last bite, Steve said, "That was really marvelous."

"*Merci.* But I'm afraid that, of the three German K's, *kuchen* is the only one I'll ever master."

"No *kinder?*"

"Not likely." She suddenly shivered.

"Are you cold?" Even in his tweed jacket, Steve had felt the chill seeping through the bay window at his back. Outside, the rain continued in intermittent bursts; the wind gusted.

"A little," she admitted. "Perhaps I should turn up the heat—or, better yet, there's a working fireplace in the living room. How would you like coffee and cognac by the fire?"

"The cognac I'll skip," said Steve, flushed and feeling a little tipsy from the wine. "But a fire sounds nice."

In Steve's subsequent reconstruction of this evening—a memory so often relived in the days ahead as to verge on what psychiatrists termed "obsessive review"—a gap of about forty minutes existed. One moment, it seemed, he was sitting back with a *cafe filtre* in his hand, Nicole an arm's length away on the ottoman, gazing with satisfaction at the roaring fire he had lit; his next clear memory, obviously much later, was of Nicole sitting nearly naked on the rug before the fireplace, head tilted back, breasts thrust out, shoulders squared, torso propped up by her arms. "Fire-bathing," she had called it; later, an illustrated confession. Whatever its purpose, it was a surrealistic scene, eerily lit, star-bursting with revelations, an erotic tableau of surpassing sensuality in the dancing reflection of the flames. It was almost as if the electrical storm outside had moved inside Steve, generating lightning bolts of sensation. If only he could remember exactly what had led up to it . . .

To the best of his recollection, it began when the freshly fed fire blazed up and Nicole, closer to it than he, started to perspire. Putting down her brandy snifter, she unbuttoned the top of her blouse and tugged its tails from her skirt. When she turned, Steve could see most of the lace cups of her bra.

"What are you doing?" he could remember asking.

"What does it look like?" she retorted, smiling to temper the sharpness of her voice. "What does your observant eye tell you?"

"That you're loosening your blouse to get cool. But if you're hot, why not just back away from the fire?"

"A logical suggestion if your premise were correct—which it is not." Calmly she undid the rest of the buttons until her blouse gaped open. "Here's additional data. Now what's your working hypothesis?"

"Nicole, stop! Either cover yourself or tell me what you're doing."

"To be exact, I'm stripping. At least, partway. I like to fire-bathe, to feel the heat against my bare body. I do it often when I'm alone. Do you object?"

He started to say yes, but feared sounding prudish. "Better to leave some things to the imagination," he said feebly.

"That depends on how active the imagination is. How active is yours, Stefan? Especially since I practically told you I loved you the other day?"

Steve couldn't speak. The evening's events had taken a dizzying turn and he needed time to regain his equilibrium, to quell the distracting tingling in his groin. At last he said, "I may be wrong, but I get the impression you're trying to seduce me."

"An unnecessary assumption!" she chided. "You taught me never to make those when a little extra effort could transform them into facts. So don't speculate. Ask directly."

"Very well," he replied wryly. "*Are* you trying to seduce me? Is that what all this sex talk has been leading to?"

"Most assuredly, yes."

"Why?" he demanded hoarsely.

"I'll show you."

To his amazement, she shed her blouse, skirt, and bra. Clad only in skimpy panties, she swung around and posed for him, head back, breasts arching, legs stretched out. Behind her the fire crackled. Tongues of flame leapt and fell, casting a golden glow that limned her body in radiance and shadow. Her nipples appeared reddish-pink in the flickering light, her face a changing mask of bronze and gold.

Awed and anxious, Steve tried to look away but couldn't. As if transfixed, his eyes roamed her nearly nude body while his libido struggled to break free from steel-bound inhibitions.

Incredible for most men but typical of him, he tried to analyze his conflicting emotions, to calm and control them through understanding. But it was no use; no insight, analogy or punishing lesson from his past could dispel his inner trembling, his voyeuristic fascination.

Finally she changed position, bringing her head forward, letting her breasts droop, clasping her right knee with both hands. It was the pose of a harem girl made famous by a painter whose name Steve could not remember—and equally enthralling.

"Very pretty," he said.

"Is that your only response?"

"What do you want me to say?"

"*Say?* Nothing! I want you to *do!* To put your arms around me, your—well, you get the idea."

"Nicole, please! It's not that I don't feel anything. I do! But I'm a creature of logic. Before acting, I must understand."

"Understand what?" she snapped. "Why I'm practically naked before you? Obviously as an invitation. Accept it or not, but don't shame me; don't make me feel like a fool!"

"Nicole, I don't mean—I would never . . . *Gott!* Why? Just tell me why?"

"All right," she sighed. "We all try to impress with what we have, *n'est-ce pas?* Well, though the quality I value highest is intelligence, mine's not fully developed; doesn't even begin to compare with yours. Which leaves my body. Not a great body, as my ex-husband kept reminding me, not even a functional one in certain respects, but better than average for a female scientist. So, with time short—I finish the formal part of my studies next week—and knowing of your monk-like existence, I thought, why not try seduction? Extreme, yes. Out of character, certainly. I assure you, I've never done anything even remotely like this before or else I might be better at it. But what was left for me after our talk the other day? After the crumb of encouragement you threw me—too attractive to work in your lab, indeed!—I was desperate, afraid I would never see you again. What could I possibly lose by offering myself this way, except empty pride? The one outcome I foolishly failed to consider was your utter lack of interest! Oh, don't bother to apologize, Stefan. It is your right, after all, not to want me in this way."

"That's not true," Steve mumbled. "I do desire you. How could I—any man—not? You're bright, you're beautiful; for some inexplicable reason you seem to want me . . ."

"It's not so inexplicable. I just haven't gotten around to it yet."

"Then, explain."

"It would help if you would hold me . . . But never mind," she sighed, seeing him tense. Lying on her back, she wiggled out of her underpants and stretched out below him. "Look closely," she said. "What do you see?"

Leaning forward, Steve observed a six-inch midline scar below her navel intersecting with a fainter one running across the top of her pubic hair. "I see two surgical scars," he said. "Sizable ones."

"Minor disfigurements. The internal scars hurt more. I've talked a lot about sex tonight, haven't I?" She sat up to meet his eyes. "But not merely to arouse you. I had more in mind—though if it led to our making love, so much the better. I thought that might make you more receptive to what I planned to tell you later. But that part of my scenario fizzled out. So, to get to the point, neither my doctors nor I know for sure, but there's a strong likelihood I'm sterile, from a condition called endometriosis. Are you familiar with it?"

"Vaguely. About all I remember from medical school, though, is that it causes non-cancerous implants throughout the pelvis, and considerable pain. Right?"

She nodded. "Not much more is known about it. Anyway, I first found out I had it in a doubly painful way—when I lost my virginity. Phillipe, my lover and later my husband, was sympathetic in his way. He took me to a doctor friend who diagnosed my condition and referred me to a well-known French gynecologist named Vauringaud. He tried various medications and, when none of them worked, he recommended a controversial surgical procedure called presacral neurectomy. The severing of certain small nerves from my spinal cord to my pelvis would make intercourse less painful. At Phillipe's urging—we were engaged then—I underwent the operation. The nerve-cutting portion of the operation went well, but Vauringaud saw endometriosis partially obstructing the openings of both fallopian tubes and removed the larger implant on the right to improve my chances for a future pregnancy. And then something went wrong. A blood vessel burst while I was still in the recovery room and I went into shock. A second operation was needed to stem the bleeding, which Vauringaud finally did, but only after removing my right fallopian tube and ovary. That left me with one partially blocked tube and a poor chance of ever getting pregnant. Phillipe swore it didn't matter; that he had no great desire to father children anyway and we could always adopt. Sex was much less painful after the operation and I was even beginning to enjoy being married to an up-and-coming film maker when the other shoe dropped. While making a movie in Spain, Phillipe suddenly became impotent, claiming overwork. It didn't take me long to discover that what was sapping his energy wasn't his strenuous shooting schedule but the starlet he was laying on the set. He even got her pregnant. So that ended my marriage and any film-making aspirations I might've had. I went back to the Sorbonne and my first love, science. My father, as you know, is a chemist and I decided to follow in his footsteps."

"Better than movie-making," Steve murmured.

"For me, anyway. Then two years ago I met Andrew at a Swiss ski resort. He had just finished his junior year of medical school and not only professed a deep personal interest in me but in my endometriosis.

One of his gynecology professors was conducting clinical trials of a new anti-hormone that showed promise as a cure. According to Andrew, six months of treatment under his professor's supervision and my endometrial implants would simply melt away, making pregnancy and all other good things possible.

"His professor was considerably less optimistic but agreed to treat me. The medicine was certainly powerful—I vomited half my meals for months. But in the end my tube was just as obstructed as before. At least Andrew wasn't the hypocrite Phillipe had been. He said he would gladly continue as my lover until he finished his internship here, but because of my sterility, marriage was out of the question. I thanked him for his candor and bid him a firm and final farewell.

"But losing Andrew didn't sadden me as much as another kind of loss. I wanted children desperately, and my inability to have them makes me feel incomplete. So I bury myself in my work. If I can't produce babies, I can at least produce new knowledge. Surely you can understand that?"

Steve nodded, but said nothing.

In the silence, Nicole looked down at herself and as if embarrassed by her nakedness suddenly folded her arms across her breasts. "Well," she said a moment later, "that's the whole sad story. You said you had to understand what draws me to you before you could respond. Now that you know, what do you intend to do about it?"

"Do?" he answered abstractedly, still trying to grasp the implications of all she had told him. "What would you have me do? Naturally I'm sympathetic . . ."

Closing her eyes as if to shut out the sight of him, she said, "I want more than your pity, Stefan. Much more."

"You want . . . for us to collaborate? For me to

serve as the symbolic father of your scientific creation?"

Nicole did not respond for a moment. Then, eyes still shut, she shook her head. "Must you always be so coldly objective? I wanted more than that; I was hoping you would, too. But I'm simply too overwrought right now to go on explaining."

When she finally opened her eyes, Steve was surprised to see tears glistening in them. "Nicole, don't! Please don't cry," he urged and got down on his knees to gather her in his arms. Sobbing softly, she hugged him tightly before lifting her face for his kiss. It was light and tender. When they kissed again, her tongue slipped between his lips, setting him tingling. He tentatively touched, then cupped, one of her breasts. The burst of pleasure he felt was intense, almost overwhelming. He was about to surrender to it, to her, when his psyche began playing tricks on him. Gwen used to kiss him this same way to excite him, give him an erection. But she was not particularly adept at it. Her tongue had plunged in and out of his mouth like a piston, and she was quick to complain when his response was sluggish. "Stefan, what's the matter with you now?" she would carp. "I'm ready—why aren't you? Maybe you ought to see a doctor." Gwen, the mortician's daughter, who had buried his masculinity for twenty years.

The memory affected Steve like bitter medicine, souring his mood and stomach. Sensing the change in him, Nicole whispered, "What is it? What's wrong?"

"Nothing's wrong," he replied, pulling away from her and sitting up. "Not with you, anyway. Believe me, Nicole, I tried to relax, to feel what any normal man would feel in the arms of a woman as desirable as you. It just didn't happen."

Her brow creased with confusion. "But Stefan, you *were* responding! I could feel it."

"Yes. For a few glorious moments, I escaped the

ghosts of the past. But they dragged me back."

"Stefan, what are you trying to say?"

"Simply that I am what I've always been, an emotional dwarf, and that it's time to go. Despite what you might think, this evening has forged a bond between us that I hope will last. But it's also made me realize—again, like your friend Isaac Newton—that science is as much a refuge, a hiding place, for me as a magical kingdom. Now I really must go."

"No, wait!" Reaching for her panties and blouse, Nicole hastily slipped them on and rose to face him. "You've had your say, nonsensical as much as it is. Now let me have mine. Obviously I'm not going to win your heart or fulfill any fantasies tonight. But I'm not defeated, either! No, don't frown. Listen! You aren't the only careful planner around here. I hoped this evening would bring us close together, and not just in bed. But I also estimated it might be a losing gamble and, with the same goal in mind, made alternate plans. Don't forget, I *am* a Sigourney Institute-trained Ph.D. I have prospects . . ."

"What prospects?" he asked, puzzled.

"Depending on the strength of your recommendation, of course, I have applied for and have tentatively been offered a year's fellowship to work with Gallo's group at the National Cancer Institute. I intend to use the time learning the latest techniques for the study of gene regulation."

"Nicole, that's wonderful! Of course, I'll recommend you to Gallo in the strongest possible terms. It's a wise career move."

"No doubt—although it's not my career I'm primarily interested in promoting. The point is, when my fellowship is over, I'm going to come back to you with a technical proficiency that few others, including your closest competitors, possess. And you'll hire me. You wouldn't dare do otherwise. However you feel about me now, or come to feel a year from now, you'll need me, Stefan!" She stared at him challengingly. "I think I'll enjoy that."

Chapter 9

DESPITE THE GRIM NATURE of his work and the appalling mortality rate among his young patients, Ted Swerdloff usually maintained a cheerful disposition. It stemmed not from any deep religious conviction nor the need to be liked, but from a fair reading of the balance sheet that summed up his half century of living. His wife, Clare, a former stage actress, was more beautiful and steadfast than he felt he deserved; his four daughters were bright and loving; his reputation as a pediatric hematologist was solid; his research was stimulating and satisfying. In short, he thought it would be unreasonable of him not to be cheerful. Yet the two weeks that followed Billy Freiborg's admission to the hospital seemed the longest and toughest Ted had endured in years. He hoped his morose mood wasn't noticeable, but after the research committee meeting Friday morning Dan Lassiter pulled him aside and asked, "What's got you down? Don't try to deny it. My syntax was more screwed up than ever this morning: I said *localize* when I meant locate, as well as other verbal atrocities, and never got a rise out of you. What's eating you, anyway?"

"I was wondering myself until I finally figured it out the other night. It has to do with Billy Freiborg, Dan, but not what you might think. In fact, just the opposite."

"I'm thinking you look depressed. So does that mean you're euphoric? You've sure got a funny way of showing it."

"It's *hope*. The old Greeks knew what they were talking about when they said hope was the last plague out of Pandora's box."

"All right, Ted," said Dan wearily. "If you want to leave that conundrum with me, I'll work on it. But if you want a more immediate response, you'd better explain."

"What it means is that hope often leads to even worse disappointment. Remember the old Flip Wilson line 'What you see is what you get'? Well, whenever I'm with Billy Freiborg, what I see is a damned nice kid who's dying fast. That time bomb ticking away inside him could go off any second. His hemoglobin is half what it ought to be, his leukocyte count's over a hundred thousand, and his platelet count is barely being maintained above the spontaneous bleeding level by the platelet packs we're giving him. So if you're wondering what makes him different from the dozens of other refractory leukemia patients I'm treating, it's hope. The hope that this time maybe I can save one."

"Okay. But what's so depressing about that?"

"The gut-gnawing fear—the almost certain knowledge—that I'm just kidding myself thinking mouse antibodies could cure *anything* in humans, let alone leukemia. Maybe if we'd gotten him earlier, at the very beginning of his disease when he still had some bone marrow reserve, maybe then . . ."

"Oh, come on, Ted, you know better! Say you *had* gotten him early—would you have had the guts to forego standard combination chemotherapy in favor of experimental treatment? Hell, we both know the 'catch-22' in the cancer business. You don't try radically new treatments on such patients until they're so far gone, their bodies so riddled with disease, that nothing's likely to work."

"I know, Dan. But I keep remembering something my dad once told me. Back in the thirties and early forties he was an internist on the voluntary teaching staff at Boston City Hospital. He said that in all his years as a doctor the worst period he ever went through was the week before the first batch of penicillin arrived at the hospital. No less than five of his patients died of infections that might've been cured if the stuff had only gotten there earlier. That's what I mean about hope being such a burden. When you've got it, it's a lot harder to shrug off failure."

"Seems to me you're talking about timing, not hope," Dan pointed out. "Speaking of timing, when do you plan to start treating Billy?"

"Well, we've been testing the monoclonal antibody Sigourney sent us with the laser cell sorter all week and it looks quite specific. Jerry Ravin wants to study its uptake by tissue sections from Billy's bone marrow next."

"How long will that take?"

"A couple of days."

"Can we wait? Can Billy? From what you just got through telling me, it doesn't sound like it."

Swerdloff sighed. "What do you suggest?"

"That we start sooner. In fact, right away, while we've still got a live patient to experiment on. How long will it take you to set up the leukopheresis machine?"

"A few hours. But I don't know, Dan . . ."

"*What* don't you know? An old pro poison-passer

like you! Don't tell me you've suddenly got an attack of pre-game jitters?"

"Something like that."

Dan smiled sympathetically. "I used to get them all the time in my boxing days. No matter how often I emptied my bladder before the fight, I still felt a terrible urge to the moment I stepped into the ring. But once the bell rang and my adrenals starting pumping, I was all right. So get on the phone and alert your team; then we'll go talk to Billy."

Having personified death for so long, Dan thought he knew how his ancient enemy operated. To thwart death, it was essential that he intercede before some invisible boundary in the dying process was crossed and internal suicide begun. Dan had learned long ago in physiology that each cell carried a structure inside it called a *lysosome*—a suicide sac, really, containing within its membrane all the enzymes needed to digest and destroy the cell, and yet still an integral part of that cell: its pre-programmed end.

Gazing down at the sleeping youth, the breakfast tray by his bed scarcely touched, Dan worried that Billy's cellular suicide had already begun.

"Billy!" he shouted, patting his cheek. "Wake up! We want your blood."

"Yeah?" muttered Billy sleepily. "How much this time?"

"All of it," said Dan. "We want to clean it up before giving it back to you."

Billy blinked. "Oh, it's you, Dr. Lassiter. I guess I was dreaming."

"About what?"

"My horse, Gustaf. I miss him."

"Gustaf? That's a funny name for a horse, even a Swedish horse. Is he from the royal stables of King Carl Gustaf?"

"Naw. But he's sleek and strong and . . . I dream

about him a lot. I'd give almost anything to see Gustaf again, but I'm afraid . . ."

Dan cut him off. "Hey, none of that. You'll see Gustaf again, even if we have to ship him in. Be a lot cheaper, though, to get you well and send you home."

Billy smiled feebly. "You better hurry."

"We're going to. We're moving you to a special room on the hemodialysis unit right now. Dr. Swerdloff will fill you in on the details and I'll see you down there in a little while."

From the pediatric floor Dan returned to his office to greet a local politician anxious to discuss, for reasons never made clear, the current outbreak of hepatitis among Boston's homosexual community, and to catch up on his correspondence. An hour later, he joined Swerdloff, his research fellow, Jerry Ravin, and two nurses huddled around Billy Freiborg to make a final check of his connections to the leukopheresis machine.

The apparatus itself, technically known as a "cell separator blood processor," was about the size of a small washing machine—which in a real sense it was. Its front was packed with various flow meters, pressure gauges, pump-speed knobs and warning lights. Its guts comprised a powerful centrifuge, intake and output pumps, and a half-pint glass bowl constructed to permit separation of whole blood into its four main constituents: plasma, platelets, red cells, and white cells.

Adjacent to the blood processor, wired to a heart monitor, a lethargic Billy Freiborg lay propped up in bed. Two thin plastic catheters threaded into large veins in each arm connected him to the machine.

"How long you plan to run him?" asked the younger of the two nurses.

"Until his leukemic cell population bottoms out. Then—" Swerdloff gestured uncertainly "—well, we'll blunder across that bridge when we come to it.

Meanwhile, it's your job to keep Billy entertained."

"Oh? And how do you propose we do that?"

"I don't know, Joan, but I'm sure you'll figure a way. Scheherezade managed it for a thousand and one nights and she never even attended one of our house staff parties."

"But he's *only* fourteen, Dr. Swerdloff!"

"I know, Joan, but like all our teenage patients, he watches the medical soaps. He understands hospital-based depravity."

"Ted, I hate to interrupt this important discussion," said Dan, "but are you going to give him extra platelets?"

"All we can get. Bleeding's still the biggest danger, unless he gets infected. The lamellar air flow should reduce that risk, and we'll maintain strict isolation procedures, but you never know . . ."

No, thought Dan gloomily, you never did. Infection went by various names under such adverse circumstances: *nosocomial*, when it was hospital-acquired; *opportunistic*, when the victim's immune system, his front line defense, was severely impaired. If Billy didn't succumb to a lightning-fast brain hemorrhage first, he would likely be consumed by the fires of an infection. Looking around, Dan could almost visualize a myriad of microorganisms hovering like vultures over Billy's vulnerable flesh.

Almost with relief, he excused himself a few minutes later and returned to his office.

Chapter 10

BILLY FREIBORG REMAINED IN MEDICAL limbo for the next several days, neither worse nor better. By Swerdloff's calculation, each eight-hour session on the leukopheresis machine removed almost a trillion leukemic cells from Billy's circulation. But it also stimulated his bone marrow to manufacture more, so that overnight his white blood cell count usually doubled. It was like trying to rake away leaves from the edge of a wind-swept forest, Ted admitted. Nonetheless, it bought precious time and he refused to be discouraged. He was already contemplating the next step—to infuse the monoclonal antibodies directly into Billy's blood stream to destroy the clusters of leukemic cells in his bone marrow; to shrivel the leaves while still on the branches without killing the trees themselves.

"When do you plan to start?" Dan asked on Friday, one week to the day since they had begun the leukopheresis procedure.

"Probably Monday. Later today I'm going over to the Dana-Farber Institute to talk to a couple of members of Schlossman's group; hear what their experience in infusing monoclonals in humans has been. Meanwhile, I'd appreciate it if you'd fill Steve Sigourney in on what's happened and see if he has any suggestions."

"Sure, Ted. I also owe Nels Freiborg a call. What should I tell him?"

"As little as possible. Billy's still alive, for which I'm grateful, but we can't keep him on the leukopheresis machine forever, and if the monoclonal infusions don't cure him within a week he's probably had it. After all, they're of mouse origin; he's bound to build up antibodies against them in time."

"Yeah," said Dan, wearily rubbing his eyes, "I see what you mean . . . Well, go on and talk to Schlossman's people. I'll talk to Sigourney and then we'll compare notes."

After Swerdloff left, Dan spent a few solitary moments contemplating the kill-or-cure nature of what they were gambling on and then put through a call to Sigourney's office. To his dismay, Steve's secretary told him that Dr. Sigourney was in New York City visiting a relative for the day, possibly the weekend, and was unreachable by phone. The best she could do was to leave a message for him to return Dr. Lassiter's call.

Dan thanked her and hung up, filled with a vague foreboding. When he tried to call Swerdloff later in the day he was frustrated again: Ted had not yet returned to the hospital.

Kris got home about nine p.m. from giving an evening lecture and over a bottle of wine Dan talked about Billy Freiborg.

"Well," she remarked after hearing his update, "at least he's hanging in there. What happens next?"

"We go for broke—infuse the monoclonal antibodies Steve Sigourney sent us directly IV and hope they achieve total leukemic cell kill. Ted went over to the Dana-Farber this afternoon to talk to a couple of researchers who've already tried something similar on a few patients to see how they made out . . ." Yawning deeply, Dan put his wine down and reached for his wife's hand. "Speaking of making out . . ."

"Yesss?" purred Kris, looking dubious.

"You interested?"

She eyed him appraisingly. "I'm always interested. But before I commit myself, how about a little negotiating? Take me to the dance at the Ritz-Carleton tomorrow night and I'll give you my all."

"Your *all* is Olympian—more than I bargained for. So's the dance. Black tie, I suppose."

She nodded. "You look great in a tux."

"And feel like I'm in a suit of armor."

"Then buy one that fits. We've already got the tickets. It's a benefit for something or other. And you certainly know your way around a dance floor."

Dan looked increasingly pained. "I don't know, Kris. I like to fox-trot. In an emergency, I could even dredge up a few jitterbug steps from the forties. But as far as rock or disco is concerned, I'm a fish out of water. I can never get the dreamy look on my face just right. So how 'bout letting me off the hook on this one?"

"No dance . . . no deal," she said flatly.

"Oh, really? That sounds like extortion."

"Well, don't stew about it. I'm still going to crawl into the same bed as you, and you know how I get after three glasses of wine."

"I've only seen you drink two."

"I'm going to have the third while you're showering. We can continue this discussion later."

Dan laughed. "All right, what time does the damned thing start? Not cocktails and dinner, but the dance itself?"

"Then you'll go!" she cried, delighted. "Thank you!"

"Don't thank me. Thank an old Prussian militarist named Karl von Clausewitz. 'If defeat is inevitable,' " he quoted, " 'lose at the least possible price!' "

Dan had no way of knowing it at the time, but he need not have fretted about the dance. At eight the next evening, he and Kris were headed for the hospital, not the Ritz-Carleton. A hurried phone call from Ted Swerdloff minutes before had forced the change of plans. Ted reported that Billy Freiborg had just suffered a teeth-chattering chill followed by a temperature spike up to 104°F. The chill was so severe that Swerdloff, fearing a brain hemorrhage from his violent shaking, had terminated it with intravenous morphine. Either from the narcotic or the high fever, Billy was now delirious.

Dan began removing studs from his tuxedo shirt while he listened. He asked Ted a few quick questions and then told him he would leave for the hospital immediately.

Climbing the stairs to their bedroom, he found Kris at the vanity table applying her makeup. On the bed was her chic new evening gown. Hesitantly he broke the news of Billy's sepsis.

"It was bound to happen," she sighed, putting down her lipstick. "Give me time to slip into working clothes and I'll go with you."

"You don't have to," he protested. "You could. . ."

"Don't say it! Going to a dance alone is almost as bad as going on a moonlit sail alone. It suggests desperation. Besides, there's a patient on the ICU I ought to check, an Englishman who took a *Tylenol* overdosage."

"Another suicidal Englishman? I thought you recently dialyzed one like that."

"I did. That was Ian. This is his soul-mate, Derick. He decided to punish Ian for not coming directly home after we discharged him last week . . . Oh, don't smile, Dan! You would't think it so funny if they were husband and wife."

"I'm smiling for two reasons: one, the realization of how much money their love-spat is costing the hospital—I assume neither has American insurance. And two, because it might well be the last time I have any cause to smile for a while. Anyway, I'm glad you're coming along. It figures to be a long night."

At the hospital, Dan kissed his wife in the elevator and got off at the hemodialysis floor. Striding down the corridor to Billy Freiborg's room, he met Ted Swerdloff coming out. "Well?" he asked anxiously.

Swerdloff took off his disposable mask and deposited it in a trash can. "It could be worse. No neck stiffness, so no meningitis . . . yet. Nothing in his lungs, heart or urine, either. The rash he's had for the last week is spreading, but it doesn't look infected. We're culturing his blood, and anything else we can, and then starting him on triple antibiotic coverage."

Dan nodded. "What's his white cell count?"

"Around thirty thousand with ninety percent leukemic blast forms. That leaves him with a couple of thousand normal cells to fight off infection—which may or may not be enough."

"That doesn't sound too bad."

"There's more."

"Let's hear it." As if bracing himself, Dan leaned against the wall.

"I suppose I should have told you this yesterday, right after I learned it myself, but I figured, why spoil your weekend, too . . . You want coffee?"

"No—facts."

"Coffee will go down better."

Dan smiled sardonically. "Okay, Ted, let me guess. The guys at Dana-Farber told you precisely what you didn't want to hear: that as far as the treatment of human leukemia is concerned, monoclonal antibodies alone may not be the way to go—may in fact be just another dead end. Right?"

Swerdloff nodded. "The monoclonal antibody infusions they've given their leukemia patients so far have worked about as well as our leukopheresis is working, and for just as short a time. By thirty-six hours their leukemic cell counts were all back to the baseline, and after a week or so of injections their patients began having allergic reactions to the stuff." He gestured apologetically. "I'm damned sorry, Dan, if my loose speculation at a staff party had led us, Billy included, down the primrose path."

"Don't take all the blame, Ted, and don't lose heart yet. To be equally honest, what you just told me doesn't come as any big surprise. Steve Sigourney predicted it."

"He did? Well, so have most of the others I've talked to. What else did Sigourney say?"

"To let him know if things went badly, which I've been trying to do since we last talked. If worse came to worst, Steve has a last-ditch treatment he wants to try, a big gun that's never been test-fired. One of his co-workers has managed to link a powerful radioisotope—an alpha emitter—to a monoclonal antibody so that it can deliver its payload directly to a cancer cell."

"What isotope?"

"Astatine, I think, but I don't recall its atomic number."

"An alpha emitter, eh?" said Swerdloff, brightening. "That's ideal. In case you don't know, an alpha particle only travels about one forty millionth of a meter—enough to destroy a cell nucleus five or six microns wide but no neighboring normal cells . . . Damn it, Dan, why didn't you tell me this before? You could've saved me a lot of grief!"

"I was tempted to, innumerable times, but Steve swore me to secrecy. After all, if this works, it'll become the standard treatment for leukemia, and I suppose he wanted to supervise its first clinical trial himself. At least he told me about it, even promised to consider letting us use it on Billy, if we begged hard enough—which I'm willing to do if only I could get hold of him."

"Keep trying! This makes a lot more sense than using monoclonals alone."

"Even so," Dan cautioned, "it wouldn't come free and clear. There are bound to be side-effects, from kidney failure to radiation poisoning. I assume you're willing to risk them."

"I am. And I'm sure Billy's parents will be, too. Now the main thing is to cure his infection; keep him alive long enough to launch Sigourney's guided missiles. Where is Sigourney, anyway? Not out of the country, I hope."

"No, somewhere in New York City visiting an uncle who doesn't own a telephone. His secretary left him a message to call me the moment he returns."

"But will he? And if he does, it won't be until Monday."

"I'm hoping sooner. If I know Steve, he works more than a five-day week."

"Well," sighed Swerdloff, "I'm going up to the lab to take a look at Billy's sputum. Any further suggestions?"

"Let me examine him first. Then I'll let you know."

Entering Billy's room, Dan asked his nurse, "How is he?"

"Burning up," she said. "I know you doctors seldom order sponge baths anymore, but at least they gave me something to do."

"Looks like you'll have plenty to do before this night's over," replied Dan, fitting his stethescope to his ears. Listening intently to Billy's heartbeat for murmurs, gallops, rubs, clicks—all the peculiar noises by which an overburdened heart signaled its distress—he fell into a sort of reverie, thinking back to other times, other critically ill patients, feeling a rekindled sense of awe at how much punishment the human body could take before its will to live was overcome. On the plus side, he knew that fever was more damaging to cancer cells than normal ones, but how much more could this frail fourteen-year-old endure?

"Easy," he urged as Billy tried to twist away from the cold stethescope against his lower right rib cage. "Just breathe deep."

Five minutes later, Dan completed his examination, thanked the nurse for her assistance and, deep in thought, trudged back to the elevator that would take him to his office. To his pleasure, he found Kris there, brewing coffee on the stainless steel espresso maker that stood on the shelf behind his desk.

"How's your patient?" he asked.

"Repentant. Also quite nauseous from all the antidote we made him swallow. How's yours?"

Dan did not reply. Instead he took the coffee cup from her hand, put it aside, and pulled her into his arms.

"Oh, by the way," she gasped as his lips sought hers, "Steve Sigourney called."

Dan's grip went slack. "When?"

"Just a few minutes ago. I wrote down the number where you can call him back . . . Hey!" she cried, feigning displeasure. "What happened to the kiss I was puckered up for? Whatever Steve wants, it can't be all that urgent, can it?"

"Afraid so. It concerns Billy Freiborg, who's critical. So please forgive me if I drop everything, including you, to call him back."

Chapter 11

AS HE LEFT HIS OFFICE for the train station Friday noon, Steve Sigourney could not remember ever needing to talk to his Uncle Anton more urgently. Though a confirmed bachelor, Anton had provocative ideas about the existential bonds between men and women. And there was no one whose company Steve enjoyed more.

Nicole had obtained her fellowship at the National Cancer Institute and had left for a European vacation the previous week. He had seen her only once in the interim, at a farewell party for the graduate students in the lab. They had exchanged searching glances, but no words. It was just as well, Steve reflected. Among her male admirers at the party, he alone had seen the beautiful body concealed by her frock. She had offered it to him in return for . . . what? Intellectual acceptance? An utterly impractical merger between brains and beauty? If only a device existed that could measure the entropy in cold thought and warm emotion, he might be able to equate the two, predict the stability of the mixture. But now that she was gone and unlikely to return, such speculation seemed pointless. Why torture himself with what could never be? Better not to think of her at all.

But that had been easier to decide than do, he discovered.

Even now, in a crowded AMTRAK compartment, his thoughts swayed to and away from Nicole as wildly as the train on the bumpy track. What he needed was perspective, he realized; someone to talk to who would make him see her not as some unattainable vision but merely unsuitable. Anton, now in his dotage, his mind consumed by the *why* rather than the *how* of life, hardly seemed his best choice for this purpose, but who else was there?

Arriving at Pennsylvania Station, spilled coffee staining the sleeve of his suit jacket, Steve took a taxi to Anton's townhouse in Greenwich Village. Outwardly drab and sooty, the three-story structure was a combination library and museum. It was also something of a fortress. Obsessed by security, Anton had installed two separate burglar alarm systems and claimed to own a mini-arsenal, including a Uzi submachine gun given him by an Israeli archeologist and army colonel. Steve had never seen the Uzi or any other weapon except for a collection of Pygmie poisoned darts and arrows mounted on a wall, but knew his uncle well enough not to doubt their existence.

Anton seldom responded to challenges based on proof of possession or personal experience. A lucid lecturer and writer, he was vague to the point of secretiveness about attributing any of his opinions to first-hand observation. As he liked to point out, "In my experience," was a phrase less favored by philosophers than by scientists. Moreover, since the brain was a trickster whose interpretation and recall of events was often as unreliable as eye-witness accounts of accidents, he refused to base argument on such faulty references. Steve's father had told him that, as a leader of the Hungarian resistance, Anton had been badly wounded fighting the Germans in World War II, but his uncle would neither confirm nor deny the story. War was mass insanity, he maintained, and those who fought and killed in one temporarily insane. Why waste time listening to a lunatic reminisce?

Steve rang his uncle's doorbell and Marianna, a shy, slim woman in her early thirties, let him in. She was the daughter of Marya, who until her death two years before had served as Anton's devoted housekeeper for over thirty years. Marya, a handsome widow, had always intrigued Steve. She had an enigmatic smile, looked intelligent, or at least shrewd, read constantly in her kitchen nook, but hardly ever spoke. More than once he had wondered whether she and his uncle were lovers and if so, whether Anton's physical and mental deterioration since her death reflected a lover's bereavement. But even if he knew this to be true, he would still find it exceedingly difficult to picture his ascetic uncle embracing a sensuous but subservient housekeeper.

Marianna took Steve's overnight bag and led him upstairs to the second-floor study. There, staring vacantly into semi-darkness, sat Anton, a stubble of beard on his usually clean-shaven face, his thick-lensed glasses in his lap. "Ah, Stefan," he said, squinting up. "Welcome!"

"Hello, Uncle," said Steve, observing with dismay how badly Anton's outstretched hand trembled. "You're well, I trust?"

"Not well, but not willing to waste breath discussing it. Are you hungry? Thirsty? No? Would you like to try some herbal tea an old friend from Cuernavaca sent me?"

"Mexican tea? Does it contain hallucinogens?"

Anton smiled. "I hope not. As Huxley showed, mescaline makes for murky philosophy . . . Marianna, a pot of regular tea, please."

She nodded approvingly and left.

"Well," said Anton, "how goes the cancer business? Have you found the cause yet?"

"Why bother?" Steve shrugged. "Whatever I find, you'll challenge by telling me that God, or whatever you're calling Him this week, is the cause."

"Only if you're boastful. Humility is not a virtue, Stefan; it's a necessity. A prerequisite to understanding."

"Understanding what?"

"Exactly! When we know what we're supposed to understand, we can be a little less humble." Anton chuckled softly. "Our usual little game, eh? Since I, too, find it tiresome, let's put it aside for today. Tell me what's happened to you lately."

Succinctly, using as few technical terms as possible, Steve summarized the progress his team was making in the cancer field, especially the series of reports (dubbed *The Sigourney Variations* by the musically inclined John Wendall, *The Sigourney Manifesto* by the more politically minded Andre Evashevski) that were now in press. Almost as an afterthought, he alluded to his brief involvement with Nicole, hoping to make it sound like nothing more than an amusing interlude. But detecting the strain in his voice, Anton was not deceived. At his insistence, Steve described his evening with her in detail.

"Remarkable," said Anton afterward, his eyes looking livelier. "And you let her get away?"

"She is very attractive, Uncle. I am not. What else could I do?"

"That absurdity is almost undeserving of an answer. Fortunately, Nature has given some beautiful women more sense; otherwise, we'd be a race of idiots. Did you not say *she* pursued *you*?"

"It was a whim, a momentary aberration. Nothing more!"

Anton frowned. "You call sharing love and knowledge an aberration? Don't you know neither can be enjoyed alone?"

"I realize that," said Steve testily. "But I am a novice at love; I need to learn the rules of the game—and I've more important matters occupying me right now."

"Your experiments?"

"Yes, my experiments. My bid for scientific immortality."

"Immortality? An interesting word choice. You want your name to live forever, though *you* have hardly lived at all."

"That's a simplification."

"Perhaps, like all great truths."

Wryly Steve said, "Forgive me, Uncle. I was unaware that you had favored me with a great truth."

Anton's eyes twinkled. "Sarcasm? Anger? Rare responses from you. I sense this woman scientist, this Nicole, has raised your emotional metabolism. Good! How convenient that she is beautiful and you are not. Gives you just the excuse you need to bury yourself again in your work.

"But before you do, Stefan, let me ask you this: do you think the world trembles in anticipation while you take the final steps to solving the cancer mystery?"

"No more than it did when you completed your translation of *The Tibetan Book of the Dead.*"

Anton rolled his eyes heavenward. "My much disputed translation, you mean. It would take the reincarnation of the original Dalai Lama, himself believed to be the reincarnation of Avalokitesvara, to resolve the points of contention. But, that aside, there is a difference. My scholarship is an avocation. My true occupation—as yours should be—is living. Experiencing. What good is a glorious sunset to a worm?"

"Another aphorism? Or perhaps a not so subtle denigration of my work? Of course I agree that life is a wonderful improbability and ought to be appreciated to the fullest. But beyond that I'm unwilling to indulge your anti-science biases. Consider the cancer-stricken, Uncle: wouldn't a cure permit them to enjoy life even more?"

Anton gestured placatingly. "Understand, Stefan, I do not deprecate your laboratory wizardry in the least. But Nicole represents another kind of experiment—one of equal, possibly greater significance for you . . ."

Anton broke off as Marianna entered the room carrying a silver tea service. "Here, here!" He gesticulated excitedly, as if afraid he would lose his train of thought, and pointed to his foot stool.

Steve thanked her and poured. "Go on, Uncle."

"Yes . . . yes," muttered Anton absently. "Where was I? Drink your tea before it grows cold . . ."

"My tea is steaming. So were you a moment ago. We were comparing experiments—mine in the laboratory, yours in the human arena, I presume. You never did say."

"Experiments? Ah! I remember now. You know, Stefan, if I were God I might be afraid of scientists as gifted as you. Find out how a cancer cell can divide endlessly in a test tube, use that knowledge to confer immortality on your fellow beings, and you force God's hand. Either He shows Himself, His power, or He becomes superfluous, which would be a pity. Then we might never know why He created us. His grand design."

"A pity for some, perhaps. As an agnostic, I'm

more curious about why cancer exists than why we do. But your thinking is obviously more universal, and you sound as if you already know."

"I suspect . . . and I am finally ready to confide my suspicions. Just as you experiment with impunity on your rats, we humans, may be nothing more than God's laboratory rats . . ."

"Not a pleasant prospect, considering the fate of dinosaurs and Aztecs," Steve interjected. "But go on."

"The Bible tells us God created man in His image. It's a sublime notion, but I doubt it, especially since the Bible was a relative latecomer in the monotheism field and needed a selling point. An even bigger selling point was the speculation by some biblical scholars that God created us for companionship. If so, He must have tired of our barbaric antics long ago. And yet we can't entirely be ignored. Every once in a while we transcend our barbarism and do something truly noble and heroic. I witnessed several such acts in the war—men, women, sacrificing their lives for the sake of others. What possessed them? What belief system was so powerful it overcame their basic instinct for survival?

"My conclusion, Stefan, hardly original or earth-shaking, is that we humans are incomplete unto ourselves. Unlike other creatures, our self-awareness, our gift for contemplative thought, make it impossible for us to exist alone. Which brings me at last to the crux of my argument: *why* we are that way? It's my hunch that mankind is, indeed, an experiment on a colossal scale—an experiment outside the scope of science as we know it, and in the less exalted realm of sexuality: the same sexuality that you are currently struggling to contain. Remember, Stefan, to make love and procreate sexually is to die! An irrevocable death sentence. Asexual organisms, from the first amoeba on, live forever; they are timeless and immutable.

Only creatures that reproduce by sexual mating, the union of sperm and egg, are ephemeral. And man is even more special, burdened as he is by foreknowledge of death. Why do you suppose that is?"

Steve shook his head.

"For the same reason that one of your inbred mice languishes in a cage dying of an implanted cancer—because some superior being has decreed that to be its fate."

"Are you saying that sex is not only the mechanism but the basic purpose for man's existence?"

"Not sex, *sexuality*—the entire gamut of male-female interactions. Perhaps Nature, in her more hostile moods, would prefer to deal with us as simple sex cells, but she can't. We are too resourceful. We are unique under the heavens: the great builders and destroyers. And should we finally succeed in blowing ourselves up, the experiment ends; its outcome is noted in God's ledger."

"As what?"

"A negative result. Other experiments elsewhere may turn out better."

"I still don't see your point. As a believer in free will, I have always viewed my life as a trial with some sort of accounting at the end. But, if I understand correctly, you're saying something quite different: that humanity is to be judged not individually but collectively."

Anton nodded. "Perhaps I can clarify it further through analogy. Apart from its instinct for survival, who knows or cares what motivates an amoeba? A flatworm? But what if we came across a group of humans, or humanoids, who reproduce asexually? How different they would be from us—no illnesses, no death, no sex, no mating drives! Can you even imagine such a group?"

"With difficulty."

"The same difficulty they'd doubtless have trying

to imagine *us*. Yet what do you do in your lab when you want to compare one biological system with another? You set up a controlled experiment."

Steve frowned. "Is that what God is doing?"

"Perhaps He has a compelling need to know. My late friend, Otto Rank, the psychoanalyst, propounded the belief that sex epitomized man's dualistic nature—the contemplative mind, the animal body. Taken one step further, sex is of the body and the body is of death. As Rank correctly pointed out, this is the true meaning of man's banishment from The Garden of Eden—one of the most profound, as well as misinterpreted, allegories in all of Judeo-Christian theology. It was the discovery of sex, not the eating of the fruit from the tree of knowledge, that caused man's downfall, bringing death into the world. The fruit of the tree," said Anton scornfully, "is nothing more than a subterfuge, a euphemistic way to avoid explaining sexual intercourse to Sunday School children. No, it was almost certainly sex that proved Adam and Eve's undoing. How else to account for their sudden, shameful nakedness? The pain promised Eve in childbirth?"

Pausing to sip tea, Anton smacked his lips at its tartness and continued. "For a long time, I resisted Rank's synthesis—his symbolic interpretation. Why, I wondered, would God be so perverse as to equip men and women for copulation, only to punish them mercilessly for it? What was there about the sex act that violated the terms of man's stay in paradise? My only conclusion—and here is where Rank and I differ—is that man was only a temporary dweller there, as a child is temporary in a home; as long as he remained sheltered and provided for, he had no stimulus to grow, to develop into something better. Sex, like the kingdom of Earth, was meant for him when he matured, when he could enjoy it in its inherent harmony. But by tasting it prematurely, he introduced shame and guilt into the act—into his very life. Instead of evolving through divine guidance, he was forced to evolve through conflict—the fearful challenges of sex and death. As sexual creatures, we must either prove our relative worth, our survivability, or perish. That, after all, is the end point of the grand experiment."

"Forgive me, Uncle, but that sounds like circular reasoning to me."

"I'm sure," said Anton tolerantly. "All metaphysical reasoning becomes circular when you adopt the agnostic's basic tenet of an unknown and probably unknowable God. So, reject my hypothesis, if you will, but don't lose sight of my reason for sharing it with you."

"Which is . . . ?"

Anton smiled. "I could say enlightenment, only that would imply I am the more enlightened. So, let's just say for future peace of mind. Go ahead and cure cancer, if you can. I wish you every success. But however you fare, remember that God does not need your help there. In the context of the grand experiment I envision, you are as insignificant and expendable as one of your laboratory rats. Cry out in anguish and rage, if you wish, remind Him of what a clever fellow you are, but don't expect any special consideration—not in this life, anyway. And since you are stuck with your sexuality, at least take advantage of its more pleasant aspects. My major regret was that I was too unyielding to do so—to marry, father children, and the like. Don't make the same mistake."

"Are you suggesting I try to get Nicole back?"

"Nicole, or some other woman. Think back, Stefan; think how you felt when you first took Nicole in your arms. It was a revelation, was it not? A discovery of self? Compare it to the thrill of a scientific discovery."

"The two are hard to compare."

"Hard, yes. But not impossible, since both relate to insights—into Nature's secrets, on the one hand, into an inner self on the other. You're staying the night, aren't you?"

"Yes, Uncle."

"Good. I've grown sleepy listening to myself ramble on. I need a nap. We'll talk more about this at dinner. In the meantime, consider carefully what I've told you. Also, this," Anton added, with a smile. "An old man is not necessarily wiser than a young one, just more desperate to be right . . . Fetch Marya for me, will you please?"

"You mean Marianna, don't you?"

Anton looked startled. "Did I say Marya? . . . Alas, my poor brain doesn't idle well anymore. When I try to slow it down, it shuts off completely!"

"A minor lapse," said Steve, patting his shoulder. "Rest well, Uncle."

Chapter 12

THE MEETING WITH THE Zairean Minister of Health had gone well, thought Gregory Carhill as he waited for Yoshio Timura in his office. While Minister Kallinga toured the Institute, Carhill had a few matters to discuss with his chief molecular biologist before going on to lunch at the Harvard Club. Timura, whom he had recruited from the University of Kyoto five years before, was proving to be one of the most brilliant thinkers in the world of molecular engineering. No one anywhere understood the subtleties of the genetic code, or how to construct complex proteins from amino-acid building blocks, better than he. Thanks to this forty-year-old Japanese genius, the Bethune Institute had not only become a leading manufacturer of synthetic vaccines but was approaching the point where such research would pay handsome dividends. It was why the Zairean Minister of Health was here. Formerly the Belgian Congo, land of Pygmies and Simbas and King Solomon's legendary mines, the strife-torn Republic of Zaire had been badly served by its homegrown leaders in recent years. But its politics scarcely interested Carhill; what did was the extraordinary prevalence of lymphoblastic leukemia in its northern provinces, making them the ideal place to field-test the leukemia vaccine he and Timura had developed. If it worked, acute leukemia might become a disease as rare as poliomyelitis and he would be hailed as its conqueror. If it failed and caused unfortunate consequences to test subjects as had happened with early batches of the Salk vaccine, well, the Institute was hardly likely to be sued by illiterate African natives.

Carhill was startled from his reverie by the silent presence of his chief molecular biologist. Timura had a habit of moving, like Carl Sandburg's fog, on little cat's feet. "Good morning, Yoshio!" he said heartily. "How did the recital go last night?" Timura was not only a brilliant scientist but a talented violist as well. Once a month, the highly regarded string quartet to which he belonged gave concerts at one of the local campuses.

Timura shrugged. "We played Vivaldi. He would not have been happy had he heard it."

"Oh, come now!" said Carhill. "My wife attended and said it was lovely."

"Please thank Mrs. Carhill for me. But the truth is, my mind was on other things. How went your meeting with Mr. Kallinga this morning?"

"Very well. He promised full support. Now let's just hope his government lasts the length of the study. Two hundred villages on the North bank of the Congo River, a total of approximately fifty thousand subjects, will receive the vaccine. An equal number on the South bank will serve as controls. Naturally, I would have preferred a 'double-blinded' study design, but Kallinga would not agree to it." Carhill sighed. "From his limited understanding of the scientific method, he thought it 'deceitful,' and I chose not to argue. Otherwise, though, a highly satisfactory arrangement. I realize it's short notice, but could you have the first batch of AL-171 ready for Kallinga to take back with him the end of the week?"

"The vaccine will be ready, Dr. Carhill."

"Good. I'm relieved to hear it. Now, let's pray it works as well on humans as on rodents." Carhill looked at his watch. "Anything else we ought to discuss, Yoshio?"

"Have you read the latest issue of *Science* yet?"

"No, but I have it right here." Carhill extracted the journal from among the magazines stacked on his desk. "Something of particular interest in it?"

"An intriguing report by Dr. Sigourney's group. Using covalent metal chelates, they have developed a technique for linking radioisotopes to monoclonal antibodies."

"Have they?" said Carhill without enthusiasm. "How extensively have they tested it?"

"They report their results in four rats with implanted colon cancers."

"Only four! That's 'salami science' if I ever heard it. What isotope did they use?"

"Indium. But they say studies with astatine are now in progress."

"Hmmm." Opening the journal, Carhill scanned its table of contents. "*That* has implications. But it's a little far afield from our work. Why do you mention it?"

Timura hesitated. "A letter from my family last week brought sad news. My uncle—my father's brother—has esophageal cancer. My father asked if there is anything American doctors could do, and I wrote back that I would talk to you. Now, after reading Dr. Sigourney's exciting paper, I am wondering if I should talk to him, too."

Carhill stiffened. "Sigourney? I really wouldn't

advise it, Yoshio. In fact . . ." He started to say that he forbade it, but caught himself. The last thing he wanted was for Timura and Sigourney to get to know each other, but he had to be tactful about it. "In fact," he amended, "I doubt if Sigourney would talk to you. He's simply unapproachable. But there are others equally skilled in that technique. Scheinberg at Johns Hopkins, for one. Let me call Scheinberg for you and see what he can suggest."

"That would be most kind Dr. Carhill."

"Not at all. By the way, Yoshio," said Carhill, holding up the current issue of *Science*, "did you read the article by Okabe and Kreisberg?"

Timura nodded enthusiastically. "I read, but did not study it. I plan to do that tonight. It is most extraordinary. I had no idea that efforts to identify the protein produced by the Simian Sarcoma Virus oncogene were so far along. I . . . I think it is a monumental piece of work."

"If true," cautioned Carhill. "Frankly, I have my doubts. You see, I was asked to referee the paper a few months ago and spent an entire evening agonizing over its validity. In the end, I decided against publication—I just couldn't imagine how Okabe had got such a complicated series of proofs to come out so neatly—but I was obviously outvoted by the other referees. Now that it's finally in print, however, and nobody can accuse me of taking unfair advantage, I want you to assign two of your best workers to try to confirm the putative existence of this cancer-causing protein. If they do, I might as well concede next year's Nobel Prize to Joshua Okabe now. If not . . ." Carhill smiled maliciously, "we can contribute to the deluge of articles, editorials and letters to the editor that are certain to follow. Do it soon, Yoshio. I'm as anxious as anyone to know the truth of the find. After all, if Okabe is right, he has done in a year what others, especially Dr. Sigourney, were unable to do in

a decade. In short, he has left Sigourney in his dust. But I certainly wouldn't bet on it; science isn't *that* unpredictable. So get your team together and assign two senior scientists to work independently on what will probably be just another wild goose chase."

"Goose chase, Dr. Carhill? I don't understand. . ."

"Merely a colloquialism, Yoshio. An idiomatic expression meaning an effort that's largely a waste of time—like the luncheon I have to host for our distinguished visitor from Zaire."

Rising, he accompanied Timura out of his office. "Rest assured, I'll call Scheinberg regarding your uncle soon, possibly this afternoon," Carhill told him as they parted.

Looking down the corridor and failing to see Kallinga and his secretary returning, he went back to his desk and started to reread Okabe and Kreisberg's article.

These were exciting times for cancer researchers, he mused. Perhaps exciting to a fault. Once scientists had years to ponder a major discovery; now they were lucky to have weeks. He couldn't help wondering if Stefan Sigourney felt as overwhelmed by all of it as he sometimes did.

From an informant in Sigourney's lab, Carhill knew what rapid progress his arch rival was making and feared that he was falling farther and farther behind. If his leukemia vaccine failed to work, he might as well concede the Nobel prize—the "Cancer Prize" as he thought of it—to Sigourney, or some dark horse candidate like Joshua Okabe.

No, not Okabe, he reconsidered. Maybe he was letting scientific snobbism cloud his judgment, but he simply couldn't take the Okabe challenge seriously. He knew the man too well. Years before, he had helped train the Nigerian born, Harvard educated biochemist and found him brainy but erratic—the type of student who would fall far behind in each of his courses only to catch up at the last moment through manic bursts of activity. He was probably manic-depressive to begin with, Carhill speculated; the nervous laugh, rapid speech, and the often unfocused look in his eyes suggested it. He also recalled that Okabe was a strict vegetarian and a religious fanatic of some kind. A *most* peculiar sort. Carhill had been glad to be rid of him. Despite his impressive grade point average and a doctoral dissertation on cell membrane regulators nothing short of brilliant, he had turned Okabe down flat when he applied for a position at the Institute. Nonetheless, he had recommended him to Max Kreisberg, founder and head of Neotech, the first commercially run biotechnical research outfit in Boston, who hired him.

Had it been a mistake to let the Nigerian go? Carhill doubted it. Okabe was young, undisciplined and unstable; a cancer cure was not going to be discovered by the likes of him. Which was not to say Okabe didn't have his uses. If nothing else, his *Science* article was bound to give Sigourney some very bad moments.

Carhill chuckled, taking perverse pleasure in the thought. Hearing footsteps in his outer office, he shrugged off his earlier self-doubts and rose to greet his African guest with his usual aplomb.

Chapter 13

FOR MOST OF THE TRAIN ride home, Steve Sigourney could barely keep his eyes open or his stomach calm. Too much acid coffee to ward off drowsiness accounted for his dyspepsia, but his fatigue remained unexplained. He had slept soundly enough the night before in Anton's antique four-poster. Maybe he was coming down with a cold, he speculated, thinking of the scruffy youth, constantly coughing and sneezing, who had sat next to him on the train to New York. Or maybe it was an after-effect of the emotional turmoil triggered by his visit. Never before had Anton been so open with him—or so disapproving.

Back in Philadelphia, Steve dropped by his office, intending to stay just long enough to look over his mail before going home to bed. But the message to call Dan Lassiter, dated yesterday, gave him pause. Since Lassiter was unlikely to be in his office on a Saturday night and he didn't have his home telephone number, Steve's initial impulse was to deal with it on Monday. But if Lassiter had phoned about his young leukemia patient, it would be unconscionable to keep him waiting.

He was almost relieved when not Lassiter but his wife, Kristina, answered the phone in his office. But five minutes later, while he was still opening mail, Lassiter himself called and Steve braced himself to hear him out. In the end, he consented to supply the isotope-antibody conjugate that represented the treatment of last resort for Billy Freiborg. He might come to regret such generosity, Steve realized, but he was too tired to argue. He even agreed to deliver the radioactive material personally and supervise its administration. Cutting short Lassiter's thanks, he wished him and his patient well and hung up. By now the ache in the back of his neck had spread through his shoulders and it hurt to hold his head up. He longed to stretch out on a bed or couch, but couldn't just yet. Wearily he telephoned his staff biophysicist, Gunther Gausse.

"Gunther," he said when the familiar voice of his young associate answered, "this is Sigourney. Sorry to bother you at home, but how many milligrams of isotope-linked TC-33 antibody do we have on hand? . . . I see . . . Yes, I'll need all that and more—enough to treat a fifty or so kilogram boy with T-cell leukemia in a Boston hospital . . . I realize it's premature, Gunther, but I let myself get talked into it. . . Will it work? Who can say? *Someday* it will work, so why not now? Besides, there's a lot we can learn; they're set up to do all the necessary studies . . . I know it's an imposition, but could you come in tomorrow and prepare as much as you can? . . . Thank you, Gunther, I appreciate your cooperation. Good night."

There, thought Steve; the wheels were in motion.

Glancing at his desk calendar, he was dismayed at the number of appointments that would have to be shifted, but with luck he could fire his magic bullets into Lassiter's patient on Monday night. In his bathroom, Steve gagged down two aspirin with a swig of chalky antacid, and at last went home.

Entering his apartment, Steve spotted the envelope that had been slipped under the door and picked it up. As expected, it was from Yuri, his precocious chess partner, and contained his next move. To Steve's relief, it was the one he'd predicted; he was in no condition to ponder chess strategy tonight. Yuri was well ahead in their latest match. Unless he made some foolish play, unlikely in an end game, the best Steve could hope for was stalemate. In the even more intricate game of cancer research, however, he still played to win—the experimental treatment of Lassiter's leukemia patient representing one of his more daring gambits.

Exhausted, he planned to sleep late the next morning. But a phone call from Gausse, reporting a snag in the conjugation procedure, roused Steve at seven, and after fortifying himself with more aspirin he dragged himself to the lab. It took until mid-afternoon to prepare new reagents and get matters straightened out. Steve felt feverish and achy throughout. On the way home he debated whether to stop by University Hospital and have one of its emergency room doctors examine him. But there would doubtless be a long wait and he felt too uncomfortable to endure it. Instead, remembering he had some antibiotic pills left over from a severe sinus infection a few months ago, he chose to treat himself, at least temporarily. If he was no better by morning, he would ask one of the M.D.'s at the Institute to take a look at him.

Fortunately, the antibiotic seemed to work. Except

for an intermittent headache and muscle spasms across his upper back, he got through his day's appointments—the last with Gunther Gausse, who had made the complicated arrangements for the radioactive antibodies to accompany Steve on his Boston flight—without much discomfort and, stuffing his briefcase with reading material, left for the airport in late afternoon.

He had last seen Commonwealth General Hospital twenty years before and did not look forward to returning there now. Knowing bitter memories of his late mentor, Curt Anders Gundersen, would be revived by his visit, he hoped it would be as short as it was successful. Gundersen, he reflected, had been a flawed and tragic talent who could bend men to his will, but not facts. Thinking back to what Dan Lassiter had confided about his wife and Gundersen, Steve wondered how many other careers the man had nearly ruined. But why brood about it now when he would soon see enough of Gundersen's ghost haunting the hospital he had almost singlehandedly created.

Taking the current issue of *Science* from his briefcase, Steve opened it to the table of contents to locate his and Gunther Gausse's report. Suddenly his eyes bulged and his neck jerked painfully as the title of the Okabe-Kreisberg article, *The Unique Protein Produced by the Simian Sarcoma Virus Oncogene,* generated an emotional jolt. What is this? he wondered. Could these two Boston-based researchers, one a man he had never heard of, the other an expert in recombinant DNA turned entrepreneur, actually have done what he himself, after years of grueling effort, had only been on the verge of doing: isolated and identified the long elusive cancer-causing protein? Steve could hardly believe it. If true, how come he had not heard about it on the scientific grapevine? If not, how had they hoodwinked the editors of *Science*? Either way, their audacity stunned him. Instead of a preliminary report, a modest bid for priority and peer consideration, Okabe and Kreisberg had published their findings as a featured article! Steve turned to it and, with mounting apprehension, began to read.

The introductory passages, mainly historical, were of little interest to him, though he did give a fleeting thought to how little of this information was known when he had begun his cancer research career in earnest nineteen years before. Since the pioneer work of Peyton Rous in 1910, the existence of tumor-causing viruses had been strongly suspected. Yet it took the discovery of the RNA-containing retroviruses more than half a century later to give legitimacy to Rous's findings. Not only did certain of these viruses produce cancers in susceptible animals, sometimes in only a few days, but their molecular mechanisms could be encoded in as few as four genes. In the virus selected by Okabe and Kreisberg for study, three of its four genes directed the production of proteins essential for survival; the fourth, the oncogene, seemed superfluous for this purpose and inherently "evil," since its only known action was to transform a healthy cell into a cancerous one unrestrained by either internal regulatory signals or external boundaries.

Presumably it did this by reactivating certain processes, dormant since fetal life, that led to explosive cell growth. Steve had once overhead Andre Evashevsky tell a group of touring students, "Picture a small community of adults where something, say some super-vitamin added to their water supply, started them growing again at the same rate as an embryo grows into a baby. Suddenly their clothes, their beds, their houses no longer fit. Ravenously hungry and lawless, they break through police barriers and spill into neighboring communities to try to satisfy their needs."

The chaos created by such rampaging mutants was horrible to contemplate. Yet something similar happened to the transformed cell. Assuming that the protein produced by the cancer-causing gene triggered these cellular monstrosities, the crucial question was *how?* Did it start at the top, affecting one master cell regulator? Or did it transfigure several lesser proteins at once? Steve favored the former hypothesis, though the identity of such a master protein still eluded him.

Now, in a series of immunological, enzymatic and structural proofs so complicated that only a few dozen scientists world-wide could fully comprehend them, Okabe claimed to have exposed the culprit. Through either incredible luck or skill, he had managed to create a monoclonal antibody that detected its molecular fingerprints.

Ignoring as best he could his throbbing head and the muscle spasms in his neck, Steve read the article through to the end, put the journal aside, and for several minutes afterward sat trance-like and stupefied. Was Okabe right? Had he actually done all that he claimed? His proof hinged heavily on the specificity of the antibody he had created to detect the abnormal protein. If others, using the same antibody that Okabe could hardly refuse to furnish them, could replicate his results, its existence would be accepted and Steve finished. An obscure investigator would not only have proved himself cleverer but would have robbed him of the surpassing thrill of discovery. For years now Steve had wooed Nature assiduously, believing that in the end she would reward him by yielding one of her most tantalizing secrets. But somehow this interloper, this Joshua Okabe, had seduced her first, leaving him heartsick and desolate. Or was it merely false bragging on Okabe's part? No one in Steve's lab had ever gotten such flurographic separations to come out so neatly. But even if the authors had "trimmed" their data a bit, it didn't much matter. The key issue remained whether the Okabe protein was the *cause,* not merely a by-product, of the cancer process, and the clincher would be if its insertion transformed a normal cell into a malignant one. In the customary scientific hedge, Okabe and Kreisberg wrote that preliminary results in that regard were "encouraging."

Maybe encouraging to them, to all of science, but not to him, Steve brooded. Having already lost Nicole, he had in all likelihood lost his bid for scientific immortality, too. All he had left to look forward to now was a favorable result in Lassiter's leukemia patient—a minor miracle from the point of view of the boy and his physicians but one for which Steve, feeling sick and defeated, had little hope.

Nor, for the moment, did Ted Swerdloff. Growing increasingly edgy as Sigourney's arrival time in Boston neared, he decided to work off some of his nervous tension by climbing the six flights of stairs from his office to Dan Lassiter's.

Dan was on the telephone when Swerdloff staggered in. Hastily concluding his conversation, he stared curiously and said, "Elevator break down? Or are you in pulmonary edema?"

"Neither," said Swerdloff breathlessly. "I'm merely substituting physical for mental exhaustion. Is Sigourney still due in here at seven o'clock?"

"Far as I know." Dan looked at his watch. "I'm going to leave for the airport to pick him up in a half-hour. How's Billy doing?"

"On the outside, okay. His four o'clock temperature was an even one hundred. On the inside, lousy. His white cell count has soared to 150,000. I just hope none of them stick together and plug up a blood vessel

. . . Damn it, Dan, I'll be glad when this night is over!"

"Me too. Billy's father just flew in from Bemidji and came up to see me. I explained the risks and he seemed to accept them. But he's got that glassy-eyed look, like a boxer about to fold, so I doubt he can take much more . . . I'm hungry. Want to join me for a quick bite in the cafeteria?"

"No, thanks. No appetite. But you go ahead. The food's marginally better here than at the airport."

"You're right," said Dan, rising and reaching for his topcoat. "See you back here in a couple of hours."

Dan had no sooner entered the airport terminal when he heard his name being paged by Eastern Airlines. Expecting bad news, either a crisis at the hospital or Steve Sigourney cancelling his trip, he went limp with relief when his caller turned out to be Nelson Freiborg. Evidently Nels' secretary considered it routine to track down people in airports. Dan gave him a terse report on what was about to happen to his nephew, promised to call back when the outcome was known, and then hurried on to meet Sigourney's incoming plane at the gate.

Steve was one of the last passengers to emerge from the jetway. From flushed face to wobbly gait, his appearance shocked Dan. "You all right?" he asked as they shook hands.

Steve shrugged. "I left Philadelphia with a head cold. Now I've got a splitting headache, an earache, and a stiff neck. Draw your own conclusions."

"You look feverish. Even your hand feels hot. Maybe I'd better check you over when we get to the hospital."

"Maybe you should," Steve said. "There's no denying I feel awful. But let's take care of your patient first."

At the hospital, they located Ted and went on to Billy Freiborg's room. There were more people there than Dan would have wanted, but since they were all involved in the case in one way or another he didn't ask anybody to leave. Almost entirely enmeshed in tubes and wires, Billy lay in bed, looking wan but expectant.

"Hi!" said Dan. "Somebody here I want you to meet. Billy, this is Dr. Steve Sigourney—a home-run hitter from Philadelphia."

Billy licked his lips and croaked, "That so? Hope you hit one tonight."

For a moment Steve didn't answer. His neck ached so badly he could barely bend it to look down at the boy. "Me, too," he finally muttered.

Billy glanced quizzically at Dan and drew him closer. "Your Philadelphia slugger doesn't look so hot," he whispered. "Who's going to inject the stuff—you or him?"

"Neither. Ted is. We drew lots in my office and he lost."

"What do you mean, lost?"

"The stuff's so radioactive it might explode. Except for you and Ted, I'm clearing the room. Maybe the entire floor."

"Oh, great!" Billy groaned. "You mean it—not about me exploding, but you leaving?"

Dan smiled under his mask. "If you want, I'll stick around a while. But nothing dramatic is going to happen. It'll take several hours, even days, before we know how well the treatment's working."

"I figured that," said Billy morosely. "Well, let's get it over with."

"Right."

Dan nodded to Ted Swerdloff. Then, directing his gaze at Steve and observing the sweat beading his forehead, he said to the nurse, "Nan, get a chair for

Dr. Sigourney, will you? He's not feeling well."

"That's not necessary," Steve protested. "I'm really quite . . ." A searing pain shot up the back of his skull as he tried to turn his head toward Dan. Suddenly his knees buckled and he collapsed.

Chapter 14

WHEN STEVE REGAINED CONSCIOUSNESS, he found himself lying on a stretcher, a flimsy gown covering his nude, trembling body. Looking down at him were Dan Lassiter and a stocky young doctor in a green surgical scrub suit. Groping for Dan's hand, he gasped, "W . . . What happened?"

"You passed out. Not surprising in view of the fact that you have a fever of 104, a low blood pressure, and a very worrisome stiff neck. This is Dr. Jim Hermanson, Steve. Jim is the pitboss in our emergency room, and you're certainly an emergency. Also he's had more practice doing spinal taps than I have."

"A spinal?" Steve grimaced. "What for?"

"We're pretty sure you have meningitis. Ordinarily that's serious enough, but with you—the research you do—it's anybody's guess what the bug is."

"Meningitis?" Steve looked puzzled. "I can't have meningitis. I'm taking antibiotics."

The surprised look on Dan's face rapidly changed

to dismay as he realized the implications of antibiotic-resistant infection. "What antibiotic? What for?"

"*Ceclor*. I had some left over from a sinus infection and started taking it yesterday . . . Not such a bright idea, huh?"

"That's an understatement." Dan knew that *Ceclor*, a cephalosporin-type antibiotic, penetrated poorly into the cerebro-spinal fluid, so the fact that Steve was taking it didn't necessarily rule out bacterial meningitis but it did make it less likely. "Steve, think carefully. Have you been working with any particularly virulent viruses or sick animals lately?"

Holding his head to stop it from throbbing, Steve said, "No, not really. Some of our hybridoma colonies were infected with mycoplasma a few months back, but we eradicated that . . . Of course, we've been heavily involved in E-B virus lymphocyte cloning."

"E-B?" repeated Dan. "You mean the virus that causes infectious mononucleosis?"

He turned to Jim Hermanson, who said, "Infectious mono can cause either meningitis or encephalitis, but it's rare . . . Look, Dan, the sooner we draw off some spinal fluid and see what's in it, the better. Why don't I go ahead and set him up for the tap while you call his lab and find out if anybody else—human or animal—has come down with meningitis lately?"

"You hear that, Steve? Who's the best person to call?"

"Andre Evashevsky," said Steve and gave Dan his telephone number.

"You'll want him admitted to the ICU, won't you?" asked Hermanson.

"That's right. Kris is at home and I don't have the heart to call her in. She's really beat. You and I'll just have to manage."

"Wait!" cried Steve as Dan turned to leave. "How did the monoclonal injection go?"

"I don't know. Been too busy taking care of you. But I would've heard from Ted Swerdloff if anything went wrong. I'll check with him first chance I get. In the meantime, Steve, try to relax and hope we find something in your spinal fluid we can treat."

Striding out of the room, Dan heard Jim Hermanson ask, "What about herpes virus, Dr. Sigourney? Have you been playing around with that lately?"

Twenty minutes later, while Steve was being transferred to a room on the intensive care unit, Dan and Hermanson huddled around Hanna Robinson in the lab as the veteran bacteriologist examined a stained smear of their patient's spinal fluid.

"Are you still betting on meningococcus?" Dan asked his emergency room chief.

"I was, until I heard the long list of deadly viruses grown in Sigourney's lab. There's another possibility, though . . ." Hermanson added. "From what little he told me before the pain shot zonked him, I gather he had a pretty bad sinus infection a few months back, so bad he nearly had to have a drainage procedure. If the course of antibiotics he took didn't quite clear it up and it's smoldered, he could have something less exotic."

"Like what?"

Hermanson shrugged. "Like pneumococcal meningitis."

"Is the pneumococcus your pick?" asked Hanna Robinson. "Well, give the doctor a cigar! You smoke cigars, Jim?"

"No, but I'll smoke one till I turn green, if that's what he's got."

"Take a look for yourself," said Robinson. "You won't see many of the little buggers, but they're there, all right."

* * *

The news that he was suffering from a common, treatable, bacterial meningitis failed to register on Steve as Dan bent over him in the intensive care unit. He was incoherent, barely responsive at all.

"Where's the ICU house staff?" Dan asked the nurse.

"They're tied up in room twelve—dissecting aneurysm that's in ventricular fibrillation."

Dan did not bother to remind her that it was a *patient*, not a piece of aorta, that was in extremis. Nor did he really need house staff help. Though it had been years since he had last treated a case of meningitis, he still remembered how and welcomed the challenge. After briefly examining Steve, he told the nurse, "Get me a blood culture kit. I'll draw the next one myself."

The nurse glanced at the name on the chart. "Is the patient a friend of yours, Dr. Lassiter?"

"A very old friend who might not be in this mess if he hadn't flown up here to do a patient of mine a favor. So please be extra good to him. I owe him one."

As a swimmer underwater perceives sound vibrations in his vicinity, Steve in his stuporous state was faintly aware of outside voices, though their speech seemed gurgling and he continued to converse with an inner self. He even felt submerged in warm water, not an unpleasant sensation after his chilly emergency room exposure. But the water temperature was uneven, almost scalding his head and leaving his body numb and cool. Was it because the membranes enveloping his brain were on fire with infection?

Am I dying? he wondered.

Do I care?

If Anton's hunch was correct and humanity nothing more than an experiment in which their lives were as insigificant and expendable as one of Steve's laboratory rats, his fate might not be so pleasant. He did not explain himself to his test animals, either. Nor did he tolerate those temperamental rodents who became listless or cannibalistic and disrupted his experimental design. Would God treat him as he did them—crack his skull with a hammer and dispose of him in a plastic bag?

His skull had felt as if it were about to crack earlier. Now the torment had eased. A good sign? Or was it the customary grace afforded a condemned man before his execution?

Pain he did not want, but otherwise he didn't really care whether he lived or died. He had no close friends; no one, except for a few loyal co-workers, who would likely mourn or miss him. And an unknown Boston scientist had apparently beaten him to the motherlode of his cancer research. Without realizing or wanting it, he had become an abrasive eccentric, a bloodless problem-solver. Whose fault? he asked himself: Was my mother's neglect and ex-fiancée's betrayal so crippling that I avoided friendship and love and, until recently, even lust—afraid to expose my true self again to another critical human being? Is that the reason I'm so skinny and ugly and blemished that I shudder at my reflection in the mirror and am ashamed to show my teeth when I smile? Believing it safer to think than to feel, Steve had never before made any effort to change.

To live or to die? Out of the confusion and uncertainty he felt, one thing seemed clear. If he survived, he would not want to live as before.

"Hey, Chad . . ."

"Yeah, kid?" Chad Petersen looked up from the magazine he had been reading. Like Billy, who was no longer encumbered by tubes and wires, he wore a flannel robe over pajamas. The light from the window was bleak and gray. Outside, it was snowing.

"What's really going on here? I mean, they bring in this doc from Philly to treat me and what does he do? Mumbles a couple of words and passes out! Right in front of everybody! Not exactly what I'd call confidence-building, would you?"

Putting his magazine down, Chad shrugged. "I gotta admit that's pretty weird."

"I'll say! Then, they shoot this stuff into me that's never been given to any human being before. Lassiter even kidded me about it being so radioactive it might explode. Jeez!"

"Hey, what're you bellyaching about? None of your other treatments worked worth a damn, so they tried something new. At least they haven't given up on you, sent in some Boston Celtic star to cheer you up by promising to sink a foul shot for you."

"I know. But wait—you still haven't heard the worst part. The stuff they shot into me was from a *mouse.* I'm not kidding. From a goddamned *mouse!* How'd you like to have mouse crap in you?" Billy swallowed a giggle. "Bet you don't even know what a monoclonal antibody is!"

Chad shrugged. "You got me there . . . *You* know?"

"Well, sort of. The way Swerdloff explained it, clones are exact look-alikes from the same mother cell. Like a bitch having a litter all identical. Only instead of a few, the cells in their laboratory can turn out trillions and trillions. Swerdloff says it's the biggest medical discovery in a long time—that pretty soon people will be talking about monoclonal antibodies like they talk now about penicillin."

"Yeah?" said Chad, yawning. "Sounds good. Hope it works."

"Me, too . . . Only what if it doesn't?"

"Then they either try something else or send you off to the cookie palace."

"What's the cookie palace?"

"A place where they serve milk and cookies laced with dope, often as you want. That way you die quietly."

"How do you know that? You been there?"

Chad didn't reply. He picked up his magazine and began to read. Finally, as if in response to Billy's unspoken question, he looked up and said, "What, kid?"

"Am I dying, too?"

"You'd know that better 'n I."

"How?"

"Your body tells you. When you're dying, you sense it somehow . . . Do you?"

"I think I did, up until a little while ago. Now it's like I got a second wind . . . But how do *you* know all this? Are you dead?"

Chad rose, stretched and went to the window. Against the light, he looked almost transparent, ghost-like. Turning, he said, "Dont' sweat it, kid. I'm here when you want, when you need me."

Billy asked, "You know Henry Wedemacher?"

"Name is familiar. Haven't actually met him, but I know he's around here someplace."

"Around where? Where's *here?"*

"Where we all are. Inside your head."

"But if you're just in my head," Billy protested, "that means you're not real."

"Everything's *just* in your head, dummy. You got to decide what's real for yourself."

"Hey, come on, Chad, cut the bullcrap! I'm confused enough already. Are you really here or not? Can I reach out and touch you?"

"Try it and find out."

"Okay, don't move. Promise?" At Chad's nod, he rose off the bed and approached within a few feet of him.

"Well?" prompted Chad as Billy stood there frozen. "What are you waiting for?"

"I don't know. I'm sort of . . . scared."

Chad gave him a disgusted look. "Then I'll touch *you.*"

Feeling a cold hand brush his cheek, Billy lurched forward and hugged his friend tightly. He felt solid . . . real.

Satisfied, Billy drifted into a deeper, dreamless sleep, totally unaware of Dan Lassiter's presence by his bed.

Dan checked on his two patients once more at midnight and went home, uneasily concluding a night's work he would long remember. Despite having taken every conceivable precaution, he expected disaster to strike at any moment. For Steve, the immediate threats were brain swelling, convulsive seizures and septic shock. Even if he avoided these complications, he still risked brain abscess or an infected heart valve. For Billy, the list was as least as long and forbidding. Dan slept fitfully that night as nightmares kept returning him to the hospital.

When twenty-four hours passed with no serious complications befalling either patient, Dan could scarcely believe his good luck. Afraid to mention it lest it change, he couldn't help wondering if some special Providence had temporarily suspended Murphy's Law. Or was he merely being set up for a crushing blow by its demon enforcers?

Under Dan's vigilant eye, Steve's fever and stiff neck rapidly responded to the intravenous penicillin he was receiving and a repeat spinal tap three days later confirmed that his meningitis was resolving. Even so, something, whether organic or psychological, seemed wrong in his head. Though he was a cooperative patient and eager for news of Billy Freiborg's latest blood studies, Steve seemed abnormally listless and withdrawn. This impression was reinforced by the nursing staff, who reported that Steve never read the papers or watched TV, but appeared lost in thought much of the time.

Dan had no idea what might be troubling him. Nor did Steve volunteer any clues, except for one he accidentally let slip while expounding on the subtle and little known politics behind the awarding of the Nobel science prizes: the frantic, often cut-throat competition among contenders in the same field to claim priority for their discoveries through early publication, and the tricky business of making themselves and their work known to the Swedish selection committee. Appalled, Dan had asked if all the time and grueling effort that went into such campaigns were really worth it. And Steve, seemingly taken aback by the question, had replied, "Why the Prize? I don't just want it, Dan, I *need* it! How else can I justify what I've become?" Pleading drowsiness, he'd ended their conversation at this point and never referred to the subject again.

Billy's behavior was the opposite of Steve's. Even though every bone in his body ached from marrow radiation and kidney-flushing drugs made him urinate gallons each day, he was so high spirited that he wore out his nurses.

Cautiously, Dan watched his patients grow steadily better, though it was not until the weekend, when Kris insisted they go sailing, that he finally dared relax his vigilance.

On Monday, Andre Evashevsky came to visit Steve. Meeting the hefty, straggly-haired, bearded Evashevsky for the first time, Dan was struck by the physical dissimilarities between the two scientists. Even their energy levels differed sharply. While Steve sat slouched in a chair, taciturn and contemplative, Evashevsky paced and gesticulated wildly, evidently frustrated by his chief's refusal to talk shop.

But Evashevsky would not be denied. Within hours of his arrival, he had sought out and questioned Ted Swerdloff, Jerry Rabin, and the technician operating the laser cell sorter. He even wanted to cross town to visit with Joshua Okabe and Max Kreisberg, but Steve strongly opposed it.

"Why shouldn't I talk to them?" Evashevsky growled. "Okabe took up a whole afternoon of my time talking to me."

"When?" asked Steve, surprised.

"Around six months ago. I told Okabe everything I knew about the sodium-potassium ATPase I was working on—maybe too much. Now it's his turn." Striding to the window Evashevsky abruptly swung back and added, "I tell you, the man is more mystic than scientist. And after our last phone conversation, I don't trust either him or his work . . . Okay, so he's flooded with requests from scientists all over the world for his monoclonal antibody and can't possibly satisfy everybody. That much, I believe. But we're the *leaders* in this field, for God's sake! Okabe ought to be eager for us to confirm his findings. And if he can't scrape up enough of his precious antibody to supply us, I strongly suspect that he doesn't intend to supply anybody, maybe because it doesn't exist! Either way, as long as I'm here, I think I should talk to him."

"Probably so," said Steve, "but I'd rather you didn't right now. Being confined to bed for so long, I've had an opportunity to think; to decide what I want to do with the rest of my life. Prepare yourself for a shock, Andre. There's a certain matter we need to discuss . . ."

When Dan visited that afternoon, Steve surprised him by asking to be discharged. Evashevsky could accompany him back to Philadelphia and arrange for his admission to a hospital there to complete the two-week course of intravenous penicillin therapy. That way, Steve argued, he would be closer to his research, now in a crucial stage, and feel less thwarted.

At first, Dan refused, suspecting that even dragging an IV pole and bottle around, Steve would sneak back to his lab or overexert himself in other ways. But when Steve bolstered his case by pointing out that further mental inactivity would only deepen his depression, Dan reluctantly gave in.

At eight the next morning, following a series of brief farewells, the last and most poignant with Billy Freiborg, Steve and Andre Evashevsky left the hospital for Logan Airport. After a final argument in the TWA departure lounge, squelched by Steve's forceful restatement of his resolve, the two embraced and parted company, Evashevsky looking on helplessly as Steve, a bottle of penicillin tablets in his briefcase to tide him over, boarded the plane for Barcelona.

He arrived in the Spanish port city after midnight. By pre-arrangement, Georgi Kosterlitz had flown in from Minorca in his private jet and was there to greet him. "My God!" the Englishman exclaimed when Steve came through customs and trudged toward him, "You look—uh—unhealthy."

"I am—or was," Steve replied. "I'm recovering from meningitis."

"So that's it! Your cablegram was so cryptic I had no idea why you were coming. You're here to rest, I presume."

"*More* than rest. Tell me, Georgi, how good is that cosmetic surgeon you hired last year?"

"Pritchard? Oh, first rate. He could make Quasimodo look presentable. A true artist."

"Good . . . Let's sit, shall we?" said Steve, indicating a nearby bench. "I'm a little lightheaded

. . . Now, as to the purpose of my visit: you would agree, would you not, that I've been instrumental to the success of your clinic?"

"Of course, old boy! No argument whatsoever. Without your biochemical brilliance, it would be just another dreary health resort."

Steve nodded. "Well, to put your mind at ease, it's not more money I'm after. A lot has happened to shake me up lately which I won't go into now. You can hear all about it, if you want, on the flight to Minorca. But the essence is, I'm tired of the way I live—and look. Regardless of how long it takes, I want to avail myself of the clinic's full range of services—dermatology, dentistry, cosmetic surgery, the works! In short, I want you to make me over. Are you willing to do it, Georgi?"

Kosterlitz broke into a grin. "Indeed I am! With the greatest of pleasure. My clinic is your clinic . . . Naturally I'm dying to hear what's behind your extraordinary decision, but all in due time. In the meantime, welcome to the world of us vain mortals, Stefan!"

PART TWO

"THE PRIZE"

Chapter 15

THROUGHOUT MOST OF THE Northern Hemisphere, October is a lovely and invigorating time of year, the premier month of fall. The pace of work and study quickens. Indian summer enchants. The nights are cool and scented by moldering leaves. Songs have been written about it.

But for an elite few, October is also a time of extraordinary suspense and tension. Appetites wane, tempers fray, daydreams disrupt concentration while sleep grows increasingly fitful. The bedside or desktop telephone, especially in the early morning hours, turns into a silent, mocking monster. Though easily surmised, the source of this intense anxiety is seldom acknowledged, even to intimates: The Nobel Prize winners are announced in October.

When Gregory Carhill heard the names of this year's winners in medicine on his car radio, he was more surprised than disappointed. Although two of the three brain physiologists were Americans, one on the Harvard faculty, their accomplishments were unknown to him. A compromise choice, most likely, he speculated; the Nobel selection committee was known to resort to these when its members were split and unyielding over the candidates they chose to champion.

Carhill had not really expected to win it this time; his masterwork on mouse leukemia had been published only a month before and the field trials of his human leukemia vaccine barely begun. Still, he couldn't help feeling wistful and a little troubled by the news, sensing somehow that this coming year represented his best—and last—chance for the Prize.

At least Stefan Sigourney had not won, he thought, while parking his car in its designated slot behind the Bethune Institute. That was some small consolation. Sigourney had his backers on the Nobel committee, Carhill knew. "The Sigourney Effect," his great discovery of almost a decade ago, remained one of the cornerstones of modern immunology—though, unlike others in the field, Carhill insisted on referring to it more properly as the "Androsh-Sigourney Effect."

Carhill still had no clear idea who this Milos Androsh was. In combing the scientific literature for a list of Androsh's publications, he had found only two, both in minor, middle European science journals. Nonetheless, since Sigourney had referred to Androsh's earlier experiments in his paper, he deserved recognition. Perhaps not the primacy that Carhill was eager to bestow upon him, but some. Never mind that this obscure Czech investigator had never published another word on this or any other scientific subject; it seemed only fair. Should others follow his lead, thereby dulling the luster of Sigourney's achievement, so much the better.

En route from parking lot to office, Carhill passed several of his co-workers, greeting each by name. Though a few stopped to chat, none mentioned the new Nobel laureates, though the names must have been on their minds. Carhill was not surprised; if not impertinent, it certainly would have been impolitic of them.

That same morning, Dan Lassiter met Nelson Freiborg for lunch at the Hyatt Regency on Capitol Hill. Bleary-eyed from lack of sleep, a chronic condition brought on by interminable budget battles, Nels half rose, extended his hand and grinned as Dan approached the table. "I spoke to Billy the other night and he's feeling fine. Just great! I don't know how I —all the Freiborgs—will ever be able to thank you."

"Don't thank me yet," Dan cautioned. "If five years from now Billy's still okay, you can do it then."

"Even so, Dan, he's home. Enjoying life again. What you and your team achieved is a real breakthrough!"

Dan grimaced. "A vastly overworked word these days. Truth is, we were lucky."

"Oh, come on, Doctor! You took a kid who was near death and restored him to robust health. You call that luck? That's being a bit too modest, don't you think?"

"I only wish it were. For a time Ted Swerdloff and I thought we'd come the closet yet to a cure for leukemia. 'The treatment of choice,' as it's known in the trade. But our euphoria ended abruptly when Ted tried exactly the same isotope-antibody combination on a second patient, a ten-year-old girl with a similar type of leukemia, and it didn't work nearly as well."

"I'm sorry to hear that," said Nels. "Can anything more be done for her?"

"We hope so. I sure wish Sigourney was around to help us out again." Looking wistful, Dan sipped the whiskey and water the waiter had brought.

"Where is he?"

"That's a good question. Nobody seems to know—

or else is under strict orders not to say. After his bout with meningitis, Steve flew off to Minorca in the Balearic island to recuperate. That was over three months ago and he's not back yet."

"Minorca? Where the Kosterlitz Clinic is? You hear a lot of talk about that outfit on the Washington cocktail circuit. A lady friend of mine went there; dropped forty pounds in two months and swears by the treatment. What's your opinion?"

"I don't have one. Rumor has it that Kosterlitz isolated some brain hormone that safely kills appetite, which is theoretically possible, I suppose, but unlikely, and the last thing Steve Sigourney needs. He's thin as a rail. So I doubt if he's anywhere near the Kosterlitz Clinic. I don't know why Steve went to Minorca, or what he's doing there so long, but I wish he'd wind it up and get back to work. He's a peculiar guy, Nels—not unstable but eccentric as hell. And he was pretty depressed when he left the hospital. Frankly I'm a little worried about him."

Freiborg ordered another round of drinks from the waiter and then said, "Well, I certainly hope Sigourney's all right. Billy wouldn't be, if it wasn't for him." He paused, then continued, "This may seem like a naive question, Dan, but no less a personage than the President is vitally interested in your answer: How close *are* we to curing cancer?"

Dan stared. "The President? Good God, don't tell me he's got . . ."

"No, no," said Nels hastily. "Far as I know, he's fine. Besides, heads of state hardly ever die of cancer—not in this century, anyway. I've no idea why, but if I had to guess I'd say it had something to do with their personalities. Look at Churchill, Franco, Tito; they took forever to die. What's that brain chemical that's supposed to kill pain and give you a high?"

"Endorphin?"

"Yeah—endorphin. Those guys must've oozed it, or whatever else the brain puts out to bolster the body's defenses. But back to my question. I know you're no cancer researcher, but try to crystal-ball it for me."

Dan's initial impulse was to avoid a direct response, but something in Nels' manner suggested that more than mere curiosity was involved. "How close are we to a cancer cure? Ten, even five, years ago the experts were still saying it wouldn't come in this century. But that was before they knew about recombinant DNA and monoclonal antibodies and the latest find, the cancer gene."

"Cancer gene, eh? Sounds ominous—the stuff of nightmares. But I sleep little enough as it is, so tell me about it."

"Well, it's been known for some time that certain viruses can rapidly cause cancers in animals. A few years back, the genetic material of one was analyzed and found to comprise only four genes. One of them, called the oncogene, does nothing but transform a normal cell into a cancerous one. Moreover, it's been discovered that we all have such oncogenes—a whole family of them—in our chromosomes, like time bombs waiting to go off. In other words, regardless of what triggers them, all cancers seem to arise through a common mechanism: the activation of an oncogene for a particular type of cell—in Billy's case, a stem cell in his bone marrow that makes T-lymphocytes. And since *one* gene directs the manufacture of *one* protein, the race is on to discover precisely what that protein is and how it works."

"What then?"

"Then, ways to block the action of this deadly protein will be sought and a cure for some, maybe most, cancers might be possible . . . What's the President's particular interest in all this?"

"Economic opportunity."

"Economic what? Last I heard, cancer was a growth, not a growth industry."

"It could be both, which is why the President dispatched an economist like me to explore the possibilities with you. Before you brought them to my attention a few months back, I'd never even heard of monoclonal antibodies. Since then, I've read dozens of items in the business sections of the newspapers about them. Just last week the *Wall Street Journal* ran an article forecasting that their diagnostic use alone would amount to a billion dollar industry in a couple more years. And an effective treatment for cancer would be worth several times more. If, along with private industry, the government got solidly behind this research, it could speed its development enormously, I'd imagine. But I'm no scientist. What do you think?"

Dan pondered. "According to Steve Sigourney, the biggest hindrance to progress in the cancer field right now isn't secrecy or crass commercialism, but duplication of effort. Take hybridoma research as an example. There are at least a dozen major problems that must be solved before their products, partly derived from a cancer cell, can be made fully safe and effective, and maybe a hundred research centers world-wide working on one or two of them—almost always the same ones! So a crash program, with an overall Czar assigning teams to specific projects, would certainly help. On the other hand, scientists—the top ones—hate to be regimented. They tend to take their work so personally they practically make love to their experiments. I doubt they'd be much interested in communal sex."

Freiborg smiled. "But a cure for cancer, Dan—a disease that's bound to strike a lot of them, their families—wouldn't that be rewarding enough?"

"Maybe. As a clinician, a treater of patients, I would hope so. But because of the nature of cancer research, a lot of workers in the field are either loners or egomaniacs. Hard to say what the best tack would be to take with them. I'd have to give it some thought."

"Well, while you're at it, please think about who the best person would be to head up such a project. What about your friend and Billy's benefactor, Steve Sigourney?"

"Steve?" repeated Dan in amazement.

"Know anybody better?"

"As a cancer researcher, no. But I don't know how good an administrator he is."

"Oh, we'd get somebody else for that. Someone with proven administrative ability . . . like you."

Dan stared. Then he laughed. "Studies show that sleep deprivation causes hallucinations, Nels. Literally dreaming with your eyes open. Which is what I think you're doing now."

"Not really. Not like when I'm telling the Congress that money stretches like bubble gum and we can balance the federal budget in a few years . . . In case you're wondering why I'm pushing this, Dan, it's not just out of gratitude for what you people did to save Billy. For weeks now, as my eyes blur going over the defense ledgers, I've been haunted by the thought that cancer could be cured for the same price as a single nuclear powered aircraft carrier. I've just about persuaded the President to appoint a commission to look into the possibility. You'd be willing to serve on that, wouldn't you?" At Dan's nod, he added, "I'd welcome Sigourney's input, too. Could you sound him out?"

"Be glad to, if I can get hold of him. His secretary still doesn't know when he'll be back."

"Well, fly to Minorca if you have to. We'll foot the bill."

"Is it that urgent?"

"No, but the President might want to talk to him.

Incidentally, I've learned a few things about Dr. Stefan Sigourney lately, and one rather intrigues me. Do you know where he gets most of the funding for his institute?"

"Haven't the faintest idea."

"Well, neither do we, since less than half a million of it comes from federal grants. That's a pretty paltry sum for a research outfit that size."

"So?" said Dan, trying to hide his surprise. "What are you getting at?"

"Nothing much. Just curious who's backing him, that's all. Makes you wonder if he made some deal with a pharmaceutical company."

Dan reflected a moment and smiled. "What *I* find curious is your curiosity."

"How so?" said Freiborg innocently.

"Well, the more money a scientist gets from the N.I.H., the more inclined he is to go along with their policies and proposals. The less money, the less inclined. Looks to me like Steve Sigourney will be standing straight up when you talk to him."

Freiborg smiled back. "A neat deduction, if a bit cynical. But to make a go of this, we'd really need Sigourney's talent in some capacity. The question is," he mused, as the waiter served their salads, "would *he* need us?"

Chapter 16

NICOLE BRUEUR BOARDED THE midnight flight from Barcelona at Dulles Airport, settled into her seat in the first-class section of the jumbo jet and sipped her first glass of champagne. Over the next hour she drank three more glasses, hoping the alcohol would blunt her sense of excitement sufficiently to let her sleep. But it was no use. Even after she stretched out on the empty seat beside her and buried her face in pillows, her brain remained stubbornly active. From time to time, she would sit up and either read the travel brochures from the Spanish tourist bureau or stare out the window at the purplish night. For a while, the eerie streaks of light from the aurora borealis held her attention, but all too soon her mind returned to its endless review of the events that had lured her on this mysterious journey.

Her month-long European vacation, taken just before the start of her fellowship at the National Cancer Institute, had been pleasant, though uneventful. She had visited family and friends in Paris, attended an international biochemistry congress in Rome, dated a handful of charming and interesting men, but slept with none of them. Each seduction attempt, however smooth, made her cringe inwardly at the memory of her failure with Stefan back in Philadelphia.

Stefan had been scheduled to conduct a seminar at the National Cancer Institute in early September. She had awaited it eagerly, planning to sit in the front row of the lecture hall, catch his eye at every opportunity, and make him keenly aware of her presence. But to her disappointment the seminar was cancelled. She was even more upset when Robert Gallo, the director of her division, told her that Stefan had barely survived meningitis and was still not fully recovered. She wondered if she should visit him, if he would welcome her, finally deciding to phone Andre Evashevsky for more information first. But in his usual brusque manner, Evashevsky was vague and unhelpful. All she really learned from him was that Stefan was out of the country, convalescing on some island Evashevsky refused to name, and would be gone for an indefinite period.

That had been almost two months earlier—an anxious interlude made bearable only by the exciting and exacting nature of her research. Then, a week ago—it seemed a year—Stefan's cryptic letter had arrived.

"Dear Nicole," it had begun. "I am completely recovered from my illness, in Minorca, and need to see you. I have changed and, if not too late, all things are now possible. I am referring, of course, to the crucial experiment you began months ago in Philadelphia. It has progressed and needs you for its end point. Please come to me."

Also included in the envelope was a round trip

airline ticket and a post office box address in Minorca where she could wire her reply.

Nicole had slept hardly at all that night. Her haggard appearance the next morning helped to persuade Robert Gallo that she did indeed need a vacation. And now, at last, she was on her way, each throb of the jet engines bringing her closer to Stefan and the explanation of his startling summons.

Landing in Barcelona in the early afternoon, Nicole changed to Aviaco Airlines for the forty-five minute flight to Mahon, capital city of Minorca. The prop-driven commuter plane, with its narrow seats and noisy engines, was packed to capacity. Sitting next to her and appearing equally discomfited by the accommodations was a tall, attractive, fortyish-looking blonde. Statuesque, thought Nicole admiringly; smart and successful, too, judging by dress and jewelry and the copy of *Harvard Law Review* she was reading. After each had requested a second cup of the strong black coffee the stewardess was serving, they struck up a conversation.

"I gather you didn't sleep much on your overseas flight, either," said the woman. "I'm Jill Rockland, by the way."

"Nicole Brueur . . . Are you a lawyer?"

"I teach law at Harvard. And you?"

"I'm a biochemist."

"Ah, two professionals. You're not going to the Kosterlitz Clinic, by any chance? . . . No, I'd imagine not," said the woman, eyeing Nicole appraisingly. "All your body needs is sleep."

"I don't understand. What's the Kosterlitz Clinic?" Nicole asked.

"You've never heard of it? I'll be damned! But then, why should you? You haven't anything to lose—weight-wise, that is."

"Oh, is it a health clinic?"

"I suppose so," said Jill Rockland, looking amused, "in the sense that Windsor Castle is a residence." She explained her meaning.

"I see," said Nicole. "It sounds extraordinary. I'm surprised I never heard of it."

"Why *are* you going to Minorca, if I may ask?"

"To meet a friend."

"A male friend?"

"Yes. He's been vacationing there for the last three months."

"Alone?"

"One hopes."

Jill Rockland smiled. "Men are so damned unreliable. My inamorato likes me thin—thinner than my fat genes permit. So here I am, and here I stay until I'm thirty pounds lighter. If that doesn't please him, I give up. Spanish men, I'm told, like big cars and big women."

Suddenly the engines were throttled back and the Seat Belt sign flashed on. "Well, nice chatting with you," said Jill Rockland, replacing the law journal in her briefcase. "Good luck with your man and hope to see you again."

Nicole nodded and turned to gaze out the window at the crescent shaped island, seemingly afloat in the azure sea below. It looked like a romantic paradise, she thought—but would it be? It depended on Stefan; no paradise could be enjoyed alone for long. But it was too late now to be overcome by doubts. Even if her fantasies about Stefan had misled her again, they were still the ones she most wanted to come true.

Hot, humid air enveloped Nicole as she descended the ramp and began the fifty yard trek to the small airport building. Heat waves shimmered in the distance and the tarmac felt soft under her feet. *Damn!* she thought, wishing the walk wasn't so long. The makeup she'd so carefully applied earlier was streaking with sweat.

Lagging behind as her fellow passengers filed into the one story building, she hoped she could sneak into the ladies room to repair her face before Stefan saw her. Inside, she glanced around, failed to spot him in the waiting crowd, and headed for the door with the senorita sketched on it.

When she emerged minutes later, the crowd had thinned to around a dozen people but Stefan was not among them. Don't panic, she told herself; if he'd been delayed for some reason, he might have left a message at the airline desk. Moving over to the Aviaco counter, she stood in line behind a man who was going over some sort of list with the ticket agent. Restlessly she looked at the colorful posters on the walls and the souvenir stand to her left before her attention was drawn back to the person in front of her by a vague sense of familiarity. Stylishly attired in a beige suit that fit to perfection, the man was tall and slim, with thick, iron-gray hair. A pair of sunglasses dangled from one hand and a keycase from the other. Was he someone she knew, Nicole wondered, or did he merely seem so because she had seen him on the airplane? She was about to step forward to catch a glimpse of his face when the agent said, "I'm sorry, Señor, but I simply don't know what has become of her." The man turned round with a puzzled frown.

Nicole gasped. This attractive man with the erect carriage and umblemished complexion couldn't be Stefan! It was impossible! He looked taller, huskier, years younger. His sudden grin displayed straight white teeth. Yet whom else could he be? A brother Stefan had never mentioned? A hallucination?

Suddenly light-headed, she swayed precariously and might have fallen if he had not seized her shoulders to steady her. "Nicole!" he said, laughing. "It *is* me—Stefan."

In her benumbed state, it took a few moments for his words to register. Then her arms flew around his neck and she kissed him joyously. After returning her kiss, he gently drew away and asked, "How was your flight?"

"What flight?" she said breathlessly. "Across the Atlantic, or this flight into fantasy?"

"It's no fantasy," Steve assured her. "Three months ago it might have been, but not now. I trained like a boxer, underwent every conceivable type of dental and cosmetic surgery just for this moment—to see the look on your face right now."

"B . . . But why?" she stammered. "I'm not only overwhelmed but utterly bewildered. *Why* did you do all this?"

Steve smiled. "How long can you stay?"

"Two weeks."

"Good. Time enough to explain."

"But Stefan, it's cruel to keep me in suspense. At least tell me *something* now!"

"All right," he said, turning her toward the baggage racks. "For a while, as my meningitis raged, I thought I was going to die. When I didn't, my entire outlook changed. Instead of seeing life as a laboratory where one either experimented or was experimented on, I began to see it as a banquet. Now let's collect our luggage and be off."

"You're staying at the Kosterlitz Clinic?" exclaimed Nicole, sliding into the Jaguar convertible he had borrowed from Georgi and squeezing his arm affectionately.

"*We* are. A lovely cottage all to ourselves."

"But I hear it's awfully expensive."

"I would hope so, considering all the worthwhile projects it supports. The Sigourney Institute, for one. It provides me with millions each year."

"Stefan—stop!" Nicole wailed. "No more riddles. You've muddled me enough for one day!"

"Very well," he said, freeing his arm to start the

engine. "Georgi Kosterlitz is an old friend and classmate. Many years ago he approached me with an idea for a clinic, a dream of his that needed a biochemical genie to make come true. When I worked the necessary magic, he made me a silent partner. Its mysterious medicine, the one that produces such painless weight loss, is my discovery."

"Fine," sighed Nicole. "So you're a partner in the Kosterlitz Clinic. You're not only handsome and dashing now, but rich! Any other secrets you've been keeping? You wouldn't also be a Hapsburg prince by any chance, would you?"

He grinned and shook his head. "The talented staff at the clinic can work many miracles, but changing one's ancestors isn't one of them.

"Well, they've certainly changed a lot. Maybe even your DNA. Stefan, *why?*"

"You promised you wouldn't ask that again until later."

"Stefan," she pleaded. "Be reasonable. Take pity on this exhausted creature."

"I intend to. First thing you do when we get to our cottage is take a nap. Then we'll go to Georgi's house and join his latest girlfriend—a charming marine biologist—for drinks and an early dinner. Georgi, unfortunately, had to fly to London this morning on business. He should be back soon, depending how long it takes him to deal with the latest currency crisis. If not, he's asked us to join him there before you return home. He's anxious to meet you."

"And I'm just as eager to meet him. A London jaunt would be nice. There's even a tumor immunology conference at King's College, Cambridge, next week that we could attend. You know about it, don't you?"

"Evashevsky wrote, urging me to meet him there." Steve shrugged noncommittally.

As they sped along the coast highway, Nicole took a silk scarf from her handbag and tied it around her hair to keep it from blowing. "One more question, and then I promise to appreciate this breath-taking scenery in silence. In the months you've been here, what's happened to your research program?"

He shrugged again. "It goes on. As acting director of the Institute, Andre Evashevsky is more than capable."

"I know. But it's such an exciting time in cancer research! The people I work with at the NCI are thrilled at the progress they're making. How can you stand to be away from it?"

"How?" Steve smiled wryly. "Maybe for the same reason I jog five or more miles each day. It hurts, my muscles cramp, I feel like I'm breathing fire, but it's healthier for me."

Nicole stared at him, trying to guess his meaning. He seemed so changed, so much in control—of the car, his life, *her* life for the time being. Soon she would be making love to this stranger. More than words and in ways only women truly understood, she hoped that would tell her how deep the change really was.

Beyond the ornate, wrought iron gate of the clinic at the end of an uphill, winding road stood their "cottage"—a five-room sandstone house nestled in a grove of almond trees and flanked by magnificent gardens.

"My God, Stefan!" exclaimed Nicole as she followed him through the door and saw the plush carpets and paintings in the living room. "Whose place *is* this?"

"Normally it's reserved for the very rich—the oil shieks and shipping tycoons—but it's ours as long as we want it."

"How lovely," she said, whirling around with her

arms outstretched. "Now lead me to the bedroom, so I can unpack."

While Nicole was in the shower, Steve concocted cognac-laced Spanish coffee in sugar-frosted glasses. He planned to make love to her that night. Depending on her willingness and his anxiety level, they would either have intercourse or merely kiss and fondle: 'sensate focusing,' in the sex therapist's jargon. At Georgi's urging, Steve had swallowed his pride and consulted the clinic's chief therapist, an erudite Englishman named Herzog with a Maharishi-like mane of white hair and beard and an obvious penchant for his work. At first embarrassed by the nature of their discussions, Steve could not help being amused and eventually intrigued by the zest with which Herzog recommended certain techniques and activities.

Tonight, he thought, after enough wine to relax but not depress his nervous system, he would find out how much he'd actually benefitted from these sessions.

But when Nicole emerged from the shower, long hair hanging damp, scrubbed face shining with girlish innocence, wrapped in a towel that barely reached her nipples, Steve was overwhelmed by sudden desire. Easily reading his thoughts, Nicole dropped the towel and came into his arms, kissing him and backing him to the bed.

"Are you sure you want to?" Steve found the breath to ask and felt the eager pressure of her lips against his in reply.

Drawing back the covers, Nicole slid between the sheets, shivering deliciously at their crisp, cool touch, and beckoned him to follow. Hastily Steve shed his clothes and with dream-like detachment lowered himself on top of her.

What happened next astonished him with its ease

and naturalness and he learned something his sexual guru had neglected to mention: that a special current flowed between people in love that made any other stimulus superfluous. It was as if their lovemaking had melded them into a single organism of limitless potential. Was Anton right about this, too? Had man and woman, sundered during some critical stage of conception for the purpose of God's grand experiment, always been one, and would be one again?

Gradually he grew aware of Nicole's gasping intakes of breath and an agonizingly pleasurable change in his own sensations and with a convulsive shudder they reached orgasm together.

For several moments afterwards they lay silently entwined. Finally, dreamily, Nicole whispered, "Oh, Stefan, it was wonderful! Too wonderful for words."

"For me, too . . . Try to sleep now," he urged, rolling off her and sitting by the side of the bed. "I'll wake you in a few hours."

She yawned and reached for his hand. "First let me look at you."

Reluctantly he rose and, sucking in what remained of his once flabby midsection, stood naked before her.

She sighed. "You're more beautiful than I am now! To hold your love, I'll simply have to improve my mind."

Steve knew it was an exaggeration, but it pleased him all the same. *She* pleased him. Let Lassiter have his world-renowned hospital and Carhill his Nobel Prize; he envied no man now.

Gathering up his clothes, he went into the bathroom to put them on. Then he quietly left the cottage to stroll down the path to the small cove in the cliffs below. The midday heat was gone, leaving the afternoon pleasantly balmy. A soft sea breeze caressed his face and the sun glittered brilliantly on the waves as Steve continued to savor another natural gift: the extraordinary sense of excitement one human being can impart to another. Their love-making had been a revelation—a discovery of self—just as Anton had predicted. He was lucky to have lived through his illness and gone on to take his uncle's advice. Lucky all around. Not even the passing cloud that blocked the sun, darkening the rippling water below, could disturb his serenity. He needed no cloud shadow to foretell an always precarious future. Having just reached a high point in his existence, it was only realistic to expect some decline. Change was an integral part of the human condition, as were the laws of compensation. After months of arduous effort to feed a vanity that, once indulged, seemed insatiable, after countless bouts of anxiety that knotted and burned his stomach until he feared he was developing an ulcer, Steve knew he had paid, in part, for his joyous reunion with Nicole. But it was equally clear that he had not paid in full.

He had not read a scientific journal since arriving in Minorca; except for tidbits in the newspapers or in Andre Evashevsky's letters, he neither knew nor felt any compulsion to know what was going on in cancer research. He hadn't even learned the names of this year's Nobel laureates until a week after their announcement. But now that Nicole was here at last, his fantasies fulfilled, he had to expect some reversion to form. How much would be permissible before backsliding totally, however, remained a major concern.

Should he go to the immunology meeting in Cambridge? An increasingly insecure Evashevsky would be so happy to see him again that he would probably greet him with a rib-crushing hug. Yet his instincts argued against it. He did not particularly want to parade himself before his peers and hear their comments about his new persona. Nor did he want to get caught up in their latest squabbles. He had been addicted to that stimulant far too long. Though Steve had no intention of abandoning research altogether, neither would he let it enslave him again. Instead, he would try to achieve a healthy balance between work and relaxation, with Nicole his partner in both. Or was he merely deluding himself by trusting in such a simplistic solution? His history, certainly, weighed heavily against it.

Perhaps he should go to the Cambridge meeting, after all. He had to re-enter the real world sometime and this would be a half step. Whether he went or not, Steve knew he had to do something to dispel the premonition, or whatever it was, that made him fearful of ever leaving his island Shangri-la.

Chapter 17

A WEEK LATER, AT Guy's Hospital in the heart of London, a senior consultant radiologist named Pitt-Rivers and a trainee named Jones sat in a cubicle off the lead-shielded computerized axial tomography room and studied the films of the body scan just taken on a middle-aged American patient referred to them by Dr. Arthur Renshaw, a prominent gastroenterologist on the staff. The hospital, one of the first in the world to purchase and evaluate the prototypical version of the CAT scanner and now in possession of the latest model, took great pride in its radiologists' proficiency with the procedure. As visitors, particularly Americans, were gently reminded, the CAT scanner was largely a British invention, developed, oddly enough, by the electronic wizards of EMI, the old Beatles' corporation. That its capabilities had revolutionized X-ray diagnosis, if not all of medicine, needed no reminder; it was established fact, as was Guy's Hospital leadership in the field. How long that would last was doubtful, however. New though computerized tomography was, an even newer invention, nuclear magnetic resonance, might soon render it obsolete.

But more than the rumor that a rival hospital had governmental approval to purchase a NMR scanner was vexing Pitt-Rivers as he studied the black and white photographs depicting cross-sectional cuts, two millimeters thick, through the patient's body from waist to groin. Since six a.m., when they called him in for an emergency head scan, the day had grown ever more hectic and exhausting. He was anxious to complete this last procedure and go home. Yawning and scratching his unshaven beard, he turned to the trainee and said, "You can spot the lesions, can't you, Jones?"

"I . . . I think so, sir."

"You *think?* What do you suppose made those holes in the liver-moths? Show me the cut through L-2 again." Wearily Pitt-Rivers waited for the trainee to mount it on the viewing box. "Ah, there it is—the primary! As pretty a picture of a carcinoma of the tail of the pancreas as you'll ever see. Damn! I wish our color coder wasn't on the blink. I'd have liked a slide of this for my teaching file."

"Could, ah, could the tumor possibly be an insulinoma, sir?" asked the trainee hesitantly.

"A malignant insulinoma, you mean," corrected Pitt-Rivers. "Now there's a fancy diagnosis for you. I'd love one of those for my collection, too. Not bloody likely, though, unless . . ." he stared hard at the trainee . . . "you know something about the patient I don't. Like a history of hypoglycemic episodes?"

Jones denied it earnestly.

"Well, pass me the referral form and let's see . . . Humph," sniffed the senior consultant. "Renshaw certainly doesn't believe in overloading us with information, does he? I can barely decipher his scrawl . . . What's this word—pelican? Oh, *American!* A something-or-other American physician with a four-week history of nausea, weight loss, and mid-abdominal pain made acutely worse at times—ah, *this* is interesting—by alcoholic beverages . . . All right, Jones, tell me what abdominal condition outside of simple peptic ulcer is aggravated by boozing?"

"Hodgkins disease, I believe."

"Quite right. So I suppose I'd better mention it in my report as a remote possibility. But I'm afraid this chap isn't so lucky as to have Hodgkins. For my money, what we're seeing is a straightforward, garden-variety cancer of the pancreas with early liver metastases and that's what I'm calling it." Pressing the foot pedal to activate the dictating machine before him, Pitt-Rivers identified himself, the case number, and glancing back at the referral form, the patient. Releasing the pedal, he looked quizzically at Jones. "Carhill? Gregory Carhill? Name sounds vaguely familiar to me. Does it to you?"

Jones shook his head.

"Well, whoever he is, he won't be around long. The mean survival time for carcinoma of the pancreas is a mere four months, you know."

Gravely the trainee nodded. "How much are you going to tell him?"

"Tell him?" Pitt-Rivers drew back in mock horror. "I'm not going to tell him anything if I can possibly help it. That's Renshaw's job. I just hope he doesn't ask."

But the patient did more than ask; he demanded to see the actual scan. And once the senior consultant learned exactly who Dr. Gregory Carhill was, he felt obliged to accommodate him, and to offer him a tranquilizer from his personal supply.

Carhill ignored the vial of greenish capsules thrust at him. Nor did he particularly appreciate the lugubrious looks of the two radiologists. If they worked for him, he thought, he would insist on cleaner frocks and tidier appearances. The pair of them—the older, tall and thin and chinless, the younger, short and squat—reminded him of the old cartoon characters, Mutt and Jeff. Hardly the sort worthy of any display of emotion. The entire scene, from the monstrous CAT scanner that had practically swallowed him whole to this obviously ill-at-ease duo seemed unreal anyway. He had come to London to attend a high-powered tumor immunology conference and to join his wife, Lenore, who had spent the summer and a little longer at their estate in Surrey—not to fall ill, to suffer the indignities of a gastro-intestinal workup that stuffed him from mouth to anus with barium like a cream-filled pastry, and certainly not to have a death sentence pronounced on him.

Intuitively Carhill knew he was experiencing a mixture of denial and anger, early defenses of the dying, but was helpless to change. He accepted their crumb of hope—that, instead of cancer of the pancreas, the lesions in his abdomen might represent treatable Hodgkin's disease—with a non-committal nod, thanked them for their courtesy, and strode out the door with the grim relief of a man exiting a dank mausoleum.

On the street, Carhill hailed a taxicab and had the driver take him to the west entrance of St. James Park. It was a crisp, sunny day and a brisk stroll in the open air might give his mind the clarity he so desperately needed. He had known that something inside him was wrong; the deep, constant pain in his abdomen told him. And for the last month a few sips of any alcoholic beverage, even his favorite wine, doubled him with cramps. But a carcinoma of the pancreas of all things! How the devil had he fallen prey to that? What loose virus in his lab or carcinogen in his diet or hereditary flaw had triggered it? It was such a nasty cancer. He remembered the shocked reaction of Boston's medical community when a friend and neighbor, a former director of the Mass. General Hospital and as vigorous a fifty-two-year-old man as he'd ever known, had died of the same cancer within a few weeks of its diagnosis, despite all the staff of the hospital he'd once headed could do for him.

The memory made Carhill wince. But no matter what it took, he wasn't going down that fast chute into oblivion. The resources at his disposal extended far beyond those of the average cancer victim, even a hospital director's. He knew the latest facts, the best people to consult; under the circumstances, they would deny him nothing. He could even hire some, put them to work at his institute to find a cure for solid tumors in general and his tumor in particular. His affliction might even turn out to be a blessing in disguise. What better reason to speed up his research and win the "Cancer Prize" than saving his own life? Above all, Carhill vowed to expend every effort to stave off the poisonous despair that arose from a spreading malignancy as smoke rises from fire.

Neither would he settle for palliative half measures, an extra year or two of semi-invalidism. Using himself as his own experimental animal, he would go all out for a cure.

Buoyed up by such resolutions, Carhill strode through the park in good spirits until he heard Big Ben strike five o'clock and the daylight suddenly seemed to dim. Time, he thought wistfully. If only he had more time . . . Nor could he devote what little he had left exclusively to himself. There were people—Lenore, his three children, his older grandchildren—he would have to inform eventually, and he dreaded it.

As well as any man alive, Gregory Carhill understood the nature of cancer. What had sprouted and spread destruction inside him was neither a ravenous parasite nor an alien invader but a betrayal of self, a breakdown of internal regulatory mechanism so severe as to cause organizational chaos, cellular anarchy. Yet even stripped of most of its mystery, there was still something almost shameful about being a cancer victim. The shame came not from within, from the ancient belief that to be diseased was to be in a state of sin, but from seeing what was reflected on the faces of family and friends once they learned of your misfortune: how much it discomfited and burdened them and altered their perceptions of you.

Just recently he had taken a veteran laboratory technician off an important research project when he found out she had recurrent breast cancer and began to perceive her, as people would soon him, as half-alive, half-dead.

And suddenly, as if deliberately delayed to a time and place when he could best absorb it, the full realization of what had befallen him, what lay ahead, hit him with stunning impact. Fear and anguish, like the icy fingers of death itself, clutched his gut, racking him with pain and nausea. He broke out in a cold sweat, his head swam, his legs went rubbery. Using his umbrella for support, Carhill hobbled to the nearest bench where he sat, huddled and shivering, until he could regain his composure.

There, he thought, as his nausea began to recede and his vision cleared, *that's better.* He wasn't dying, after all. He had merely experienced a panic attack and now it was over. He would rest here a while longer and then be on his way. But a bare moment later, while looking across the Thames at the Big Ben tower jutting up majestically from the spired silhouette of Parliament buildings, it struck him that he might be seeing such a favorite sight for the last time ever and his eyes filled with tears.

A uniformed park attendant, seeing Carhill's distress, approached as if to offer aid, but his glower turned the man away. Ungracious though it was, this small act of defiance helped Carhill regain self-control. All right, he sighed, you've had your little cry and it's nothing to be ashamed of. Now get back to Surrey and draw up a list of the researchers who can help you the most. Let's see, he thought, there's Milstein at Cambridge and Baldwin at Nottingham, Gallo in Washington, Levy in Palo Alto, Scheinberg in Baltimore and even Sigourney wherever he is now and whatever he's doing.

Ah, Stefan Sigourney, he thought ironically, as he rose shakily to his feet. Would I grow to love him or resent him even more if he was the one who helped the most to keep me alive?

Chapter 18

UNLIKE HIS NEMESIS GREGORY CARHILL, who was facing disaster that day, Steve Sigourney was enjoying the most idyllic time of his life. Even if Georgi Kosterlitz had not returned from London that morning, he and Nicole had decided against joining him there; their moments together on the island were simply too precious to squander on medical meetings or travel.

They would usually wake shortly after dawn and have breakfast on the terrace in their robes: orange juice, coffee and oven-hot croissants, delivered to their door by a clinic waiter. Then, hunger sated and warmed by the rising sun, they would go back to bed and spend the next hour or two making love and exchanging confidences. Sexual experimentation ceased between them when Steve confessed that what he liked best was to be on top of her, seeing her hair spilled over the pillow and the look of rapture on her face.

He never seemed to tire of gazing at her nude or scantily clad body. One pose in particular—Nicole, legs straddled and back arched, brushing her hair before the bathroom mirror—filled him with possessive pride. She, in turn, would often watch with amused wonder while he blow-dried his hair. He could hardly blame her: in his forty-six years, he had never before spent more than a few minutes a day with a comb or brush in his hand.

Following breakfast and love-making, they would usually spend the cool hours of the morning exploring the twenty-mile-long island. Unlike Majorca, its larger, better developed neighbor, Minorca attracted few tourists, though it was equally enchanting and even more of an archeological treasure trove. Its western end especially was studded with megalithic monuments from remote pre-history, none more spectacular than the *Naveta dela Tudons*, a boat-shaped stone structure believed to mark a seafaring warrior's grave. Because Mahon, the best natural harbor in the Mediterranean, had once held such strategic value, Minorca's cultural heritage, from Moorish and Carthaginian conquerors to the eighteenth century under the British, was richly varied, too.

Steve and Nicole spent half a day roaming the well preserved farm that had once belonged to Lord Horatio Nelson, the bantam-sized naval hero of the battles of Niles and Trafalgar, and his long-time mistress, later wife, Lady Hamilton. Steve had no particular fondness for imperialistic Englishmen, but Nelson, who accepted social ostracism as the price of his scandalous love for a friend's wife, was a man of impressive accomplishment and complexity.

"Would you sacrifice so much for the woman you love?" asked Nicole as they wandered out of the farmhouse's tiny master bedroom.

"That remains to be seen," said Steve, peering

again at Lady Hamilton's matronly portrait in the pamphlet they had purchased. "I wonder what she really meant to him? A mother figure?"

"No," asserted Nicole with authority, "merely the mother of his courage."

Steve looked askance at her. "What do you mean?"

"Maybe a scientist like Isaac Newton can be a recluse, but not a military hero. He'd need someone to love deeply to fully realize and value life. I'm sure it made little difference to Nelson how others saw his lady; he saw her in his own way and, through her, himself."

"Interesting," murmured Steve.

"Thanks," she said, pouting, "but I'm no longer your student, remember? My observations deserve more of a response than that."

"Granted. But what makes you snap?"

"Oh, I don't know. Maybe because you're not Lord Nelson. No history book can tell me how well or how long you'll love me."

"What does your intuition tell you?"

"What it has all along," she said, taking his hand and moving on. "That we have—possibilities."

Georgi's return that morning made them postpone the caving expedition they had planned. Instead, they met him for lunch in Mahon at a beachside restaurant famous for its seafood.

"At last," said Georgi, his eyes gleaming with admiration and approval when Nicole was introduced to him. Hugging her with one arm while holding his linen napkin with the other, he kissed her cheek. Then, turning to Steve, "I understand your motivation much better now!"

Steve winced, expecting Georgi to gush compliments and possibly confidences. When he did neither, merely sat and beamed benevolently, Steve was reminded again of his flamboyant friend's surprising sensitivity. "How did your London trip go?" he asked.

Georgi shrugged. "Oh, about as expected. A lot of boring bank luncheons, drinks at clubs, that sort of thing. But the pound is holding, thank goodness, and our investments seem safe." Abruptly he faltered and looked anxiously at Steve. "Does, ah, does Nicole know about our little arrangement?"

"Not so little, I hope," said Steve, "and not to worry."

"Good," said Georgi, after sipping water. "I must say you look happy, Stefan. Your transformation was worth the effort, I take it."

"Every effort," affirmed Steve, grasping Nicole's hand under the table.

Georgi chuckled. "Actually I could use pictures of you two for the new clinic brochure. You know the sort—in tux and evening gown sipping champagne at sunset. What do you say? Would you consider it?"

Steve glanced briefly at Nicole before saying, "It would be ungrateful of me not to. But wouldn't it be more effective to use before and after pictures?" He reached in his back pocket and handed Georgi his passport. "Take a peek to refresh your memory. I resembled some wild-eyed terrorist, don't you think?"

Nicole stretched to catch a glimpse of the passport photo. "I'd almost forgotten how you used to look," she said softly.

"Does it distress you?"

"Hardly. It's the face of the man I fell in love with. Does it distress *you*?"

Steve smiled wryly. "I'm afraid it does. I never want to be that man again. If I do, it will be a devastating defeat."

"Not much chance of that, I'd say," said Georgi,

and at Steve's lack of response, added, "Well, is there?"

"Here, no. Away from here . . ." Steve shrugged. "But I can't stay forever."

"You could, you know. Naturally, it would take some doing, but there's no real reason you couldn't relocate your research institute here."

Steve looked wistful, but shook his head. "Maybe some day, Georgi, but not now. No matter how I package myself, I can't run away from what I am, what I do best. Nor can I afford to take much more time off. With all that's happening in cancer research these days, I'd never catch up. So I must leave, and soon."

"How soon?"

"Nicole flies home in another week. I plan to accompany her to Barcelona, where I'm meeting Andre Evashevsky for the day. Depending on what he reports regarding certain projects, I'll either go back with him, or wait a week."

"I see," said Georgi solemnly. "I'll miss you greatly, you know—both of you. It's been wonderful having you here."

"For me too, old friend," said Steve, dropping his gaze to the table. "I'm very grateful."

"Nonsense. You're a partner. It's your due . . . Well, let's order, shall we? But not too much. I'm planning a gala reception tonight in honor of you both. You know how I love to throw parties, Stefan, and what better reason than to celebrate your obvious good fortune?" He bowed to Nicole. "You are stunning, my dear. A natural beauty. And Stefan here—who, as the song goes, "must've been a beautiful baby!'—is a reclaimed work of art." He turned to Steve. "Please say you won't object if I invite all the clinic people who had a hand in your restoration. Have they all met Nicole by now?"

"Not all," said Steve.

"Has Ben Herzog?"

"Especially not Herzog. I wanted to do everything possible to win Nicole for myself before I introduced her to him."

"Understandable." Georgi winked. "What's that word you used to describe Herzog—leonine? Yes, leonine. An old lion who hasn't lost any of his roar. I was lucky to lure him here, if only to help me deal with my own emotional problems. I'm terribly fickle, you see, as was my philandering father, and his father before him. A good thing for them Britian was a far-flung empire in their day. But enough of that. So it's settled then; I can invite them all?"

Steve nodded and picked up a menu.

Their love-making that afternoon, though satisfying, was less leisurely than usual. Nicole could feel the extra tension in his muscles and almost cried out in pain, not pleasure, at his final thrusts. Sensing that for the first time the outside world had penetrated their sanctum, she was left disturbed and mystified. She especially missed the prolonged hugs and murmurings that usually floated her back to earth from orgasm. But she refrained from saying so, hoping to find out what was troubling him without a confrontation.

Later, after shampooing her hair, she joined him on the terrace. "Nervous about tonight?" she asked, after observing that the liter-sized carafe of white wine at his elbow was half empty.

"A little," he admitted. "Even with you along, I'm bound to be the center of attention."

"And that bothers you? Why?"

"Because it will make me feel even more artificial than I already do."

Nicole sighed with exasperation and relief. "Is *that*

what's upsetting you? It shouldn't. They made you into what you wanted to be, didn't they?"

"What I *thought* I wanted to be. I overdid it. I used to avoid looking at myself in mirrors. Now . . ." He grimaced.

"Well, despite what you may think, Stefan, you aren't the least artificial to me—just a man of extremes. All I ask is that you don't revert completely to your old ways. Besides," she said, pouring wine for herself, "don't be too sure you'll be the center of attention tonight. You haven't seen the new gown I'm going to wear!"

Nicole's prediction was borne out. The family of clinic professionals was made up predominately of men who, while pleased to see in Steve the culmination of their best efforts, were dazzled by his escort. He should have expected it, Steve thought. For men whose livelihood depended on making their clients more attractive, Nicole, in a backless floral print gown that showed her lissome figure to full advantage, needed absolutely no improvement. Roland Pritchard, the clinic's chief cosmetic surgeon, his gaze flickering back and forth from her face to her bosom, hung around Nicole all evening like an art dealer around an El Greco. Hoyt, the orthodonist, his eyes level with her smile, seemed equally captivated. Only Ben Herzog, wandering away from the knot of men about Nicole after introductions were made, seemed more interested in conversing with Steve.

"What's your reaction?" asked Steve as they stood by the bar.

"She's lovely, of course . . . Is she loving?"

"Yes. Very."

"A problem?"

"Yes. It makes me afraid."

Herzog nodded. "And you—does the new you

make *her* afraid?"

"I suspect so."

"Good. The necessary tension."

"How necessary?" asked Steve, uncertain of his meaning.

"A certain residual tension is as necessary to a relationship as to a muscle. Otherwise it goes flaccid. You wanted her enormously, you know. You must have, to put yourself through all you did. But be careful that you don't love an idealized version of her."

"Oh?" said Steve. Herzog had never mentioned this possibility before. "Why would you think that?"

"Because you tried to transform yourself so that she'd love *your* idealized version of *you*. Now that I've met your Nicole, I can understand why. She's almost too beautiful."

"I thought that once myself. I refused to consider her for a permanent position in my lab because of it. There are times when I wish I could keep her hidden from the whole world—but of course, I can't."

"You plan to marry?"

"Should I?"

"It's optional. Wedlock isn't much of a lock anymore. Nor does it necessarily enhance love—merely institutionalizes it. But if you want children, certainly."

"She tells me she's infertile. From endometriosis. I don't care either way."

As they talked, Herzog had noticed that Nicole kept glancing in their direction, as if more concerned about Steve's enjoyment than her own. "Tell me about your love-making," he continued. "I don't mean to pry; it's simply what I know how to analyze best."

"It's gentle . . . unimaginative . . . and satisfying. I was uncomfortable with some of the variations you recommended."

"They're not meant for couples in love. Most

aren't, you know . . . You have no hostile thoughts?"

"For the first time, today I did."

"You thought of her with other men?"

Reluctantly Steve nodded, acutely aware that a person's thoughts during sex were even more private than the sex act itself.

Herzog shrugged. "It's common enough. In my experience, personal as well as professional, jealousy—the terrible need to *know*—is an unavoidable penalty for the lovers of beautiful women. Fortunately, there's a simple remedy . . ." Before he could elaborate, he saw a flush-faced Georgi Kosterlitz bearing down on them and said hastily, "Come see me again before you leave the island, Stefan."

"I will," said Steve and turned in time to brace himself for Georgi's affectionate *abrazo*.

Late that night, as Steve and Nicole began the walk back to their cottage, he asked, "Did you have a good time?"

"Marvelous! What a fascinating group of people. Especially Georgi and Isabella and that Dr. Pritchard."

"Obviously Pritchard found you equally fascinating."

"His admiration was strictly professional. He wants photos and a cast of my nose . . . What did you and Dr. Herzog talk about for so long?"

"What we always talk about—sex."

"Had he anything new to say?"

"No. Just new people to say it about."

She stopped to gaze up at the sky. "Oh, I love this place so! I never want to leave."

"My problem, too."

"But you will leave, won't you?"

"Either that, or import a new woman every few weeks."

"Really? When does my turn come up again?"

"I'd have to consult my schedule."

"Well, in that case, I'm glad Pritchard made you jealous."

"So was I, in a sense. Herzog says a little uncertainty creates the necessary tension to keep the ties between us taut."

"Is that so? Well, let me know if they slacken; I'll tell you about the men I dated this summer."

"Tell me now," he demanded.

Nicole glanced curiously at him. "Rest easy. I wasn't involved with any of them—sexually or any other way. I might've been, if not for you . . ."

"Me? I wasn't there. What did I have to do with it?"

"Oh, you were there, all right," she said ruefully. "A constant sentinel. Like any major frustration, you were never out of my thoughts . . . What about you? You must've met other women in your months here. Herzog probably encouraged it."

"Not strongly. He knew I was in love with you."

"That's reassuring. But does the leonine Dr. Herzog believe in love?"

"As in saints and prophets—with a lingering element of doubt."

"I see. And you, my glib friend, what's your opinion?"

"It's an adventure, like exploring a deep cave. It's exciting going in, scary as you wander lost, and then . . . I don't know . . ."

"Nor I," she said, as they began to walk again. "But if it's caving you want, we'll explore to your heart's content."

The huge cave, burrowing deep into the southern cliffs, was known locally as "The Devil's Mouth." Like Minorca itself, it attracted few visitors. An underground lake rimmed by thick marble draperies and roofed by icicle-like stalactites, flowed through its depths. Steve had explored the cave a month before with a guide and been awe-struck by its ethereal beauty. Now, in heavy sweater, jeans, boots, and steel helmet, a small knapsack slung over his shoulders and a powerful electric lamp in his hand, he was preparing to lead Nicole, similarly dressed and equipped, through the cave to the subterranean lake whose serene splendor still haunted him. Going without a guide was foolhardy, he knew, but it was Nicole's first cave exploration and for reasons he could not fully fathom, he wanted to be alone with her.

In the cave entrance, where sunlight streaming in on twisting spirals of calcite and shimmering crystal straws filled the eyes with dancing radiance, Nicole gasped, "Oh, Stefan, it's wonderful! A fantasyland!"

But when they left daylight behind and negotiated a narrow passageway toward the first grotto by the pallid beams of their flashlights, she was less enthusiastic. "Are there bats?" she asked.

"No bats," he assured her. "Just ghosts."

"Oh, well. Ghosts don't get in your hair . . . You've seen them?"

"Faintly. But I've felt them brush against me; their cold breaths on my neck."

"Really?" Coming up close behind him, she wrapped her arms around his chest and nuzzled him with her chin. "Well, I hope you know what you're doing, since I'd rather not join them!"

As the passageway widened, a dank, musty odor welled up and the ground turned oozy under their boots. "You didn't say it would be muddy," she accused. "What else didn't you tell me?"

"Look." Steve shone his flashlight on a pair of worm-like creatures, three inches long, curled in half moons on the rocky floor.

Nicole wrinkled her nose. "What are those things?"

"Millipedes. Flip one over with your toe, if you like. They have row upon row of little legs."

"No, thanks," said Nicole. "I'll leave them alone, hoping they'll do the same for me. Speaking of legs, mine are getting weary. How much farther is this lake?"

"Beyond the next grotto, I think."

"And if not, will we turn back?"

Busy trying to establish how far they had come from the cave entrance, Steve did not answer. From his previous exploration, he remembered how the muddy earth ahead had suddenly become a ledge dropping away into seeming nothingness. If he wasn't careful, he could easily stumble or slide down the ten-foot drop to the jagged rocks below. "We'll have to go slow here," he warned.

"Why?"

"You'll see. Trust me."

"Always. But for your information, I'm looking very dubious right now."

Abruptly he stopped, flung out his arms to restrain her, and gingerly brought her forward. "This is why," he said, shining his light down. "It's the only pitch."

"*Pitch?* You mean pit!" She clung to his arm. "How do we get down?"

"With this." Unslinging his knapsack, he opened it and took out a rope ladder. He anchored its ends as he remembered the guide doing and said, "I'll go first. It's only about fifty feet on to the lake."

"I'm down!" he shouted a moment later and held his light so that Nicole could descend the ladder. When she did, he gave her a quick hug and then led the way through the narrowest passage yet, its walls slippery-wet with condensed moisture and its dankness so pungent it stung their nostrils.

Wriggling through, they emerged at last into a

spacious cavern containing a pool of sea-green water. With ivory-white stalactites spiking down over the water like crowded teeth, it was a spectacular sight, as otherwordly as if the earth had actually swallowed them up through "The Devil's Mouth" and propelled them into its belly.

"Well?" he asked, flashing light from water to shining stalactites and back again. "Was it worth the trouble?"

"Oh, yes! It's breathtaking! I'll never forget it." She hugged him. "How far does the lake extend?"

He shrugged. "If we'd brought an inflatable raft, we could find out."

"Oh, let's do it! Let's come back with one."

"And a guide," he added.

"Yes, a guide. Why didn't we bring one this time?"

"I . . . I wanted to be alone with you."

"Oh? Why?"

"Because I had never seen such hidden beauty before. It made me believe in . . . eternity. Some things do last a long, long time."

"What things, Stefan?" she asked, refraining from shining her light at him, though she wished she could see his face.

"There's no good reason for us to marry, you know."

"No," she replied, a sudden catch in her voice. "I suppose not."

"I mean, children are unlikely."

"I know. I only wish it were otherwise."

"It doesn't matter."

"Not to you, perhaps, but that sad fact changed the course of my life."

"So you've said. But you can't make research your whole existence, Nicole. Nobody knows that better than I."

"I'm well aware of it. What's your point?"

In the distance, they heard an ominous cracking sound, but were so deep in conversation that neither mentioned it.

"Marry me, Nicole!" he said, the words bursting forth. "Even if there's no reason to, I want it. Very much!"

In the penumbral light from their down-pointing beams, Steve could barely see her face. But he sensed the tension there as his words registered in Nicole's brain. Mistaking her silence for reluctance, he asked anxiously, "Will you?"

"Oh, yes," she said huskily. "Of course I'll marry you! For no reason and every reason . . . ."

He clutched her in a fierce embrace, but their kiss was light as a wisp of wind against their lips.

"Do you want to?" she asked as his hands caressed her bare skin under her sweater.

"I'm torn . . . At a moment like this, I want to give you love, not sex."

"They're the same for you, Stefan. Which is why I cherish you so . . . Who minds a little mud? I'm willing, if you are."

Before he could respond, a loud rumbling reverberated through the cave. Nicole cried, "*Mon Dieu!* What's that? Is the place caving in?"

"To trap us forever? Would you care?"

His teasing tone reassured her. "Frankly, yes. I'm like the French—I'm willing to live for love, not die for it. What *was* that noise?"

"Thunder, I think. It's probably pouring outside."

"Good," she said, her lips brushing his. "If we're going to get soaked, let's get muddy first. The rain can wash it off."

Chapter 19

THE FOLLOWING MONDAY, A few hours after bidding Nicole a wrenching farewell in the TWA lounge, Steve sat at a sidewalk cafe in downtown Barcelona having coffee and a one-sided conversation with Andre Evashevsky. Fresh from the tumor immunology conference in Cambridge, Evashevsky was brimming over with news from that and from their institute.

Steve was genuinely glad to see him. Though even less interested in talking shop than he expected he would be, Evashevsky's babble helped distract him from his sadness over Nicole's departure. Even so, he could only concentrate on his deputy director's words for a few minutes at a time before his mind took him elsewhere . . .

He and Nicole had returned twice more to "The Devil's Mouth"—once with a guide, once alone. Each time they had brought along inflatable rubber rafts to follow the course of the underground lake as far as the cave's passages permitted: an unforgettable experience, suspenseful and exhilarating, like floating down a dark, seemingly endless tunnel in a dream. Never before had Steve known such a sense of timelessness and antiquity . . .

Now, Evashevsky was trying to lure him back into another dark tunnel, one in which he had lost himself for years, and he resisted as long as he could.

"Stefan, you must come back with me," Evashevsky urged at the end of a long, rambling review of the highlights of the Cambridge meeting. "There's so much to do!"

"Not so much," said Steve, shrugging. "A few loose ends to be tied up, I suppose, but otherwise what else is there?"

Evashevsky stared. "Stefan, tell me the truth—are you sure you're completely over your illness? You seem so different, so distant. I can hardly believe you're the same man I've known all these years—and I don't mean just physically. That was enough of a surprise. I don't pretend to understand why you did it; your vague explanation only compounds my confusion. But that's your business. Mine is research, and I desperately need your help."

"For what?" asked Steve. "What can I do that you can't?"

"You can't be serious!"

"But I am. In my area of investigation, what's left to do that I or somebody else hasn't already done? Nothing of importance."

"Not true!" Evashevsky almost shouted. "There's more, much more, that you—*we*—must do!"

Steve shrugged. "Why so emotional, Andre? Don't you like being director? Your own boss?"

"I neither like nor dislike it," said Evashevsky stiffly. "But we were a *team*. Without you, I'm only half as good. So stop playing games, for God's sake, and tell me the real reason you're reluctant to come back."

"It's not reluctance so much as lack of direction. A definite goal. You've said nothing so far about Okabe's and Kreisberg's oncoprotein. I assume their findings have been confirmed by now?"

Suddenly, unexpectedly, Evashevsky's teeth flashed in a wide grin. "You do, huh? Well, for once, you assume wrong. There *is* no Okabe protein. Never was!"

"What?" Steve's head jerked forward. "What are you saying? How's that possible? Damn it, Andre, stop looking so smug and tell me!"

Evashevsky laughed. "I figured that bit of news would jolt you back to life. It was just as I suspected all along. The reason Joshua Okabe refused to supply me or anybody else with the monoclonal antibody to detect his oncoprotein was because *it didn't exist.* Not the antibody, not the protein—nothing! It was all a fake, a fraud, an insane invention of an insane mind. Need I say more?"

"You'd better! Why didn't you tell me any of this in your letters, your phone calls? It changes everything!"

Evashevsky shrugged. "In all good conscience, I couldn't. I mean, rumors about Okabe's weird behavior have been circulating for months; every meeting I went to was buzzing with them. But until Max Kreisberg's letter of retraction appeared in *Science* just last week, nothing was definite. Obviously you haven't seen it."

"No," said Steve. "I haven't read *Science* for months. Do you have a copy of it with you?"

"Right here." Evashevsky patted the briefcase by his feet. "Want to look it over now?"

Steve hesitated. "No, I'll get to it later. But are you quite sure all of Okabe's work has been discredited?"

"Totally. By Max Kreisberg himself—a terrible blow to his otherwise solid reputation. Composing that letter must've been sheer agony for him. You can almost feel it in his words."

"I repeat, Andre, have *all* of Okabe's claims been repudiated?"

"Maybe not all, but the main ones certainly: the entire proof of the oncoprotein's existence. In fact, Kreisberg stated that he personally could not confirm any of the immune precipitation data."

"What about Okabe? How's he handling the uproar?"

"Like the lunatic he is and probably always was. Phil Puestow, associate director of Neotech, was at the Cambridge meeting. Kreisberg sent him to read a prepared statement to the group, which he did. Later, over drinks, Puestow confided that Okabe had suffered a complete psychotic break and is a patient in one of Boston's psychiatric hospitals."

"Which one, do you know?"

"The Faulkner, I think."

Steve nodded. "Did he become frankly psychotic before or after Kreisberg exposed his fakery?"

"Before. For three days and nights, Puestow said, he locked himself in his laboratory. They finally had to get security guards to break in. There was Okabe, sitting in yoga position on top of his workbench, raving about his mystical communication with the sun, or sun people, or some such nonsense. Of course, they'd suspected something was fishy with his data long before that—as well they should! No one, not even fellow scientists at Neotech, could even begin to confirm his findings. When Okabe told him that he had exhausted his supply of antibody. Kreisberg gave him an ultimatum—either produce more in two weeks or face dismissal. It was shortly afterward that Okabe went to pieces."

"I can imagine the pressure he must've been under. Too bad it had to end this way."

Evashevsky frowned. "You sound almost sympathetic. Why?"

"I read Okabe's article with great care, Andre, and, up to a point, I agreed completely with his reasoning. I've no doubt he was onto something. Maybe a key experiment went wrong and he got impatient? Or maybe he was simply too exhausted from overwork to think clearly, consider the consequences of premature publication? Obviously he duped Kreisberg and the editors of *Science*. But until I know whether or not he duped *himself*, I prefer to withhold judgment."

"Sometimes you amaze me, Stefan. I would've thought that a meticulous scientist like you would damn him the most. After all, it was you—your life's work—that he tried to negate by publishing first."

Steve shrugged. "Isn't it enough that he failed; that the race for the cancer-causing protein is still on and we're in the lead again? I don't deny I'm terribly excited by this bizarre turn, but as for Okabe himself, I can afford to be charitable."

"More so than most. The people at the tumor immunology meeting were really up in arms about him and not in the least impressed by Kreisberg's apology. Gregory Carhill seemed particularly incensed by the whole affair."

"I'm sure," said Steve, thinking that Carhill had ample reason. Not only was the image of all medical scientists tarnished by such a scandalous episode, but Okabe's downfall re-established the Sigourney Institute's lead in this line of research.

"Speaking of Carhill," said Evashevsky, after ordering more coffee, "there's something strange going on with him."

"Oh? Explain."

"Well, for one thing, he looks . . ." Evashevsky groped for the word " . . . unhealthy. He's lost considerable weight, his face is drawn and he lacks his usual bounce. They're field-testing his leukemia vaccine in Zaire, so I don't know if he's simply overworked or what. What I *do* know is that he's recruiting like mad. He even talked to Gunther Gausse about joining him. Several times, in fact."

"Gunther? Why would Carhill want a biophysicist? Especially one whose expertise in the cancer field is limited to isotope—antibody conjugates? I wasn't aware that Carhill was doing research in that area."

"Nor is anybody else. But I have to warn you, Stefan, we may well lose Gausse. He's been increasingly unhappy in your absence—I simply can't give him the direction you could—and Carhill made him an extremely generous offer: his own section at double his present salary and a job for his librarian wife."

"That *is* generous. What do you make of it?"

Evashevsky gestured uncertainly. "If Gausse were the only one he went after, I might hazard a guess. But I heard he also made offers to Hahn from Geneva, Sedgwick from Milstein's lab, and Billings from Nottingham. Along with *L'Affaire Okabe*, Carhill's recruiting forays were the talk of the meeting. He seems almost desperate. I'm no medical doctor, Stefan, but there were times when I couldn't help wonder . . . well, never mind. It's merely conjecture and I know you don't like to discuss Carhill."

"Usually not," said Steve. "But since this seems to be a day for surprises, go on. You thought what?"

"That he looked like a dying man—perhaps a man dying of cancer. It's nothing more than a feeling, understand, but it would explain why he's trying so hard to hire certain people. They're all doing hybridoma research and, like Gausse's, their work has therapeutic implications . . . Oh, before I forget, when I phoned the Institute on Friday Marta made me promise to give you a message. Dan Lassiter needs to speak to you. Not about his patient, but something else. What, I don't know."

"All right. I'll phone him from Minorca."

"Then you're going back?" Evashevsky said glumly.

"Only for a few days. Before our meeting, I was undecided whether to or not. But you decided me."

"Me? How?"

"By tellling me about Okabe. I need a day or two by myself to mull that over so when I do get back, I'll know exactly what I want to do." Steve drained his cup of espresso. "Anything else in your bag of tricks?"

"Nothing of comparable magnitude."

"Well then, I have one for you. You remember Nicole Brueur, of course. An exceptional graduate student, wouldn't you say?"

Evashevsky nodded vigorously. "I was surprised you didn't offer her a permanent position."

"I couldn't at the time. But I have now. We're going to be married next summer." With amusement Steve watched Evashevsky's facial expressions reflect first incredulity, then wonderment, then enlightenment. "In all our years together, Andre, this is the first time I've ever seen you speechless. You have nothing at all to say?"

"I . . . I'm delighted for you, of course. She's—uh—she's . . ." Evashevsky faltered, flushed.

"She's what, Andre?"

"She's lovely, a dream!" Evashesky flung out his arms. "What can I say? She phoned me a month ago, you know, to ask how you were."

"I do know. Yet you suspected nothing?"

"Not a thing. I received many such calls . . . But you and Nicole—I'm still dazed. This . . . this calls for a drink!" Evashevsky's bark brought a waiter on the run. He returned shortly with two snifters of cognac.

"What should I toast?" wondered Evashevsky. "Your happiness, naturally, but what else? A future

Nobel Prize? A little Sigourney?"

"Neither," said Steve. "It would make me nervous."

"Then, *L'Chaim!* It means *health* in Yiddish."

Thinking back to his collapse at Commonwealth General Hospital and to Evashevsky's morbid speculation about Carhill, Steve nodded and clinked glasses.

Chapter 20

AT EIGHT A.M. THAT SAME Monday, Dan Lassiter received Gregory Carhill in his top-floor office. Carhill had telephoned from London the previous morning to request the appointment, his tone conveying an underlying sense of urgency his words never adequately explained. Surprised by Carhill's call and busy frying an omelet in his kitchen, Dan agreed to the meeting without pressing him as to its purpose. From what little he did say, Dan had the impression Carhill knew of his recent conversation with Nelson Freiborg—not surprising in view of Carhill's extensive Washington connections—and wanted to discuss the matter with him. But he obviously had more in mind than that; otherwise, why would Gregory Carhill, a man he hardly knew and had reason to dislike, phone him at home on a Sunday morning?

Between the time his secretary, Hedley, informed him of Carhill's arrival to the time he buzzed her back to show him in, Dan reflected on their last meeting four months before, when he had gone to the Bethune Institute on Billy Freiborg's behalf. Now their roles were reversed; Carhill evidently needed something from *him*, and although Dan meant to keep their meeting brief so he would not have to play catch-up with his other morning appointments, he was undeniably curious.

When Hedley escorted Carhill in, Dan left his desk to meet him at the coffee table by the bank of windows that ran the length of the office. Though the sky was so overcast it cast a grayish pall over everything, Dan was still struck by Carhill's sallow, sickly appearance. His face was gaunt, his clothes hung loose, his shirt collar seemed inches too large. Clearly the man was, or had been, ill, thought Dan as they shook hands. Was that why he was here?

Dan offered coffee and when Carhill politely declined, Hedley turned to leave. At the door, she said, "It's rather gloomy in here, don't you think? Want the lights on?"

"Go ahead," said Dan, "and please hold all calls."

The indirect lighting, blending with the grayness, did not so much brighten the room as impart a twilight glare to it that subtly heightened the tension between the two men.

"Well," said Dan, sitting across the coffee table from Carhill, "how's London these days?"

"Pleasant. Almost too pleasant. England is more than a floating museum, you know—at least, to me—and this time especially, it was hard to leave . . ." Carhill's voice trailed off and a distant look showed in his eyes.

Before Dan could speak to fill in the awkward pause, Carhill cleared his throat and continued. "It's kind of you to see me on such short notice. Very kind, indeed, considering that our last meeting didn't end very happily for you."

"No," said Dan, "though eventually it all worked

out. Billy Freiborg, the leukemia patient I told you about, is in complete remission right now."

"So I understand," said Carhill, "and I'd like to congratulate you on your innovative treatment; your courage in even attempting it. I remember our discussion about your patient well and I apologize for my attitude. At the time, I thought I was only being sensible, but I must have seemed terribly cold-blooded to you."

Dan shrugged. "Maybe a little, but you did steer me to Steve Sigourney, who proved extremely helpful."

"Stefan Sigourney is the reason I'm here," said Carhill, uncrossing his legs and leaning forward. "I understand you saved his life, too."

"With a big assist from Alexander Fleming. But go on."

"I need to meet with Sigourney as soon as possible. Could you help arrange it?"

"Me?" said Dan, taken aback. "I don't understand . . ."

"No," sighed Carhill with a wintry smile, "I don't expect you do. But before I launch into a long explanation, please answer this: do you know where Sigourney is these days?"

Dan hesitated. Though Carhill's conciliatory manner seemed forced, his intensity did not. He must have undergone some great upheaval in his life; his pride-swallowing desire to meet Sigourney was proof of it. "I don't know if he's still there, but last I heard, Steve was convalescing on an island off the coast of Spain—Minorca. Are you familiar with it?"

Carhill shook his head. "Not first-hand. He's been there all this time?"

"As far as I know."

"For medical reasons?"

Dan shifted uneasily. "Not that I'm aware of. Frankly, Dr. Carhill, I don't know why he's there, nor would I want to guess, but I'm as anxious to get hold of him as you apparently are."

"I doubt it," said Carhill morosely. "As I implied on the phone, I know something about your recent discussion with Nelson Freiborg and his interest, shared by the President, in a crash program to cure cancer. I know this from friends at the National Cancer Institute, some of whom are intrigued by the idea, and others vehemently opposed. If you want my personal opinion, I'd be glad to give it to you. But I have higher priorities for the moment—foremost being contacting Stefan Sigourney. Can you help me?"

Dan sighed. "I'm not sure. I spoke to his secretary last week and practically begged for his phone number, but it got me nowhere. She did, however, promise to get Andre Evashevsky, who's supposed to be meeting with Steve today, to urge him to call me. Let's hope he does."

Carhill frowned. "I wish I'd known where Sigourney was while I was still in Europe, or that Evashevsky was joining him; I might have made other arrangements . . . But no matter. Circumstances dictate that I either see him soon or not at all. Again I ask, can you help me?"

"Perhaps if I understood why . . . "

"The *why* is simple, if confidential for the moment. I have cancer of the pancreas, Dr. Lassiter. I only found out about it a week ago, at Guy's Hospital in London, and since then have been making arrangements—not to die but to be cured! That's why I need to see Sigourney. It's no secret I've never liked the man, but that's not to say I don't respect his abilities. Perhaps too much . . ."

"And you want to see him for what reason?" asked Dan.

"I'm undergoing exploratory surgery in two to three weeks. Slater, at Mass. General, will do it. He's a decent sort, knows damned well he can't cure me with his knife, and is willing to go along with whatever I suggest. Even so, I would gladly forego surgery if I were not so in need of biopsy material from the cancer and direct access to its arterial supply. Needless to say, I plan to make quite a production of it—which is where Sigourney fits in. I want to discuss intra-operative and post-operative strategy with him."

Dan's eyebrows lifted. "I see."

"Do you?" Carhill scrutinized him. "I would certainly like to think so. After all, you're the one who took on a hopeless leukemia patient and pulled him through. And I'm sure you agree that what I'm doing beats sinking into morbid despair."

"I certainly do," said Dan, "and I'll help any way I can."

"Excellent! I'll be on the West Coast for the next few days, but should be back no later than Friday. If you can contact Sigourney somehow and set up a meeting soon after that, I'd be most grateful."

"I'll do my best. His secretary expects him by the end of the week. If not . . . ?"

Carhill shrugged. "It's another imponderable. I doubt if I have the time—and I mean that literally—to fly to Minorca looking for him. But I'm sure you'll argue my case persuasively. Well," said Carhill, starting to rise, "I've taken enough of your time."

"Wait," said Dan. "Before you go, I'd welcome your views on a crash program to cure cancer."

Carhill relaxed back in his chair. "Since you ask, I do have an opinion, though it's somewhat clouded by my personal predicament. Such a project might succeed or it might backfire—get so bogged down in organizational squabbles and red tape as to actually hinder progress. A better idea might be to take two or three leading research institutes—mine and Sigourney's, for example—and combine them under some federally financed umbrella. In fact, I plan to suggest something like that to Sigourney, if and when I see him. Your friend Nelson Freiborg is certainly right about one thing, though—a cancer cure would be immensely profitable." This time Carhill stood up and Dan with him.

"How can I get in touch with you in California?"

"Call my home or office. Both my secretary and housekeeper will know where I am at all times."

Dan glanced out the window at the dark sky. "You're flying out today?"

"No, in the morning. I'm still not over jet lag, or whatever's making me so tired."

Dan made no comment. After ushering Carhill out, he returned to his desk and began wondering what more he could do to locate Steve Sigourney.

At six the next morning his bedside phone rang and Dan groped for the receiver. He came awake abruptly when the overseas operator told him who was calling. "Steve! Where the hell are you?"

"In Minorca. But I can hear you okay. No need to shout."

"Maybe not for that, but I have other reasons!"

Steve chuckled. "Well, I'm feeling fine; have been all along or else I would have let you know. But I've grown very lazy. Sloth is the most addictive of the deadly sins, you know. I'm returning to work very reluctantly."

"When?"

"Probably Thursday. I saw Andre Evashevsky yesterday and he said you needed to talk to me."

"*Do* I!" said Dan, sitting up in bed and glancing at Kris who had just seized his pillow to cover her head. "Let me get to another phone, Steve. Kris is still asleep." In his den, he said, "Okay, I'm back. I hope you're comfortable; we have a lot to talk about."

"First tell me how Billy Freiborg's doing."

"He's healthy as his horse. Ted plans to re-admit him over Thanksgiving to run more tests, but every blood report from his hometown doctor has been normal."

"Good . . . What's next on your list?"

"What do you think of a federally funded crash program to cure cancer?"

Steve laughed. "Did somebody blow up the National Cancer Institute while I've been away?"

"No, but the President wants to explore the possibility for fun and profit."

"Are you serious?"

"You bet I am. Nelson Freiborg and I met a couple of weeks ago to discuss its feasibility. Now Nels and the President want to hear your views."

Steve sighed. "I don't know. Sounds a little utopian. Exactly what do they have in mind?"

"A centrally controlled, massively funded project to push the new technology until it pays off with a cure."

"Where does that leave the existing programs?"

"Under new management, I suppose; less democratic and more dictatorial. Know any good dictators?"

Steve ignored the question. "Is this the urgent matter you wanted to talk to me about?"

"It was, until yesterday when Gregory Carhill came to see me. Only it was you, not me, he was really after. He wants a meeting with you, Steve, and it *is* urgent. A week ago, doctors in London made a presumptive diagnosis of cancer of the pancreas on him—presumptive only in the sense that he hasn't been operated on yet—but he sure looks like he's got it."

"So he *does* have cancer," Steve mused. "Andre Evashevsky saw him recently at a conference and guessed he might . . . I'm sorry to hear it. Really! Our differences have been strictly professional. In an odd sort of way, I suppose I'll miss him."

"Well, don't bury him yet. From what he said, he plans to put up a hell of a fight. With your help, he might just win."

"My help? He actually *asked*?"

"That's why he came to see me. Through me, he hoped to set up a meeting with you. You'll do it, won't you?"

"Under the circumstances, I could hardly refuse. Exactly what does he want, do you know?"

"Not in detail. All he said, and these are pretty much his exact words, was that he wants you to help plan his intra-operative and post-operative treatment. With monoclonal antibodies, I presume. He goes under the knife in a couple of weeks, so time is short. What should I tell him?"

"Tell him okay. We'll meet."

"Where? His place, your place, or mine?"

Steve hesitated. "You could do me a favor, Dan. Is the name Joshua Okabe familiar to you?"

"Okabe? . . . No— Wait a minute! Okabe and Kreisberg, co-authors of a headline-making article in *Science* a few months ago and an even more sensational retraction last week, right? Ted Swerdloff told me about it. They're calling Okabe the biggest scientific scoundrel since Lysenko. What about him?"

"He's gone psychotic, I understand, and been hospitalized at the Faulkner. If he's still there, would you pay him a visit?"

"What for?"

"I'd like to know what kind of shape he's in. If he's coherent—and amenable—I might want to visit him myself. In that case, I'd meet with Carhill in Boston. Could you possibly see Okabe today or tomorrow and let me know?"

Reluctantly Dan replied, "I suppose—though psychiatric wards, even my own, aren't exactly my favorite places. Swerdloff said that Okabe's work has been totally discredited. Why would you want to see him?"

"Because I'm not sure he's wrong. When Okabe's report first came out, I bought his findings completely; I as much as conceded the next Nobel Prize to him, and I'm not usually fooled that easily. Maybe it's just ego, but it bothers me. It bothers me enough to want to know what drove Okabe to falsify data when he was so close to the real answers."

"All right," sighed Dan. "I'll call over there and find out what's what. If Okabe is up to it, I'll visit him. Either way, I'll let you know."

"Thank you. When?"

Dan smiled mischievously. "Oh, before bedtime, my time; six a.m. your time. Sleep well, Steve—while you can."

That evening Dan Lassiter drove out to the Faulkner Hospital in Jamaica Plain where he met staff psychiatrist Dave Sonneborn, an acquaintance from county medical society committees. Over sandwiches and coffee in the doctors' section of the cafeteria they discussed Joshua Okabe.

"I'm not sure how much help I can give you, Dan," said Sonneborn. "I tried to get hold of Jack Enright, Okabe's private therapist, but he's out to dinner somewhere. But I took a quick look at Okabe's chart and can tell you some things. For one, he's almost certainly manic-depressive. Enright brought him down on heavy doses of *Haldol* and maintained him on that plus lithium ever since. He's responded well—so well that Enright plans to discharge him any day now. I only hope he has sense enough to stay away from the wrong people; namely, reporters. His cancer research has gained him quite a bit of notoriety, I understand."

His mouth full, Dan nodded.

"He's also a Nigerian Ibo, by the way. Remember the Biafran revolt?"

"Not as well as I probably should. What's the significance?"

"Okabe was a student at the University of Lagos when the bloodbath started. They drafted him into the Nigerian army and he deserted to fight on the side of the Biafrans. At our staff conference, Enright got him to talk about atrocities he saw. It helps explain his paranoia."

Minutes later, Dan followed Sonneborn into Joshua Okabe's large, comfortably furnished room. Only the heavy metal mesh over the windows distinguished it from one in a college dormitory. For some reason, Dan had pictured Okabe as a diminutive, bespectacled, deliberately mannered man. In fact, he was physically imposing—six foot two or three, muscular, flat featured and ebony-skinned. Instead of robe and pajamas, he wore brown gabardine slacks, a tan cashmere pullover and polished black loafers as if he, too, were a visitor.

"Do I know you, Dr. Lassiter?" he asked after Dave Sonneborn introduced them and left. "If I do, please forgive me; the medication I'm on seems to affect my memory."

"No," said Dan. "I don't believe so."

"Hmmm. Lassiter . . . Lassiter. It has a familiar ring."

"I'm general director of Commonwealth General Hospital."

"Oh!" Okabe's lips pursed. "My, my. A famous hospital, that . . . Please sit," he said, nodding at the easy chair by the bed, "and tell me why you've come to see me. Not about my work, I hope?"

Dan sat and leaned back to look up at Okabe perched on the bed. "Not directly, Doctor Okabe."

"*Don't* call me that! I've renounced the title of

doctor and all it connotes. I want none of it anymore. I was but a simple man when I came to this country and I shall leave it the same way."

"You're planning to leave?"

"Oh, yes! It's expected. I'm an embarrassment, you see: a messy smudge on the annals of American science. They'd like nothing better than to blot me out." He shrugged. "At Harvard, I was always an outsider. Now I'm something worse—a pariah. It matters not at all that I happen to be right."

"*Are* you right?" asked Dan softly.

Okabe smiled mockingly. "Are *you* qualified to judge? How much immunology, enzymology, biochemistry do you know?"

"Not much," admitted Dan. "I'm an internist primarily, with a peripheral interest in cancer research. But I'm curious about your side of the controversy."

"Then let me satisfy your curiosity as best I can . . . Does the cell-transforming protein I described exist? Oh, yes! As surely as good and evil exist. I hunted it for years, laying trap after trap, but it always eluded me. Then, after mastering the new technology—monoclonal antibodies, molecular hybridization, and the like—I built more efficient traps and in a moment of dazzling clarity—of divine inspiration, if you will—it revealed itself, its evil nature, to me. Only it wouldn't be captured. Each time I tried, it either transmuted or simply vanished. But I had *seen* it, Dr. Lassiter! I knew the oncoprotein existed as surely as you and I do. But existence, depending as it does on perceptions of the mind, is a tricky matter to prove. Spirits might be as plentiful as radio waves in this room right now, but since our senses cannot detect them we conclude they don't exist . . . Am I being too abstract, too metaphysical, Dr. Lassiter? Or am I, perhaps, boring you?"

"Neither," said Dan. "But you are straying off

course a little."

"Ah, yes—proof. I didn't quite have it. I admit it. And as a well trained scientist, an ethical human being, I never would have dared submit my findings to peer review until the proof was firmly in hand. But I knew I was right. I *knew* it!" said Okabe, wagging a finger. "And when I was told to publish, I did."

"You were *told?* By whom?"

Okabe smiled tolerantly. "By God, Dr. Lassiter. By the Almighty Himself! He commanded it; chose me as His messenger to present this gift to the world. Like Moses, like Muhammad, who was I to refuse God's command? Especially since it answered so many other nagging questions for me. So I published; I gave humanity the benefit of my inspired discovery, hoping all the while that through more hard work, another miracle, I could prove my case before the nay-sayers and nihilists, the vultures of science, tore me to pieces. I *am* right, you know, though I'm certain you don't believe me. You think I'm quite mad. Don't be embarrassed to say so. I would probably feel the same way in your place."

The slight lilt to Okabe's deep, reasonant voice was almost hypnotic. Crazy or not, thought Dan, he was certainly articulate: a well-reasoned argument by a seemingly reasonable man. But, like the arguments of other psychotics Dan had known, it hinged on a faulty premise: that Okabe had been commanded by God. If one accepted this premise, his logic was flawless; if not, it fell apart.

"You said before that publishing your findings under the circumstances you described answered other nagging questions for you. What questions?"

"Oh, many: Why I was drawn to science. Why I still lived when most of my family, my friends, my people are dead. I am an Ibo, a Biafran, Dr. Lassiter. Not many Americans know what that is—or, if they ever knew, have forgotten. Between 1966 and 1970, almost three million Biafrans were slaughtered, and yet they've forgotten! That's what I had to change, to redeem: by being the first to identify the oncoprotein, the common denominator of all cancers; by winning the Nobel Prize. Then, as Joshua Okabe, Ibo and Nobel laurate, I would command the necessary respect, the forum, the following, to carry out my greater mission. Do you follow?"

"Not exactly," said Dan.

"All right. Say, instead of Ibo, I told you I was a European Jew, a child survivor of the Nazi death camps. You would know exactly what that meant, wouldn't you?" At Dan's nod, Okabe smiled fleetingly. "In fact, because of their ambition, their shrewdness in business, the Ibos have been called 'the Jews of Africa.' It's pejorative, I think, but no matter. The Jews are a highly literate people. Their writers, playwrights, film-makers have made sure that the horrors of the Holocaust are never forgotten. But who writes or cares about the near genocide of the Ibos? Where is the diary of a Biafran Anne Frank to stir the conscience of the world? My own thirteen-year-old sister hid in the bush for a year before she was caught, tortured, and butchered. Who, besides me, echoes her cries? So you see, Dr. Lassiter, when God commanded, I listened. I still listen, though He speaks no more. Perhaps it is because the drugs I'm taking make me deaf. Or because I've proved unworthy . . ."

"What will you do now?"

"I don't really know. Make inquiries about the political situation back home. Return to Nigeria, if I'm welcome. Otherwise . . ." Okabe shrugged forlornly. Leaving the bed, he went to the window, looked out, then swung round suspiciously. "But you say you're not a cancer researcher. What is *your* interest in all this?"

"I'm acting as a sort of intermediary. Dr. Stefan Sigourney is a friend of mine. He's out of the country right now, but will be returning this week and he'd like to see you. I'm here to find out how you'd feel about such a visit."

Okabe's eyes bulged. "Dr. Sigourney, you say? Dr. Stefan Sigourney wants to visit me?" he asked, his voice rising shrilly.

Dan nodded, not knowing what to make of Okabe's apparent agitation.

As if sensing his bafflement, Okabe said, "Obviously you don't understand. That man is my idol! There's no living scientist I respect more. I've read almost everything he's ever written, heard him lecture many times, though I've never mustered the courage to introduce myself to him. Now you say *he* wants to meet *me?* Why would he want to do that?"

"I don't really know."

"Oh, come now, Dr. Lassiter. You're no errand boy. Dr. Sigourney simply didn't order you here. He must've given you some reason."

Dan exhaled wearily. "This seems to be my day for vague explanations. All I can tell you is that Steve—Dr. Sigourney—has questions about you and your work that he wants to ask in person. Will you see him?"

Okabe hesitated. "Not here. Not in a locked psychiatric ward. It's . . . undignified. But I'll gladly meet him elsewhere."

"Fine. Where?"

"A friend has a cottage on Cape Cod she is lending me for a while. I'll draw you a map. Tell Dr. Sigourney I will meet him there."

"All right. When?"

"I'm due for discharge tomorrow or the next day. So let's say Friday. Friday evening. Is that possible?"

"It might be a little too soon, but I'll find out and let you know."

"Please do. And please tell Dr. Sigourney I will be honored by his visit. I thought a lot about him—the injustice I might be doing him—when I first submitted my article for publication. But I had no choice."

"Shall I tell him that, too?"

"Tell him whatever you wish, Dr. Lassiter," said Okabe haughtily. Then he smiled. "I fully appreciate your dilemma. Either you believe that I've been directed by God, or that I am insane. But there's a third possibility: that all mortals directed by God appear insane. Even a fourth—that I'm simply a scoundrel. The choice is yours."

Dan rose, glanced at the titles of the history books stacked on Okabe's bedstand and offered his hand. "Goodnight, Doc—uh, Mister Okabe."

"And a good night to you, Dr. Lassiter," replied Okabe with exaggerated formality.

Chapter 21

STEVE LEFT BARCELONA FRIDAY morning and, with the time difference and a stopover in New York to change planes, landed at Logan Airport in early afternoon. More than curiosity about Joshua Okabe had prompted him to fly directly to Boston. This way he postponed for a few days the ordeal of homecoming, the inevitable fuss and receptions and mounds of mail to answer. At least Evashevsky had sworn to keep his engagement to Nicole secret; news of that, on top of his altered appearance, would have halted work at the institute for days.

From the airport, Steve took a taxi to Commonwealth General where he spent a few hours with Dan Lassiter and Ted Swerdloff going over data on the three leukemia patients treated with his monoclonal antibody. Then, gratefully accepting the loan of a hospital car, he left for Cape Cod and his visit with Joshua Okabe.

It was a clear, cool day, the traffic outside of Boston

light, and as he drove, his throughts centered mainly on the man he was about to meet. Lassiter's description of Okabe had both fascinated and appalled him. Steve wondered how he could possibly discuss science with a religious fanatic. What disturbed him even more was the realization that he would be dealing with a perverted intellect. His betrayal by Curt Gundersen twenty years before had taught him that it was better to listen to an ignoramus, a man who knew nothing, than to one to whom truth had lost its precious value.

In waning daylight, Steve followed a two-lane highway through mile after mile of sea marsh and dune grass to his destination—Truro, a tiny village on the outskirts of Provincetown. He stopped twice—once for coffee to combat his mounting fatigue, and then for supper at a motel restaurant.

His waitress was a big-bosomed, slim-waisted young blonde with large expressive eyes, a quick smile and a shy, self-conscious manner. Her smile was contagious, thought Steve, as she brought him a second cup of coffee. When she lingered, he looked up quizzically. "Yes?"

"Excuse me, sir, but mind if I ask you a question?"

"Ask away."

"Are you . . . European?"

Steve stared. He thought he had rid himself of his Hungarian accent years before. "Why? Do I look it?"

"Not in any bad way." She brushed back an invisible strand of hair from her forehead. "I don't know what it is—but you kind of do."

"I'm from Philadelphia," said Steve, expecting her to look disappointed.

"Oh! I've never been . . ."

"Where are you from . . . Sheila?" he asked, reading the plastic nametag pinned above her left breast.

"Here. Born here, went to school here, never been out of New England. But I hope to travel someday, which is why I like to talk to customers who look foreign, or at least interesting."

"And you think I look interesting?"

"Oh, I'll say! The way you dress. That gorgeous briefcase . . ." Suddenly she faltered and flushed. "Hey, I don't mean—I hope you don't think I'm coming on to you?"

"Coming on?" he repeated. "What does that mean?"

"You know, trying to make a date with you. I just wanted to talk. Look, if you'd rather not . . ."

Steve gestured placatingly. "I don't mind at all. I only wish I had more time. But I have to meet a man in Truro. Could you tell me how to get there?"

"Oh, sure. I live out that way myself. It's a little tricky once you leave the highway. I'd be glad to show you if I weren't on duty. But . . ." She shrugged, drew breath, and gave him directions. "Well, it's been nice talking to you, Mr. uh . . ."

"Sigourney. Stefan Sigourney."

"You *are* foreign!" she exclaimed, looking pleased. "I *knew* it. Are you an actor, too?"

Steve laughed. "Afraid not. Merely a research scientist. Well, thanks again for the excellent service."

"Oh, that's okay. I'll be on until midnight if you want more coffee."

"Then maybe we'll see each other again?"

"Hope so," she said, looking wistful. "You're really *interesting.*"

Smiling to himself, Steve left a dollar tip on the table and walked toward the cashier. No waitress before had ever paid him the slightest personal attention. Had his looks improved that much? Or had she somehow tuned in to his newly acquired sexual confidence? Could women actually sense that? He would have to ask Nicole. He felt obligated to tell her about the amusing incident. In their last session together, Herzog had explained sexual jealousy as being not so much fear of betrayal as fear of not knowing. Herzog's remedy: lovers should tell each other everything, even the most trivial happenings involving the opposite sex. Total honesty, he maintained, not only allayed suspicion but developed lines of communication too good to be broken by infidelity.

But Steve was not quite ready to dismiss the young waitress from his mind. Her slight flirtation had lightened his mood, distracted him from the serious business ahead. Impulsively he strode to the motel registration desk and took a room for the night.

In the darkness, Steve drove down a dirt road paralleling the beach until he came to a cluster of houses. When he pulled into the driveway of the last one, his headlights revealed a shadowy figure at a side window. Moments later, the lights over the front door came on and a large black man in a turtleneck sweater stepped out to greet him.

"Dr. Sigourney? A great honor, sir. I'm Okabe."

Tentatively he extended his hand and Steve shook it. Okabe ushered him into a small living room lined with book shelves. A quaint spinning wheel stood in a corner and a coal fire blazed on the hearth.

"Charming," remarked Steve, looking around.

"I think so, too. The house belongs to Janet Mumford, a dear friend of mine. Maybe you've heard of her? She's a television personality; has her own interview show on a local channel. Current events and that sort of thing . . . May I offer you a drink, Dr. Sigourney? I have beer, wine and bourbon whiskey."

"Perhaps a small glass of wine. I left Barcelona only this morning and I'm really too tired to do much drinking."

"Of course. Please sit anywhere you're comfortable. I'll be right back."

On his way out Okabe flicked a switch on a wall-mounted record player and the next moment Steve heard the opening violin solo of Rimsky-Korsakov's *Scheherazade*. Leaning back on the leather couch, he gazed at the fire on the hearth, imagined Nicole before it, and sighed. He literally ached for her. He shut his eyes, hoping to sharpen the image, and fell into a pleasant reverie . . . Sensing Okabe's huge form hovering above, he came awake with a start.

"Your wine, Dr. Sigourney," said Okabe with no change of expression. "I can shut off the record player if it distracts you." At Steve's head-shake, he smiled. "Symphonic music soothes me more than tranquilizers. No doubt Lassiter told you about my illness. I'm surprised you came here at all."

"I came to discuss your work, not your mental condition," said Steve firmly. "Nor do I intend to humor you. If anything you say sounds crazy, I'll tell you so, as I would anybody else. Otherwise there's no hope for a serious discussion."

"Well said, Dr. Sigourney. I have been humored quite enough in recent days—by professionals. But let me make sure I understand the precise purpose of your visit. You want—what?"

"To find out two things. First, how much of your oncoprotein theory was based on solid evidence. And second, why you didn't keep on in the direction you were going. You were a step ahead of me, Okabe. Ahead of the whole pack! Another year's work and you might have solved the cancer mystery once and for all. So why didn't you stick with it instead of committing scientific suicide as you did?"

"Didn't Dr. Lassiter tell you?"

"He told me," said Steve disdainfully. "You did a good job of convincing him you really believe God commanded you to publish. But Lassiter's no researcher; he doesn't know about all the strange whispers we hear when we're working late at night in our labs. I do, and I have a less mystical theory." Throat dry, he paused to sip his wine while Okabe, a cushion apart on the couch, watched him intently.

"Biafran or not," Steve went on, "I think you just got stuck and couldn't get unstuck. It happens to the best. You lose your way, your grasp of the problem, and maybe waste more time on shortcuts that turn out to be dead ends. So what do you do? You take long walks, hope that through meditation or ridiculous pacts with God you'll find your way again. Well, maybe you got more direction than you bargained for."

"A shrewd guess, Dr. Sigourney. It might even be correct. I really can't say. I no longer trust myself to distinguish fact from fancy . . . It's true, I did reach an impasse. I worked furiously to get around it, isolated myself totally, hardly slept . . . Then, one day while watching the sun rise over the Bay, it seemed to sail straight up to the center of the sky, swell bigger and bigger, until it burst. And out of the blinding flash came this voice, this incredible voice . . ." Okabe broke off to stare vacantly at the hearth for a long moment. Then he shook his head and smiled. "But I see that I'm making you uncomfortable. Obviously you've never . . ."

"Heard voices?" interrupted Steve. "I hear them all the time. But they've never been so compelling that they control me, make me self-destructive."

Okabe nodded. "Perhaps I'm a weaker person than you, or else I know something you don't: how very peaceful psychosis can be. Anxieties disappear, doubts vanish, you seem to exist on a separate plane from ordinary people. If only your body could make the leap, too, instead of being so dependent on others for its care. That, of course, is the main drawback—literally what drew me back. So now I can feed, bathe and dress myself. I can even feel some measure of remorse for the wrong I've done. But I won't deceive you; I'm not fully recovered. A part of me still yearns to go back."

"To what?" snapped Steve. "To a vegetative, meaningless existence? What good are you to yourself, to your people, then?"

"A wicked question. I wrestle with it constantly. But a famous man like you—why concern yourself with my problems?"

"I don't. Make no mistake, I'm a scientist, not a Samaritan. If there's anything to salvage from the shipwreck of your folly I want to know it. My only purpose for coming here, my only concern, is to find the oncoprotein—if, in fact, one exists—and be done with it."

"You sound as impatient as I used to be."

"I probably am. I've been at it longer than you. It's obsessed me long enough. There are other things I want to do with my life."

Okabe looked pensive. Then he sighed. "I cannot help you, Dr. Sigourney, not in any active sense. But I'm glad you're here, that I finally made your acquaintance, and for that alone I feel I owe you something. If you wish, I could supply you with a complete set of my data books and let you judge their worth for yourself?"

"You have them here?"

"I'll get them for you."

Okabe left the room. He returned shortly with a large cardboard box which he laid at Steve's feet. "It's all here and, I assure you, all factual. I give it to you as a gift."

Steve shook his head. "I'll look it over gladly. But I couldn't possibly accept."

"But I insist. I'm through with it—with science—forever. I know that a man's work bears his mark as surely as his children do; he can never completely dissociate himself from it. But it would be more cruel than kind of you to make me think I could continue on with it. So take what you will. Another glass of wine, Dr. Sigourney?"

Steve hesitated. His inclination was to plead exhaustion and leave, then expend what little remained of his energy going over Okabe's data. But he felt pity for the man, his ruined reputation; the least he could do would be to stay a while longer and be sociable. "All right," he finally said, "if you'll join me."

Steve left around nine p.m. and returned to his motel. After a cold shower to clear his head, he sat down with Okabe's data books, intending to spend no more than an hour on them before going to sleep.

Two hours later, he was still reading and taking notes furiously.

At midnight he broke off reluctantly, crawled into bed, and tried futilely to sleep. At one a.m., after paying the night clerk ten dollars for the loan of his percolator, a pound of coffee, and a carton of milk, he returned to his room and his reading.

Shortly before six, Steve turned the last page of the last cloth-bound book, shaved, and showered again. When the night clerk informed him that the restaurant would not be open for another half hour, he turned up his coat collar and went for a bracing walk. Before him the early November day was spreading silver light across the horizon and a pair of squawking seagulls foraged the beach for breakfast. Steve scarcely noticed them.

He hadn't expected Okabe's data books to be so absorbing, and at first they weren't. But as he was about to put them aside for the night, he came across an intriguing item: a query in Okabe's small, neat script alongside an experiment whose clear-cut outcome was at variance with the theory being tested.

Unlike Okabe's bafflement, the results made immediate sense to Steve, who had run similar though less sophisticated experiments himself. The more he thought about the peculiar phenomenon the two had independently observed, the more intrigued he became. Had Okabe modified and repeated the experiment, as his note to himself had recommended? Steve wished he could phone and ask, to save himself the trouble of going, page by page, through the remaining data books. But he couldn't remember the name of the woman who owned the beachhouse and in any case, it was too late to call.

It was two a.m. when he finally discovered Okabe's follow-up experiments and from then on sleep was out of the question.

Now, in the chill bleak dawn, Steve re-examined his find. Evidently before an oncoprotein, a rampaging monster enzyme, could be unleashed on an organism, a much smaller key-like structure—a peptide, not a protein—had to free the monster from its chains. Okabe had failed to recognize this because he lacked Steve's hard-won experience in trying to breed lymphocytes in tissue culture. Those infernal white blood cells simply would not grow without a molecular signal, a prod, a hormone-like growth factor that he had finally isolated from the blood of a patient with leukemia. There was little doubt in Steve's mind that the protein fragment Okabe had isolated and described almost in passing was similar, if not identical, to his own lymphocyte growth factor and that the implications of this kinship were staggering.

But that remained to be seen, and what preoccupied him now was more a question of ethics than science. Okabe had done more than allow him access to his data: he had given it to him as a gift. Should he accept? With the clue it had provided, Steve felt more confident than ever that he could identify the cancer-causing growth factor. Together with his team at the institute, he could do it faster and better than any researcher alive. But where did that leave Okabe?

Why should the man's fate even concern him? he asked himself. After all, he knew the rules of scientific fair play and he'd broken them. Any attempt to restore Okabe's tattered reputation would likely be at the expense of his own. Why risk it when he already had what he wanted?

If only Okabe hadn't opened up and confided so much of his personal life in their last hour together. The image of his young sister, too scab-ridden and emaciated to be raped, but broken in bone and spirit and discarded like a ragdoll in an incinerator, still harrowed Steve. Okabe had blamed greedy British oil barons whose ruthless meddling in his country's politics had fomented civil war. Would not the Biafran consider Steve equally ruthless and damnable if he usurped his findings?

No. That was precisely the problem; Okabe would not. He might actually be grateful.

So it was settled, Steve thought with weary resignation. Okabe must be enlightened, rehabilitated to the extent possible, given his fair share of future rewards.

He glanced at his watch: 6:32. He had to be back in Boston to meet with Carhill at 10:30—just time enough for either a nourishing breakfast or to see Okabe again.

Damn! Hadn't he complicated his life enough already with Nicole? Did he have to make it even more unmanageable by being fair-minded as well? And there was still more to come: how much would he have to forgive and forget where Gregory Carhill was concerned?

All right, all right, he conceded, looking Heavenward. You've been good to me. I can afford to give a little back. But must I do it all in one day? I merely want to be a candidate for the Nobel Prize, not sainthood!

Chapter 22

STEVE WAS TEN MINUTES late picking up Dan Lassiter at his hospital so that the two could ride together to the Bethune Institute. "Mind driving?" he asked as Dan got in the car. "I'm really beat."

"I believe it," said Dan. "You're quite a chameleon, you know. Yesterday you arrive from Spain looking like a movie star and ten years younger. Today . . . well, today you look more like your old, haggard self. How did it go with Okabe?"

"Quite well," Steve yawned. "We had a friendly talk."

"Just friendly—that's all. You look like he kept you up all night."

"Not Okabe, his data books. I'll fill you in as we ride."

"Fascinating," said Dan, after Steve gave him the gist of his new theory. "So there's no oncoprotein, after all?"

"Not a *single* one, anyway. Probably a number of proteins, dormant since fetal life, are activated by the growth factor. We'll know soon enough."

"Hmm. Sounds like exciting times ahead. I'm happy for you. I'm less happy about your intention to include Okabe. How does he feel about it?"

"He's reluctant to chance it, as well as he should be. He knows perfectly well the reception he's likely to get from people at my institute, Andre Evashevsky in particular. It's hard to regain professional acceptance after being denounced all around. I know," said Steve ruefully.

"Richard Nixon seemed to manage it."

"Nixon was a unique president—easy to condemn, hard to replace. Unlike politics, however, where a little deceit is not only tolerated but expected, science must be sacrosanct. We're certain of precious little as it is . . . No, Okabe will need more persuading. I'm going back to see him this afternoon. Okay if I keep the car?"

"Sure. But do you think that's wise, Steve? After all, the man's barely out of a psychiatric hospital. To plunge him back into a lab under such adverse circumstances might be too much pressure."

"Possibly. But I've agonized over what to do about him long enough. If Okabe wants a second chance, he'll get it. If not, my conscience is clear. Now tell me what to expect from Carhill."

Dan shrugged. "A red carpet, certainly. A little remorse over past squabbles and a lot of bravado. Ought to be an interesting session."

"Who else will be there?"

"No one, except possibly Yoshio Timura, Carhill's right-hand man. When we last spoke, Carhill was undecided whether to include him or not. Do you know Timura?"

"Only by reputation. I hope he *is* there. I'd like to exchange ideas with him."

"One last question," said Dan, as he parked the car at the edge of the Bethune Institute's rotunda. "How much of this new stuff about the growth factor are you willing to reveal?"

Steve smiled. "Ironic, isn't it? Ordinarily Carhill would be the last person I'd tell. But if he really wants my help, he'll get it—all of it. Knowing Carhill as I do, though, I won't be surprised if he pooh-poohs the theory to my face and then borrows it for some research of his own. Some very rushed research! They don't award Nobel Prizes posthumously, you know."

Dan shut off the ignition. "You think he's still trying to beat you out for that?"

"Why not? There's mortality and then there's *immortality*. I'd probably do the same in Carhill's place."

The meeting of the two research titans, with Dan as moderator and Joshio Timura as a taciturn participant, was held in the elegantly furnished conference room next to Carhill's office. At the outset, Dan felt uncomfortably like the referee at the start of a prize fight summoning the opponents to the center of the ring, but the meeting got off to a smooth start. Steve helped himself liberally to the sweet rolls laid out on the credenza and sat sipping coffee and munching while Carhill stood at the blackboard outlining his proposed treatment plan.

It was a remarkably cool performance, thought Dan. A casual observer would never guess that when Carhill spoke of "the cancer" or "the tumor mass" he meant his own. When the question of Gunther Gausse's future services came up, Steve accepted the news graciously that he had agreed to work for Carhill. He even offered to let Gausse take whatever materials he wished with him.

"Thank you, Stefan," responded Carhill. "It's a

time-saver, and I need as much of those as I can get. I only hope the isotope-antibody conjugate works as well on me as on your animals."

Steve shrugged. "The leukemia data is encouraging, although solid tumors, with their fibrin coats and uncertain blood supply, present an entirely different set of problems. I do, however, like your idea of injecting the antibodies intra-arterially so that they come in contact with the tumor almost immediately." He turned toward Dan. "That way it's less likely the isotope will be split off the antibody prematurely or that circulating macrophages will sop them up."

"Exactly," said Carhill. "I'm hopeful, of course, but I doubt very much if the initial injection will eradicate every last cancer cell, especially those buried in the less vascular interior of the tumor mass. So I plan to leave a catheter in the hepatic artery more or less permanently for follow-up treatment."

"Chemotherapy?" asked Steve.

"Preferably not. It's so indiscriminate. What would you say to massive infusions of straight monoclonal antibodies? An allergic reaction to the mouse protein is unlikely for the first week or so, and I'm willing to risk the other potential side effects if you think it's worthwhile."

Steve grimaced. "I don't know . . . Monoclonal antibodies alone haven't been too effective against intestinal cancers. Without a radioactive bombload, they simply aren't good killers. I do have a minor suggestion, however. Just before I fell ill, John Wendall and I were getting some interesting results by mixing monoclonal antibodies with activated macrophages just before injecting them. Essentially, what we did was this . . ."

While both Carhill and Timura took notes, Steve outlined his procedure for isolating macrophages, giant scavenger white blood cells, from the blood, and the anti-cancer effects he had observed with them.

"A neat suggestion," remarked Carhill afterwards. "What do you think, Yoshio?"

Timura nodded. "I'll start working on it immediately."

Carhill smiled. "Yoshio's my heir apparent. He's earned it. But he's as anxious as I am to see me cured since he hates administration. Which reminds me, Yoshio took part of his training under Professor Bashioto at Kyoto, whose life's work has been the nature of cancer metastasis. Evidently they just don't seed haphazardly; they're organ-selective. And there's recent evidence from a number of groups that they won't go anywhere at all unless they contain a certain glycoprotein that shields them from the immune system. So Yoshio's heading up a team to look into that angle. Perhaps by creating an antibody against the glycoprotein, it's possible to prevent a cancer from spreading. I might end up looking like a pregnant woman, but at least I'd be alive. Stefan, might you and your group be interested in working along those same lines?"

Steve hesitated. "I could assign people . . ."

"You don't look too enthusiastic."

"It's not that. I know of Bashioto's work and I think it's promising, but . . ." Again Steve hesitated.

"Yes?" prodded Carhill. "Please speak your mind."

"Well, suppose for argument's sake that every cancer, regardless of cause or type, has a common feature so essential for survival that it represents its point of maximum vulnerability."

Carhill stared. "An oncoprotein? Surely you're aware of how unpopular that theory has become? It's sunk as low as its contemptible champion."

"You may as well know," said Steve, "that I've just returned from a visit with Joshua Okabe. The man was—and is—mentally disturbed. His frantic efforts to find the oncoprotein probably precipitated his breakdown. But some of the work was done while he was quite sane and that much at least deserves to be taken seriously."

"You've studied it?" asked Carhill.

"In considerable detail."

"Well, I'd be interested in your opinion, of course, but I still believe in the computer programmer's maxim: 'Garbage in, garbage out!' " When Steve kept silent, Carhill sighed, "please tell me. I'm grasping at straws as it is."

Reluctantly Steve did. Beginning with the marginal note in Okabe's data books that had first piqued his curiosity, he went on to explain his new hypothesis.

Checking reactions with Timura from time to time, Carhill listened attentively. When Steve concluded, he asked, "And you say your paper on lymphocyte growth factor is in press?"

"Yes. It's due out in the next few weeks. I'll send you a typescript on Monday."

Carhill nodded and stroked his chin. "All very interesting and—at least the part originating from your own lab—important. But I would discount Okabe's findings entirely. I wouldn't even waste time trying to repeat his experiments. I know the man. I helped train him at Harvard, and I saw trouble coming even then. But I never imagined how much!"

"I'm not offering excuses for what Okabe did," Steve answered. "Nor am I particularly happy that this idea I'm so keen on pursuing was originally his. But I'd keep an open mind about it if I were you. Of all people, you can't permit personal prejudices to blind you to anything where cancer research is concerned. What if Okabe's right?"

The color rose in Carhill's face. "He's *not* right. With his character, his background, he couldn't be!"

"No," snapped Steve. "Nor could a man as puny

looking as Mohandas Gandhi lead half a billion people to independence. No class of human beings has a monopoly on ideas, Carhill. Ideas are democratic; they arise out of brain power, nothing else, and they stand or fall on their own merit. I'll know soon enough how solid Okabe's data is on the growth factor. And by my standards of fair play, I have to offer him the chance to collaborate."

Carhill shook his head. "You're making a serious mistake. Any work involving Okabe will be tainted, and so will you. Your colleagues will not only be horrified by such a collaboration, but unforgiving. It will seriously damage, if not destroy, your standing in the scientific community. And regardless of past differences, I would not wish that on you, especially now. I had even hoped . . . well, no matter. Your suggestion regarding macrophages was most welcome and I do appreciate your coming here. Would it be permissible for Yoshio or me to consult you again from time to time?"

"Of course," said Steve, rising.

Dan wished he could see their faces as they shook hands, but Timura, who had come forward, blocked his view. In the suddenly tense atmosphere, Dan was glad Carhill did not repeat his invitation to tour the institute. After a final round of handshakes, he and Steve left.

In the car, Steve sighed, "Well, I did my best. I withheld nothing."

"No," said Dan. "Nobody could accuse you of that."

"It went badly at the end, didn't it?"

Dan shrugged. "My hunch is, Carhill wanted to propose a merger of your two institutes. But you bringing up Okabe killed that."

"A merger?" said Steve. "How would that benefit me?"

"You'd be in charge of it all when he died."

"Oh, no! Carhill's tricked me before. What if I agreed, and he refused to die?"

"You need sleep, Steve. I'm taking you home with me."

"Why? Because I made bad jokes?"

"No. Because I'm a tightwad administrator and I'd hate to see a hospital car wrecked!"

Chapter 23

A SENSE OF FAMILIARITY makes sex even better. It was Steve's last conscious thought before dozing off and, as sometimes happened when he was so exhausted, it kept repeating. A sense of familiarity makes sex—no, *love*—even better . . .

His eyes opened into darkness. Where was he? Whose soft body was lying half over his? Kris Lassiter? He knew he had warm feelings for her, but he'd never expected to be in bed with her! What would Dan say? Shocks of guilt quivered through him. With Dan out of the house, he should never have spent the night there.

But wait—he hadn't. He had driven back to Cape Cod around suppertime. He relaxed. This must be some confused dream.

Steve woke again sometime later to the sound of a toilet flushing, and a panel of light across the bed. Nicole was propped on an elbow gazing down at him. "What . . . ?" he asked.

"She was right, you know—that young waitress. You *are* exotic-looking. And every bit as good a lover as she imagined," she said.

"Stop!"

"I won't stop," she teased. "You're mine. I'll bring you all the coffee you want. No waitress can have you that cheaply."

"Be serious."

"No! I feel kittenish; I want to play. I don't *want* to be serious."

Steve grinned. Her playfulness was just the antidote he needed for his somber mood. He was happy to forget Carhill, Okabe, science itself, for a while. But he wouldn't spoil the fun by admitting it.

"Please!" he cried as Nicole sprawled over him, kissing his chest. "I'm not a sex object!"

"I just can't help it, Stefan. I can't control myself around exotic-looking men, especially when they show up unexpectedly on a Sunday afternoon and take me right to bed."

"I called first."

"Finally! You were supposed to call Saturday, remember? I hung around here all weekend waiting. Then what happens? You invite me to dinner at a fancy restaurant; I spend hours fixing my hair, ironing my dress—for what? We haven't even been out of bed!"

"I tried hours ago to get out of bed. You wouldn't let me."

"I wasn't finished with you." She laughed. "I'm still not. But to prove my forgiving nature, I'll fix us something to eat."

Afterwards, as they sat in her dinette sipping cognac, Steve asked, "What time must you be up in the morning?"

"Six. I have a busy day planned. Now that I've more or less mastered the technique of 'in vitro mutagenesis,' Hollis Reed and I are plunging into a series of retrovirus experiments."

"I'm glad you're working with Reed," said Steve. "He's clever, seasoned—and old."

Nicole shrugged. "Sixtyish. Not so old. His eyes still light up when a pretty technician prances by, and we sometimes walk hand in hand when we go out to lunch. Hollis has worked with Okabe, you know. They've spent time in each other's lab. He's still puzzled by the whole sad affair."

"Puzzled? Why?"

"Well, at first he, like you, believed Okabe was right. Crazy perhaps, but right. Even after Kreisberg's retraction letter, Hollis wasn't convinced the oncoprotein didn't exist. You see, several months before, he had sent Okabe some coded specimens to test for it and the results were impressive. Is it all right if I tell him about you sponsoring Okabe?"

Steve shook his head. "It's not definite yet. He wants time to think about it, talk it over with his psychiatrist. In the end, though, I'm pretty sure he'll accept. And when word gets around that Okabe's at the institute, there's bound to be a commotion. Carhill was shocked; Evashevsky will probably be apoplectic."

Nicole compressed her lips. "Stefan, I don't like it—the way it's going to complicate your life. It scares me."

"Why? I've ignored convention before."

"I know—with a vengeance. That's what troubles me. You seemed so relaxed, so carefree, on the island. Now, you're beginning to brood again. Why? You're merely borrowing an idea from Okabe, not any great body of data. Why do you feel so obligated to him?"

Irritably Steve said, "I thought I'd explained that."

"No! Everything *but* that. Maybe because you haven't explained it yet to yourself. But don't be cross. It's late, we're both tired, and I'm so glad to see you. When will I see you again?"

Looking subdued, Steve said, "Next weekend, every weekend—whenever you wish."

"What are *your* wishes?"

"I *must* see you. I have to relax."

"I know," she said softly. "Now come to bed. This time I may even let you get some sleep.

Nicole was right, thought Steve on the train ride to Philadelphia the next morning. His reasons for sponsoring a known psychotic and fraud like Okabe made little sense. What really kept him from taking a small portion of Okabe's data without taking responsibility for the man himself? His own rebellious nature? Or because it was the decent thing to do?

Though thinking about little else during the two-hour train ride, he arrived at no satisfactory answer. Events would simply have to provide one, he reflected, as he strode through the seedy grandeur of the railroad station to the street.

Chapter 24

"HAVE YOU HEARD FROM Steve lately?" asked Kris Lassiter as she and Dan sat in Symphony Hall waiting for an Andre Watts piano recital to begin.

"Not for the last couple of weeks. I'll call him tomorrow when I get back from Carhill's surgery. I promised him I would."

"You're going?"

"I might even scrub in. Yoshio Timura invited Ted and me."

"Invited?" repeated Kris dubiously. "Will there be a reception afterward?"

"Possibly. After all, it's an event—a Carhill extravaganza. If the treatment works, it might even be a medical milestone: the first case of abdominal cancer cured by monoclonal antibodies."

"Well, because I'm a doctor and a nice sort of person, I hope it *does* work. I've lost enough cancer patients. . . . Anyway, I rather miss Steve. And I'm dying to meet his girlfriend."

"Me too. He might never have mentioned her if you hadn't figured it out. A neat bit of detective work on your part."

"Cherchez la femme? Elementary, my dear Lassiter. But I want to meet her, and soon. I'm sure it wasn't easy making Steve so likeable. I wonder how she did it?"

Dan eyed her curiously. "How likeable?"

"Well, if you must know, Steve and I had a friendly little chat while you were off playing handball."

"About what?"

"Oh, men and women—why some are joys to be with and others are about as comfortable as hemorrhoids."

"Hey!" said Dan, protesting her look. "I'm here, aren't I? I even turned off my beeper. The hospital could blow up while I'm listening to Rachmaninoff and I wouldn't know it. But you and Steve being buddies—that's a switch."

"I *did* dislike him, but I don't any more. I'd really like to see him again. And if Nicole's half as attractive as he says, *you'll* like seeing *her.*"

"Okay," said Dan, as the footlights dimmed and the orchestra began tuning up. "I'll see what I can arrange."

Steve had waited for Okabe's acceptance letter before broaching the subject of his employment with Andre Evashevsky. Even then, he kept putting it off until, with Okabe due in Philadelphia in two days, he could delay no longer. At the staff dinner that Friday—the last and most boisterous of his homecoming parties—after personally plying Andre with liquor, Steve took him aside to tell him.

Evashevsky was smiling when Steve first mentioned Okabe; surprisingly, he kept on smiling—

a sad smile, Steve came to realize. "I already heard," Evashevsky informed him.

"You what? From whom?"

"From Gunther Gausse who heard it from Carhill who heard it from you."

"Then why didn't you say something?"

"I was waiting for you! But I'm not upset anymore. Now it just saddens me."

Steve frowned. "That bad?"

Evashevsky nodded. "When is Okabe starting?"

"On Monday."

"The same day I leave on vacation. Good! Maybe he won't last. Maybe he'll be gone when I get back. If not, I don't know. I honest to God don't know . . ."

"I need you, Andre, more than ever before. The next few months could be the most exciting ever here."

"Stefan, don't! Don't cajole, con or pressure me. The months I took over for you were a strain, but this is worse. You knew my feelings about Okabe, yet you went ahead and hired him anyway. So let it be. When I get back from vacation, we'll talk."

"If there's any chance of losing you, I'd prefer to talk now."

"There *is* a chance. But any discussion now would only increase it. And this is supposed to be a celebration—an outpouring of joy at our leader's return." At Steve's wince, Evashevsky patted his shoulder. "I'm a great sulker, Stefan. I was as a kid; I am now. So instead of begging our friendship, let me sulk a while longer. And drink."

Glumly Steve nodded. "Let's go back to the bar."

The look of melancholy in Evashevsky's eyes—or was it rebuke?—still haunted Steve as he waited at the Union Station gate for Joshua Okabe, a huge suitcase in each hand, to climb the stairs toward him. He had found an apartment for Okabe, arranged for laboratory space and technicians and a generous salary; what he couldn't arrange was a congenial working atmosphere. As director, Steve could only spare him psychological shocks from above; he could not shield him from his peers.

Breathlessly Okabe reached the landing, put down his luggage, and extended his hand. "Dr. Sigourney!" he rumbled. "I'm happy to see you."

"Welcome," said Steve, and over Okabe's protests, picked up one of his suitcases. It would be the least of his burdens, he thought.

The following Sunday, while Nicole was visiting, Steve invited Okabe to his apartment for drinks. She had been curious to meet him and Steve was curious about her impressions. Although Nicole and Okabe appeared wary of one another at first, they eventually found common interests and the hours passed pleasantly.

"Well?" asked Steve after Okabe had left. "What did you think of him?"

Nicole hesitated. "A very intense, very attractive man."

"Attractive in what sense? Physically?" At her nod, Steve looked bemused. "I've never thought of him that way."

"You wouldn't. You're not a woman."

"And you do?"

"Oh, yes! Very sensitive, very sexy . . ." Suddenly, she grinned. "Oh, Stefan, stop gaping! It's a standard woman's ploy to get back at a man for putting her through an ordeal—and this was, at least at the beginning. After a while I got used to his intense manner and warmed up to him. I almost wish he *were* sexy—so sexy that the females at the institute couldn't keep away from him. Maybe then he wouldn't seem so lonely. Or so anxious for your approval."

Steve shrugged. "I'm his boss, after all."

"You're his friend. His only friend . . . How's he progressing in the lab?"

"It's taken time for him to set up. We begin work in earnest next week."

Steve invited Okabe over again the next Sunday, and the ones after that, until his Sunday afternoon visits became part of their weekend routine. Nicole did not object. It was only a few hours out of the twenty-four she and Steve had together and she rather enjoyed their scientific discussions. Okabe was unfailingly polite, but opinionated, gleefully playing devil's advocate to Steve's more unorthodox views. With mock disdain, Steve labeled his arguments "The Boston Fallacy," and any Nicole dared voice, usually based on information from her National Cancer Institute colleagues, "The Party Line."

At first, Steve made a conscious effort to include Nicole in the conversations, although both realized she lacked the breadth of knowledge that would make her an equal partner. But as their research intensified, so did their discussions and Steve sought her opinion less and less.

Nicole well knew that the task they had taken on was Herculean: there were countless cancer-causing viruses and at least thirty separate oncogenes, each for a different type of cancer. To find one, or at most a small group of growth factors that all cancers shared—a final common pathway—was not only a colossal undertaking but quite possibly insuperable. Realizing this, she tried her best to be tolerant of Steve's increasing lapses into a world from which she, though not Okabe, was excluded.

One Sunday in early December, however, as snow swirled outside the windows and Nicole sat curled up on the couch half listening to Steve and Okabe debate the nature of the hepatitis B virus, she finally forced herself to accept a hard truth: Steve was not only slipping back into his old habits but by her accomodations, sexual and otherwise, she was actually making it easier for him.

" . . . I don't care!" Steve was almost shouting. "I don't care what Messerlich says. I tell you, Joshua, hepatitis B is a retrovirus in disguise, which is why it's associated with liver cancer. Messerlich is just being pig-headed about it because he didn't realize it first. And just because Finlander tends to agree with him, you'd think he'd been blessed by the Pope! But we mustn't make the same mistake. We must be ruled by logic, not consensus."

"I'm trying," sighed Okabe. "I'm trying to present as coherent an argument for the opposing view as your continuous interruptions permit."

"Then go ahead. Don't let my interruptions interrupt you!"

Okabe smiled tolerantly. "Well, for one thing, a retrovirus genome is much larger than the hepatitis virus genome. And . . . " He broke off suddenly. "You look . . . pained."

"It's my tooth." Steve pointed to his left upper lip. "It hurts. There must be decay under the cap." He glanced guiltily at Nicole. "I have a dentist appointment Tuesday morning, so don't nag."

"*Do* you?" she remarked. "How sensible! It's only been hurting for weeks."

Steve gestured helplessly. "No time . . . But back to that ridiculous assertion of Messerlich's . . ."

No time! mused Nicole fretfully. On Minorca Stefan always had time—to listen, to play, to stay fit and healthy. He had stopped jogging three weeks ago and was thickening again around the middle. He needed a haircut, household supplies, a new winter coat. Worse yet, his facial rash, a sensitive indicator of excessive stress, had come back, though medication was controlling it for the moment.

Face it, Nicole told herself. This was not merely a

phase, a frantic effort to catch up after his long absence. It was the path of least resistance; the way he had been before and, because of its familiarity, was bound to be again. In part, she blamed Joshua Okabe—not for any specific act but because his presence at the institution and in their lives increased the pressure on Stefan to succeed.

On the Saturday before Christmas, six weeks after Okabe's arrival in Philadelphia, Nicole's frustrations boiled over and she confronted Steve. He had come home hours late from the institute looking as haggard as she had ever seen him. No sooner was he through the door than he was on the telephone to someone in the hybridoma lab. Then, muttering curses, he rushed into his den and rummaged through the desk for a research report. Before he could pick up the phone again, Nicole thrust a glass of wine in his hand and demanded a few minutes of his time.

"Stefan," she began, "I don't mean to carp, but it's five o'clock. You asked me to be here by two so we could go shopping, remember?"

"I know," he sighed. "I'm sorry. I lost track of the time."

"That's not all you've lost track of. You say you need me to relax, but you don't *want* to relax. Nor do you seem to want to make love anymore. What *do* you want?"

Steve winced. He was aware of his recent lack of ardor; only that morning he had resolved to make amends. But coming home hours late was obviously not how to go about it. "Nicole, please," he said wearily. "You don't run an institute. Evashevsky is still away doing God knows what with Bach in Paris. Gunther Gausse is stealing my ideas right and left. Wendall and Okabe are feuding. I'm trying to direct ten labs simultaneously. And if that weren't enough, I'm expecting the delegation on Wednesday."

"The delegation? You mean the people from the National Academy?"

"The Academy, the NIH, the Scientific Advisory Council—maybe even the Ku Klux Klan! I told Haskell to limit the group to half a dozen. I don't want to be overwhelmed by numbers."

"Does Joshua know about it?"

"No! Not from me, anyway. But I'm sure he suspects. Who do those jokers think they are—a scientific Curia? If this were Hungary, I might understand: visits by Communist vigilante committees are common enough there. But this is America! If they're so unhappy that Okabe's working here—that he's even in this country—why don't they take it up with the immigration authorities? What do they want from me? What do *you* want?"

Nicole smiled wistfully. "Remember the 'Devil's Mouth,' Stefan? The lake . . ."

"Yes!" he hissed. Then, softly, "Yes . . . I think about it often before I fall asleep at night. But old habits are harder to break than I thought, especially around here. A jungle is a bad place for a man trying to get over malaria, a bar for an alcoholic . . . It's not Okabe's fault, Nicole. At first I was afraid to push him too hard in the lab. But he seems to thrive on the work. It's me, not him, that's acting crazy. *He's* worried about *me.*"

"He's not the only one."

"All right, all right. I'm overdoing, I admit it. This has been the worst week yet. If only everyone in the field would stop publishing for a month—a single week!—I might be able to catch up, make some sense out of what we're doing. But that's like asking the earth to stop spinning. The staff's complaining about the work load, too. Some are even calling me *Scrooge.* So it's Christmas week. People are still going to get cancer."

"And ulcers and coronaries and nervous breakdowns."

Steve laughed mirthlessly. "Okay, I get your point. But what would you have me do? Phone Ben Herzog and have a talk with him? No, better! Much better! See him! We'll spend Christmas with Georgi and Isabella. What do you say?"

"I'd love to, Stefan. But it's foolish to go all that way for a weekend, and I can't take much more time off."

"All right, how much time can you take? Three, four days? Then take it! We'll go someplace closer, just the two of us. We could visit the Lassiters in Boston. You like them, don't you?"

"Very much."

"Good. It's settled then. I'll clear my schedule. Book a suite at the Ritz-Carleton. Call Dan . . ."

"Stefan, please! Keep away from that telephone. All I want you to do right now is relax. Do you want to eat in or out?"

"Out! We'll go to that new French restaurant, whatever its name is. You know, the one Wendall's been raving about. You make the reservation while I shower."

Springing to his feet, Steve hugged her, apologized again for his recent thoughtless behavior, and left the room humming.

Nicole stared after him. A swank restaurant, an impromptu trip to Boston—the grand gesture. It was becoming Stefan's style. But he needed the break, she needed to be alone with him, and though she barely knew the Lassiters, she liked them enormously. She'd let Stefan indulge her with his grand gestures a while longer, she reflected. It might turn out to be a very pleasant holiday, after all.

Chapter 25

THREE DAYS BEFORE CHRISTMAS and all Boston glittering merrily, thought Dan, glancing out his office window at the skyline glow of dusk. He had hardly gone downtown or done anything in a yuletide spirit this year. While the hospital emptied of all but critically ill patients and its staff caroused at departmental parties, he struggled with paperwork. Ironically, whenever a federal agency adopted one of his Health Care Cost Commission's recommendations, his reward was a batch of new forms to fill out. Back at his desk, he was attempting to decipher another one when his secretary buzzed.

"Ted Swerdloff's out here, Dr. Lassiter. He wants you to come out to meet someone."

"Can't they come in?"

"I already asked. Ted says it'd be better if you came out."

"What would? . . . Oh, never mind. It'll be quicker just to do it." He rose and strode to the door.

"Okay, Ted. What's . . ." Abruptly Dan stopped and did a double take. Next to Swerdloff, grinning from ear to ear, stood Billy Freiborg, barely recognizable as the frail youth Dan remembered. His straw-blond hair had grown long and full and his lank frame was at least thirty pounds heavier. In buttoned-down shirt, maroon tie and navy blue blazer, he looked like a member of some prep school glee club.

"Good God!" Dan exclaimed. "What've you been giving him, Ted—growth hormone?"

"He's no taller, just fatter. No more fat-doctor jokes, okay, Billy?"

"I guess. Nice to see you, Dr. Lassiter."

"Same here. How're you doing?"

"You tell me. Ted's taken his usual quart of blood."

"You owe us more than that," Dan said. "How much more, I don't know. I'll have to check your account . . . Where were you Thanksgiving, by the way?"

"Couldn't make it then. Too busy at school. Besides, it's easier this way. My folks are spending Christmas in Washington."

"Washington, eh? Must be nice having a big-shot uncle."

"You bet. How's the homerun slugger from Philadelphia doing?"

Dan looked baffled momentarily. Then, "Oh, Steve Sigourney! Fine. In fact, he'll be in town tomorrow night. How long's Billy going to be with us, Ted?"

"I'm going to grab some bone marrow first thing tomorrow morning and run a tracer study on him. I sort of promised him we'd be through in time for Billy to catch a five o'clock plane."

"Too bad in a way. Steve would get a kick out of seeing him again."

"I'd like to see him, too," said Billy. "He really

came through in the clutch. Thank him for me, will you, Dr. Lassiter?"

"Sure thing," said Dan, giving Billy's shoulder a squeeze.

"Speaking of teamwork," interjected Swerdloff, "tell Dan what Dr. Nestor asked you to do."

As if suddenly shy, Billy said, "*You* tell him."

"Tom Nestor, his pediatrician back in Bemidji, wants Billy to help counsel some of his leukemic kids. Be a sort of big brother to them."

"Great idea," said Dan. "You going to do it?"

Billy shrugged. "Maybe. I'm still thinking about it."

"Remember the deal we once made: no Gray Ladies, no O.T., no medical gobbledegook. Just straight talk and no bullshit," Dan reminded him. "You could help negotiate the same kind of deal for them."

"I suppose," said Billy, shifting his feet awkwardly. "Least I could do is spread the good word about monoclonal antibodies."

"Billy, why don't you go down to the ward and wow the student nurses," said Swerdloff, "while I have a quick word with Dan."

"Sure. Student nurses are what I dream about these days," Billy said with a grin.

"I thought you dreamed about your horse," Dan accused.

"Gustaf's a stallion," said Billy. "He understands. See you guys later."

Taking Swerdloff in his inner office, Dan asked, "How's Carhill going?"

"So-so. His liver metastases are no longer visible on scan and his main tumor mass has shrunk. But it's far from gone and he's lost more weight."

Dan frowned. "How is he mentally?"

"Sharp. Still works at his desk a few hours a day. Yoshio's going crazy trying to come up with the antibody Carhill wants, the one to the metastatic factor. He's testing another batch on mice with implanted tumors today."

"Tell him I wish him luck. Anything else?"

"Carhill would like to see you sometime after the holidays."

"Fine. I'll phone him then and set it up. Know what about?"

Swerdloff shook his head. "Every time I run into him at the Bethune he asks about you and then Steve Sigourney. So my guess is it has to do with Steve."

"Does he know Steve's visiting us?"

"No. Do you want him to?"

"Definitely not," said Dan. "Steve's supposed to be on vacation."

Yesterday morning the dentist, today the delegation, thought Steve, as he sat across the conference table from the three men. At least a local anaesthetic had deadened the pain of the dentist's drill. Nothing, except possibly boredom, could numb the sting of their self-righteous accusations.

He had not been surprised to learn that the original six-man delegation had shrunk to three. He personally would have never taken time from work to engage in such a thankless task. What did the underworld call such men—enforcers? Except for their formality and academic titles, these three could have been Mafia enforcers. Steve regretted that Franklin Haskel, a grand old man of science, had to be their spokesman. In his late seventies, Haskell was a tall, stooped, wizened-faced but clear-eyed gentleman whose distinguished career included pioneer research on radiation-induced cell injury and many years as chancellor of the University of Chicago. The curse of retirement, thought Steve; Haskell must have accepted this assignment more out of boredom than conviction.

At Haskell's right, David Kavachek, a molecular biologist from M.I.T., evoked different feelings in Steve. Sucking, sometimes smacking, the stem of an unlit pipe, Kavachek was young and bearded and brash. Steve almost ached to vent some of his pent-up hostility on him.

He felt neutral about the third member of the delegation, Robert Whitson, once a senior editor of *Science* and now publisher of the popular *Research Reports*. From what he knew about the man and could now observe, Whitson struck him as rigid—in posture, prose style, and beliefs. To his later regret, Steve chose to ignore him.

From the burnished tabletop and fingernails that needed clipping, Steve's eyes roamed the ceiling while Haskell opened the proceedings by praising his institute's recent accomplishments. "Please understand," he concluded, "it's only because of our high regard for you, Stefan—and for science—that we're here today."

"I do understand," said Steve. "You want me to fire Joshua Okabe."

"We prefer that you hear us out first. After that, we're confident you'll do the proper thing."

"The proper thing?" repeated Steve. "Wouldn't the 'proper thing' be to hear Okabe out, too? After all, since Magna Carta a man has had the right to face his accusers."

Haskell compressed purplish lips. "We discussed that among ourselves earlier and decided it was neither necessary nor advisable. Our sole concern is for your reputation, not his, and . . . and . . ." He looked at David Kavachek for assistance.

"And Okabe is a confessed faker," said Kavachek. "What's he doing here, anyway?"

Steve smiled disarmingly. "I don't know how they do things at M.I.T., but we try to emulate Heaven here."

"Heaven, eh?" Kavachek smirked. "What's that supposed to mean?"

" 'There's more joy in heaven when one sinner repents than when ninety-nine good men . . . *et cetera.*' But let's not waste each other's time. You say your sole concern is for my reputation and for that, I suppose, I ought to be grateful. However, I've no intention of firing anybody. I don't condone what Joshua Okabe did, but I do think I understand why he did it. We all have a breaking point, gentlemen, and for reasons I won't go into, Okabe reached his. He came to what he *thought* was the truth—which may yet turn out to *be* the truth—intuitively, not objectively. His mistake was publishing it. Now he's trying to redeem himself for that folly. Why not give him the chance?"

Haskell cleared his throat. "Stefan, this has been said so often I know it sounds trite, but scientists are like holy men. They must either keep the faith or be banished from the temple forever. Half measures won't do, and the old safeguard, reproducibility of results, is no longer enough. There's simply too much going on in every field these days. Unless an experiment is truly important, it might take years before anyone tries to repeat it. So we *must* be strict in our standards and severe in our condemnation of the rule-breakers."

"No doubt," said Steve. "But you all know the ludicrous story of French physicist Rene Blondlot and his magical N-rays, supposedly emitted by all living matter to brighten nearby objects. For a time Blondlot's discovery was the glory of French science, the source of over a hundred related papers, until it was finally proven that his N-rays were nothing more than an optical illusion and non-existent."

"As you said, Stefan," interrupted Kavachek, "we all know that story. What's your point?"

"That though French science suffered a near

mortal blow because of him, not a single colleague ever questioned Blondlot's honesty or sincerity, only his powers of observation. Okabe, too, made a crucial misperception. Must we be less forgiving than the French?"

With the smirk back on his face, Kavachek was about to reply when Haskall, with a restraining gesture, said, "Ordinarily, I would say, no. But the work you're doing here is too important to be tarnished by controversy. And after the series of scandals that have rocked science lately, cancer research in particular, we can't afford to give the public further cause for disillusionment."

As Haskell sipped water, Kavachek added, "You know what Machiavelli said: 'One who deceives will always find those who allow themselves to be deceived.' It's good advice, Stefan."

"Is it?" replied Steve coldly. "I've never read much Machiavelli. Being outside the Harvard-M.I.T. axis, I never felt any need. Nor will I allow outsiders, whatever their motives or the pressures they bring to bear, tell me how to run my institute. Speaking of pressures, though, I'm curious. Apart from peer disapproval, what else do you have in mind? Oh, come now, gentlemen! This was no spur-of-the-moment visit. Pressures from somewhere brought you here."

In the ensuing silence, Steve scanned their faces: Haskell, obviously discomfited; Whitson, expressionless. Only Kavachek seemed unfazed. "How much NIH money are you getting?" he asked.

Steve smiled sardonically. "That's irrelevant, I would think. But . . . perhaps not. Why do you ask? Do you want to compare grants like children comparing toys?"

"Hardly," said Kavachek through unsmiling lips. "And it's not idle curiosity either. Those Congressional investigations of fraud in biomedical research can be rough, believe me. They really raked the head of the NCI over the coals for some trivial impropriety not so long ago. Who's to say they won't do even worse with you, if you insist on sponsoring Okabe?"

Steve shrugged. "That's a risk I'll simply have to take."

"Nonetheless, I'm curious about your NIH funding. I hear it's surprisingly small."

"It's a matter of public record. If you can't contain your curiosity, look it up."

"I will," replied Kavachek. "*Is* it small, Stefan?"

Steve sighed wearily. "Comparatively. Most of my operating funds come from private sources."

"Well, don't you feel some obligation to them?"

"Of course, I feel an obligation—to do the best work I can!"

"You know what I mean, Stefan."

Though Steve usually liked informality among his colleagues, Kavachek's use of his first name, along with his badgering, was beginning to grate. "My sources aren't complaining, *David.*"

"Maybe they don't know enough to complain."

"Gentlemen, please!" Haskell urged. "This is getting us nowhere. Let's stick to the business at hand."

Seething, Steve said, "Fine. Joshua Okabe, being my employee, is my business. Mine alone. Despite your objections, he will continue in my employ until he either completes his work or gives me reason to fire him. Now, do you have anything better than the NIH to threaten me with?"

"No threats, Stefan," said Haskell somberly. "It was never our intention to threaten you in any way. But we do have legitimate concerns. Robert here publishes an important journal; David and I serve on the editorial board of others. Certainly you can appreciate the difficulties we'll have evaluating any paper with Okabe's name on it."

"A burden, to be sure," conceded Steve, "but all the more reason to make our proofs iron-clad. There's enough of dubious value being published as it is, especially by cancer researchers. They could use more of that same discipline."

"Most assuredly." Haskell paused reflectively. "Is there nothing—nothing at all—we can say to get you to reconsider your relationship with Okabe?" He turned to Robert Whitson. "Robert, we haven't heard from you yet."

Whitson nodded. "I'm still a little puzzled about your motive, Dr. Sigourney . . ."

"Motive for what?" asked Steve.

"For championing Okabe. It wouldn't by any chance have to do with some special empathy you might feel for him based on personal experience, would it? I'm referring—reluctantly, I might add—to a report you and Curt Gundersen published back in the early sixties on an erythropoetin assay. A second paper by Gundersen, along with numerous others, disproved the worth of the assay, though its original claims were never retracted."

Steve stiffened. "The work came out of Gundersen's lab. If he felt a retraction was called for, he should've written it."

"Yes, but you were first author on the paper. *You* should have . . ."

"Enough!" Steve barked. He scribbled a number on a piece of paper and flung it at Whitson. "This is Dr. Daniel Lassiter's office in Boston. Phone him and repeat the charge you just alluded to; he can enlighten you. You can use the phone here or in my secretary's office."

"Well," said Whitson, faltering under Steve's glare, "I don't . . . I'm not really sure that's . . ."

"I warn you, do it now or else this meeting is over!"

As the others seemed to shrink back in embarrassment, Steve continued to glower at Whitson, who sat motionless, frozen with indecision. "That's it, then!" Rising, Steve stalked out of the room, leaving the three scientists looking bewildered.

Steve strode fifty feet down the corridor to his office to tell his secretary to cancel the luncheon planned for his guests. Finding her away from her desk, he shouted, "Marta! Marta, where are you? . . . *Kristus Jazus,*" he muttered in Hungarian, a language he reverted to only under extreme duress. "Mar—" Behind him, someone cleared his throat. Steve whirled around.

From a chair between two file cabinets, a wide-eyed, straggly-haired young man leaped to his feet clutching a manila folder to his chest. Taking note of his soiled lab coat, open necked shirt and faded jeans, Steve assumed he was a new graduate student. "Who are *you*?" he snapped.

"Uh, Modreski, Dr. Sigourney . . . John Modreski. I, uh, work in Jorgeson's lab."

"Since when?"

"Uh, what?"

Steve stared with distaste at the slovenly, acne-scarred student until he remembered that was how he himself had looked not too long ago and would again if he didn't shape up. "I said, since when have you worked here?"

Modreski gulped. "Since July. We haven't met."

"So it seems . . . Are you waiting for me or my secretary?"

"Uh, you, I guess. I heard you were interested in cancer of the pancreas and I'm doing my thesis on it. On ectopic hormone production by pancreatic neoplasms. I thought you might like to, uh, take a look at what I've done so far."

Steve sighed. The poor student looked so flustered that he began to take pity on him. Had he ever been so frightened of a superior? "All right, let's see what you've got." Snatching Modreski's folder, he read the table of contents and flipped through the pages. "Who told you I'd be interested in this?"

"Uh, Ingrid—Dr. Jorgeson. Was she wrong?"

Steve shrugged. "I know someone it would interest much more." He was about to hand the folder back when he heard footsteps coming down the corridor. Afraid it might be one or more members of the delegation, Haskell, in particular, wanting to make a last appeal, Steve seized the startled student's arm and said, "Come into my office and tell me more about this—this interesting project. Maybe I can offer a few suggestions."

"Would you, Dr. Sigourney? I'd . . ."

"Not here. Inside!" Steve thrust him forward and shut the door behind them.

Chapter 26

FROM TURKEY TO TABLE TALK, Christmas Eve dinner at the Lassiters was a great success. More relaxed than Nicole had seen him in weeks, Steve regaled them with descriptions, complete with mimicry, of the three-man delegation and the hapless graduate student, literally quaking in his scruffy boots, he had dealt with the morning before. Between laughs, however, Steve detected worry in Dan's eyes. After dinner, while Kris took Nicole for a walk in the woods back of the Lassiter house and the two men sat in the living room sipping twenty-five-year-old Scotch, Steve asked him to explain the look.

"Well," said Dan, "I know Kavachek from lectures he's given at my place and, to quote Ted Swerdloff, he's 'the sort of guy who gives arrogance a bad name!' So I don't blame you for lashing out at him. The others, though—I have to wonder how much grief they and the organizations they represent can cause you."

Steve shrugged. "Not much. No doubt they'll sharpen their knives for the next time I present a paper at a national meeting, but other than that I don't see how they can hurt me. I'm well past the stage where belonging to a particular society or publishing in a particular journal means much."

"Even so," said Dan, "you might have been a bit more tactful."

"How? Nothing short of firing Okabe would have satisfied them."

"What about Okabe? How's he behaving?"

"Extremely well," said Steve without hesitation. "Quiet as a mouse at staff conferences, but bursting with new ideas when we're alone. I never cease to marvel at how his mind works. He thinks empathically."

"Empathically? I don't understand."

Steve smiled. "Nor did I, at first. But I'm beginning to. I'm sure you've heard it said that great detectives learn to think like criminals. Well, Okabe tries to *think* like a cancer cell. Just the other day, I wandered into his lab and found him gazing out the window. Without turning, without even confirming my presence, he said, 'Stefan, I've been thinking: If I were a cancer cell and given three wishes, what would they be? First, to grow big and strong; to suck dry every blood capillary in my vicinity for the necessary nutrients. Second, to protect myself from my host's defenses. After all, I'm a mutant, a non-self. And being so tiny, I'd either have to find somewhere to hide or disguise myself so I wouldn't be recognized by its cellular police. Later on, when I'm bigger and easier to spot, I'd need protective armor—a fibrin cocoon—to shield me from their immunological bullets. Finally, after gobbling up all the nutrients locally available, I'd invoke my third wish: To spread far and wide, realizing too late that by destroying my host, my food supply, I've also destroyed himself.' An analogy to our nuclear age, eh, Dan? But let's not get into politics."

"Lord no! The threat of getting cancer is depressing enough. But back to Okabe. What else has he come up with?"

"When he gets bored thinking like a cancer—a very simple, very primitive cell type really—he tries to imagine himself an embryo."

"Male or female?" asked Dan, amused.

"Undetermined, as yet, but with this incredible potential to stretch out its primordial DNA millions of miles and grow from one cell into trillions. You see, Dan, there's overwhelming evidence that the cancer process is essentially a crude, misguided attempt to return to fetal life. But something goes awry, some crucial determinant is lacking. So instead of recreating itself as a fetus, it grows into a shapeless, omnivorous mass."

"Any idea what's missing?"

"An organizing or integrating factor of some sort; a blueprint that not only permits a cell to reproduce itself but to mature into something recognizable and useful. Take leukemia, for instance. Recent experiments have shown that one can convert primitive leukemia cells into mature white blood cells by incubating them in a soup of organizing factors extracted from normal lymphocytes."

"Yes," said Dan, "I'm vaguely familiar with that work. Any clinical application?"

"Perhaps for leukemia victims, where you're dealing in part with cells that float free in the blood stream. But the problem of how to supply organizing factors to the densely packed cells of solid tumors is vastly more complex. Nonetheless, the results of those leukemia experiments tend to reinforce my beliefs about the basic nature of cancer. Imagine a robot-operated automobile assembly line that can construct an automobile from its component parts in under six minutes. Without blueprints translated into computer language and fed to the robots, all it would make is junk."

"But from what little I know of oncogenes, cancer cells have blueprints of a sort, don't they?"

"Maybe for the early steps in the assembly process, not the finished product. Still, activation of the oncogene is essential for turning the machinery on. What happens next of course is the crucial question."

"You mean the oncoprotein, or growth factor, or whatever you're calling it these days? How close are you to identifying it?"

Steve gestured uncertainly. "Some days I think my next experiment will give me the answer. Other days it seems as far away as the next century. Being a gene product, the key substance has to be a protein of some sort—but what a protein! The granddaddy of all hormones . . . Speaking of hormones, Dan, how's Gregory Carhill doing?"

"Not so well, I hear. But I seem to have missed something. What's the connection between Carhill and hormones?"

"I've been thinking about his case lately. Remember Modreski, the graduate student I told you about earlier, the one I bumped into in my office after my meeting with the delegation? Well, he's found that as many as fifty percent of pancreatic cancers manufacture and release chorionic gonadotropin—a hormone, as you well know, that's seldom detected in the blood of anyone other than pregnant women."

Dan's brow furrowed. "Why would a pancreatic cancer make that? Because it really wants to be a fetus?"

"Perhaps. But Modreski, who's evidently much smarter than he looks, is accumulating evidence to suggest that chorionic gonadotropin suppresses the immune system to some extent, a necessary step for a cancer to thrive."

"Makes sense," said Dan. "After all, a fetus, with half its chromosomes from its father, is something of a foreign body and must prevent the mother's immune system from rejecting it. But what's all this got to do with Carhill?"

"It might be a good idea for whoever is taking care of him to survey his blood for the presence of any unusual hormones, chorionic gonadotropin in particular. If one is found, it could be useful both as a measure of his cancer's activity and as a potential point of attack."

"An interesting suggestion. I'll pass it on to Yoshio Timura and see what he thinks. Nice of you to be so concerned about your old nemesis."

"Why not?" said Steve sardonically. "He seems to have sustained his interest in me. I have no proof, but I strongly suspect the delegation that descended on me was largely Carhill's doing. Knowing I would never let myself be pressured into firing Okabe, it was his way of making mischief." He sighed. "As if I didn't already have enough on my mind these days."

"So Nicole tells me. She says you're pushing yourself harder than ever."

"She has a right to her opinion, I suppose."

"*Are* you pushing too hard?"

Leaning forward and clenching his fists with determination, Steve said, "I'm so close, Dan! I feel it in my bones. All I need is one key insight, one solid clue, into the nature of the growth factor and the whole picture might become clear to me . . . I don't know exactly how to say this, but I feel as if I've been given a second chance in more ways than one. So how can I stop now or give it less than my all? Why would Nicole even want me stop, since it's her life work, too?"

"Nicole doesn't want you to stop. She just wants

you to pace yourself better. Damn it, Steve, she's a lovely and loving woman; better than you deserve, just as Kris is for me. So let's give them their due. Life's too short to spend it all on problem-solving even if the problem's as important as a cure for cancer."

Steve's pensive expression gave Dan hope that he was getting through to him. But his next words made him wonder if Steve had heard him at all. "You raise an interesting point. Life *is* too short. Did it ever occur to you that cancer might be much more than a scourge? That through it, Nature may actually be trying to tell us the secret of immortality?"

"Immortality, huh? While I'm trying to get you to slow down, you're trying to figure out how to go on working forever!"

"I'm serious."

"I'm sure . . . Just hold the thought while I pour us a refill."

Steve nodded, but instead of pausing while Dan went to the bar, he continued. "Well, as you know from the work of Hayflick and others, human cells are only capable of dividing approximately fifty times. After that, they simply wear out, or else commit suicide by activating a death gene. Cancer cells, on the other hand, are immortal; either they escape such preprogrammed senescence somehow or they lack a self-destruct button. Now, what do you think happens when you fuse an old cell, one on its last legs so to speak, with a cancer cell?"

"I don't know," said Dan, handing him a tumbler of Scotch.

"Some of the time, the normal cell turns cancerous. Other times, it's rejuvenated, able to keep on dividing many more times. What do you think of that?"

"I think it's wonderful, Steve. I think, for some cells and some people, immortality might be just swell. But I have to tell you, there are days when I feel so damned burdened and depressed and fed up with it all, my greatest worry is that there might actually *be* life after death!"

Chapter 27

ALONE IN THE DOWNSTAIRS library of his spacious Chestnut Hill home, Gregory Carhill sat staring at the embers in the fireplace. Lay a shawl round his shoulders and a Bible in his lap, he reflected wryly, and he would be the very picture of a hell-fearing dotard on death's brink. Actually he had on the same three-piece suit he'd worn at dinner with his family and there was a copy of Susan Sontag's *Illness as Metaphor* in his lap.

Unsentimental by nature, Carhill had not so much enjoyed as tolerated the Christmas ritual in previous years. Even tonight, in what might well be the last gathering of his three children and five grandchildren he would ever live to see, he resisted any backsliding into sentimentality. Freud once wrote that it was impossible for an individual to contemplate his own death; that, however he envisioned it, he would still exist as an observer. Without delving into its nuances, Carhill knew this to be true. Except as an event to be postponed as long as possible, he had no clear metaphor for death. Instead, he personified pain. The two had reached an understanding: he would tolerate a lot of it briefly or a little for a long time. In an odd way, its presence made him feel brave and alive. But if pain dared exceed those limits, that would be the end of it. He need only consult an anesthesiologist who would insert a tiny, permanently indwelling plastic catheter into his spinal canal. To it would be attached a miniaturized, battery operated drug pump to continually infuse morphine in amounts too small to impair him physically or mentally but enough to render him pain-free.

You hear that? Carhill warned the twinges he felt. *Then take heed. If you can't control yourself, I'll vanquish you forever.*

He no longer found it queer that he talked to various parts of his body—liver, pancreas, spinal ganglia. They were all in the same leaky boat and without cooperation they would sink into oblivion together. And pain was their most insistent way of talking back. "I think; therefore, I am," may have been appropriate for Descartes; for all his anxieties, he had been a well man. But *I feel; therefore, I am* was more to the point for someone in his situation.

Yet apart from pain or its absence, what *did* he feel? mused Carhill. Regret? Well, yes, but not to any overwhelming degree. He had contributed knowledge to society, helped perpetuate the species, had his share of ups and downs. What more might he have done? What great goals had he missed?

The obvious one, of course, was the Prize. No matter what it demanded of him and his doctors, he was determined to last until October—a mere eight months away, but double the mean survival time for one with his cancer.

A morbidly amusing notion made him chuckle. What if it took an artificial life-support system for him to meet that Nobel Prize requirement; would the selection committee still consider him eligible? Like pro- and anti-abortion groups pitted against one another, he could just picture them wrangling over the murky metaphysics of life versus non-life.

At one time or another Carhill had met all five members of the selection committee. He knew three rather well, and with the exception of Kurt Eliasson, an innovative neurologist and bon vivant, found them unimpressive. Certainly not the Olympian arbiters of talent much of the world believed them to be.

For a scientist, the Nobel wasn't the only prize worth winning. There was the American equivalent, the Lasker Award, and the Israeli government's Wolf Prize. Unlike the stodgy Swedes, the Israeli judges did not shy away from controversy; they might give the Pope their prize if he came up with any solid proof of Genesis. But there was no denying that the one Carhill longed for most was the Nobel.

Pressure from a full bladder cut his reverie short. Struggling up from his easy chair, Carhill lumbered to the hall bathroom to relieve himself.

On his way back to the library he paused briefly in the living room doorway to gaze at the glittering Christmas tree banked by piles of presents. Doubtless there were gifts galore for him—books, jewelry, articles of clothing—their sales slips all carefully filed away in case he should die before Christmas morning and they had to be returned.

Well, he had never been an easy man to please with gifts. Too bad his intolerance for alcohol prevented family and friends from giving the most sensible present for a dying man. Only Yoshio Timura could provide him with the one gift he wanted. Pitifully thin to begin with, Timura had worked so tirelessly on his behalf in recent weeks that there were times when Carhill thought he looked the more likely to expire. He hoped Timura would at least last out the week.

His heroic effort to create a monoclonal antibody to the metastatic factor had reached a crucial point. If this current experiment yielded favorable results, Carhill would insist on receiving the antibody without delay.

Then there was another present in the offing: encouraging word from Zaire on his leukemia vaccine. After only six months of use, it seemed to be fulfilling its promise. By a clinical investigator's cold-blooded stroke of luck, there had been a recent jump in the number of cases of African variety B-cell leukemia among the unvaccinated villagers south of the Congo River and no new cases whatsoever among those vaccinated. It might be pure chance and certainly the numbers were too small for any meaningful conclusions, but the trend was heartening and had not gone unnoticed by the Zairian Minister of Health. Rumor had it that the Zairian government was about to award him a medal. If so, they had better hurry it up. Though he wouldn't be able to accept in person, he would make sure that a press release reached the Stockholm newspapers.

Carhill picked up the Sontag book again, both because it interested him and because he felt he ought to think about something other than the Prize. But his brain was not quite ready for a switch. There was still Stefan Sigourney to consider.

From his unwitting spy, the Pakistani cousin of one of his section chiefs who worked for Sigourney, he knew that his arch rival was busier than ever, though making little apparent progress toward identifying his putative growth factor. In fact, thought Carhill, savoring the image, he seemed to be spinning his wheels, stuck in the ditch that Joshua Okabe had landed him in.

News of the outcome of Sigourney's meeting with the *ad hoc* delegation had not surprised Carhill. He had soured on the whole idea after suggesting it to David Kavachek and wished now it had never come up. Not that he had lost total interest in making life difficult for Stefan Sigourney. Only the other day, Lenore had mentioned that Jill Rockland, a lawyer friend, had met Sigourney in Minorca; the two of them had been patients at the Kosterlitz Clinic. Intrigued, Carhill had urged his wife to invite Rockland to their open house on Sunday so he could find out more details. Intellectually vain though Sigourney was, he'd never before given a damn about his appearance. So why would he spend three months at a health resort? It made no sense, not unless some secret connection existed between Sigourney and the Kosterlitz Clinic. Carhill rather hoped one did; at the least, it would make for amusing gossip.

Hearing the soft ping of the grandfather clock in the living room, Carhill realized it was one a.m. He had kept his promise to his grandchildren to stay up past midnight and tell Santa Claus what presents to leave. But there was no Santa Claus and consequently no cure for his cancer—though how he wished there were!

Yawning deeply, he decided to read a half hour longer and then go to bed.

Chapter 28

HANGING UP THE PHONE after his early morning conversation with Nicole, Steve grabbed his hat and coat from the hall closet and set out for work in a light snowfall. Yesterday bright sunshine, today snow; the February weather was as changeable as his moods. Steve wasn't sure if he was disappointed or relieved to know Nicole could not join him that weekend. Though her absence would give him more time in the lab, it might only heighten his frustration. Exploring the inner workings of a cell was like exploring a jungle; the deeper you moved into its interior, the more impenetrable the tangle. Without Nicole, he would probably not relax at all. Better that, though, than to inflict his irascible moods on her.

There was no denying that since Christmas their relationship had again become strained. His fault, no doubt. Though he had kept his New Year's promise to stay out of the lab when she was in town, his Sunday afternoon discussions with Okabe had grown longer and longer. More often than not, Nicole did not join in, retiring to the den instead to read or analyze data from her own project.

Okabe was getting to be a problem, too. Madge Cohen, the trusted employee he had picked for Okabe's lab supervisor, was giving him disturbing reports. The man was working impossibly long hours. If not wild-eyed, he looked bleary-eyed much of the time. Fearing that, despite the medication he swore he was taking, Okabe was becoming manic again, Steve had forbidden him from working in his lab after eight p.m. But how could he ban Okabe from the library, even though the usually placid librarian complained that he was overwhelming her with demands for obscure foreign-language publications?

Steve had repeatedly urged Okabe to take a vacation, and though agreeing each time, he kept postponing it. So next month he was sending Okabe to an important scientific meeting in Geneva as his personal representative. Which reminded him to give Okabe the newly arrived book of abstracts to study. Steve made a mental note to do it right after the weekly inter-departmental conference that morning. Maybe if one of his teams reported favorable results, it would put him in a better mood.

As it turned out, the staff meeting only brought more frustration, and Okabe wasn't even there. Afterward, Steve strode up to Madge Cohen and demanded: "Where's Okabe?"

"I don't know," she said as they walked along. "But the lab was a mess when I came in this morning. Looked like the coffee pot had boiled over, among other things."

"You think he was there all night?"

"Sure looks that way."

"But—but . . ." Steve spluttered.

"I know, Dr. Sigourney, and I'm sorry it happened. But I've got a family to take care of and he's a grown man. I can't be his keeper!"

Steve entered Okabe's lab ahead of her. It was empty and he swung around, scowling. Then, seeing John Wendall coming out of his next door lab, he asked, "John, have you seen Joshua this morning?"

"Briefly. He was coming out of the building as I went in."

"Out? Out where?"

"Out of his mind, probably," snapped Wendall. "He certainly looked it. No hat, no coat, nothing but a sweater and a scarf and that clipboard he always totes around."

Steve stared. "Are you serious, John? Forget personal antagonisms for the moment. You know his history."

Wendall nodded. "He did look strange—stranger than usual. If he didn't get back soon, I was going to tell you."

"*Thank you* for telling me now," said Steve coldly. Then, to Madge Cohen, "Be sure to let me know the moment he returns."

In his outer office, Steve told his secretary, "Please call Dr. Okabe's apartment to see if he's there," and waited by the window while she dialed. The snowfall was growing heavier. "Well?" he asked a minute later.

"No answer, Dr. Sigourney."

"Damn!" he muttered and went into his office. It would be futile to try to concentrate on anything else while he was so worried about Okabe. Madge Cohen knew his schedule; she would have told him if Joshua had any outside appointments that morning. So where could he be?

Suddenly Steve remembered Okabe saying that he got some of his best ideas watching the sun rise; his favorite spot was the park half a mile away. Nobody could have seen the sun behind this morning's snow clouds, but better to look than to wonder, Steve concluded.

"Stefan! I can't believe it!" cried Okabe as he encountered Steve at the entrance to the park. "Just this instant I decided to go see you and as if by magic, you appear!"

"No magic. I came looking for you. Why weren't you at the staff conference? What are you doing here?" A sheepish expression came over Okabe's face and Steve exploded, "Good God, man, look at you! Snow in your hair, sticking to your sweater. If I didn't know you, I'd think you were a bum looking for a handout. Damn it, Joshua, with all my other problems, I don't need you acting crazy!"

"Crazy? Is *that* what you think?" Okabe shrugged. "It may be, but the truth is I've never felt more sane."

"Fine," Steve snapped. "I'm happy to hear it. Only let's discuss it in my office."

"Wait!" cried Okabe as Steve turned to leave. "There's something I must tell you now, while it's still together in my mind. Something that needs your total attention. Let's go for coffee around the corner."

"Wherever," said Steve, shivering, "as long as it's got a roof and a stove."

"All right," said Steve, a cup of cafeteria coffee in his hand. "What's this all about? And why were you in your lab all night? I've warned you about that."

"I know, and I didn't mean to. But last night I got to thinking about a new approach to the problem that has us stymied and needed my notes from the lab. Once there, I simply lost track of the time. Then around six or seven this morning, my thoughts all came together in some sort of glorious harmony. I tell you, Stefan, it was wonderful! Like cerebral bells chiming! I tried to phone you, but the line was busy.

So I went for a walk. I'm sorry about the staff meeting. I completely forgot. Even now, my brain's in something of a whirl . . . How to explain?"

"Why not calmly and simply?" said Steve. "No reason to get flustered. It's just a friendly discussion."

"You don't understand; you don't realize the importance of what I'm trying to communicate!" Suddenly Okabe's face brightened. "That's it! The analogy I was looking for. Take what we're doing right now: one speaks, the other listens. How? Through ears—receptors of sound. But voice-ear is a primitive way to communicate. If you were in your apartment and I in mine, we'd use the telephone, a more sophisticated system. If you were here and I in the Nigerian bush, we might use radio, more sophisticated yet. And just as people have different means of communication, so do cells. After all, they must talk to one another somehow, by an endocrine system 'radio' or a paracrine system 'telephone.' But how do embryonic cells, who have no heart, circulatory system or nerve network as yet, communicate? Do you see what I'm getting at?"

"Haven't a clue," said Steve tolerantly. "Maybe if you gave me the gist of your idea first, then explained it . . ."

Okabe drew a breath. "All right. We've spent almost four months now searching frantically for a growth factor unique to cancer cells that may or may not exist. Well, even if it does, it may be of only secondary importance."

"Secondary to what?"

"To the cancer cell's primitive communication system, the one between membrane and nucleus. *That's* what we ought to be concentrating on!"

"You mean receptors? Is that what this almost incoherent chatter is all about?"

"Exactly. What good is the most powerful radio transmitter in the world without receiving sets? Or, more to the point, a cancer-causing growth factor without cell membrane receptors to fit it? That's where we may have gone wrong in our thinking, Stefan! Instead of the growth factor, what if the oncogene coded for something even more special—a protein key that unlocked the door of its receptor, opened it wide enough to receive growth factor molecules that may have been around all the time but targetless, unable to act elsewhere. Then, once the two fit together, a signal is sent to the nucleus to divide."

Impatiently Steve said, "I still don't see . . ."

"Wait! Let me explain a bit further. The special receptor I envision is only open during fetal life; it must be to permit such rapid cell growth. Then, as soon as the fetus reaches a certain size, it snaps shut and stays shut unless, perhaps, some massive tissue injury occurs that requires repair. Wouldn't a flood of keys from an oncogene, special keys that open the receptor in such a way that it can't close again, create havoc?"

"Perhaps," conceded Steve. "But how do you study such a system?"

"Ah, that's the question that had me stumped, sent me to the textbooks to learn all I possibly could about embryology. But the information simply wasn't there. So instead of concentrating on the patriarch, the fetal-cell receptor, I began looking for what you might call its progeny—those receptors that persist into adult life because they're needed for cellular repair."

"And you found one?"

"Yes! It's not ideal, but it may do for a start. I'll show you the references when we get back to the institute."

Steve sipped his coffee. "Good. But before you go on, let me make sure I've understood what you've said so far. That unlike the endocrine system; where hormones released into the blood stream transmit cellular messages over long distances, the embryo—and by analogy the cancer cell—uses a much more primitive system to communicate between its outside and inside worlds. And since the crucial component to this system is the cell membrane receptor, it's likely that the oncogene codes for a protein that affects this, making it accessible to the growth factor—the combination of the two firing an inappropriate or excessively strong signal to the cell nucleus to divide."

Okabe nodded.

"Therefore the supposedly unique growth factor we've been searching for may not be so unique, after all; instead, it may be the receptor-opening protein that's unique?"

At Okabe's second nod, Steve sighed, "All right. I have problems with that theory, but I'm willing to be convinced. One thing, though: I want your solemn promise. No more night work! And I'm still sending you to Geneva next month. Despite all you've accomplished, I want no further challenges to my hard-won reputation as chief eccentric around here, understood?"

Okabe grinned. "You have my word. And I'll go to Geneva gladly. Just tell me this—do you think there's a chance I'm right?"

"Frankly, I think you're all wet."

"Oh?" Okabe looked crestfallen.

"Snow melts in warm environments, you know. Go home and change. I'll see you in my office in an hour."

Chapter 29

NAUSEA RACKED CARHILL'S STOMACH as he sat at the breakfast table contemplating the poached eggs on his plate. They looked like a pair of giant, enucleated cat eyes, he thought. What was making him so nauseated—cancer or just plain fear?

A nightmare had wakened him permanently around four that morning. In it, an injection from an incredibly sinister-looking Yoshio Timura had bubbled through his blood until it blew the top of his head off. His skull had literally exploded, bits of hair, bone, brain matter, flying in every direction. The memory made Carhill shudder.

For weeks he had looked forward to receiving the monoclonal antibody to the metastatic factor that Timura had created for him. It was his last and best hope. He had wanted to receive the infusion at once, but Yoshio insisted he wait until his team could purify the antibody further, making it less likely to provoke an allergic reaction. At last they had done so, and at ten this morning, in the large animal surgical lab at the Bethune Institute, with perhaps a dozen physicians and scientists in attendance, Carhill would make medical history again.

At the Bethune Institute, Yoshio Timura could not finish breakfast either. Not even Ted Swerdloff's calm presence could quell his jitters. Though other medical doctors, including Slater, the surgeon, would be present when he infused the MF-12 antibody into his superior, Swerdloff was the only one he felt he could confide his fears to. Timura remained silent until Swerdloff had wolfed down his eggs and bacon. Then, with a glance at the cafeteria clock, he said, "We should leave now. Dr. Carhill will be arriving any minute."

"I'm ready," said Ted. "Let's go."

Timura started to rise, but stopped. With jaw trembling, he asked, "Are you certain, absolutely certain, we've taken every conceivable precaution?"

Ted smiled and gave the same reassuring answer he had five minutes before. "Relax, Yoshio. The main danger, as you well know, is an allergic reaction to the mouse-derived antibody and I simply can't think of any counter measures we've overlooked."

"An allergic reaction?" repeated Timura as if hearing of it for the first time. "Yesss," he hissed, "I worry about that greatly. What do I do then?"

"Just step aside and let Slater and his team take over. But I'm telling you, Yoshio, chances of anything like that happening are pretty remote . . ."

Carhill reckoned the odds against a life-threatening allergic reaction the same way as he lay on a padded metal table in the animal surgery room. His nausea had receded for the moment and he felt remarkably calm. Being the center of attention was a familiar experience, but being an object of pity was not, and he tried to ignore the circle of familiar faces peering down at him by fixing his gaze on the operating table spotlight.

At last, the bent heads parted to permit Yoshio Timura to approach with a large syringe in hand. Carhill tried to say something encouraging to his protege, but his mouth was too dry. Instead, he managed a smile.

Sweat beading his forehead, Timura attached the syringe to a connection in the intravenous tube dripping a balanced salt solution into Carhill's arm vein and slowly injected its contents. The circle of faces bent closer, but no one spoke. For almost a full minute, the only sound Carhill heard was the steady, reassuring beep of his heart monitor. Finally Timura asked, "You all right, Dr. Carhill?"

"Fine. Just . . ." Suddenly the air in Carhill's lungs seemed to grow heavy, harder to push out; he had to grunt and strain to expel it. Faintly he heard the beeps from his heart monitor speed up and grow irregular, as if someone was sending a message in Morse code, until the roaring in his ears drowned it out. Something had gone wrong, he thought. Opening his mouth, he shouted a warning at Yoshio, but no words came out. It was as though a gag obstructed his oral cavity, growing larger and larger until it began blocking his windpipe. His right hand flew to his throat, pulling the attached IV pole and bottle with it. A firm yank ripped the needle from his wrist vein. Vaguely Carhill realized what he had done but told himself it didn't matter; he had to do something to remove whatever was suffocating him, never realizing it was his own massively swollen tongue.

Suddenly the circle of faces above him dissolved into blurs of motion. A babble of voices penetrated the roaring in his ears. Out of it he managed to understand two words: *anaphylactic shock*.

Of course, thought Carhill, unable to move or

breathe, but giving up the struggle. As if more observer than victim, he understood exactly what was happening to him. His bodily defenses, under the evil influence of his cancer, had resisted the intruding antibodies in the most extreme way possible: by closing down all portals of entry—throat, larynx, bronchial tubes, blood vessels. Instead of cancer, allergic shock was going to kill him. He had seen patients go that way before, gasping, thrashing about, turning blue, clutching their throats as if to try to loosen some strangling cord, seemingly in the most horrible agony. But now that it was actually happening to him, Carhill knew such appearances were deceptive. Inwardly, it wasn't agonizing at all. It was . . . rather peaceful . . . .

"Jesus!" groaned Dan Lassiter later that morning in his office as Swerdloff described the calamity that had befallen Carhill. "What happened next?"

"They pumped him full of epinephrine and cortisone. I thought he was a goner for sure when his heart stopped. Though nothing was said at the time, Ed Slater later confessed that for a moment he had serious doubts whether he ought to even try to resuscitate him. But he went ahead anyway."

Dan sighed. "A familiar dilemma . . . Too bad about Carhill though. Sounds like he's reached the end of the line."

"Most likely. But . . . maybe not. I passed on your suggestion about surveying Carhill's blood for oddball hormones to Yoshio and he followed through on it."

"Not *my* suggestion, Steve Sigourney's," Dan corrected. "But go on. What did he find?"

"High titers of human chorionic gonadotropin."

"Hmm. That's interesting—though, I suppose, strictly academic at this point."

Swerdloff shrugged. "Maybe not. Look at it this way, Dan. If *only* Carhill's cancer cells are making chorionic gonadotropin, as seems a fair assumption, that's a difference we may be able to exploit, say by making a precursor to the hormone, one that would be picked up preferentially by the cancer, and then loading it up with radioactive bombs."

"Ted, between the two of us, wouldn't it be more humane just to stop? Let the man die in peace?"

"That's for Carhill, not us, to say."

"Think he will after what happened this morning?"

"Who knows? He's tough, tenacious, and more than willing to experiment on himself. What would you do in his place—have yourself a last fling? Or use the resources of the hospital you run to the fullest in hopes of a cure?"

Dan reflected and shook his head. "I don't know. I don't even like to think about it. Which is why I'm calling a halt to this conversation and getting back to work. I'll let Steve Sigourney know what happened and if he has any more suggestions I'll pass them on."

Apart from conventional regrets, Steve expressed no other sentiments when Dan phoned about Carhill that evening. But in the subsequent small talk, Dan sensed an exuberance in Steve's voice that he finally got around to explaining: results from the first set of experiments testing the validity of Okabe's receptor theory were just in and highly promising. It looked at last as if his team was on the right track and might be first across the finish line.

"How long before you'll know?" asked Dan.

"For one man in one lab, it would probably take years. But running ten labs as I do, I hope to have the proof in a few months."

"That's wonderful, Steve. But I'm still not clear on one thing: do the cancer-causing genes you're studying code for the growth factor or for the receptor-opening protein?"

"A good question. It's already split the workers around here into two camps."

"What do *you* think?"

"I'm sticking with my original theory for the time being, mainly to provide Okabe with a loyal opposition . . . Ah, here he is now, fresh from the library and ready to do battle again. Say hello to Kris for me, Dan. We'll talk again soon."

Steve was in the same high-spirited mood when Nicole joined him in Philadelphia the following Friday. To her surprise, he met her at the train station, whisked her off to a special exhibit of Chinese art at the University Museum and then to dinner at a small, charming French restaurant. Though delighted, she was puzzled and a little annoyed when he refused to divulge the cause of his euphoria. Her curiosity was further whetted when he mentioned that Okabe would not be dropping by Sunday—too busy in the lab—and would not elaborate.

Later that evening after love-making as tender and satisfying as they had ever known, she sighed, "God, I love you, love you, *love* you! . . . But I won't be put off any longer. I know something's happened—you haven't been in this good a mood for months—but what? It can't be another woman; even if it is, I can only be grateful to her for the change in you. The Nobel Prize winners won't be announced till October. And you can't have come into a fortune; you already have one. So it has to be something in the lab . . . No, don't touch me there. It's my curiosity, not my libido, that needs to be satisfied. Tell me, damn you! Oh, *please* tell me, Stefan!"

Steve laughed at the girlish plaint in her tone, but still said nothing.

"Are you going to tell me or not?"

"Tell you the greatest scientific secret of the decade, possibly the century? How do I know you can be trusted? That you're not some kind of medical Mata Hari?" Steve teased. "After all, the people you work for, your government employers, would pay a bundle for such information. With it, they could wheedle more millions out of Congress. They might even force it out of you. You say you love me, love me, *love* me, but how well could you stand torture?"

"Better than this drivel!" sighed Nicole. "All right, *don't* tell me. I don't care." She shrugged, pouted, then slowly smiled. "Just give me a little hint."

"That would be like giving a hungry cat a whiff of frying fish."

"I could resent that comparison—resent *you*—but I won't. I won't even harp on the fact that we once promised to tell each other everything. . . No, don't touch me!" Rolling away from him, she seized a pillow and turned on her side.

"All right, a hint," Steve sighed. "In seven weeks, at the American Cancer Society meeting in Washington, I'll be giving one of the state-of-the-art lectures, supposedly on monoclonal antibodies. But if Okabe and I are right, if our new theory of cancer cell receptors pans out, I'll be reporting on that and it could be memorable. There's nothing more to say until we collect enough data for a paper. When it's written, I promise you'll be the first person I show it to."

As he spoke, Steve returned his hand to her inner thigh. Nicole tried to ignore it, but felt herself becoming aroused. "When do you think you'll have it ready?" she asked in a quavering voice.

"With luck, another month."

"All right. I'll just have to wait until then. In the meanwhile, either quit what you're doing to me or do it all!"

The weeks passed like a dream for Steve. It was his

happiest time ever in research. With word of new discoveries rippling through the ranks almost daily, old antagonisms and feuds were forgotten in a harmony of shared purpose. Even the resident iconoclast, John Wendall, was caught up in it and willingly collaborated with Okabe on certain projects. For the first time in years, the Friday interdepartmental conferences were fully attended and often ran hours overtime. By popular demand, Steve began holding them twice a week; even then, he could not fit in all the team reports. He tried to guard against overconfidence. As he had learned early in his career, Nature has a devilish way of rebuking the unwary, the driven, the disrespectful. But as favorable evidence mounted, he too began to succumb.

At eight every morning, Steve and his sections chiefs met to review and plan that day's activities. He encouraged those with literary ambitions to keep personal diaries. If cancer was finally to be conquered, it was essential that accurate accounts be kept of all aspects of the campaign. Steve's only regret was that Andre Evashevsky was not there to share in the excitement. In his letters, Steve repeatedly urged him to cut short his sabbatical year in Paris and rejoin them. But Evashevsky, well aware of Okabe's rising star at the institute, refused.

The evening before Okabe was to leave for Geneva, Steve gave a small party for him. He hoped it would be well attended by senior staff and it was—final proof of Okabe's redemption and acceptance.

Midway through the festivities, Okabe took him aside and asked, "What should or shouldn't I tell the gathering in Geneva about our work?"

Steve shrugged. "Tell them whatever you like. We're far enough ahead of the pack by now that it wouldn't matter."

"They won't believe me anyhow."

"Probably not," said Steve, perceiving the hint of

sadness in Okabe's smile. "But if we're right, Joshua, they'll wish they had. You know you'll receive full credit for your contributions in all our papers."

"I know," said Okabe, "and I'm grateful. But what matters most to me is that I've been of some small service to you—your program."

"Not so small," Steve corrected. "Though I still think you're wrong about the receptor activity being more important than the growth factor."

"So I've heard," said Okabe with a grin. "It's certainly courageous of you."

"Courageous? Why?"

"To go on defending such a vulnerable position in the face of an avalanche of facts!"

"Facts?" scoffed Steve. "Facts are supposed to be hard, Joshua. Like steel. Not those putty-soft creations you keep coming up with to plug the holes in your theory. Take your rather naive concept of autophosphorylation, for instance . . ." As Steve propounded his argument, his guests began to gather round. It didn't surprise him. Their colleagues, particularly the younger ones, liked nothing better than to hear him argue with Okabe. It was like a prize fight between the champion and the leading contender. This latest bout, begun in relative sobriety at nine p.m, ended two hours later when their panel of self-appointed judges halted it on the grounds that both contestants had grown drunk and repetitious.

Throughout the week Okabe was gone, Steve worked hard on the paper he was going to give at the American Cancer Society meeting. Though the data he decided to include achieved spectacular levels of statistical significance, its interpretation was another matter. How far dare he go before so critical a group? He could always hedge, pepper his discussion with choice phrases from the compendium of ambiguous and obfuscatory remarks, but he was loath to do it. It would be like describing Nicole as rather pleasant-looking rather than breathtakingly beautiful. And there was a sort of beauty to Okabe's receptor theory. If true (and Steve had few remaining doubts) it meant that the critical step in the cancer process was external, at the cell membrane level where a variety of therapeutic bullets could reach it, and not so deeply buried inside the nucleus as to be practically invulnerable. It could—*would*—open the door to all kinds of new treatment approaches.

On Thursday, Steve labored past midnight to complete the first draft of his paper. Marta would type it up in the morning and he would present it triumphantly to Nicole that evening. He could hardly wait for her to read it.

When finally she did, Steve was tense as a first time father-to-be in the waiting room of a maternity ward. He tried to sit quietly across the room and peruse a medical journal, but it was no use; he felt too fidgety. Maybe the data wasn't as convincing as he thought. Maybe he had gone overboard in some of his conclusions . . . Why was Nicole frowning? Because she didn't understand something or didn't agree with it?

At last, seemingly hours, not minutes, after she had begun, Nicole finished reading, sighed deeply and lay the manuscript aside. Looking across the room at him, she smiled.

"Well?"

"Parts of it are brilliant, Stefan. Simply brilliant. But . . . there are problems."

Chapter 30

LIKE A FIRE REKINDLED BY periodic bursts of wind, their argument went on into the early morning hours. Though Steve tried to keep his emotions in check, he seethed with hurt pride. His ill advised attempt to make love did not help matters. Hardened by hostility, he entered her too quickly and thrust too deep. Nicole received him with stony silence. He had opened his eyes, seen he was inflicting pain, not pleasure, and withdrawn. Now, lying apart from her in bed trying futilely to sleep, he felt doubly frustrated.

He himself had taught her the cardinal rule of the Persian rug weaver: *Never leave loose ends for busybodies to tug on, lest the entire rug unravel.* Admittedly, there were loose ends to his thesis—minor ones. Why couldn't Nicole see that? Because she had been misled by the lesser talents of the National Cancer Institute? Hollis Reed, an able but too cautious investigator, was obviously a bad influence. Despite her long hours in the lab, Nicole was little more than

Reed's technician, seldom given any opportunity for original work. For her to take issue with him on theory would be like Brahms' piano-tuner disputing the maestro's construction of a symphony. Though he would never be so crude as to tell her this, she must know. So why wouldn't she just admit she was too inexpert to offer a valid opinion?

She had, of course, several times. Only her disclaimers were too general. To bolster his ego, Steve needed her to yield on specific points.

"All right," he spoke aloud without really intending to, "let's take up the matter of tyrosine phosphorylation one last time . . ."

"Oh, Stefan, *please!*" she groaned. "I'm really exhausted, aren't you? Try to sleep."

"I have tried. No use. Not until we get one thing settled."

"If only it were just *one* thing . . . . But obviously you won't be satisfied until I concede each and every point!" Suddenly she sat up and stared accusingly at him. "What do you really want from me? Total, slavish submission to your superior intellect? Is that what will make you feel secure again? All right, you have it! I hereby amend my initial opinion: It's not parts of your paper but *all* of it that's brilliant! The most brilliant scientific synthesis since Newton's Laws or Avery's work on DNA. The scientific world is yours, the Nobel Prize is yours, and *I'm* yours! Now can we please get some sleep?"

"If only Okabe had been here to answer some of your technical criticisms. He knows the new chromatographic procedures better than I. I really wish he were here . . ."

"Where?" she cried exasperatedly. "In bed with us? He is, Stefan! He has been for weeks and weeks."

"What's that supposed to mean?"

"You want me to put it more graphically? I almost feel his . . . Oh, never mind! Just forget it."

"No, go ahead; be as graphic as you like. Tell me."

"Stefan, I've taken a lot from you tonight, but I won't be provoked into being a complete bitch. You know my feelings about Joshua; you have all along. Personally I like the man; I admire your attempt to rehabilitate him. But don't you see what's happened? He lives only for you—to please you, to justify your faith in him. You're his love object, his god! No, don't shake your head. I know the signs only too well; I once felt the same way about you. And you—you're so touched by such loyalty, such devotion, you'll go to almost any length to reward it, even to reach conclusions favorable to his theory that are unsupported by facts. Don't you see, Stefan, it's excessive. It could backfire. Instead of restoring Okabe's scientific reputation, you might destroy it forever. And your own."

"Perhaps," he admitted. "But my every instinct tells me we're right. For the first time ever, I can look beyond the next ridge, the next set of experiments, and see the peak. After so many years, so long a climb, would you really have me creep, not run, to it? I can't quarrel with the extra experiments you suggest. But that's the long way. It might take years, and word is already out about our new receptor theory. What's to stop a rival group from doing a few quick experiments, adding a conceptual wrinkle or two, and rushing into print to claim the theory as their own? It's been done before, you know."

"I'm not asking that, Stefan. Go ahead and present your data. Publish it. But let others, not you, draw the sweeping conclusions. Just having Joshua Okabe as co-author will draw criticism enough."

Grudgingly Steve nodded. "In a wishful sort of way, I'd hoped to overwhelm the critics by the sheer beauty of the receptor theory." He paused to rub his eyes. "I still want to . . . and I will! I won't let your jealousy of Okabe dissuade me."

"Jealousy?" Nicole drew back. "Is *that* what you think?"

"What else can I think after your insinuations a moment ago? If not jealous, what?"

She shrugged sadly. "Honest concern. Caring enough about you to risk your temporary displeasure —or *is* it temporary? Perhaps I've outlived my usefulness. It's almost April now and I haven't heard a word about that July marriage we talked about at the airport in Barcelona . . . But maybe it's just as well. I'm a bit tired of having to adjust to your wild mood swings. Two weeks ago you were so high you exhausted me, sexually and otherwise. Tonight, one wrong word from me and you plummet like a punctured ballon."

It was at this point that Steve made a disastrous mistake. Nicole's mention of Barcelona had somehow reminded him of Evashevsky's work on cell membrane ATP*ase*, a point that he had neglected to include in the discussion section of his paper. Brooding on the oversight, he did not hear Nicole ask if he still wanted to marry her.

"Well?" she snapped, stung by his silence. "Do you or don't you?"

"Do I what?" he replied absently.

Five minutes later, despite all his conciliatory efforts, she was dressed and gone.

The next morning Steve tried repeatedly to reach her by telephone. He should have gone after her, he reproached himself. He should have swallowed his pride and risked public embarrassment, rejection—anything—to show how remorseful he was, how much he cared.

By five p.m., after a wasted day at the institute, Steve was so frantic to speak to her he was on the verge of calling Hollis Reed to inquire about Nicole's whereabouts, even to ask Reed to intercede on his behalf. But he couldn't quite bring himself to do it.

He decided instead that if he failed to contact her that night, he would take the first train to Washington the next morning to beg her forgiveness in person.

Steve slept so fitfully that he woke feeling as if he hadn't slept at all. At Union Station by seven a.m., he bought a Sunday *New York Times* to read on the train. Listlessly, he sat with the thick newspaper on his lap until the conductor punched his ticket. Then he began to leaf through its inside sections. Suddenly he grunted as if he had been struck a heavy blow in the stomach. There, on the cover of the Sunday magazine section, his image constructed from thousands of variously shaded dots, was the grinning face of Joshua Okabe sandwiched between the masthead and the caption: THE FRAUD THAT FOOLED CANCER RESEARCHERS—AND MAYBE STILL DOES?

With trembling fingers, Steve turned to the story and was sickened further on learning that it was written by Damon Frick, a deceptively mild mannered man with an odd turtle-like shape: disproportionately small head and short limbs attached to a rotund body. Frick was a freelance science writer who had once interviewed Steve. Actually he hadn't come off sounding too badly, thanks largely to having being forewarned of Frick's reputation for viciousness and duplicity.

Opening with the Abraham Lincoln cliche about fooling people, the article was long, pretentiously erudite, and scornful of both Okabe and the "top experts" he had duped. The unscrupulous Frick had even wrangled an interview with a male psychiatric nurse who allegedly had befriended Okabe during his locked-ward hospitalization at Faulkner. Some friend! He made Joshua appear not only deranged but diabolical, the maddest of mad scientists.

Too angry to be fearful, Steve raced to the portion of the article involving him. Frick did not disappoint.

Not once did he use Sigourney's name without such modifiers as "eccentric," "reclusive" or "driven." Though irked by it, Steve knew that his innuendo about the Sigourney Institute's "mysterious financial support" was too vague to be libelous, and he found it ironically amusing that even with help from Carhill, Kavachek and Max Kreisberg, Frick had failed completely to figure out why he had ever employed an apparent lunatic like Okabe. The search for scientific truth had apparently never been considered.

With his American Cancer Society lecture a week away, the Frick exposé couldn't have come at a worse time, Steve reflected. Still, for him it was merely one more complication; for Okabe, it could be a devastating setback.

Poor Joshua. Due back on Tuesday, and this waiting for him. How would he react? Withdraw deep within himself, as in his first days at the institute —or worse? Steve considered phoning him in Geneva with some pretext to keep him in Europe and away from *New York Times* readers a while longer. It would only delay the inevitable, of course, but at least it would be something positive to do.

Trying to stave off gloom, Steve thought of Nicole. He could hardly wait to see her, hold her, convince her by any means possible, including immediate marriage, that he loved and needed her. Never again, he vowed, would he let the pressures and frustrations of work diminish his joy in her.

Arriving by cab at her Bethesda apartment, Steve let himself into the building with the extra set of keys Nicole had given him. If she meant to turn him away, she'd have to do it on her very doorstep. But even that dismal prospect faded as he pressed her doorbell again and again. If she was asleep, why didn't she wake up? If she was home, why didn't she answer? Worriedly he thrust the key in the lock and turned it.

The one-bedroom apartment was empty; her bed hadn't been slept in. Dejectedly Steve turned and trudged back to the elevator.

The train back to Philadelphia was packed and noisy, preventing any possibility of sleep. The ride seemed endless. Numb with fatigue and disappointment, Steve tried not to think at all. He had already phoned Joshua in Geneva and persuaded him to stay in Europe another two weeks. There was nothing more he could think of to do for either Okabe or Nicole. For himself, all he wanted was sleep.

But he had no sooner returned to his apartment when Nicole phoned. "Where are you?" he rasped. "Are you all right?"

"Yes, fine. I spent the last two nights in New York with a friend—a *female* friend . . . Did you see today's *New York Times?* Oh, I hope you did! I'd rather not be the one to . . ."

"I saw it," he interrupted.

"Stefan, I'm sorry. After some of the things I said about Joshua Friday night, you might not think so, but I really *am* sorry—about that and other things."

Steve nodded, as if she could see him. A part of him longed to tell Nicole that he forgave her, that he had even gone to Washington to beg *her* forgiveness, but a more prideful part restrained him. The day's tumultuous events had left him too drained to cope with more emotion. His need to be alone and at peace so overwhelmed that he wanted to shout, *Enough! I have nothing left to offer you!*

"Stefan? Are you there?"

Her voice seemed to come out of a dream. He didn't answer.

"Stefan, please!" she implored. "Speak to me!"

Don't you see, he remembered her saying about Okabe, *you're his love object, his god. I know only too well; I once felt the same way about you . . .* It was too much, he thought. Too big a burden. Better to be alone, a disappointment only to himself.

"Goodbye, Nicole," he said wearily and hung up.

Chapter 31

ON THE AFTERNOON OF THE American Cancer Society meeting, Dan Lassiter had planned to reach Washington by two, get together privately with Steve at the Shoreham Hotel at three, and then hear his lecture there at four. But heavy rain along the East Coast delayed his flight and he did not land at National Airport until three-thirty. The long line of cab seekers would have held him up even further if Jimmy Dallesio had not been on hand to meet him.

Slender, slouch-shouldered, perpetually squinting at the world through thick-lensed eyeglasses, Jimmy's physical appearance belied his importance as a Pulitzer Prize-winning columnist whose column was syndicated in over two hundred newspapers. Though he divided his time between Boston and Washington, Jimmy was Dan's closest friend. With ties extending over two decades, each considered the other "family."

Outside the terminal, Dan asked, "You driving, or

—I pray—a chauffeur?" Actually Jimmy was a good, safe driver made cautious by poor eyesight.

"A chauffeur."

"Good. Lead me to him and let's hope he can get us to the Shoreham by four."

"In this soup? We'll be lucky to get over the Fourteenth Street bridge by then!"

Dan scowled. "Damn! I really wanted to be there on time. Think you can get us a ride in a patrol car?"

"Sure. Just expose yourself. Or smash a window—though they'll probably want to stop off and introduce you around the precinct." Stepping to the curb, Jimmy beckoned and a sleek black Cadillac rolled toward them.

"Better," said Dan. "Much better."

"All right," said Jimmy after he had directed the driver, promised to pay any traffic fines incurred en route, and turned to Dan in the roomy back seat. "Reassure me that the reason you're dragging me to the Shoreham to hear this Steve Sigourney is that he's going to announce a cure for cancer."

"Did I say that?" replied Dan innocently.

"Come to my office. I'll play you the tape."

"Well, I doubt if I used the word *cure*, but I admit to something like that. How else could I get you to a lecture on the molecular basis of carcinogenesis? And after last Sunday's *Times* story, Steve needs all the good publicity he can get. Aside from that, I honestly think he's made the basic discoveries that will someday lead to a cure."

"How soon?"

"Oh, in our lifetime."

"I'll give him ten years. After that, I'm going to really raise hell with you about this."

"Fair enough. But Steve's talk today is only half your story. The other half will be the audience's reaction. A lot of them don't want to see anybody, especially an independent operator like Sigourney, win the cancer sweepstakes. It could cost them their grants or their jobs."

Reaching the Shoreham at 4:15, they hurried to the ballroom on the mezzanine floor. To Dan's relief, the afternoon session was behind schedule. Its chairman, Dr. Arnold Axelrod, was just in the process of introducing Steve to the vast audience when he and Jimmy took up places against the back wall. Diagonally across the room, Dan could see Steve, speech in hand, standing at the far end of the front row waiting for Axelrod to finish before mounting the podium. At a table immediately above Steve sat the honorary chairman of the session, 1937 Nobel laureate Dr. Albert Szent-Gyorgyi, looking alert and fit at ninety. Feeling his muscles grow tense, Dan realized he was empathizing with Steve. He knew from their phone conversations what a hellish week Steve had been through and was pulling hard for him to triumph.

In contrast, Steve himself felt an almost trance-like calm. He had given dozens of such lectures before and considered this one no different. Moreover, the pressures of the last three days and nights had been so great that he had barely had time to think, let alone worry. The new findings from Wendall's and Jorgeson's labs reported to him on Tuesday had been a godsend, not only for their thrilling implications but by distracting him from his personal problems. Steve did not feel he had exaggerated when he confided to Dan Lassiter that their combined data supplied the last missing piece to the cancer jigsaw puzzle. Just in the nick of time, too, since it saved him from a major mistake.

At the time Steve had shown the manuscript of his talk to Nicole, he, like Okabe, was more or less convinced that overproduction of the receptor-opening protein was the crucial step in the cancer process, and the still elusive growth factor of lesser importance. Now, based on these latest findings, he knew that a second oncogene, the one coding for the growth factor, had to be turned on as well before a cell turned cancerous. Thus, the "two gene hypothesis."

At last, Axelrod finished reading highlights from Steve's career resume and beckoned him onto the podium. He stopped for a warm handshake from Szent-Gyorygi, whom he had first met in their native Hungary in his youth and long admired, then stood beside the lectern while Axelrod attached his neck microphone.

He arranged his papers, drew a breath, and turned to Axelrod. "Thank you, Mr. Chairman, for your kind introduction. Thank you also for permitting my last minute change in subject matter.

"Dr. Szent-Gyorgyi, colleagues, ladies and gentlemen. Instead of sticking to my assigned topic of monoclonal antibody therapy, I'd like to take this rare opportunity to present new findings from my institute that has led us to formulate a unified theory of cancer causation . . ."

A murmur swept through the audience. From the whispers on either side of him, Dan was uncertain whether it denoted anticipation, disapproval, or merely surprise.

In a fast-paced forty minute talk, Steve took his audience step by step through the reasoning behind his new theory. Though Dan was no researcher and got lost at times in the complexities of molecular biology, he was soon caught up in the web Steve spun out of speculation and hard data, and marvelled at its clarity. Checking from time to time, Dan found that even Jimmy could follow the gist of Steve's argument, though he repeatedly reminded Dan of his promise to explain it all in lay language later.

" . . . In conclusion," said Steve, "it's my belief,

based on the admittedly incomplete evidence I have presented, that the focus of the cancer-causing process is not the cell nucleus, as long supposed, but rather the more accessible cell membrane. Once damage to the control regions of at least two oncogenes, one coding for the receptor-activator and one for the growth factor, occurs, a chain of cell-transforming events is set in motion.

"Obviously, much more work needs be done before this two-gene process is fully delineated and clinical counter-measures devised. Yet, as I hope you'll agree, its formulation represents another step forward. Perhaps—to paraphrase Winston Churchhill—not merely the end of the beginning but the beginning of the end—for cancer."

As Steve paused, several members of the audience, responding to what they mistook to be his dramatic close, applauded. Holding up his hands to quiet them, he quipped, "I ran out of breath, not words. . . One final one: Many outstanding talents at my institute contributed to this work and I would like to acknowledge and thank them. Last slide please. . . ."

Dan winced slightly at Joshua Okabe's name heading the list; he feared it might blunt the impact of Steve's talk, and it did. The applause, begun by the chairman as he strode to the lectern, was lukewarm.

"On behalf of the Society," intoned Axelrod, "I would like to thank Dr. Sigourney for his most provocative lecture and for finishing on time. We've ten minutes for questions."

Almost simultaneously a dozen members of the audience raised their hands and, after a moment's indecision, Axelrod pointed to David Kavachek in the second row. Stuffing his ever-present pipe in a pocket, Kavachek sidled out to the aisle microphone. "As you say, Arnold, a provocative talk. But, like Swiss cheese, full of holes. We all accept the concept of oncogenes. Their discovery, first reported at this meeting several years ago, has stood the test of time. And we know that *all* cells, not just cancer cells, need growth-promoting hormones—insulin, somatotropin and the like. But Dr. Sigourney would have us believe in a unique, almost magical *growth factor* that sets off intracellular fireworks whenever it fits into its own exclusive receptor. What's the nature of this receptor? He doesn't know; he hasn't actually located it yet. The nature of the growth factor? Doesn't know that either. When, I wonder, Dr. Sigourney, *will* you know these things? Specifically, how long do you estimate it will take to identify the oncogene coding for this putative growth factor, clone it, insert it into a normal cell and see what it does? As for methodology . . . ." In rapid order, Kavachek fired off several more questions.

Steve's half-smile never wavered. "Thank you, Dr. Kavachek, for your—uh—intense interest. But I was expecting a query or two, not an hour examination. It would probably take that long to answer you. Nonetheless," he turned to Axelrod, "if the chairman approves, I'll make the attempt."

To the chorus of nays from the audience, Axelrod shook his head and called on a researcher from the Rockefeller Institute. His question, though tactful and concise, was equally critical.

As if made bold by Steve's tempered reply, more questioners assaulted his theory. Although he defended it as best he could, the growing sullenness of his tone revealed how discouraged he felt.

"One last question," announced Axelrod and chose the president-elect of the Society to ask it. His query was not hostile, merely irrelevant.

Steve answered with a terse, "I'm sorry, I've no information on that matter." Then, unhooking his neck microphone and laying it down, he gathered up his papers and was turning to leave when he heard

Szent-Gyorgyi's gravelly-deep voice boom over the loudspeakers. "Stay a moment, Sigourney, and permit me a word or two . . . My goodness, the audience has certainly given you a workout! I, too, would have liked to tweak your gorgeous theory in a few tender places, but fun is fun, and enough is enough! Cancer is serious business, and I would hate for anybody in the audience to leave here without fully appreciating what they have been privileged to hear this afternoon. As for the old timers—though none so old as I—if I didn't know better, I'd think not one of them supports your ingenious theory." He turned to the hushed audience with scorn. "You know, I know, and this Society had better know, what remarkable insights you've given us today. I remind you all, especially the skeptics and scoffers who used this microphone, that Sigourney and his marvelous institute don't need our guidance—*we* need *his!* Do you honestly think you've raised one legitimate doubt or inconsistancy about Sigourney's unified theory he himself hasn't already considered? Of course not! So, where are the congratulations, the encouragement, the acclaim? You know, Stefan," said Szent-Gyorgyi mockingly, "some here actually think you've allied yourself with the devil!" He chuckled. "I myself would have done so long ago had I only known what wonderful secrets the old rascal had to offer. After dabbling in cancer research for over half a century, I had hoped to live long enough to see the cancer mystery solved. Now I think maybe I have. I would like to be sure, however, so work a little faster, if you can. Don't squander precious time at too many meetings . . . Anyway, congratulations, my friend."

Szent-Gyorgyi half rose to shake Steve's hand again. As he did, several in the audience, Dan included, broke into lusty applause.

"May I, Albert?" said Axelrod, smiling and

reaching for the table microphone. "The last lecture of the afternoon will be given by Dr. Ronald Levy of Stanford University . . ."

Looking straight ahead, Steve strode up the aisle and out the ballroom door. Dan caught up with him in the foyer. "Steve!" he began. "That was . . .."

"Not here!" rasped Steve, eager to escape the premises. "Room 1212. I'll see you and your columnist friend there."

Though he was visibly exhausted, Steve gave Jimmy a lucid twenty-minute interview. When Jimmy finally shut his notebook and rose, Dan did, too, indicating his willingness to leave with him. But Steve asked him to stay.

"Well," he asked Dan when the two were alone, "what did you think of my little talk?"

"I thought it was fantastic!"

Steve eyed him dubiously. "Fantastic as in 'from an unrestrained imagination'?"

"You flatter me if you think I'm that clever with words. Rough day, huh?"

"Rough *week* . . . Did you see Nicole in the audience?"

"No. But I was standing way in the back. Did you?"

Steve shook his head.

"Plan to see her while you're in town?"

"No plans."

"Do you want to?"

Steve hesitated. "I suppose so . . . Even if dear old Szent-Gyorgyi hadn't come to my rescue, I never would've yielded an inch to that bunch down there. But to Nicole I would. She warned me what to expect. I was naive to think it could be otherwise."

"Don't tell me, tell her!"

"How?"

Dan grinned. "Kris and Jimmy's wife, Nora, are in

town. They flew in early this morning to see the Chagall exhibit at the National Gallery. Nicole is meeting us all for dinner at the *Lion d'Or* at eight. . . Hey, don't give *me* the fish eye; I didn't arrange it. Kris did. She's the fixer in the family. You will join us, won't you?"

Steve gestured uncertainly. "I'd like to, but I'm really bushed. I wouldn't want to doze off in the middle of dinner. Let me catch a short nap and see how I feel."

"Fine," said Dan, rising and moving to the desk. "I'll jot down the restaurant name and address. If you're not up to joining us, call. In case Nicole missed your bout with the Cancer Society, I'll tell her how bruising it was. Do I have permission to say you still love her? You're a first class fool if you don't!"

Steve nodded and smiled. "First, you struggled to save my life. Now, my love life. And all because I once gave you a batch of monoclonal antibodies. . ."

Dan shrugged modestly. "Some might call it meddling, but go right on thinking about it your way. See you later, I hope."

When his traveling alarm clock woke him at seven, Steve felt considerably refreshed. A shave, shower, and coffee from room service revived him further and he decided to go on to the *Lion d'Or*. Patting a flesh-colored ointment over his facial rash, he thought about what he would say to Nicole—first in the company of others, then alone. One thing seemed clear: like a beginning juggler, Steve could manage to keep two balls in the air. With practice, he might become adept with three—his institute, his research, and Nicole. Yet that was stretching his capacity to the limit. Any attempt at more and he would surely drop them all.

Realizing he was running late, Steve was hastily knotting his tie when he heard a soft knock on the door and went to open it, expecting either the waiter returning for his tray or the night maid. Instead, looming tall in the doorway, stood a somber-faced Joshua Okabe.

"Stefan, I'm sorry to surprise you like this," he said, "but we *must* talk."

Steve struggled to overcome his astonishment. "Of course, Joshua. Come in. You're back earlier than I expected."

"Yes. I landed at Kennedy this morning, and knowing about your lecture, came directly here."

"Did you hear it—my talk?"

"I . . . I would have liked to, very much. But I felt I didn't dare show my face."

"Then you know about the *Times* article?"

"It's the reason I'm here."

"I see," said Steve. "Well, sit down and let's discuss it. Have you eaten?"

"Eaten? Not since breakfast."

"Here." Steve handed him the leather bound room service menu. "Order whatever you like."

Okabe took the menu but did not open it. "Why, Stefan?" he said after a tense pause. "Why the subterfuge? Do you want me to leave the institute? All you need do is ask."

"No!" replied Steve emphatically. "I most certainly do not want you to leave. Especially now, when we've so much work to do. I sent you to Geneva because you desperately needed a vacation but kept putting it off. Then, when the Frick article appeared, I thought a few weeks longer might help you weather the storm when you got back. Believe me, Joshua, that's all there is to it."

After a brooding silence, Okabe said, "I'd like to believe you, Stefan. I truly would. But I'm terribly confused right now. I simply don't know whether it would be best for you if I stayed or left."

"*I'm* hungry, Joshua, even if you're not. Let's order some dinner and talk about it."

"But, uh, you look as if you're dressed to go out," said Okabe. "I wouldn't want to spoil your plans."

"They're of no importance," Steve lied. "I'll call and cancel. It's more important that we talk."

Chapter 32

DAN WAS NOT SURPRISED when Nelson Freiborg phoned the next morning. Having just read Jimmy Dallesio's column about Steve in the *Washington Post,* he expected that Nels' interest in a government-sponsored crash program to cure cancer would be revived. Though Kris demurred, Dan agreed to meet him for breakfast at the Capitol and, if possible, bring Steve along. But when he phoned the Shoreham, he was told Dr. Sigourney had already checked out.

Remembering Nicole's subdued manner at dinner, Dan again regretted Steve's absence. All he had offered by way of explanation was that Joshua Okabe had come back early from Europe and they had urgent business to discuss. From Steve's hushed tone, Dan had guessed Okabe was listening and did not press him. He only hoped Steve would have sense enough to phone Nicole later to explain more fully—though he wouldn't have bet on it. From what little Nicole had confided at dinner, he gathered that Steve's relationship with Okabe had contributed to their rift.

Without Steve's presence, Dan and Nels' breakfast conversation was mostly a rehash of their earlier one, though it ended on a disturbing note. "Remember the last time we talked?" Nels said as the busboy cleared the table. "I mentioned being curious about how the Sigourney Institute is funded, since less than half a million comes from the NIH. Well, this year Sigourney hasn't even reapplied for that."

"So?" said Dan.

"Nothing. It just gets curiouser and curiouser."

"Jesus, Nels, you're not going to sic the IRS on him, are you?"

Freiborg gestured innocently. "All I'm asking for is a meeting, not an audit. But, if you do happen to know how he's financed, I'd appreciate your letting me in on it."

"I admit that since our last talk, I've wondered about that myself, but figuring it was none of my business, I never asked. I can assure you of one thing, though: Steve's as ethical a guy as I know, so I wouldn't worry about it."

"Who's worried? I'm just trying to make an honest buck for our government and maybe give the President's humanitarian image a boost . . . By the way, Dan, this is unofficial but it looks like Sigourney's about to come into a little more money. A friend of mine, a General Motors vice president, told me recently that Sigourney will be one of this year's winners of the Alfred P. Sloan Prize for meritorious cancer research. Don't say anything yet, but when it's announced, give him my warmest congratulations—Billy's too."

Dan was delighted about Steve's upcoming award and only wished he could tell him; it would give him a much needed lift. As for Nels' persistent inquiries into Steve's finances—understandable, in a presidential advisor seeking every edge in future negotiations—Dan couldn't believe Steve capable of any fiscal chicanery and dismissed the possibility from his mind.

Yet two weeks later, during a tense discussion with Gregory Carhill, the accusation surfaced again. Though Carhill had recovered from his life-threatening allergic reaction and was back to work on a limited basis, he had asked Dan to visit him at his home.

A maid led Dan through the art-rich and chandeliered front hall to the downstairs study where Carhill sat waiting. To Dan's discerning eye he looked wan and wasted, though not enfeebled. Shaking hands and sitting opposite him, Dan remarked, "You're looking well."

"I'm far from well," replied Carhill, "but all things considered, I'm not doing too badly, thanks in no small measure to you. Yoshio informs me it was your suggestion to look for chorionic gonadotropin in my blood, and you again who gave him Harland Verrill's name. Harland's a very clever biochemist. I can easily understand why Andrew Schally refuses to part with him, or even lend him out for more than a short time. Harland was up here a few weeks ago and supplied me with a chorionic gonadotropin antagonist that I've been taking by nasal spray, the idea being that if I show any significant response, he'll load up the compound with a radioisotope and inject it intravenously. Well, I'm happy to say I've not only responded biochemically but clinically. My appetite's picked up and my pain is definitely less. It may just be wishful thinking—the vaunted placebo effect but no matter. In the shape I'm in, I'm grateful for any help I can get."

Had he paused longer, Dan would have said it was Steve Sigourney, not him, who rightfully deserved his thanks. But Carhill immediately went on to say,

"However, that's merely an aside and not the reason I've asked you here." Taking a manila folder from the end table beside him, Carhill handed it to Dan. "I've written an editorial of sorts and would very much like your opinion."

Dan opened the folder and read the title of the editorial: SCIENCE, PATENTS AND PROFITS: THE HIDDEN LEDGERS.

Coyly, Carhill asked, "Does the subject interest you?"

"I'm not sure—yet. Why do you want my opinion?"

"Two reasons. If you think it's suitable, I plan to submit it to *The New England Journal of Medicine*. And its inspiration, so to speak, is none other than your friend, Stefan Sigourney. By an odd coincidence, I've tumbled to the secret source of his funding and it's really quite shocking. Or do you already know?" At Dan's headshake, Carhill added, "Surely you must have wondered about it?"

"Not especially." At least not until recently, thought Dan. "Assuming it's not organized crime that's backing him, what difference does it make? What interests me more is *why* you're doing this?"

"Because I want the Nobel Prize," answered Carhill bluntly. "I deserve it. Sigourney probably does, too, along with three or four others in the cancer field—and that's precisely my problem. If they award this year's prize for cancer research as well they should, only three can win. Sigourney's won the Sloan Prize, you know. And I hear we're both leading candidates for the Lasker Award. But it's the Nobel I'm after, and I can't help feeling my chances would be considerably improved if Sigourney were out of the running."

"And you think this . . ." Dan tapped the manila folder in his lap "might knock him out?"

Carhill shrugged. "It certainly won't help him any.

You really know nothing about Sigourney's tie-in with the Kosterlitz Clinic?"

Again Dan shook his head. "Only that Steve was a guest there while he was recuperating from meningitis. Georgi Kosterlitz is an old friend from medical school days."

"Then it may interest you to know that Sigourney was a little more than Kosterlitz's 'guest.' He's his partner! That exorbitantly expensive clinic provides him with the millions it takes to run his institute—the reason Sigourney can thumb his nose at the NIH and other federal funding agencies. Though it took some doing for my British banking friends to dig this out, I can assure you it's all true. A curious arrangement, wouldn't you say?"

"Exactly what are you getting at?" demanded Dan.

"Just this. Kosterlitz didn't make Sigourney a partner out of friendship, but from necessity. His clinic's reputation was built on exclusive possession of a magical medicine, an anorexia-producing peptide, for which Sigourney and Kosterlitz jointly hold the patent. Don't you see, Dr. Lassiter? Sigourney made a major breakthrough in the treatment of obesity, one that might have benefitted millions. But instead of publishing it, he kept it secret to use for his own selfish ends."

"If you can consider cancer research selfish," Dan pointed out.

"For Sigourney, it's probably nothing more than an intellectual challenge. A means to an end. What does he *really* know of the horrors of cancer? How much do most laboratory-based researchers know? Whatever Sigourney's motivations, there's simply no excuse for his actions. He's not in weapons research, after all; by keeping his discovery a secret, he's committed an unpardonable scientific sin and I intend to call him on it. My arguments are all in the editorial

I've written. I think you'll find them sound."

"They'd better be," warned Dan. "Otherwise your attack on Sigourney could be perceived as self-serving and vindictive, hurting your chances for the Nobel Prize as much as his. Before you proceed any further, I strongly urge you to carefully reconsider what you're doing and why . . . and while you're at it, consider this: earlier you thanked me for certain suggestions concerning your care you erroneously thought I'd made. They weren't mine at all—they were Steve Sigourney's. He, not I, came up with the idea of surveying your blood for the presence of any unusual hormones; it was Sigourney who recommended that you consult Harland Verrill. I merely passed the suggestions on by way of Ted Swerdloff. I'm glad you're feeling better as the result, but it's Steve Sigourney you should be thanking, not me."

"I see," said Carhill slowly. "I . . . I had no idea. In view of the unsatisfactory outcome of our meeting last November, it never occurred to me that Sigourney would take any further interest in my case."

"You really don't know the man at all, do you?"

"No," said Carhill, looking chagrined. "Apparently not."

Dan lifted the manila folder from his lap and held it out. "Want this back?"

Lips taut and trembling slightly, Carhill stared at the envelope in silence. "No," he said at last. "I still want you to read it. Regardless of your personal opinion of me, Dr. Lassiter, there's something to be said for consistency."

A cold wind gusted in Dan's face as he strode down Carhill's front walk to his car, but he hardly noticed. The chill he felt went far deeper. It was almost impossible to believe that Steve had actually isolated and synthesized an anorexia-producing hormone, a feat that had frustrated endocrinologists for decades and, instead of announcing it, was using the secret to enrich himself and Georgi Kosterlitz. It simply didn't fit what he knew of Steve's character. But whatever the truth, he would have to warn Steve what Carhill was scheming. Loath to broach such a sensitive subject on the telephone, Dan decided to wait until they saw one another again.

The opportunity came ten days later, on the occasion of the Alfred P. Sloan Awards Banquet in New York. Dropping by Steve's hotel room beforehand, Dan was shocked by his haggard appearance. "Jesus," he exclaimed. "You look awful! Like you're going to the gallows, not an awards ceremony. You feeling all right?"

"Physically, okay. Mentally . . ." Steve shook his head. "For one thing, Joshua Okabe's left—gone back to Nigeria. When he told me yesterday he was going, I asked—practically begged—him to think it over. But this morning he was gone."

"For God's sake, what happened?"

"Nothing dramatic. Certainly nothing as bad as the Frick article. Just an accumulation of little things piling up to more than he could bear. Joshua's first week back at the institute was hell, of course. The senior people already knew about his fraudulent report in *Science* and how hard he had worked to make amends, so they were supportive. But the technicians and graduate students with their smirks and whispers, and the constant harrassment by the press made it a horrible ordeal. I tried to occupy his mind by assigning him the crucial project of creating a monoclonal antibody to the growth factor. I even worked side by side with him in the lab. My God, how we worked—in shifts, night and day, for weeks! Then, three days ago, we thought we'd finally succeeded and gave it to John Wendall to test independently. I still don't know what went wrong, Dan, but in Wendall's hands it proved worthless. Joshua was crushed, took all the blame on himself, insisted he was more hindrance than help to me. I tried my best to talk him out of resigning but obviously failed."

"What will he do now?"

"An old friend who's now the dean of a college in Lagos has offered him a teaching position there. It would be a tremendous waste of talent, but who knows? Maybe he'll be happier."

"Maybe you will, too."

"May be." Steve laughed mirthlessly. "Until the next major crisis. Okabe or no Okabe, I still have to come up with that damned antibody. Without it, I'm stuck. Instead of blossoming in full glory, my unified cancer theory will wither on the vine."

As Steve paced restlessly, Dan asked, "Have you seen or spoken to Nicole lately?"

"No, but we've corresponded. After I stood her—all of you—up in Washington, she wrote me a letter. Not exactly an ultimatum but close . . ."

"Mind telling me about it?"

Steve stopped pacing and sank dejectedly onto the bed. "It's painful, Dan. Almost too painful to talk about. But I suppose I ought to unburden myself to someone, and Anton, unlike you, has never met her. Have I ever told you about my uncle Anton?"

"A little. He sounds . . . sagacious."

"Oh, he is! And as reclusive as the Dalai Lama. Even though I'm in mid-Manhattan now and he's in the Village, I just can't drop in on him. I have to wait until my audience with him next Wednesday. His ways are maddening, but I like and respect him enormously. If it weren't for Anton's last bit of advice, I might never have become involved with Nicole at all. Now I'm depending on him to read my psyche again and tell me what needs repairing in order to get her back.'"

"Is it such a mystery?"

"The mystery," said Steve, pointing to his head, "is up here. Beneath this thick Hungarian skull lies a brain that's not only convoluted but tightly compartmentalized. One problem at a time, please! In her letter, Nicole said she doesn't expect me to give up anything—not my research, my dealings with Okabe, my quest for the Nobel Prize—but she wants nothing concealed from her. In other words, she wants us to talk out everything." Steve flung out his arms. "Easy, huh? Not for this brain of mine. 'You want Nicole?' it whispers. 'Fine. But first you must do this, that, and the other thing. . . .' Oh, it has a *super* ego, all right. Absolutely tyrannical!"

"Steve," began Dan gently, "if you ask me, you're overdoing again. This confusion you're feeling may be nothing more than exhaustion. I'm glad you're going to see your uncle; he's obviously a good influence. But in addition, why not take a brief vacation? That might help you sort things out, too."

Steve nodded. "I'm considering it. Right after my visit with Anton, I'm flying to Paris to consult with Jean-Francois Bach and talk to Andre Evashevsky. Now that Okabe's gone, I may be able to persuade Andre to cut short his Sabbatical and return to the institute. God knows, I need him. I'd planned to be away only a few days, but I'm thinking of staying longer. I might even spend a week in Minorca. There's a psychiatrist I know there and it wouldn't hurt to have a few sessions with him . . . Yes, I might just do that. Good idea, don't you think?"

Dan didn't answer. Abrupt as an alarm clock's jangling, the mention of Minorca woke him to the realization that, however precarious Steve's mental state, they had more unpleasant business to discuss.

"Well," said Steve, glancing at his wristwatch, "enough of that. I've been so busy pouring out my troubles I never thought to ask what you wanted to see me about. What say we go down to the bar and discuss it over drinks?"

"Be better if we ordered up drinks and did our talking in private. I'm afraid I have more bad news, Steve. . ."

Unnerved enough before Dan Lassiter's visit, Steve felt numbed afterward. The two-hour-long awards banquet was almost a complete blur. No formal acceptance speech was required of him and none was given. Good thing, too, he thought later. With Lassiter's words playing and replaying in his brain, he would probably have been incoherent.

Always a risk-taker, Steve knew it was inevitable that some day he would take one too many. But his deal with Georgi Kosterlitz had been struck so long ago that it seemed almost as if it involved another self. Small wonder that his efforts to defend his actions to Lassiter sounded so feeble. How could he adequately recapture for anybody, even himself, his state of mind fifteen years before; the seemingly unattainable needs and ambitions that ruled him then? He had long known that his silent role in the Kosterlitz Clinic had to become public knowledge one day. Some reporter or—as had actually happened—some enemy would ferret it out. But even if his entire world should crumble as a result, it would not happen soon; not unless he himself precipitated it. What he faced now was discouragement, not defeat. Like the desolate stretch of New Jersey landscape he saw outside the window of the train carrying him back to Philadelphia, this latest string of setbacks must come to an end. Maybe it already had, he thought dully. With Okabe gone, Nicole alienated, Carhill gloating from his deathbed, what else could possibly go wrong?

As Steve unlocked his apartment door, he heard the phone ringing inside. But before he could reach it, the caller had hung up. He stripped to his undershorts and opened a bottle of *Mersault*. Postponing the reading he had to do by tomorrow, he sat in his living room sipping wine and brooding.

Some time later, the phone rang again and a whispery-soft voice asked for him. "Who is this?" Steve demanded. "Oh, Marianna. How are you? How's Anton? . . . What? I can't understand. Why are you sniffling? . . . Dead? Anton's *dead?* Oh, my God!"

Chapter 33

"DAN," BEGAN NELSON FREIBORG breathlessly the moment Hedley put his call through, "sorry to interrupt your trustees meeting, but I've just come out of a conference with the President and some of his top science advisors on Sigourney's cancer work, and I need your help. Once they got to arguing among themselves, I didn't understand half of what they said—and neither, I'm sure, did the President. But the upshot is, they want to wait for Sigourney to prove his theory before proceeding further. The President doesn't. He wants to meet with you and Sigourney right away. Can you arrange it?"

"What's his hurry?"

"I know this sounds ridiculous, Dan, but his favorite aunt, a retired schoolmarm who had a big influence on him when he was growing up, was just operated on here for breast cancer. She's doing fine post-operatively. In fact, she's probably cured. But the President wants to do something more for her—for all maiden aunts everywhere. So . . ."

"I understand. It's not ridiculous, Nels, it's very human. But the last time I broached the notion of a crash program to Steve he had a lot else on his mind and wasn't too receptive. Now I've not idea where he is or how to get in touch with him."

"What do you mean? He's got to be somewhere!"

"His uncle died last Friday and after the funeral he just took off. Even his secretary doesn't know exactly where."

"Doesn't know or won't say?"

"It's my guess she really doesn't. But ask her yourself, why don't you? Invoking the President's name might work wonders."

"All right, I will. But if you happen to hear from Sigourney in the meantime, please have him contact me right away. Well, better get back inside. Anything I can do for you?"

"Just take time to smell the cherry blossoms, Nels. They should be in full bloom about now."

"I'll have to sneak a whiff. What with our soaring trade deficit, anything Japanese isn't too popular around here these days . . . Take care, Dan."

It had rained all night. Unable to sleep, Steve had listened to its soothing patter on the cabin roof. In the morning, thick mist clung to the hillside and filled the deep valley below like white smoke, until around nine o'clock the sun broke through the clouds to dispel it. At the end of a stroll through the birch forest behind the cabin, Steve saw a glorious rainbow in the azure sky which lifted his spirits. There was a certain solace in despair, he thought, especially when circumstances were so overwhelming that one was forced to cease struggling for a while.

He had come to the cabin high up the eastern face of Mount Marcy four days before. With no telephone or postal delivery route, it was utterly isolated, known in the village ten miles below only as the Sigourney place. Anton had either built it or bought it thirty years before and had spent every summer there. Now the cabin and its acres of wilderness, its clean air for clear thinking, belonged to Steve—a legacy from his uncle.

From the books Anton had left behind, Steve had learned about this section of the Adirondacks, the Indian tribes who had once lived here and the famous battles over old Fort Ticondaroga, now the nearest town of any size. Through his reading, he had hoped to become sufficiently familiar with his surroundings to rid himself of the sense of aimless drifting that had overcome him since his uncle's death. Invigorated by the morning sun and cool air, he considered climbing mile-high Mount Marcy—*Ta-ha-wus*, the Cloud-Splitter, in Indian lore. But it began to drizzle again as he was cooking breakfast and he went back to bed instead.

Loud claps of thunder and the downpour on the roof woke him four hours later. He built a fire in the fireplace and brewed fresh coffee. Then, as he had done every day since coming to the cabin, he read Anton's farewell letter before turning to his private journals.

"Dear Stefan," it began. *"A bequest or two and a final word. Yes, final, in the sense it will be the last time that I ever speak directly to you. By the time you read this I will be changed—to what I don't know, but I use the verb deliberately, not merely as a euphemism for death.*

We Westerners have trouble with the concepts of beginnings and endings—understandably, since there are no *such events. Nothing is ever created* de novo. *Nor obliterated. From matter to energy, things either continue on or they change. I won't belabor the point except to say that I believe strongly that the essential core of my being, my piece of God, cannot be annihilated. It can only be transformed into something else . . .*"

On first reading this passage, Steve had not quite understood it. From his sketchy knowledge of "steady-state" physics he knew that matter was continually being tranformed into energy and that somewhere the process was reversed, but Anton's description of his indestructible core as "a piece of God" puzzled him until he came across its explanation in a discourse on *Paradox* in one of his uncle's journals.

"Just as the brain corrects the inverted images from the eye," Anton had written, "*Paradox* and *Inversion* are as much a part of our perceptions as visual images and must be compensated for before we can hope to solve the riddle of human existence. Like dreams, people and things are seldom what they seem. I once thought that religious practices and belief in a Supreme Being were antithetical; that organized worship obscured more than it revealed. Yet lately, through the principles of Paradox and Inversion, I have begun to conceive of God in a very different, though no less majestic, way.

"What if, instead of the biggest living force in the universe, God is actually the tiniest? Not the towering cathedral pointing the way to Heaven, but the smallest mote of mortar in its construction?

"Eberhart Kruger, my biochemist friend at Columbia and cribbage partner, keeps telling me what wonderful stuff DNA is. He can remove strands of it from a cell, dry it, store it for months on a shelf, pound it with a hammer or do virtually anything he wants with it, then put it back in a nutrient solution and presto! it immediately comes to life and starts reproducing itself. You long for proof of magic? Eberhart says smugly. Study DNA, the most magical stuff that ever was! If only Emerson and Thoreau and the other New England Transcendentalists had known about DNA, how much more convincing their theology might have been!

"Yet, I ask myself, if God is as tiny as a single DNA molecule, how can He then be so omnipresent and all-powerful? The basic tenets of computer science help me here. Imagine a computer whose information storage bits are as tiny as molecules and its capacity so large that it fills, not rooms and buildings, but planets and solar systems, and one can perhaps begin to grasp infinite intelligence; how, because we are alive and life is DNA, we are all a piece of God.

"Still, egotist that I am, I worry: does this concept of God make Him impersonal? Prayers futile? Quite the opposite. It represents a schema whereby all prayers can be heard, weighed, coordinated and acted upon. Just as satellite computers are linked to central ones, so are we linked with God. Our thoughts are instantly His thoughts; our hopes and desires, if deemed worthy, are transmitted to others through Him. And if our fragile egos demand free will, the network I envision allows for it. Just as an individual computer bit can respond to a given stimulus by magnetizing or not magnetizing, so can we respond positively or negatively to a given situation. Through DNA, we are not only one with Him who has created us, but as necessary to Him as each tiny microcircuit is necessary to the proper function of even the most complex computer."

If not wholly convinced by Anton's reasoning, Steve was fascinated and more than a little amused by it. For all his anti-science biases, Anton had not hesitated to borrow analogies from the work of Steve's computer science brethren. And as for the importance of paradox in the proper perception of the ways of God and the universe, Anton's life exemplified that far better than any of his theories, as the rest of his letter made clear.

I confess, Stefan, that only in the last few years have I been the recluse you believed me to be. Before that I was simply too busy with my teaching, my writings, my life, to pay much attention to what went on in the outside world, or with you. It's time I told you the truth about Marya and me. It may surprise you to learn (or, to your credit, it may not) that we were lovers for almost thirty years. What a magnificent human being she was—brilliant, passionate, voluptuous. We first met in Budapest during the war. Her husband, a shy, studious man determined to be brave, was a member of my resistance group. He was killed on a demolition mission I sent him on. Despite her infant daughter, Marya took his place. After the war, we emigrated together to America. (More about that in my early diaries.)

Why have I not told you about us before? I don't honestly know. Possibly because I was afraid you would neither understand nor approve. We should have married, of course. Instead, we nutured each other. Marya taught me how to live, and even how to die. I was still learning from her in our last hours together.

Your cancer research is important, Stefan. I've never denied it. Nor have I applauded it as lustily as you would have liked. With Marya as my laboratory, I compared experiences, observations, conclusions, and found yours too limiting. Doubtless this was unfair of me, but I can't possibly convey in mere words the bountiful rewards Marya and I received from one another. Suffice it to say, most of my best ideas came from her, either because she thought of them first or drew them out of me. Our life together passed through many phases, each better than the last. This final phase of remembrance and recapture is much like rereading a favorite book—though nothing in it changes, everything can be savored to the fullest.

It was only after Marya's death that I became truly reclusive. Impatient to die, I began my separation from life. Nonetheless, our last visit together was special. If I seemed unduly harsh with you, forgive me, though I must admit at the time I feared I was not being harsh enough. Seeing in your Nicole, or someone like her, your salvation, I was determined, by whatever means available to me, to make you see it, too.

If you are so wedded to purpose, Stefan, I suggest you spend a few moments observing an ant gathering food. It is so intent, industrious, even ingenious—not unlike yourself. Watch it a while and you will come to appreciate what a marvel of raw ambition it is. You can, of course, toy with it, deflect it from its task, even crush it under your shoe; otherwise, it will ignore you. What importance are you, a creature it is incapable of understanding, compared to a twig, a leaf, a morsel of food? Yet it, too, is animated, purposeful, and has collective intelligence. Which raises the question: Are we humans anything more than God's ants? Alone, probably not. Alone we lose all significance as a man forever abandoned on a desert island. But let him be joined by one other person and each gains more significance than ever before; they become one another's entire world. My point: Alone, we are nothing. Paired, our programming circuits are complete. Our billions of nerve connections are given us not so much to do as to understand the ways of the universe, ultimately God. What an exciting journey!

Yet in all my years, I've come to a partial understanding of only two things—Marya and myself, the entity we were together. It was enough, a surpassing experience! My most fervent wish now is for you, my closest kin, to know this same thrill of discovery.

Poor Marianna! The material goods I've bequeathed to her cannot even begin to compensate for the burden I've been these last few years. Now, at last, she will be free to marry her fiance, a not untalented composer, live with him wherever they wish, and start a family of their own.

Knowing you have no need of money, I have left you my diaries and private journals for whatever they're worth. Also, my cabin in the Adirondacks. It sits on top of a mountain, not the world, though it often seemed so to me. No stars I have ever seen elsewhere shine so brightly as the ones above it; no lakes and valleys are so restful to the eye as the ones below. I wish to be buried there, to have my nitrogenous remains enrich the soil. I have already made the necessary arrangements and, if you choose to accompany my corpse, I urge you to stay awhile. You won't learn anything new about cancer there, but perhaps other things. And if perchance you sense my presence around the cabin—if anything other than the artifacts I have left behind brings my memory strongly to mind—it is probably echoes of past happiness. In such event, you may consider the cabin enchanted. Take advantage of it with your Nicole.

So, farewell, Stefan. I regret I will no longer be around to goad and confuse you, but I leave you a glorious world. Be grateful for all it offers, even its terrible injustices and tribulations. Never mind adversity. It stimulates, it strengthens, it sharpens the mind, and eventually it passes. Your father was very proud to have you for his son—though he told me, not you. In my own selfish way, I have loved and been proud of you, too.

Anton

With an aching sense of loss, Steve put his uncle's letter down and sipped coffee. Each time he read it, its message sank deeper into his psyche. Yet, with his need for solitude waning and few of Anton's journals left unread, Steve knew he must soon decide what to do next. Should he go to Paris to see Bach and Evashevsky, or return to the institute? This time he had left John Wendall in charge. When the rain let up, he would drive to the village and phone Wendall. Could he find the courage to phone Nicole, too? Ever since learning the truth of Anton and Marya's relationship, she had been constantly on his mind. But was he ready to talk to her, tell her? Uncertain of how forgiving she might be of his recent neglect, he decided to write her first.

The letter took almost two hours to compose to his satisfaction; once it was finished, Steve wanted to mail it right away. Despite the continuing downpour, he put on his raincoat and hat, climbed into his rented Toyota, and drove down the mountain.

Almost at once he regretted his rash action. The winding dirt road was thick with mud and the windshield wipers so worn that he could barely see ten feet in front of him. Twice in the first five miles he swerved dangerously around sharp curves; another time he stalled the engine after slamming on the brakes. But to drive slower risked getting mired in mud-filled ruts.

Nearing what appeared to be a small hill, Steve downshifted and speeded up to make the climb. At the crest, surprised to see how steep the downslope was, he abruptly hit the brakes. The small car shuddered violently and went into a skid. Cutting the steering wheel back and forth, Steve fought to straighten out. From previous trips down this road, he knew that some of its embankments dropped off steeply into rocky ravines. But, caught in some sort of groove, the car continued to slide sideways. To his horror, an almost hairpin curve loomed ahead. Frantically, he tried to veer into the trees at his right or plunge into the ditch at his left, but could do neither. Letting go of the wheel, he fumbled for the seat belt latch, intending to leap out, but before he could release it, he was into the curve. *Kristus Jazus!* he gasped. Was this how he was meant to die? In bleak moments, he had contemplated the possible ways his life might end, but because he drove so little, an automobile accident was never one of them. It hardly seemed fair—if fairness was ever a factor in such happenings—not after Anton had reached out from beyond the grave to enlighten him. Foolishly, Steve had assumed he still had time, years and years, to make amends. Now, as terror numbed him, he realized that what was left of his life might well be measured in milliseconds.

Tipping at a steep angle after skidding off the road, the Toyota seemed about to flip over. Steve ceased struggling with the seat belt and braced himself for the series of impacts to come as the car tumbled down the embankment into whatever lay below. Instead, he heard metal grate harshly on metal and was jolted sideways, then forward, his forehead slamming against the windshield. A shower of scintillating lights exploded on his retina and he blacked out.

When his brain began to work again, Steve's first impression was of peace. He felt profoundly, almost blissfully, peaceful. Was it the peace of the dying, he wondered, or simply the absence of terror? He blinked several times but couldn't orient himself. Rain fell on his face and he saw gray sky ahead; the bandlike pressure around his waist told him he was suspended somehow. It took him another few moments to realize that the car door had sprung open and, anchored by his seatbelt, he was hanging halfway out. Struggling into a sitting position, he shut off the engine and looked around, scarcely able to believe what he saw. Ten feet down the embankment, the Toyota had smashed into the rusted hulk of an abandoned truck. If it hadn't, it would have plunged forty or fifty more feet into a rock quarry.

Painfully Steve extricated himself from the front seat and, slipping and sliding, climbed back to the road. Head throbbing and shoes sloshing in mud, he set off toward the village of Westmont. Shortly after reaching the paved highway that ran through its center, he hitched a ride in a delivery van to the village's only garage, where he arranged to have his car towed in as soon as road conditions permitted, cleaned up as best he could, and used the pay phone to call his secretary.

"Dr. Sigourney!" cried Marta. "I've been so worried. Are you all right?"

"Fine," Steve replied. "But why worry? You knew where I was."

"I knew *approximately*. But there was no way to reach you and so many people have been trying: Wendall, Dr. Lassiter, Nicole Brueur, even a man named Freiborg who said he was calling for the President of the United States!"

"The President, no less . . . Maybe he could send a helicopter for me. I could use one."

"A helicopter? Where are you calling from?" asked Marta.

"A garage in a very rainy village. But never mind that now. Please switch me to Wendall's office, Marta."

"I will, Dr. Sigourney. But first there's something I'd better tell you. Nicole called several times. She's very anxious to talk to you—about what I don't know."

"All right," said Steve, suddenly apprehensive. "I'll call her back."

"There's more. Maybe I shouldn't have, but she seemed so upset that I told her where you were."

"When was this?" Steve asked.

"Early this morning."

"It's all right, Marta. You did the right thing. I'll call her as soon as I get through with Wendall."

"And don't forget the President."

"I won't. I voted for him, after all. Now, please get me Wendall."

"Stefan!" blurted the usually imperturbable immunologist a few moments later. "I'm so relieved you finally called. I'm afraid I have very upsetting news. Damn! I don't exactly know how to put this . . ."

Wondering what else could possibly go wrong, Steve snapped, "Please, John. Out with it!"

"It's about the monoclonal antibody you and Okabe created to the growth factor. It's all right! The fault was at my end, in the assay material I used. I simply can't believe my carelessness in not . . ."

"Skip the apology," interrupted Steve. "Are you sure?"

"Quite sure. We've triple-checked. It works fine. It's everything Okabe claimed it would be."

"I see," said Steve, feeling more relief than elation over Wendall's news. Okabe must be told at once, though Steve doubted it would be enough to persuade him to return to the institute now.

In their subsequent conversation, Steve gave Wendall suggestions for what to do next and told him he would probably fly to Paris in a day or two. Immediately upon hanging up, he tried to reach Nicole, first at her apartment, then at her lab. There was no answer at either place. With deep uneasiness, he walked away from the phone wondering why Nicole had been so anxious to talk with him. Dan or Kris Lassiter might know, he speculated, but before calling them he had the garage owner drive him to the motel at the far end of the village.

When he arrived, Steve signed a registration card and passed it back to the desk clerk along with a credit card. The clerk, a moon-faced middle aged man, glanced at the form, then up at him.

"You're a doctor, too, huh?"

"Yes," said Steve, puzzled. "Are you?"

"Me!" exclaimed the clerk with a deep chuckle. "Hell, no. But we got another doctor staying here tonight and she's from the same neck of the woods as you."

"Oh?" Intense interest enlivened Steve's face. "What's her name?"

"Wal," drawled the clerk, "don't know's I ought to be giving that out. But she's in the restaurant right now, if you want a look at her. She's worth a look, too."

Steve turned and strode quickly through the connecting doorway. It couldn't be, he thought; Nicole couldn't possibly be here. But there she was, in jeans and heavy turtleneck sweater, looking as lovely as he had ever seen her, at a table in front of him.

"Stefan!" she gasped on seeing him. "Thank God!"

"For me, too," he muttered, his throat tight with emotion. "But what are *you* doing here?"

"What?" she repeated, recovering her poise and with it, her resentment at his recent behavior. "Oh, nothing. It was a slow day in the lab, so I went for an automobile ride. A three hundred mile ride! And as long as I was at it, I decided to search the Adirondacks for a missing researcher I used to know . . . Damn you, Stefan! I know how much your Uncle Anton meant to you. And when Dan Lassiter told me how depressed you were the last time he saw you, I was frantic with worry. I called you and called you, until finally dear, sweet Marta took pity on me and told me where you were. I would've driven up to your uncle's cabin, but they told me the road was washed out, so I stopped here for the night. Any more questions?"

Still astonished at finding her here, Steve merely shook his head.

"Good. Then sit down. You can at least buy me dinner." She smiled ruefully. "I used to think you were so brilliant, but you're really a fool. An *idiot savant* who happens to know a little science. And I'm an even bigger fool for chasing after you like this. Oh, sit down, will you please? You look ridiculous, standing there wagging your head. I'm sure the motel clerk—who's spying on us from the doorway—thinks so, too. At least take off that soggy raincoat."

"I'm just as soaked underneath," said Steve.

"Why? What have you been doing? Don't you have sense enough to come out of the rain?"

"Evidently not," he said, sitting next to her.

"Well," she said, feigning indifference, "now that I'm here, what do you intend to do about it?"

Steve grinned. "At last a question I can answer! I know exactly what I want to do—marry you, if you'll still have me, and take you to Paris."

"Hmm," murmured Nicole, maintaining a neutral expression with difficulty. "A reasonable proposal—which I accept. But you'll have to explain it all to the motel clerk."

PART THREE

THE LETTER

Chapter 34

LIKE ALL LARGE PARIS hospitals whose architecture had to comply with strict city height restrictions, the Hôpital Necker comprised a sprawling complex of two- or three-story buildings around a central courtyard. At the reception gate, Steve got directions to the unit that housed Jean-Francois Bach's immunology laboratories and set out along the path that led to it between beds of violets and petunias.

Andre Evashevsky's office was barely large enough for a bookcase, a desk, and his bulk. Leaning back in a swivel chair, eyes on the ceiling, Evashevsky seemed lost in thought when Steve appeared. Standing in the doorway, Steve almost expected him to bark, "Now what!"—Andre's usual response when anyone dared interrupt his reverie. Instead, he blinked and cried, "Stefan! It's good to see you, *mon vieux.*"

Fifteen minutes later, they were ordering lunch at the sidewalk cafe across from the hospital entrance and trying, through small talk, to ease their way into serious discussion.

"Well," said Steve, putting his menu aside, "how do you really like working here?"

Evashevsky shrugged. "I've learned a lot of immunology. As for the rest—if you like French politics, you'll like French science."

Steve smiled, but did not question his meaning.

"Have you met with Jean-Francois yet?" Evashevsky asked.

"No, I wanted time with you first."

"Well, he's anxious to talk to you. He's program chairman of the next international cancer congress and he wants you for a featured speaker."

"When and where is it?"

"Second week in January in Madrid. Interested?"

"Hmm. Eight months from now. I might be, depending how well the work goes in the meanwhile. I might even make it my swan song."

"You're giving up lecturing? Or do you mean more?"

"I haven't quite decided. With or without you, I'm going to push ahead to try to find proof for my unified cancer theory. I'm giving myself six months, no longer. After that—I don't know."

"You'd never divorce yourself from science completely, would you?"

"Not science—scientists. Cancer researchers. I've run with the pack for a long time now and I'm weary. So I'm going to muster all my remaining energy for one last sprint. If after six months I still haven't crossed the finish line, that's it."

Evashevsky regarded him with concern. "What's happened?"

"A number of things, some good, some bad."

Steve began by telling him about Joshua Okabe's troubles at the institute, concluding with the incident that had forced his needless resignation.

"So his monoclonal to the growth factor *was* good, after all," mused Evashevsky. "Guilty but let off leniently for one crime, he was wrongfully punished for another. Ironic, isn't it? Does Okabe know?"

"Not yet. But he will. I cabled him."

"Will he return to the institute, do you think?" When Steve hesitated, Evashevsky shrugged. "Well, let him. I still think he's crazy. But craziness is an entire other world. Evidently there's useful information there, too."

"Say Okabe does return," Steve ventured. "Will you?"

Evashevsky grinned. "My bags are already packed. They have been ever since I read the manuscript you sent me on your two-gene hypothesis. It's brilliant, Stefan; even if it's all wrong. But therein lies the fun—finding out."

Steve sighed deeply. "Thank you, old friend. I'm greatly relieved. I don't mean to rush you, but how soon can you wind up here and be back at the institute? There's so much to do."

"Any time. I can even fly back with you, if you want. When are you leaving?"

Steve smiled slightly. "My original intention was to be in Paris only a day or two. Now I'll be here at least a week. You see, I'm on my honeymoon."

"You and Nicole? You finally did it?"

Steve nodded and braced himself for Evashevsky's exuberant expression of approval. Instead, he looked a bit perturbed.

"When did all this happen?"

"Three days ago."

"I see. Well, heartiest congratulations. But as your friend, colleague, and confidant, I'm a little hurt that I wasn't invited to the wedding."

Steve laughed. "My apologies, Andre, but it was a spur-of-the-moment thing and very exclusive; the entire wedding party consisted of a justice of the peace and a motel clerk and his wife."

"Why such a rush?"

Steve looked into the distance for a moment. "You know the expression, 'living on borrowed time.' Well, without quite realizing it, I've been doing that for a long time now. It took a severe jolt to remind me." He described his close call on the mountain road outside Westmont.

"And when you limped into town, Nicole was just sitting there? Amazing! Your runs of luck, good and bad, are truly extraordinary. Let's hope the good luck continues . . . You and Nicole must be my guests tonight. I know a small Vietnamese restaurant with fabulous cuisine—though we could go anywhere else you wish." At Steve's enthusiastic nod, he said, "Good! Now back to your two-gene hypothesis. Obviously, the next step should be . . ."

At dusk that same day, a Lagos postman on a bicycle delivered a cablegram to Joshua Okabe at the guest house of St. Mark's College where he was residing temporarily.

Okabe thanked the postman for his perseverance in tracking him down, tipped him generously, and seeing that the cable was from Stefan Sigourney, went into his bedroom to read it in privacy. He still felt guilty about leaving Philadelphia without giving Stefan a last chance to dissuade him. But after his monoclonal antibody's devastating failure to pass John Wendall's tests, resigning from the institute had seemed the only honorable course. Okabe had even urged Stefan to delete his name from all publications to which he contributed, but Stefan refused. The mere suggestion of it had upset him so that Okabe reluctantly agreed to reconsider his situation and his future worth to the institute, and to discuss it again in the morning. But believing Stefan was acting out of kindness, not conviction, Okabe was unable to sleep that night and by dawn had decided to spare them both further anguish. He was sure his friend and chief would understand. By entrusting him with a crucial project, even working side by side with him in the lab to help bring about its success, Stefan had given him every chance to prove his scientific mettle, and he had failed—or so Okabe thought until he read Steve's cablegram.

Staring with disbelief at the words, Okabe sank into a chair and began to chuckle with almost hysterical relief.

Would he consider returning to the institute? Stefan had asked.

"No, my dear friend," Okabe said aloud. "Perhaps someday when curiosity seizes me again and there are things I must know. Until then, let my account with you remain as balanced as it is now."

But imagine John Wendall, that infuriating fussbudget, making such an amateurish mistake! Still chuckling at this ironic turnabout, Okabe went into the bathroom to shave. For the first time since his arrival at St. Mark's, he felt like joining his fellow faculty members for dinner.

Eight days later, with Nicole back at the National Cancer Institute for the last two months of her fellowship, Steve and Dan Lassiter met Nelson Freiborg in his office in the West Wing of the White House. Having just received word that, because of the current Middle East crisis, the President had cancelled all his morning appointments, Freiborg advised the two doctors that the President would probably not be able to see them until early afternoon and then only briefly. "After all I've told him," Freiborg went on, "he'll probably just want to eyeball you two."

"For Chrissake, Nels," Dan protested, "Steve cut short his honeymoon for this *urgent* meeting. Is that all you got us down here for?"

Blandly Freiborg replied, "You know how things work here, Dan. Even if all the President says is, "Hello, Doctors. Nice to meet you. Keep up the good work,' it's a necessary preliminary. The real meeting will take place afterwards between the three of us and whomever else you want. Mind you, though, I'm just saying it *might* happen that way. Could be the President will find you guys so fascinating he'll skip his nap to keep you talking."

"You think that's likely?" questioned Dan.

Freiborg shrugged. "Two weeks ago when I first tried to set up this meeting, he was all fired up over the idea of a crash program. Now, I don't know how enthusiastic he'll be. But I can assure you my feelings are the same. I can't forget what you two did for Billy, and with two good friends currently battling cancer, I'm as eager to get going as ever. Hell, if it were up to me, I'd give you both a wheelbarrow and the keys to Fort Knox and let you buy whatever you need—the NIH establishment be damned! Anyway, now that I've finally got you here, Dr. Sigourney, let me ask you bluntly: is an all-purpose cure for cancer even possible?"

Steve, his mind elsewhere until that moment, smiled tolerantly. "Depends on what you mean by 'cure.' Will we be able to treat most cancers someday as successfully as we now treat pulmonary infections? Probably. But, remember, people still die of TB and pneumonia. What I'm trying to say, Mr. Freiborg, is that if my two-gene hypothesis proves correct and agents can be developed to block the action of the protein products of these genes, similar steps would then be possible with cancer."

"I see," said Freiborg, "and I certainly hope your theory proves out. Let's say it does, and let's say further that the President decides to launch a crash program to conquer cancer. Would you be willing to run the research end? I'm speaking hypothetically, of course."

Steve smiled and shook his head.

"Why not?"

"In science, Mr. Freiborg, you can't speak hypothetically for long. To maintain credibility you need proof, and the proof for my cancer theory is not easy to come by. Not only are my efforts to find it at a crucial stage, demanding all my time, but they're crucial to the outcome of your proposal. If my two-gene hypothesis is wrong, you won't want me. And if it's right—if it pays off therapeutically as I'm hopeful it will—you won't need me. From that point on, the steps to translate theory into effective treatment would be almost cookbook-simple. You'd be better off with a good organizer for your top man."

"Perhaps," Freiborg conceded. "But I'd prefer to withhold judgment on that until I hear how your theory actually pans out. How long do you think it'll be before you'll know?"

"Within six months. The proof is exceedingly complicated, but if we don't find it by then, it's unlikely we'll find it at all."

"All right, Dr. Sigourney," said Freiborg, standing up and stretching. "In six months, we'll meet again. Now, let me check with the President's secretary to see when he might be free and then we can get some lunch." He reached for the phone and paused. "Oh, by the way, I have the heads of the NIH and NCI standing by in case you'd like to meet with them later today. Would you?"

"No," said Steve. "Not this time. I don't mean to sound rude, but I'm simply not ready to talk to them, not in any convincing way. And I've had more than my fill of skeptics lately."

"I understand, though they're both fairly new in their jobs and might benefit from getting to know you better. Dan was right about you—Billy, too. You're not at all the fire-breathing eccentric some of the President's science advisors would have him believe."

"Marriage has mellowed him," Dan said. "But for how long nobody can say. There's still a lot of fire left in his belly."

"I'm sure," said Freiborg, smiling and reaching again for the phone. "I only wish there were in mine."

Chapter 35

SWELTERING OUTDOORS, STICKY INSIDE despite the central air-conditioning, the senior staff of the Sigourney Institute would never forget that August day.

At breakfast, Nicole had sensed that Steve was on edge, but said nothing about it. By contrast, the usually volatile Evashevsky, in and out of Jorgeson's lab a dozen times that day to consult, seemed subdued, almost prayerful. At four p.m., when Nicole went to the cafeteria for a carton of milk, she found Steve, Evashevsky, Wendall, Jorgeson and two others in intense conversation at a corner table. Spotting her, Steve jumped up and came over to kiss her cheek, unusual behavior for him.

"What's going on?" she demanded.

"We're having a highly theoretical discussion."

"Theoretical? It looks conspiratorial. If you weren't already chief, I'd think you were plotting a *coup d' etat.*"

Steve smiled. "Perhaps a *coup* of another kind."

"Tell me!"

Steve glanced at his tablemates. All eyes were on him. "I will—later."

"What time will you be home?"

"I don't know, but not too late. I'll explain it all then."

At nine that evening, Steve phoned excitedly. "Nicole, could you come back to the institute please? I—we—have something to show you; something so beautiful I'm at a loss to describe it. Oh, and bring champagne! The two bottles in the cabinet."

"You've found it!" she cried. "You've found the gene for the growth factor!"

"We think so. But come and see the data for yourself. And hurry!"

Hanging up the phone, Steve went to his office window and looked out at buildings in the eerie twilight. Somewhere out there a baseball game between the Philadelphia Phillies and the St. Louis Cardinals was in progress; he had heard the security guard listening to it on a transistor radio as he made his rounds. At Evashevsky's urging, Steve and Nicole had attended their first major league baseball game two weeks before and enjoyed it; they would go again soon, he thought. Elsewhere in the hot city, cab drivers parked at the airport or around hotels had their front doors open and their radios blaring the game broadcast; on beaches or in cars, lovers waited impatiently for full darkness to conceal their intimacies; in parks and dim streets, muggers and junkies were on the prowl. Steve even envisioned nuclear submarines on patrol under the seas, and SAC bombers high in the sky—the entire gamut of human diversity and complexity. Like *Brownian motion*, the irregular, zig-zag movement of particles suspended in solution, so many people, so much activity—while here at the institute he had founded fourteen years before, an epochal event had just taken place: a tiny bit of DNA, hunted, trapped and taken prisoner, had been tricked into revealing its true identity and would now be forced to lead them to the cancer high command in the cell nucleus. What a triumph! He could hardly wait to share it with Nicole, the one person who best understood the steep price he had paid for it. He would have also liked to share its richness with cancer researchers everywhere, but knew he never could. In standard form—introductions, materials and methods, results, discussion—he would describe his discovery to them in due time: what he could never hope to convey was the enormity of this introspective, exhilarating, humbling and terrifying moment.

Hearing the click of heels in the corridor, he turned from the window and rushed to the door. Seeing Nicole, he swept her up in his arms.

"Where is everybody?" she asked, holding a champagne bottle tightly in each hand.

"In Evashevsky's lab. Now that they think they've solved the cancer mystery, they're debating what to tackle next."

"Then what are you doing here?"

"I wanted—needed—a few moments alone . . . No, don't look at me like that. I'm perfectly all right, just in need of a breather. But come and let Andre show you his immunoprecipitates, so you can *ooh* and *ah* over him. Then, let's pop the champagne!"

Later that night, after Jorgeson and Wendall had left and Nicole and Madge Cohen were talking quietly in a corner, Evashevsky refilled their plastic cups with the last of the champagne and said, "Want to hear something funny, Stefan? I've only met the man once, and much as I've despised him for what he did, I almost wish Okabe were here."

"Oh?" Steve had been thinking the same thing,

along with more complicated thoughts. "Why's that?"

"It was his antibody, after all, that paved the way for me to do what you initially doubted I could. You thought my short-cut wouldn't work; that plodders like Wendall and Jorgeson would find the gene for the growth factor first. Well, thanks to Okabe's monoclonal, I proved you all wrong."

Steve smiled. "So you did. But if you're that grateful to Okabe, why not write and tell him so?"

"Maybe I will. In spite of all the grief he brought on himself and on you, he did us a valuable service. We could have done without his antibody, of course, but it was faster this way. That much should be acknowledged."

Sensing some hidden message behind Evashevsky's words, Steve asked, "What do you mean, 'that much'? He contributed ideas, too."

"I know, Stefan. You've told me. But how can you attribute an idea to only one person? It's like bouillabaisse—a lot goes into it, but it takes careful seasoning to keep it from tasting too fishy. Besides, didn't you say that before he left, Okabe urged, even pleaded with you, to omit his name from all future publications to spare yourself needless controversy?" At Steve's reluctant nod, Evashevsky added, "It's good advice. It'd be best if you took it."

"Best for whom?"

"For you . . . for science. You'll be presenting our definitive findings at the cancer congress in Madrid soon; they're bound to cause a sensation in ten languages. You know as well as I do that the sooner they're accepted as fact and other labs begin to search for substances to block the action of the growth factor, the sooner one will come up with a treatment to benefit cancer patients. Like it or not, Stefan, leaving Okabe's name off your paper will hasten its acceptance."

Before Steve could answer, Nicole came up to him and said, "Why are you frowning? Because we're out of champagne? Then let's all go to our place and keep on partying. Oh, come on," she urged in response to his half-hearted shrug. "How often do we get to celebrate something this exciting?"

It was past two a.m. before their guests finally left and Steve and Nicole could go to bed. But try as he might to relax, to dispel all but the most soothing images from his brain, Steve couldn't sleep. Waiting for Nicole's breathing to grow deep and steady, he stole out of bed and went into his den. Picking up a pen and writing pad, he began the report he intended to submit to the journal, *Nature.* The title came easy: *The Two-Gene Hypothesis of Malignant Cellular Transformation.* But the next line, the list and ranking of authors, gave him pause. Evashevsky, Jorgeson and Wendall would have to be included, of course, along with one or two others. But what about Joshua Okabe? Where, if at all, should he rank?

Damn Andre! he thought. Before tonight he had almost forgotten Okabe's plea that his name be omitted from all future publications and didn't welcome being reminded: it was too tempting an out. Nor had Evashevsky needed to warn him that acknowledging Okabe's contribution would cause controvery—the hostile response to their preliminary report in *Science* on the growth factor had already proved that.

Steve rose and paced restlessly, tracing his sense of *deja vu* back to the small motel outside Truro and the chill dawn on the beach when he had wrestled with the same ethical dilemma: what to do about Okabe?

Doubtless Evashevsky was right. Untainted by Okabe's name and notoriety, his new theory would be accepted quicker, bear therapeutic fruit sooner. Untold numbers of cancer victims, their disease beyond control by current treatment methods, might benefit. Shouldn't his sense of fair play take their welfare into consideration? And then there was the scientific stir his forthcoming report in *Nature* would generate—a stir bound to reach the Nobel Prize selection committee well before they took their final vote.

Steve laughed ironically. Did he still covet the Prize as much as ever? Hadn't he convinced himself yet that Nicole's love was reward enough for his labors? Well, yes, but his practical side argued that one blessing need not exclude the other. Since it took no extra effort, why not have both?

After all, he mused, wasn't he selling his own abilities short by crediting so much of his recent success to Okabe? While it was true that a marginal note in one of the African's data books had refocused his attention on the potential importance of a cancer-causing growth factor, it wasn't that clear a clue. And Okabe's brilliant notion regarding cell membrane receptors was only partly correct. As Steve had suspected, and Wendall and Jorgeson subsequently proved, the receptor-opening protein alone wasn't enough to trigger the cancer process; it took the growth factor, too. So why be so protective of Okabe's interests? Why keep on agonizing over him?

And, as always, when faced with the problem of apportioning credit for a scientific discovery, Steve had the ghost of Milos Androsh to contend with. Wryly he reminded himself that, among his peers, only Gregory Carhill insisted on referring to the phenomenon Steve had described a decade before as the "*Androsh*-Sigourney Effect." Carhill was acting out of envy and spite, of course, but with more justification than he realized.

In preparing to publish his momentous find, Steve had painstakingly reviewed the world's scientific literature on the subject and come across an article in a

Czech biochemistry journal by a Milos Androsh that reached similar, though far less definitive, conclusions. Androsh's report had evidently been ignored; Steve could not find a single reference to it in any related publications. Did he dare ignore it, too?

In Prague for an immunology congress the following month, Steve decided to look up this Androsh, find out how much theory he actually knew. But when he phoned his university, there was no listing for him, nor any record of previous employment.

Puzzled but persistent, Steve finally found Androsh's name and address in the telephone book and went to his home. He soon wished he hadn't. An elderly woman and her young granddaughter met him at the door. The woman sadly explained that her son Milos and his wife had been arrested by Soviet security police three years before and had not been heard from since. Only Steve's conscience stood in the way of his ignoring Androsh's earlier report, but it was enough. He could not possibly cheat a man as good as dead out of the only recognition his life was ever likely to have.

But Okabe's case was different, Steve told himself. To show him the same generosity as he had Androsh would simply cost too much. Deeply agitated, he went to the kitchen for a glass of wine, hoping it would calm him, but all it did was remind him again of the Prize and how close he was to winning it. This report in *Nature* could make or break him. If he shared credit equally with Okabe, it would do little good. Averse as they reportedly were to controversy, the Nobel selection committee would award neither the coveted prize.

So it was settled, Steve thought with relief. Okabe would have the obscurity he seemed to want and he himself would go on to reap the rewards for his research unencumbered . . . Still, Steve knew that without Okabe's insights, tireless work, and companionship through the long winter, he never would have made such swift progress. The least he could do was write the poor man a tactful letter.

Back at his desk, another glass of wine by his elbow, Steve found the letter exceedingly difficult to compose. Words he wanted to use, knew existed, eluded him; those he wrote seemed blatantly insincere. He might possibly deceive his trusting friend into believing such self-serving arguments, but he could not deceive himself.

Tearing the letter up, he began another to an influential man of science he had never met. Unlike the first, this one practically wrote itself. . . .

Chapter 36

BOUND TO HIS DESK DOING paperwork most of that rainy Labor Day weekend, Dan Lassiter was delighted when his old friend, Kurt Elliason, a member of the Nobel Prize selection committee, phoned from Stockholm Sunday evening to say he would be in Boston next month for a neurology meeting and would like to get together with him. Dan agreed at once and asked if Kurt would be willing to give grand rounds at his hospital.

"Why not?" replied Elliason amiably. "But I must warn you, Dan—since becoming so political, my knowledge base has shrunk to the point that I'm only able to talk intelligibly on one subject: senile dementia. Unless, of course, you'd rather hear propaganda about the Swedish Health Service. That's the spiel I give in place of anesthesia to my poor-risk surgical patients."

Dan chuckled. "A talk on dementia would be fine,

though I'm sure you haven't slipped as much as you say."

"Oh, haven't I! The truth is, I'm growing duller by the day. Two years ago I gave up my mistress, last year my horses, and this year, if the damned bureaucrats don't get off my back, I'm just giving up! But seeing you again is bound to cheer me. Is there anything else I can do for you?"

"No . . . except maybe one thing. Let me know who this year's Nobel winners in medicine are soon as you can. A friend of mine might be in the running."

"Gregory Carhill?" Elliason asked.

"No! Definitely not Carhill. What made you think that?"

"Well, for one thing, you're both in Boston. And for another, I recently got a letter from him. He wants the Nobel badly, of course—understandable, since what else has he to look forward to?—and went on and on about a new treatment he had just received, some radioactive hormone that's supposed to destroy cancer cells selectively. Also about his leukemia vaccine, which seems to be working out well—at least against African-variety, B-cell leukemia. How prevalent that is elsewhere, I don't know, but Carhill's method for making artificial vaccines is really quite ingenious. Just the thing for multiple sclerosis, if we can ever pin it down to a virus or a family of viruses. But if not Carhill, who are you pulling for?"

"Steve Sigourney," said Dan.

"Ah, Sigourney! He is, indeed, in the running—though more I cannot say."

"I understand. But please phone me once your selection is made. Because of my friendship with Steve, I have more than a passing interest in this year's winners."

"I will, Dan, and I'm looking forward to another

great evening with you and your beautiful Norwegian wife. I know all about beautiful Norska women—and unfortunately they know all about me. See you next month."

Chapter 37

THOUGH THERE WAS NO FIXED time for it, announcement of the winners of the physiology and medicine prize, traditionally the first in the Nobel Foundation's annual awards, was usually made the second Monday in October. The judges held their final discussion on the weekend, slept a night on their choices, and voted the next day. This year, however, the announcement was inexplicably delayed.

On Wednesday of that week, at five p.m. Stockholm time, Dan phoned Kurt Elliason to inquire about it, only to be told by his secretary that Dr. Elliason had been in committee all day and might be all night, but would return his call as soon as possible.

When no call had come by midnight, Dan and Kris went to bed.

Something—some internal jolt—woke Gregory Carhill in the early morning. Was he really awake? he wondered, unable to get his thoughts together. He felt woozy one moment, clear-headed the next. His life force seemed to be flickering like a fluorescent light about to burn out. Was he dying or just dreaming of dying?

Dream or not, something at his core was on the verge of happening that seemed to require a conscious choice: his wasted body, its cellular fuel exhausted, was urging him to let it happen; his brain was urging him to resist. Was the Angel of Death so shy that it waited for an invitation? He was so weary in spirit, so tired of seeing the looks of pity or worse in other people's eyes. Hadn't he prolonged his struggle to stay alive long enough? Wait—what day was this?

No, enough! he screamed silently at the obstinate element in his psyche that refused to give up. As if in angry support, his heart palpitated, his head swam, he heard a roaring in his ears like jet engines. Then a ringing sound, intermittent, insistent. He groped for the bedside telephone. Before he could bring it to his ear, his heart flip-flopped several more times and he dropped the receiver on the bed. What was happening now? Was he going into fatal ventricular fibrillation? Fight it! he thought. Pound the center of your chest with your fist!

Again his instincts pleaded, *No—enough!* He was too feeble to do it, anyway, too helpless to do anything but die.

"Dr. Carhill?" he heard, as though from very far away.

"Dr. Gregory Carhill?"

"Yes," he muttered faintly.

"Dr. Carhill . . . Dr. Gregory Carhill?"

It sounded like a page over the hospital loudspeaker.

"Yes," he said louder.

"One second, please."

Oh, go away, he thought. I'm in the midst of dying. I don't *have* a second.

Now he heard another voice—masculine, thickly accented. I'm being bombarded by strange voices, he thought. Next I'll probably hear a Heavenly choir!

"Dr. Carhill, this is Lars Carlson calling from Stockholm. Congratulations on winning the Nobel Prize!"

"Ah, yes, the Prize," said Carhill dreamily. "I've waited a long time for this honor . . . But I must sleep now. I really must sleep . . ."

The same old dream—always a happy one, thought Carhill, but he mustn't let it excite him. He must lie very still, lest his heart start fluttering again.

Suddenly the bed, the floor, the very foundation of the house, seemed to collapse and he was falling . . . fallling . . .

Kurt Elliason finally telephoned when Dan and Kris were at breakfast. Dan's fingers tightened around the receiver when the overseas operator told him who was calling.

"Hello, Dan! Elliason reporting in. Forgive the frog voice but, unlike my fellow judges, I tend to yell at the top of my lungs when I'm excited. But the excitement's over for this year . . ."

As Elliason paused to clear his throat, Dan blurted, "For God's sake, Kurt, tell me!"

"Well, it wasn't easy, but at least I got them to make it a 'cancer prize.' The winners are Silberg and Lambert for their pioneer work on oncogenes . . . and Gregory Carhill for his leukemia vaccine."

Dan repeated the names to Kris and then said, "Well, Kurt, I'm sure you had your reasons, but I have to tell you I'm disappointed."

"And I have something to tell *you*, Dan. After reading most of his publications, I've become a great admirer of your friend, Sigourney. I tell you this first —what's your American expression? 'up front'?— so you won't think I'm being unreasonable when I also tell you I think he's an *arrogant son of a bitch!*"

Dan laughed and glanced at Kris. "I've heard Steve called that before, though not lately. What's he done now?"

Elliason sighed. "No doubt you can appreciate the pressures we Nobel judges are under; we take a solemn vow never to discuss our deliberations with outsiders. Well, what I'm about to tell you will either be stretching or breaking that vow. Six weeks ago, the chairman of our committee received a letter from Sigourney, a really outrageous letter! I only wish I could show it to you, let you see for yourself the incredible nerve of the man. But essentially what it said—*demanded*—was, either we make Sigourney and Joshua Okabe co-winners of the medicine prize or remove Sigourney's name from consideration."

"Steve did that? Jesus! I don't know whether to laugh or cry."

"Emotion I can do without; it's an explanation I want. If you have one, please tell me."

"I'm not sure I do. I don't expect you to fully understand this, Kurt, but my relationship with Steve Sigourney goes beyond friendship—it's become almost a second career! But I'll find out what I can and let you know when we see each other next week. Now hold on . . ." Dan passed the phone to Kris so she could say hello to Elliason.

When she hung up, he asked, "Well, what do you think?"

"Carhill's winning surprised me. Is he still alive?"

"Far as I know. Maybe just barely, but alive. I'm sure I would've heard from Ted if he weren't."

"Are you going to call Steve and tell him?"

"When I get to the office. He and Nicole are in Minorca, you know."

"What's he doing there this time?"

"Analyzing all the clinical data he and Kosterlitz have collected over the years on his anorexia-producing peptide and getting it in shape for publication."

"So he's finally going to publish! Through you, Carhill must have scared him into it."

"Could be. I don't know whether my arguments helped persuade Carhill to back off from that scrap or not, but I'm damned glad he did. Anyway, it's all over now. Want a ride to the hospital?"

Kris eyed him curiously. "Last time I looked, I still had a car in the garage."

"I know. I just crave your company."

"Feel let down over Steve not winning?"

"A little," Dan admitted.

She smiled sympathetically. "Me, too."

Picking up the telephone to call a friend, Lenore Carhill winced at the shrill sound coming from it. A receiver must be off the hook somewhere. Slipping on a robe over her nightgown, she crossed the hall to her husband's bedroom and entered quietly, so as not to wake him if he slept. At the foot of his bed she waited for her vision to adjust to the dimness.

Ah, there it is, she thought, seeing the phone on a pillow. As she bent for it, her eyes swept past her husband's face, paused, and jerked back. Jaw slack, mouth gaping, right arm dangling over the side of the bed, he lay on his back, silent and motionless.

Hesitantly at first, then with frantic haste, Lenore moved to the windows to open the drapes. Sunlight flooded the room, yet Gregory did not stir.

Steeling herself, she moved close to him. Under the two- or three-day stubble of beard, his face looked ghastly, sallower than she had even seen it before. Too squeamish to touch him or feel for a pulse, she pulled the blankets from his chest and looked for signs of breathing. There were none. Oh God! she thought. It couldn't be! While he lived, there had always been hope; he was so clever. But there seemed little doubt.

"Oh, Gregory!" she shrieked as intimations of

endless loneliness shuddered through her. How could she bear old age without him?

As she closed her eyes in pain and fear, Carhill opened his. "W . . . What, dear?" he croaked.

Lenore braced herself against the bedpost, weak with relief. "Oh, Gregory! Oh, my dear, you gave me a terrible fright! You really *must* shave today; you're beginning to look seedy. And why is the phone off the hook?" She replaced it in its cradle.

Carhill looked baffled. "I . . . I don't know, unless . . . I had this . . ."

The phone rang.

Lenore answered it and he heard her say, "Who? . . . the *Globe?* . . . Congratulations on *what?* . . . He *did!* Are you sure? Oh, how splendid! How absolutely wonderful! Excuse me a moment, please." She clamped her hand over the mouthpiece. "Gregory, Gregory, darling! You won the Nobel Prize! You, Silberg and Lambert. You did it, darling! You hung in and did it! I'm so *enormously* proud!"

Carhill blinked in astonishment. So it hadn't been a dream, after all.

"Did you already know?" his wife asked.

Carhill hesitated and shook his head. It would take too much breath to explain.

"What do I tell this reporter?"

"Get his name and number and tell him I'll call back."

Carhill could hardly wait for Lenore to finish her hugging and gushing and go instruct their cook to fix breakfast. He desperately needed time to think.

He had nearly died in the night; he remembered that much clearly. But by some miracle, he hadn't. Like a marathon runner in the last mile, his heart had struggled on. Now, from a burst of adrenalin or endorphin or whatever, he seemed to have gained a second wind.

Almost as sweet as winning the Nobel Prize was knowing that Stefan Sigourney hadn't. It surprised him; Sigourney's two-gene hypothesis had been gaining wide support. His foolhardy collaboration with Okabe had obviously cost him dearly.

Would it embitter Sigourney? Carhill hoped not. Now that he was a Nobel laureate, he had a new goal: to attend the awards ceremony in Stockholm. A month's hyperalimentation at home or in the hospital would fatten him up and a few blood transfusions restore his color; that much was easily accomplished. But getting to Stockholm would take more than that. He'd have to ask his old nemesis again for help, learn all he could about how to block the action of the cancer-promoting growth factor. It was his last and best hope for remission. But would Stefan respond as generously as before?

Carhill was glad now that he had listened to Lassiter and not exposed Sigourney's partnership in the Kosterlitz Clinic. Though his reason had been selfish—not to look petty and vindictive to the Nobel judges—Sigourney ought to be grateful to him all the same.

Perhaps he should write Stefan saying that he considered it rank injustice that he wasn't a co-winner of the Prize. Such a letter would have to be carefully phrased, lest it sound patronizing. But he could do it, and it might just work. It *had* to work. He was a Nobel laureate; he deserved to live.

The pediatric lounge at Bemidji Community Hospital was empty when Billy Freiborg entered. It was the last place in town he wanted to be on this sunny October afternoon, but he tried not to think about that. Picking up a discarded newspaper, he scanned the headlines. A story captioned NOBEL

PRIZE TO THREE CANCER RESEARCHERS caught his eye and he looked for the winners' names, feeling a sharp sense of disappointment when Steve Sigourney was not among them. Just then, Leonard Olsen's nurse stuck her head in the doorway and said, "He's awake, Billy. You can go in now."

"Thanks, Mrs. Erickson."

Billy stood up, smoothed down his sweater, and sighed. This would be the third kid with cancer he had counseled, but he still felt like an intruder. All Dr. Nestor had told him about this Leonard Olsen was that he was about Billy's own age, came from Cass Lake, and was a newly diagnosed case of leukemia. Would Billy drop by to talk to him before he was transferred to Mayo Clinic? Billy almost wished he had refused. But doctors weren't too good at getting into the heads of kids with leukemia; they just couldn't imagine the crazy thoughts that came from knowing you had a trillion cancer cells floating around in your blood. Billy knew, all right, and wanted to forget; he might have forgotten except for this volunteer work. He wasn't exactly sure why he had taken it on, only that he had debts to pay and memories to honor—one memory, in particular, that even now kept driving him hard.

"Hi!" said Billy casually as he strode into Leonard Olsen's room. The pale youth propped up in bed stared at him, but did not reply. Oh well, thought Billy, unfazed by the silent reception. Olsen wasn't from town. What did he know of local celebrities?

Looking around and spotting a basket of fruit on the dresser, Billy took a red apple from the pile, inspected it for worm holes, polished it on his sleeve and put it back. Then he turned to the boy.

"I'm Billy Freiborg, Len—okay if I call you Len? They must've told you about me."

"Told me what?" asked Olsen sullenly.

"That I'd be in to see you . . . and here I am."

"Never heard of you. What do you want?"

"Oh, nothin'. Just came by to watch a little TV, eat some of your fruit, and talk if you want. That's about it."

Leonard Olsen stared at Billy incredulously. "Who said you could come in here?"

Billy shrugged. "Nobody, really. But they all know me around here."

"Maybe *they* do, but *I* don't! So just cut out. I got leukemia, you know. You could catch it."

"How?"

"How should I know? Maybe by eating an apple I touched."

Picking up the apple he had polished, Billy held it at arm's length a moment and then bit into it.

"That's dumb!"

Billy chewed and swallowed. "No, it's not. I can't catch leukemia 'cause I already got it . . . Yeah, that's right. A year and a half ago I was in this same hospital, this same floor, and a lot sicker'n you. Want to hear about it?"

Leonard Olsen hesitated and then shook his head. "Naw, not really. If it's real inspirational, maybe I'll read about it someday in the *Reader's Digest.*"

Billy chuckled. It was a pretty good line; Chad Petersen would have loved it. He took another bite of the apple and said, "Suit yourself. Only you might be missing out. Certain things I know about leukemia, you don't."

"You a doctor?"

"No, but I been around. Almost three months at Mayo's, another month at Commonwealth General Hospital in Boston. You might not believe it, but I was a four-tuber for a while."

"A what?"

Billy pretended disgust. "You been here two, three weeks and you still don't know what a four-tuber is? That's the number of tubes they stick in, down, or through you—how you know how sick you are. For instance, you've got no stomach tube, no bladder catheter, no arterial line, nothing but a measly IV right now. Which makes you a one-tuber. No big deal."

"Up till a few days ago I had a tube in here." Leonard pointed to a spot just below his right collarbone.

"A CVP catheter. Nothin' special about that. I had plenty of them. All that makes you is a two-tuber. Only don't feel bad. Seven tubes and you're a goner. Nobody I know of ever survived seven, except one guy—Chad Petersen, my first hospital roommate." Billy smiled wistfully. "He was really something, Chad was. Talk about tough! No hospital flunky dared to mess with him. Long as Chad was my roomie, no Gray Ladies or other busybodies pestered us. Nobody but The General himself told Chad what to do. 'The General' was what we called Dr. Henley, chief of the Mayo Clinic's leukemia ward. You see, Chad had this med. student girlfriend, Madeline, who kept him posted on his tests and stuff so nobody, not even The General, could bullshit him." Billy drew breath and sighed. "Lots of stories I could tell you about old Chad, but . . ." he shrugged ". . . since you don't feel like talking, guess I'll just mosey along . . ."

"No, wait!" cried Olsen as Billy turned slowly away. "This Chad guy had leukemia, too?"

"Yeah. He was in his third year and had it bad."

"What happened to him?"

"Uh-uh," said Billy, shaking his head. "One thing Chad taught me: if you don't know, don't ask! When they ship you to Mayo's, you'll get a roommate, too—probably more'n one—and believe me, it's better not to know."

Leonard Olsen frowned. "You mean, after rooming

with a guy for a month, you don't know if he's alive or dead?"

Forcefully, Billy said, "This is a leukemia ward we're talking about, not summer camp! Leukemia's like war—you got to expect casualties."

"I still don't get it."

"Yeah, well, neither did I at first. But it was Chad Petersen's number one rule, and since he was right about everything else, I went along with it. Want to know what rule two was?" Billy pulled a chair up to the bed and sat down. "Well, like I said, you're in a war, kid, and you got to get all the intelligence reports you can. For instance . . ."

"Beautiful though they are, sunsets always make me sad," said Nicole as she and Steve sat on the terrace of their cliffside cottage, watching the brilliant colors flare and fade. "I'm not sure why. Maybe because they symbolize the end of something . . . Like your not winning the Nobel Prize. You never will now, will you?"

"Probably not." He laughed. "Not unless they give it to Georgi and me for our fifteen-year study of the anorexigenic peptide. Imagine Georgi in Stockholm, resplendent in high hat, sash and tails, looking even more regal than the King!"

"Be serious," admonished Nicole, though she, too, smiled.

"Serious? All right, I will. Like the Japanese, I'm a great admirer of symmetry: things and events fitting together in proper proportion. Take my long feud with Gregory Carhill. Whether he lives another minute or not, Carhill got what he wanted most in the world—and so did I. Only I got it earlier; when my rented car skidded off the road and I thought I was a goner. I don't remember having any profound thoughts then—they came later. I asked myself what

I would have missed most: my chance to pin down the cause of cancer? Win the Nobel prize? Scientific immortality? No, it was you, Nicole; the life we're enjoying together now. With minor lapses, I've been gratefully content ever since."

"I'm glad, Stefan." She squeezed his hand, gently at first, then almost painfully. "But there's something you're not telling me . . ."

"Is there?" he replied, raising his brows.

"You know damned well, so stop playing innocent! When Dan Lassiter phoned about the Prize winners, he said to ask you about the letter you wrote to the Nobel selection committee."

Steve scowled. "How the devil did he know about it?"

"He didn't say. But he's a very fair man and a good friend to us both. He thought that before I smother you with affection to try to allay your disappointment, I ought to ask about the letter."

Steve emitted a half-grunt, half-laugh. "Just goes to show you can't trust anybody anymore—not your friends, your doctor, not even the supposedly sphinx-like Nobel committee." He sighed. "I *was* going to tell you about it after dinner, or at least after a little wine."

Nicole seized the wine carafe on the table, poured two glasses, and pushed one towards him. "Here's the wine. You supply the truth."

Steve took a sip. "All right, I admit I did write a letter. It wasn't the one I started to write—that was to Joshua Okabe thanking him for all the good ideas I planned to claim as my own. Instead, I wrote the Nobel committee chairman to advise—no, to *tell* him —that, should I happen to be one of the finalists, they either award the Prize jointly to me and Joshua or drop me from consideration."

Nicole gasped. "You didn't! For God's sake, *why?*"

"It was necessary . . . a way of burning bridges to a state of mind I never want to return to again."

"I still don't understand. Didn't you *want* the Prize?"

"I wouldn't have refused it. No one yet has had the independence of spirit to do that. But I no longer needed it, not the way I once did." Steve winced, remembering. "A good thing, too, since it was almost within my grasp. All I had to do was omit Okabe's name from my paper in *Nature* and there was no stopping me . . . nor turning back."

"Ah," she murmured. "I'm beginning to understand—maybe even to agree. But be honest: did Okabe really contribute so much?"

"Tell me how to measure genius and I'll answer that. All I know is that I rode a long way on this. To pretend otherwise would be to give in to my worst instincts. Nor would winning the Prize be the end of it. Who knows what I'd want next, or who I'd betray to get it? No. I simply couldn't risk it. I suppose I should've told you about the letter long before this, but I was praying that, by some miracle, the Nobel committee might see it my way."

Nicole shook her head in wonderment. "You're amazing, Stefan—a true Hungarian in your need for making the grand gesture!"

"I'll try to reform," Steve said with a smile. "But if as you say, it's in my blood, I can't promise."

"Then promise me something else: that when we're in Madrid for the cancer congress, you'll go with me to the plaza—I forget which one—where there's a statue of Cervantes and Don Quixote; let me snap a group picture of the three of you!"

"Is that all?" he asked dubiously.

"That's all. A fair price for my forgiveness, wouldn't you say?"

Steve shrugged, pondered; finally he grinned and touched his glass to hers in a silent toast.

* * *

That evening, giving up his favorite TV show to finish a letter he had begun the week before, Billy Freiborg wrote:

> ". . . Anyway, as I told you on the phone, I've been visiting kids with cancer at the hospital here, mostly as a favor to Doc Nestor, my pediatrician. Today I spent a couple of hours with a fifteen-year-old leukemic from Cass Lake. His name's Len Olsen and it was really tough going for a while. Like me, at first, he was pretty scared and withdrawn and didn't want to gab with a guy he'd never met before. I guess, being from Cass Lake (which is even smaller than here) he'd never heard of the famous Freiborgs of Bemidji. So what did I do? Give up? Did Knute Rockne give up when Notre Dame was way behind Army in their big game? No way! What he did was dig into his bag of tricks and pull out the story of George Gipp. Which is kind of what I did. Only instead of The Gipper, I told Olsen about my old Mayo Clinic buddy, Chad Petersen. Never mind what I told him. It worked before and, by golly, it worked again! I know I didn't mention anything about this on the phone, and I sure didn't want to wait to tell you in person 'cause you might take a poke at me. So, figuring I was sort of obliged to, I'm writing it. Naturally, Olsen asked if the legendary seven-tuber was alive or dead, but I ducked the question. More dramatic that way.
>
> Truth is, Chad, for a long time I thought you really were dead. I'd still think so if I hadn't told Doc Nestor about you and he hadn't asked The General how you made out with your bone marrow transplant. Boy, was I ever glad to hear you're still alive and kicking and back home in Milwaukee!
>
> I'm really happy your treatment worked and

that your mom's marrow found a home in your bones. Only doesn't it feel a little weird to know all your blood cells have female chromosomes? You don't get any strange urges to wear dresses or put on lipstick, do you? (Just kidding!) I'm no one to talk, since it took a whopping dose of mouse antibodies to cure me and some might still be around. In fact, the fuzz on my upper lip twitches whenever Blacky, our cat, prowls my room.

I read in today's paper where three cancer researchers got the Nobel Prize. The Freiborgs, me especially, were rooting hard for Steve Sigourney to win. He's the doctor from Philly who put together the stuff they gave me in Boston. I only met him once and I doubt if he remembers me 'cause he was pretty sick himself at the time, but I'm really grateful for all he did. Hope he's not too disappointed, though he probably is. I would be, too, I suppose, if I spent my whole life on one thing and then missed out on the big prize. Wonder if he ever stops to think there's a kid up in Bemidji, Minnesota, who owes his life to him? I sure think a lot about him. Do you, about the doctors who came up with your bone marrow treatment?

Funny how getting and licking leukemia changes you. I know I'm not cured, that it could come back any time, but even so, it's taught me a lot. For one thing, I'm never bored. Not ever. Not even when I'm telling the story of seven-tuber Chad Petersen for the umpteenth time. Maybe I ought to take guitar lessons and set it to music. Okay, okay. I'll get off it before you really get pissed.

Can't wait for you to come visit during Christmas vacation. I know that, compared to the Beer Capital of the U.S., Bemidji probably seems like dullsville, but we'll find lots to do. I can't promise to fix you up with any hot dates. Having trouble finding any myself. People around here, same as people everywhere, I guess, have weird ideas about leukemia. Some kids at my school treat me like I'm some kind of hero for licking it and others act like I could be contagious. Ever ask a girl out and have her turn you down 'cause her mother told her she could catch leukemia from kissing you? I tried telling one it was just the opposite—that my spit was so loaded with antibodies that a lot of kissing would protect her from leukemia forever. Nearly had her convinced until she asked our science teacher about it.

Well, that's about all the news for now. Oh, one more thing. I think it's great you want to be like your Dad and make the army your career, and I know getting into West Point is tough, but I hope you're wrong that they won't want you just 'cause you had leukemia. If anything that unfair and dirty ever happens, let me know. Maybe my Uncle Nels can fix it by promising the army an extra billion or two for accepting you. Seriously, though, if Nels is still the President's number one money-man two years from now, he might really be able to help you out.

Finally, I'm not much of a writer, so don't expect all my letters to be this long. Just happens I had a lot to tell you this time.

Your friend from the war,

Billy.